HEART OF STEEL

CATHLEEN COLE
FRANK JENSEN

Copyright © 2021 by Cathleen Cole

All rights reserved.

No part of this book may be reproduced in any form or by any electronic or mechanical means, including information storage and retrieval systems, without written permission from the author, except for the use of brief quotations in a book review.

Any references to historical events, real people, or real places are used fictitiously. Names, characters, and places are products of the author's imagination.

Publisher: C&J Novels LLC

Cover designed by: Kari March Designs

ASIN: B08S2WH8L6

This book is dedicated to the most perfect partner in crime — my husband. Thank you for pushing me to be my best, for supporting me through everything, and for always having my six no matter what. I'm grateful to you for helping me write this book and checking another item off our bucket list. Thank you most of all for your love.

CHAPTER 1

Remi

"Jesus Remi!" Bridget gasped as I peeled into the university parking lot. I whipped my car into an empty space, about two feet in front of the car that was waiting to pull in. A long blast of the other vehicle's horn told me exactly what the driver thought of my stunt. I couldn't be late for my first class of the morning.

"Sorry Bridge, but we're going to be late." I stepped out and gave the other student a semi-apologetic smile and a shrug. Opening my back door, I grabbed my backpack and slung it across my shoulder.

"So what?" Bridget said, with a careless shrug as she slammed the door after grabbing her own bag.

I eyed her stylish clothes and high heels. Bridget was majoring in fashion. Her dad was the former mayor of Austin, so she'd gotten used to dressing a certain way. As a kid, it was expected that she always looked well put together. That had carried on into college. There were times I wished I had the desire to dress like her. Once I'd become the owner of my late father's company, Mackenzie's Trucking, I'd let her talk me into a shopping trip. Now I owned more business clothes than I could ever wear but I still mostly wore jean shorts, tank tops, and sneakers.

"Your professors may not mind you walking in late. But this is the class where the professor locks the door right at eight a.m." This hadn't been the first time I'd been late and therefore been locked out of class. I needed to pass this class so that I could start its consecutive course next semester. I was desperately trying to finish my degree a year early.

If Uncle Caleb had to spend another year running Dad's business, I'd likely lose the only family I had left. Or the only family I chose to recognize. Sorority girls had started passing out Mother's Day flyers, in preparation for the upcoming holiday, and it had been making me think a lot about the mother who'd abandoned me hours after giving birth to me. She tried coming back every year, usually around my birthday, but I refused to see her.

It had to have hurt Dad to have her come around, but he never complained. He never spoke badly about her, just encouraged me to let go of the past. He never tried to force me to see her, but he'd said it would be healthier for me to forgive her, for myself, if not for her.

Normally, I found it easy to ignore thoughts of Rhonda but with the bubbly college girls popping up around every corner and reminding us to 'take care of the special ladies in our lives', it was getting harder to do. I shook the old memories out of my head as we moved across the parking lot.

I watched in amusement as people started calling out greetings to Bridget. She was, by far, the biggest social butterfly in my group of friends. She had always drawn people in, and the rest of us were happy to let her have the limelight. Not that I had trouble making friends, I just didn't seek it out like a moth to a flame the way Bridget did.

"Oh, they hate it when I'm late. I'm just better at getting myself out of trouble than you are." Bridget stuck her tongue out at me, and I rolled my eyes. She wasn't lying, Bridget could charm the pants off damn near anyone.

I didn't bother to respond to her but increased my speed across the parking lot. Bridget huffed a little as she had to double-time it to keep up with my long legs. At five-four she was having a hard time keeping up with my five-eleven frame.

Bridget darted in front of me to cut between two cars. We were finally reaching the end of the lot where the road met up with the buildings. She would have to head past the building directly in front of us to go to her class, but luckily mine was here. I had to give it to her. It impressed me that she could run in those heels.

I glanced at the thick leather watch on my left wrist and groaned. Ten minutes. I had ten minutes to get into my class. "Fuck!" I bellowed in surprise when I slammed straight into Bridget's body. She had stopped suddenly when I wasn't looking.

She let out a squeak as she stumbled forward. I yelped, more in surprise than pain, when she smacked the back of her hand into my stomach. "Quit walking so fast and you wouldn't be in danger of mowing me down."

"Don't stop so suddenly when we're rushing to get places." I glowered at her when she just smiled at me and dug in her purse for some gum. I was boxed in on three sides by her and the cars. I could go around, but it would be faster to just wait her out. This was going to be a shitty day, and it was only eight a.m.

Finally, Bridget started moving again, but stopped a few steps later. I groaned, and she shot me a dirty look. She jerked her head in the direction of the road. "Who brought the delicious man candy?"

I stepped forward and followed her gaze. Sitting at the curb were six huge men on motorcycles. They were wearing jeans, white or black t-shirts, and leather vests. Bridget was practically drooling now. The last two had females sitting behind them on the bikes. In Bridget's world that meant the first four were hers for the taking.

I rolled my eyes. "Seriously? I don't want to be locked out of the classroom. Let's go!" I trotted across the road and felt a stab of relief when I heard the click of her heels behind me. The dean was rushing out the side door of the building adjacent to the one my classroom was in as we crossed the road. He paused when he saw me and glanced at his watch. Looking back up at me, he frowned and held up his watch. Most students would never meet the dean. I, however, was one of the unlucky few that he knew personally.

Rolling my eyes, I slowed and nodded my head. Mr. Richards was a dick. He really didn't like me, and he took every opportunity to point out when I was doing something wrong. Normally, I would try to stay off the radar of any of the faculty, but right before my dad died there'd been an...incident. I'd ended up punching a girl in the cafeteria. She'd had it coming, and I had a hard time controlling my temper in the best of times.

That hadn't been the best of times, so when she'd bumped into me on purpose, causing me to spill my lunch on myself, I'd kind of snapped. Rachel had gone to the same high school as me. She'd been the typical cheerleader bully. On top of the fact that she enjoyed picking on kids, Rachel had also been in love with my boyfriend, Scott. We'd just broken up, and she'd thought that it was the perfect opportunity to make me look like an idiot in front of him without incurring his wrath since I'd embarrassed him by dumping him.

College hadn't humbled her at all, and it certainly hadn't made her smarter. I'd broken up with him. If she'd wanted him, I wasn't standing in her way. I'd like to think giving her a black eye had knocked her down a peg, but now most of the faculty of the University of Texas in Austin, knew exactly who I was and *that* I didn't care for. The idea that they all knew who I was and thought I was a troublemaker made me cringe.

"Ms. Jordan!" Richards yelled across the courtyard, and I realized I had lost Bridget somewhere along the way. I turned and groaned. At the motorcycles. I'd lost her at the motorcycles.

Well, rather at the bikers, I thought wryly. Bridget was standing there, twirling her pale blonde hair around her finger and batting her lashes at a guy on one of the bikes. She completely ignored the dean yelling at her across the walkway. Bridget was a bit of a princess around here. Everyone knew her and clamored to be her friend. She sucked people in like a black hole.

The biker leaned his motorcycle to the side and swung a leg off of it. His gait was smooth, like stalking prey, as he moved toward her.

The guy has to be six-three. What is it about bikers? They're always huge. They usually have huge personalities to match, I thought sourly. Not that I knew any bikers, but they had a reputation. The guy dwarfed Bridget as he stood in front of her and leaned down to whisper something in her ear. She giggled, I gagged. Not that the guy wasn't gorgeous.

He was, I thought as my eyes roved over him in appreciation. The guy was ripped. It was her overly high pitched, sugar-sweet giggle that had me rolling my eyes.

They look like Barbie and Ken. Well, if Ken is a tough-looking biker with a bunch of tattoos. He had blond hair and bright blue eyes. The smile he gave Bridget could probably knock the panties off a girl at ten paces.

I couldn't help but laugh as they stood there flirting, completely ignoring Mr. Richards and everyone around them. They should look ridiculous, Bridget in her short skirt, flowy long-sleeved top, and stupidly expensive high heels, and this guy in dirty jeans, boots, and a leather vest. But strangely, it worked. I tilted my head and studied them like they were a lab experiment until a movement drew my gaze.

Glancing over, I noticed Richards's face turning an alarming shade of red as he stormed toward them. I trotted back and grabbed Bridget by the wrist. She glanced at me over her shoulder, but the massive biker glared at me. His eyebrows were slashed downward over those incredible blue eyes as he glowered at me. I tugged Bridget backward, making her stumble a bit. "Sorry, we have to go."

He moved forward, crowding into my space, and wrapped his huge hand around Bridget's opposite arm. "I don't think you do." He said the statement calmly, but dread curled in my stomach at his tone. I looked down at my hand on Bridget's wrist. This probably looked like a Rottweiler and a Chihuahua playing tug o' war with a bone. I was not going to win that battle. I glanced over at Bridget quickly and her eyes were wide, as she stared at him.

Bridge laughed nervously at the guy's intensity. "We actually do have to go so…"

He looks like he is going to throw her over his shoulder and stalk off to his cave.

"Gunnar!" Both Bridget and I jumped as a voice bellowed from the vicinity of the motorcycles.

Behind Gunnar was an equally big man, still sitting on his bike. His arms were crossed loosely over his chest, legs stretched out. At first glance, you'd think he was relaxed and waiting to get on the road. Those intense, pale gray eyes said that you would be wrong in that assumption. He was coiled, like a snake ready to strike.

That stare was piercing and made me more than a little nervous, especially when it landed on me. My heart started pounding in my chest as I felt his gaze move over me. He was tan and had black, short hair, trimmed close to his head, and a beard that was trimmed equally close to his face. He was ruggedly handsome, but the grim line of his mouth made him seem dangerous.

Who am I kidding?

It didn't take the slash of his mouth to tell me that. Danger oozed off him. I swept my eyes down his body. His biceps were as thick as my thighs and he had a sleeve of tattoos that came from beneath his sleeve on his left arm and went down over the back of his hand. He even had tattoos on the fingers of his left hand.

My eyes kept following the line of his body downward, where his waist tapered down to his hips and flared out again at his muscular thighs. My gaze was drawn back up and I stared at his throat where a fully colored tattooed skull stared back at me. I swallowed nervously and met his eyes. He was watching me, unblinking.

Okay, that's not creepy at all. It was his penetrating stare that made me uncomfortable more than anything. Otherwise, he was gorgeous, and his tattoos were beautiful. They were bright and vibrant against his tanned skin.

Since gray eyes had stepped in, Gunnar released his hold on Bridget. "I'll text you later, baby girl." I could only describe the look he gave Bridget as a smolder.

We turned and ran toward the building. I let her go through the door first, then glanced back and watched the dean talk to the bikers. His hands were waving around. Gunnar stepped menacingly toward him and the breath caught in my throat. He said something that had Mr. Richards backing up quickly.

Finally, Richards hurried back toward the building he'd come out of, shooting wary glances over his shoulder the whole way. A tingle zipped down my spine and my gaze flashed back to gray eyes. He was still staring at me and an unwelcomed zip of excitement shot through my body. I twisted my lips and frowned at him, then bolted through the door.

CHAPTER 2

Steel

We pulled up in front of the campus and I cut the engine on my bike. Leaning back on the seat, I stretched my right leg out. We had a job later this afternoon to handle for the club's president, Cade, but Drew and Trip had to drop their old ladies off at the school. Both women were attending the University of Texas, trying to finish up their degrees and helping the club out by doing a little dealing on the side.

This was amongst the many things that set Cade aside from the old president. Cade could think ahead. Dealing was just a way to get some easy cash today. Degrees in finance and economics were ways to get cash tomorrow. Anytime one of the women of our brothers showed interest in obtaining a college degree the club helped them out as much as we could. It gave us a good return on our investment and helped their family out as well.

Movement caught my eye and my hand immediately went to the small of my back. I palmed the butt of my gun. Two females rushed past, and I slowly relaxed. I smirked when the blonde glanced over, then slowed down when she caught sight of Gunnar, my main enforcer. It didn't surprise me when she glanced at her friend's retreating back, then changed direction and strolled over. Gunnar had that effect on women.

While she started flirting with my best friend, I watched the second girl, who was still booking it toward the main building. A small man, with a comb-over, approached her and shook a watch at her. The girl stopped to acknowledge him. She was tall, at least five-eleven, maybe more. Her long dark brown hair was piled on top of her head as if she'd just rolled out of bed and thrown it up to get it out of her way. I couldn't see her face from here, and I'd only caught a glimpse of it when she ran past. I'd seen enough to want her to turn around.

She did exactly that, searching for her missing friend. Her brows lowered and a look of aggravation passed over her pretty features. Her full lips thinned; whiskey-colored eyes narrowed. I raked my gaze down her body. She was stacked. She wasn't petite, like her friend. A full pair of tits held my attention for a minute. Then my eyes continued their path downward. She had an athletic build, I could see the muscles in her arms and legs, thanks to the jean shorts and tank top she was wearing. I wasn't sure why I found that sexy as fuck, but it worked on her.

My eyes raised back up to her face as she trotted forward to grab her friend. Gunnar was glaring at her, not wanting her to drag his newest flavor of the week off.

"Sorry, we have to go." Her voice was lower-pitched and sexier than I thought it would be. I shifted slightly as my dick hardened. I wanted to hear that voice moaning my name.

Gunnar closed the gap between them and grabbed his girl's arm, tugging her back toward him. Both girls' eyes widened, and the brunette's mouth dropped open. I imagined my tongue tracing the shape of those lips. Gunnar said something to them in a low voice that I didn't catch. Worry passed over both of their faces. I sighed; we didn't have time for this.

"Gunnar!" I bellowed. It was more of an order than anything else.

Both women jumped at the sound. The brunette's eyes shot over to mine. I watched her quietly as Gunnar muttered something to the blonde. I locked eyes with her until she averted her gaze. I took the opportunity to appreciate her body again, slower this time, as I waited for Gunnar to tear himself away from his girl.

I could tell I was making the woman in front of me nervous, but I liked that. I liked how tense she'd gone when she'd realized I was watching her. I wished I didn't have somewhere else to be so I could find out more about her. She was trying to pretend that she wasn't noticing me, but she was. I saw her eyes tracing my tattoos. Finally, Gunnar broke apart from the women.

They turned and ran to the building. My eyes tracked her, the way a wolf would a wounded doe. Watching the play of muscle in those long legs as she sprinted across the courtyard I shifted on my bike, trying to relieve the restless feeling growing inside of me.

She paused by the door, watching Gunnar threaten the administrator who was trying to kick us off of the campus. I tried to suppress the wicked grin when her eyes found mine again. Her eyes widened slightly before she frowned at the challenge she found there. Then she rushed into the building, disappearing from sight.

"Let's go," I yelled back over my shoulder and started up my bike. I saw my brothers' two women walk toward class, laughing and talking together. I waited until they went into the building. Gunning the engines, we took off down the road. Students looked around at the sound of the Harleys and stared as we drove past.

CHAPTER 3

Remi

I slid on the floor a bit as I rounded the corner at a run. My sneakers were making a squeak, squeak, squeak, sound with every step. I saw the door of the classroom ahead of me. Standing there, scowling was Mr. Mancini. He looked down at his watch and his face softened slightly in smug triumph.

Watching in horror, I raced down the hall, as he shut the door and locked it. I thumped into it three seconds later. I tried the handle, nope, locked. Our gazes clashed through the glass, mine pleading. He just turned away and went to take his place for the lecture.

Dick! I can't believe he just did that.

I turned my back to the door then slid down to the floor, dropping my bag next to me as I sat there trying to catch my breath. Letting my head fall back onto the door with a thump, I prayed there wasn't a quiz today. My grade couldn't afford to miss many of those. I held up my watch; it was one minute past eight.

"Asshole," I muttered. *He could have let me into class.*

I considered my options. I could go to the library to study. *Meh.* I stood up, picked up my bag, and made my way across the buildings until I found Bridget's class. I watched through the window until the professor turned her back to the students and I quietly snuck in and plopped in the seat next to Bridget.

She looked over at me and gave me a sympathetic and slightly guilty look. "Got locked out?"

I nodded quietly, half-listening to the professor excitedly chirp about contrasting colors and color palettes.

"I'm so sorry, Rem. I wouldn't have asked for a ride last night if I'd known I'd oversleep."

I looked at her and shrugged. "It's not that big of a deal. I'll try to get some extra credit to see if I can bump up the grade."

Now we had a chance to sit and talk about what had just happened. I knew she thought the biker's actions were hot. I found them downright scary. Bridget tried to control the excitement in her voice and keep it low so she wouldn't alert the professor.

"Those guys were so sexy!"

I frowned at her. "Yeah, they were, but that guy was really intense." I didn't elaborate on which man I was talking about.

She rolled her eyes at me. "They're bikers. That's how they are. His name is Gunnar." She all but sighed his name out.

"The blond?"

"Of course, who else would I be…"

"Something to add ladies?" The professor glared at us. We both quietly shook our heads and the lady eyeballed me.

She's trying to figure out if I am in her class, I realized.

"You noticed one of them," Bridget whispered accusingly after the professor turned back around. A girl sitting in front of me turned and gave me a heavy frown, as if I was the one speaking. Bridget made a shooing motion directly in front of her face and I had to smother a chuckle.

I just shook my head at her, but pursed my lips together. After a few seconds of suspicious silence, I glanced over and couldn't help but sigh. She was sitting there staring at me like I was a circus freak.

Granted, I hadn't paid guys any attention for the last year. It had been a hellish one for me, so men had been pretty far down on my list of priorities. Apparently, one making a blip on my radar shook Bridget speechless. I wished I had the ability to make that happen more often.

"Which one?" she hissed loudly at me once she found her voice again.

When the professor turned to glare at us again, we quieted down and listened to the remainder of the lecture, but Bridget's meaningful looks told me that this conversation wasn't done. *Yay for me.*

CHAPTER 4

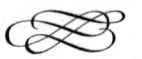

Steel

We pulled up to a warehouse later that afternoon, and I glanced around as I got off my bike. It looked abandoned, but belonged to the club. This was one of the locations that we used for our drops. Two prospects were waiting there for us with a cage ride. They were in charge of bringing the truck so we could transport the merchandise. I hated driving anything that wasn't a bike, most of us did, which is why we called them cages.

"Doesn't look like they're here yet." Gunnar lit up a cigarette as he stopped at my side. He offered me his pack, and I took one and lit it before handing his lighter back. I shook my head when he ran a hand through his short blond hair. We were constantly giving him shit about being too pretty to be a biker. I would have started ribbing him, it was my favorite pastime and had been since we were kids, but I needed to focus on the drop about to happen.

"We have a few minutes." I watched as the prospects opened the rolling door on the warehouse and drove the truck in. The rest of us followed them in on foot. Gunnar and I paused by the door to finish smoking.

"Steel." He nodded toward the entrance as our buyer drove up. We both flicked our cigarettes away and Gunnar motioned for them to pull in. As soon as the door was closed behind us the front and back doors of the car opened. Two men in suits got out and strode forward toward us.

I leaned against the truck and watched as they approached. The air was thick with tension. Gunnar stuck close to my side as he always did, insisting on taking a position that allowed him to cover my back. He was one of the few men I knew I could trust with that task.

"Good to see you again, Steel. Gunnar." Alexis, the taller blond man shook our hands. "Enzo was happy with your shipment last time. We're looking forward to continuing to do business together." The man spoke with a heavy Russian accent.

I felt my lips twist in a smirk when I remembered one of the prospects, Scout, imitating the accent, but talking about fluffy bunnies and cute puppy dogs. He'd insisted that even when these guys talked about harmless things, they sounded dangerous.

He wasn't wrong about that. Both Alexis and Enzo were dangerous. They'd contacted us, interested in forming a mutually beneficial relationship between our organizations. They got our guns; we got their cash. Our deal with the Bratva was new, but it was proving to be very lucrative.

Enzo was the Pahkan of the Austin Bratva, so we hadn't met with him directly, yet. I'd been organizing everything with his second in command, Alexis, since Enzo had reached out to Cade a few months ago. Eventually, Cade would insist on a face-to-face meeting between all of our officers and his if we were to continue our relationship. But he was happy to do things Enzo's way, for now. We would soon become indispensable to the Bratva.

Our club, Vikings MC, was responsible for eighty-five percent of arms dealing on the west coast. That, drugs, stolen vehicles, and a few legit businesses were how we made our money. We never got into prostitution, or human trafficking. There were some lines even we wouldn't cross.

The Bratva was attempting to edge out the local Italian Mafia Don. We were happy to supply the weapons for that war. We had our own to deal with. The Lycans MC wasn't only our rival, but they were stupid enough to be making a power play for our territory.

There had been a shakeup with our MC last year. Our former president, Dagger, hadn't been willing to do what was necessary to grow the club. Our new president, Cade, along with Gunnar, my brother Riggs and I had been members, but when the opportunity to take over had presented itself, we'd done what was necessary.

It had ended with a significant amount of bloodshed and over half of the surviving members of the club leaving. That didn't matter to us. We'd already had a core group of guys that were waiting for us to take them on.

It was a little over a year later and we had thirty-five members and six prospects hoping to patch in. Business was booming for us. As word of the takeover spread, we'd fended off a few of the local clubs who'd tried to take advantage.

Anytime there was a big shift in a motorcycle club there were growing pains and that tended to make people sloppy. Cade wasn't sloppy. At thirty years old, he was considered young to be the president of an MC. All of our officers were young, between twenty-six and thirty, but every one of us was ruthless. We had no problem killing to protect our investments, or our club.

We owned territory that contained all the main shipping routes to the west coast. It's why we took over the club, instead of moving on and forming our own. It was also highly coveted by the other local MCs. The mafia organizations didn't bother with us, luckily. That was an additional problem that we didn't need. They preferred to buy from us rather than start another war and attempt to edge us out.

Nodding to Alexis, I folded my arms over my chest. "We're happy to supply Enzo with as many weapons as he needs." I glanced over and watched as our prospects and his man loaded the crates of M4s and pistols from our vehicle to theirs.

"The payment is being sent." Alexis watched the exchange as well. We stood silently as the deal wrapped up. I appreciated that he was a man of few words. That quality probably made many men nervous, but it took a lot to throw me off my game.

I pulled my phone out of my pocket when it vibrated.

Rat: Payment is made.

I turned toward Alexis. "Let us know when you need the next shipment."

Alexis nodded. "I'll be in touch." Both Russians got in the car and waited for a prospect to roll up the door so that they could leave.

Gunnar walked up and clapped a hand on my shoulder as we watched the car turn the corner. "Do you have to head back to the garage?"

I nodded, finishing a cigarette. My brother, Riggs, and I owned a local mechanic's shop. We built custom bikes and repaired both bikes and cars. It was work we both loved and gave us the freedom to come and go for club business.

"Did you invite your little college girl to the party tomorrow night?" I asked, thinking about the brunette from this morning.

Gunnar chuckled. "Of course."

"Tell her to bring her friend." I ignored the way Gunnar's brows shot up and the shit-eating grin that spread over his face. It'd been years since I'd shown any interest in a female, other than fucking the club bunnies who hung around at our parties. I didn't want to listen to whatever he had to say, so I hopped on my bike. That was the cue for the rest of the crew to move.

My enforcers followed me out, but once we hit the highway I split off, heading for our business, Valhalla Choppers. I was ready to get back to the shop. I didn't like leaving it alone without either Riggs or I there. As the sergeant at arms, it was my job to see to club security — and all that entailed — which meant I often had to skip out during the day to handle situations as they arose. Riggs wasn't much better since he was the vice president. We had a few employees who were all club members, so we knew we could trust them. But I still preferred one of us being there, when possible. Hiring club members just made the most sense for us. Not one of our guys questioned our comings and goings, and with the club, we were constantly on the move.

Gunnar took the lead back to the clubhouse, which was located about thirty minutes outside of Austin. We owned a big stretch of land, which was perfect since we didn't want neighbors all up in our business. I gunned the engine, trying to force my mind toward the bike waiting for me at the shop. Instead, a pair of whiskey-colored eyes kept creeping into my thoughts.

CHAPTER 5

Remi

"Ugh, when I said that we needed to do something together a few nights a week, this is *not* what I had in mind," Bridget complained, glaring around at our group of friends.

Plopping down onto the mats ass first, I let out a heavy sigh, catching my breath while I readjusted my boxing gloves. I looked over to where she was sprawled on her back, her blonde hair fanned out around her. Anna was crouched next to Bridget, elbows on her knees, head lowered, dark hair covering her face.

Ming and Julie stood next to the other girls, arguing back and forth in Chinese. I wasn't sure how the sisters had the breath to argue. I was still trying to catch mine after the last exercise.

Our parents had placed all of us into our school's Chinese immersion course. That first day was how we'd met each other as young girls. The course went on to teach us both English and Chinese, and our parents had been thrilled. We'd started from the time we were in kindergarten and continued through our senior year of high school. I wasn't fluent the way Ming and Julie were, but I could follow a conversation well enough.

Anna snapped something at the sisters from her spot on the mats, and it brought me back to the conversation in front of me. Ming was lecturing us about the need to remain healthy. I rolled my eyes, although good-naturedly. Ming was only a few years older than us, but she often acted more like a mother than a friend.

"I meant we should be going out to a club or a bar together," Bridget wheezed again and Julie just grinned at her.

I said nothing. I couldn't respond. My lungs were currently fighting to provide me with enough oxygen so that my body could go on living.

"This is way better than a club." Julie had a prim look on her face, and damn her, she was barely even breathing hard. Her dark brown eyes clashed with Bridget's baby blues. She'd switched back to speaking English.

"Exercising is very important for our bodies and health." This came from Ming. She was in her last year of residency and was about to become a doctor at our local hospital's ER. That meant we were never safe from her health lectures.

"And we learn how to defend ourselves." Both Bridget and Anna groaned, expecting to hear the same speech we'd gotten a few nights ago from Julie. I swear, she'd only gotten Anna to agree to this so she'd finally stop talking about how important it was that we were careful and safe.

I didn't mind that we were here at the gym, though. I glanced around and inhaled the smell of leather and sweat. The sound of other people punching bags and the clang of the weights hitting racks and the floor was strangely comforting. I missed playing sports. I'd spent all of high school playing on various sports teams. I'd always been athletic, and it was something that my dad and I had shared. He'd gone to all of my games and we'd often stay up late, talking strategy on how to beat some of the better teams.

Unfortunately, a little less than a year ago, my dad had passed away from cancer. I felt the familiar lump tighten in my chest as I thought about him. He'd been the love of my life. A single dad who had taken on the challenge of raising his little girl with no help. He would have liked that I'd taken up boxing. A former Marine, my dad was never one to back down from a fight. He would have liked knowing that I was training to take care of myself.

He was the best. My heart clenched in my chest.

"Earth to Remi!" I jumped when Julie leaned down and waved a hand in front of my face. I shot her a sheepish grin.

"Sorry. Brain took a vacation for a minute."

Her gaze was sympathetic, her look mirrored Bridget's and Ming's. Anna's might have been as well if she hadn't changed positions. She was now lying face down on the mats. I wrinkled my nose. "People sweat all over those, Anna." She just muttered something and rested her cheek on the mat, eyes closed.

These girls were my family and had been since Bridget had first marched up to us that first day and declared that we all would be friends. We'd grown up together, in the same neighborhood, us younger girls went all the way through high school together, so it was no surprise that we were now at the same college and were also roommates. We'd opted for a house off-campus, since Ming was no longer in school, and couldn't live on campus. Plus, there was no way we were going to chance being split up, which would be the case if we lived in the dorms.

"Thinking about your dad?" Julie asked, soft enough the other girls couldn't hear from their positions on the ground. I nodded, my mouth thinning into a grim line. I couldn't figure out how she could always tell when I was thinking about him. Julie was a psychology major. She was going to make the best therapist one day. Until then, we often had to put up with her psychoanalyzing us.

I avoided her gaze and watched as a guy squatted an impressive amount of weight across the room. His thighs looked like they could crack a coconut between them. I was mentally avoiding the talk Julie was attempting to have, and I knew it.

She opened her mouth to say something, but cringed when Sergio bellowed at us from the sidelines. He'd given the women in the self-defense class a ten-minute break while he'd gone to answer a phone call.

"Get off the mats! You don't lay down when you're tired! Stand up. Bridget. Anna, if you need to, put your hands over your head and breathe deep."

Both girls grumbled and glared at Julie and Ming for getting us into this mess, but gamely got to their feet. "We just did so much punching I couldn't lift my arms over my head if I wanted to," Bridget grouched and I couldn't help but laugh.

Now that we were juniors, and we were all hitting our stride in higher education, Bridget had suggested we come up with something the five of us could do together at night. We'd all been pulled in so many directions it wasn't unusual to only see the girls in passing, for a few days at a time, despite living together.

She'd been mentioning for a while that we needed to take the time to socialize together, but had waited until last week to insist. It had taken me a lot of time to not only grieve for the loss of my dad, but to get my life situated now that I owned the only other baby he'd had in life—Mackenzie's Trucking.

He'd retired from the Marines fairly young and with a teenage daughter to provide for he'd pooled all his resources to start his own trucking company. It'd exceeded his expectations in every way, and after his death, it became mine. There'd been a lot of family drama over the company, but things were starting to smooth out a little.

I was finally in a better headspace, back on track with my business degree, and learning how to deal with the business. Things were busy, but I was managing to deal with Dad being gone which was why Bridget sprang her plan on us.

"Seriously, we could go home, shower and change, and still make it in time for the huge frat party at Delta Sigma Phi," Bridget muttered unhappily.

Now she's pouting. Glancing over in amusement, I watched Bridget pick imaginary lint off her pants. Normally, Bridget wouldn't mind these classes, but not when the football team's fraternity was having a kegger.

We all knew she meant we should go drinking or dancing. She liked to gripe about the fact that none of us acted like irresponsible twenty-one-year-old college kids. Sure, we'd gone out for each other's birthdays, well, except for mine since it was on the day my dad had passed. I remember that birthday for a very different reason than most kids my age. They went out and celebrated the fact that they could legally drink. I'd just tried to find a way to make it through the worst day of my life. Now my twenty-second birthday was looming, and I wanted to be able to fast forward and completely skip the day.

"Drop it, Bridge." Julie all but growled at her.

Bridget's mouth twisted into a disappointed pout and she flounced off to go stand next to Anna. Julie sighed, then side-eyed me. Before she could say anything, I responded to the question she hadn't asked.

"I'm fine, Jules. I promise." Her concern had nothing to do with drinking or the gym. I didn't bother to get upset about the fact that Julie constantly checked in with me. They all did.

I hadn't handled my dad's death well in the beginning. It'd taken months to pick myself up. Luckily, my Uncle Caleb was the manager at Mackenzie's, and he'd been doing both his and my dad's jobs while I pulled myself together. Now, I'd been slowly learning the ropes so that I could take over and Uncle Caleb could go back to doing the manager position he loved. He never envied my dad being the owner, something he'd told me many times before. Our relationship had been strained thanks to Dad's death and him running everything.

"Break's over!"

Bridget groaned when Sergio came over and started setting us up with focus mitts to punch. This wasn't a normal self-defense class. Julie hadn't been lying. It was a workout. But while we sweated, Sergio made sure he taught us everything we'd need to know to be able to defend ourselves. At least he taught us enough so that we could escape. None of us, including the other ten women in the class, had any delusions that we could go toe to toe with a man in a fight and win right now. Sergio was going to help change that.

We practiced punching, we did cardio, we punched some more,

then finally Sergio had us circle around so that he could demonstrate the new move he wanted to teach us during this lesson.

When we limped into our house that night, with the exception of Julie and Ming, we all went our separate ways. The first thing I wanted was a blistering hot shower. Then I had a ton of homework to do for my classes. Two nights a week, and all day Wednesdays and Saturdays I worked at Mackenzie's. It was more work than I had ever thought it could be.

Between that and school I hadn't been around as much, which is why the girls had mandated the hangout sessions. Anna agreed with Julie when she'd vetoed Bridget's idea of going dancing. I'd shrugged and said I didn't care what we did. It was just nice to be around my friends. Anna was likely going to regret agreeing to the defense class, but she'd stick with it, we all would. Most weeks it was only one night a week. Sergio wanted two in our first week so he could get everyone signed up and all the paperwork filled out.

I started the shower and began planning a to-do list for tomorrow. As steam filled my room from the attached bathroom, I pulled all my books from my bag and got all my homework laid out on my bed. I dropped the empty bag on the chair next to my desk and hesitated.

Picking up the picture frame, I stared at my dad's laughing face. I looked so much like him. We had the same wide smile, the same light brown eyes, and dark hair. He'd been such a handsome man. I grinned remembering all the times he'd gotten hit on at the PTA meetings and the grocery store. It had made him so uncomfortable.

He'd just wanted to be the best dad he could be. For so many years he'd put his life on hold for me. I wanted to make him proud by taking over his company and making sure it continued to grow and flourish.

The knot that had been residing in my chest for the last year tightened so fiercely I sucked in a breath. Tears pricked my eyes as I set the photo back down. "I miss you," I murmured.

A knock on the door interrupted my thoughts and before I could say anything Bridget burst through the door, bouncing on her toes. "He invited us to a party tomorrow night!"

"What?" I chuckled, watching her in amusement as she happily danced around the room. "Who did?"

"Gunnar. The biker from this morning. They're having a party at their MC's clubhouse." At the look on my face, her expression turned mutinous. "We're going."

The smile had slipped off my face at the idea of meeting her bikers at a party. "I don't know, Bridget. I don't think that's a very good idea."

"It's a perfect idea. It's Friday night and you don't have to work. I want to spend time together somewhere other than at a boxing gym. Do Anna and Julie have to work tomorrow?"

Both girls worked at Mackenzie's part-time. It was the perfect setup for all of us. It allowed us to have a job that worked around our school schedules.

"Anna is on shift. The other girls have dinner with their parents."

"Well, then, it's just you and me. We're going," she repeated with a firm tone. Before I could argue she flounced from the room, leaving me to finally take my shower.

CHAPTER 6

Steel

"Church in ten minutes!" Cade bellowed up the stairs of the clubhouse and a couple of the guys hanging out in the hallway groaned. It was four p.m. on Friday afternoon and Cade had called us all back to the clubhouse. Something must be up, and I could see the guys were wary as they trudged down the hallway toward the stairs. We all worked hard during the week.

The club had multiple legit businesses that we owned and ran. Then there were the activities that stayed off the books. We were a bigger club, but the workload kept us all hopping. Friday nights signaled the weekend. It was time to let loose and they didn't want anything to get in the way of the good time planned for tonight.

Gunnar fell in step beside me. We'd come home and immediately headed up to our rooms, hoping to shower before the meeting. "Any idea about what's going on?"

"Nope," I replied. Normally, I would know, but Riggs'd had other stuff to do this morning, so he hadn't been at the garage. When I asked

Cade, he'd just said he'd tell me what was going on in church with the others.

Gunnar didn't say anything else as we headed down the stairs and filed into the kitchen, which doubled as our meeting spot for now. I slid onto a stool at the island, setting the beers I'd grabbed from the fridge down. The clubhouse was in the middle of renovations. We were adding in more bedrooms for the brothers who chose to live here and a meeting room that the officers could hold church in.

The members who weren't officers went outside, giving us space. I saw Cade leaning against the wall that separated the kitchen and living room. He acknowledged me as Riggs, his vice president and my brother, walked in the front door.

Riggs clapped a hand on my shoulder as he passed, and I handed him one of the two beers I had sitting in front of me. He accepted it with a grunt of thanks. Riggs was two years older than me. He's the one who had brought me into the club. Our dad walked out on our mom a few years after I was born and it was my brother who taught me all the important shit, how to ride a bike, how to roll a joint, and that I should use a condom unless I wanted my dick to rot off. The memory of that talk made me grin as I watched him walk over to Cade. They clasped forearms in greeting and sat talking quietly.

My brother was a big motherfucker. He had finally topped out at six-six. Add that to muscle upon muscle packed on his frame, and most men didn't want to take him on. If he wasn't so important to Cade as VP, he would have continued to be an enforcer. Not that I was much smaller. I was six-four and thanks to the grueling workouts Gunnar put us through in the morning I was almost as big.

As the rest of the officers filed in and sat down, Cade sat at the end of the table and Riggs took the seat next to me. "Alright, let's get going." Cade looked around at his officers, his most trusted men.

"Steel, how did the drop go yesterday?" His green eyes met mine. I'd already given him my report, but he had me repeat it for everyone else.

"No problems. According to Alexis, Enzo is happy with the product and plans on ordering more."

Cade nodded. "Good, that's going to help a lot with cash flow for the club. Let's make sure we stay in good standing with the Bratva. We don't want to piss those guys off." Everyone sitting at the table nodded in agreement.

"Absolutely," I agreed.

"Anything new to report from the field?" Cade and his VP looked around expectantly.

"We came across some Lycans last night," Axel, our road captain, spoke up. I tensed, wondering why I was just hearing about this now. As the sergeant at arms, my enforcers and I should have been contacted to take care of that problem.

Axel shot me an apologetic look. "Sorry Steel, but they took off as soon as they saw us. We lost them downtown. I would have called, but I knew you were busy with the drop. I would have still called, even with the drop happening, if we'd been able to keep up with them."

I nodded and took a long swallow from the bottle in front of me. It was a good call, which is why Cade trusted Axel to be the captain.

"What were they doing?" This came from Riggs.

"Honestly, I'm not sure. We spotted them coming out of an alley. By the time we got close enough they were on their bikes, had seen us, and booked it through late afternoon traffic." Axel ran a hand through his short black hair and blew out a frustrated breath.

The Lycans were getting ballsier by the day. It was starting to piss us all off. No other club should be encroaching into our territory.

"Probably dealing," Trip, one of my enforcers, chimed in. Cade had asked him and Drew, another enforcer, to join the meeting today. "There's been rumors of a new drug circling the local clubs and the campus." We all listened intently. This wasn't good news. "My old lady said a few college kids were sent to the hospital thanks to something that was passed around at a campus party a few days ago."

"Fuck," I muttered. Sure, we sold drugs, too. But our shit was clean. We never cut our product with stuff that would kill people. It was bad for business to kill off the clients. This was more of that forward-thinking that made Cade a better president. Plus, we didn't need a bunch of irate parents connecting their kids' deaths to our MC.

"Alright. Steel." I focused on Cade. "Get a plan together to see if we can get a hold of this new drug. Begin a rotation to keep an eye on both the campus and a few of the more prominent nightclubs in the area. If you see a Lycan, I want them alive so that we can question them. We need to figure out what their play is and go from there."

"Yup." I nodded and looked over when Gunnar nudged me.

He smirked. "I volunteer to watch the campus." A lecherous grin spread over his face. I frowned and shook my head.

"Keep it in your pants, asshole. I'm not putting you at the campus or clubs. I have another job for you. One that won't let you get anywhere near that number of females." We all knew it was pointless to expect Gunnar to get anything vertical done when women were around.

"We can put a few extra members on it if you need more manpower," Riggs spoke up again. "Hell, even the prospects could babysit the campus."

I nodded in acknowledgment of his offer. We had six prospects right now. Four had been with us for close to a year. It wouldn't be long until they were patched in, so we trusted them with handling our business. The other two were fairly new. He knew there was no way I'd trust the two new prospects with that kind of responsibility. Hell, they weren't even allowed to guard the clubhouse alone yet.

"I'll get it done," I spoke to both Cade and Riggs. They nodded.

"Drew, Trip, speaking of drugs. How's our product moving?" Both men grinned at our president.

"Great. It was a brilliant idea to start up at the campus." Everyone rolled their eyes. Of course, Trip thought it was a good idea, it was his. Dealing at the campus could blow up in our faces, but it was hard to deny that it was working out well so far. That's what had brought in the two new recruits. Plus, our drugs were flying off the shelf. College kids loved to party.

The back door to the clubhouse slammed open and a younger kid in khaki shorts and a white t-shirt strolled in. He paused when he saw all of us sitting there staring at him incredulously. "Hey, guys!" An insolent grin crossed his face.

I was up, out of my seat in an instant. Storming around the island, I grabbed him by the back of the shirt and started dragging him out the door. I heard voices start back up in the kitchen again as I walked him around the side of the building.

"What the fuck man? Let me go, Steel," the kid whined.

"What the fuck? You just walked in on church, Prospect." The kid struggled, but he was a buck fifty to my two twenty and I easily overpowered him.

"You guys rarely have church this early. I just figured you were hanging out before the party tonight." He jerked again, and this time I let him go and watched as he stumbled away from me.

"With all of our officers there? You're a dumbass, but you're not that fucking stupid. Do that again and you'll regret it," I growled at him and felt slightly appeased when his face lost a little color. We were standing in the parking lot out back, where we parked our bikes. We absolutely hazed our prospects, but as long as they were fitting in, we didn't let it get too out of hand. After all, what good was a prospect if he was crippled? Kids like this, though?

I eyed him up and down and scoffed. He didn't belong here. He was a preppy college kid who was just here trying to be a badass and get easy access to coke. "Where the fuck is your cut, Prospect?"

He flinched. "That's what I was going in to get. It's in my room." He fidgeted in front of me and it set my teeth on edge.

"There's no reason it shouldn't have already been on you. You'll know when church is done, then I suggest you grab it and make yourself scarce tonight."

His head shot up, eyes wide. "But what about the party?"

His whining voice was sending my blood pressure through the roof. I slammed a fist into his gut, knocking him back on his ass. He crab crawled backward as I advanced on him. Stopping his retreat, he held his hands up in an appeasing manner.

"If you want to take a chance and come to the party after pissing all of us off, be my guest. But there will be more of that waiting for you if you do." I watched as he stood up.

"Sure thing, Steel. I'll stay in my room." His voice was condescending and still had a whine to it. He shoved his hands in the pockets of his shorts.

I tilted my head to the side, studying him before I spoke again. "No. Join Bass for his rounds tonight." We had the prospects patrolling the compound in shifts tonight for the party. His face turned red, but he kept his mouth shut.

"Get the fuck out of my sight," I told him as I turned to head back inside. I shook my head as he stalked off to find Bass. This kid wasn't going to make it into our club. He didn't fit in, and no one liked him. I wasn't sure why he was still here. Opening the door, I noticed everyone was still sitting and were now quietly waiting for me at the table. I nodded at Cade and sat back down.

"Alright, you all have your assignments," Cade said, effectively dismissing everyone now that the meeting was over. "Let us know if you need anything." Everyone except Cade, Riggs, and Gunnar stood and shuffled out. I followed behind them, mind already on my assignment.

"Steel, hold up a minute." I paused when Cade called to me, then sat back down.

Cade raised his brows and Riggs scowled at me. "Everything okay out there?"

"It's fine. I explained where he messed up."

That made Cade chuckle. "I'm sure you did."

"He need any more reminders?" I met Riggs's dark gray eyes.

"I handled it."

"Good," Riggs grunted, leaned back, and crossed his arms.

"Heard you invited a new girl to the party tonight." It wasn't a question, but there was curiosity in the statement. Cade was staring at me, waiting on the reply to his question. I noticed Riggs giving me the side-eye as well, and I narrowed my own.

"Fuck you, Gunnar," I muttered and shot him a glare. It shouldn't surprise me he'd told Cade and Riggs that I'd invited her. He just grinned at me. The condescending prick was enjoying this.

Cade laughed, and even my brother chuckled, then said, "I don't know how you pulled a college girl. That ugly face usually scares them off."

I flipped them off and stood to head up to my room. As an officer, and a member of the club, I was expected to attend all of the functions, and I did. It didn't mean I stuck around for long at most of them. At the family functions, I closed the parties out. I wanted to be respectful to the guys' families. But the parties like tonight? I stayed long enough to get drunk, fuck, then kicked the girl out and stayed holed up in my room upstairs. None of the guys gave me too much shit about it, normally.

"Can't wait to see who you invited," Riggs smirked at me, his words stopping me in my tracks.

"I didn't invite her, Gunnar did."

Riggs rolled his eyes. "Because you told him to."

Cade slid a knowing look at Riggs before speaking to me. "If she doesn't belong to you, then you won't mind if the rest of us take a shot at her?" He flipped open a switchblade and used the tip to clean under his nails.

I spun back around and slammed my hands on the surface of the island. "Hands off," I snarled.

All three men wore smug looks on their faces thanks to my outburst. The four of us had been friends forever. I'd never speak this way to Cade or Riggs in front of the rest of the group. I had to set an example for the rest of the members. But in private? They were just my dick head brother and his friend who had hung out at our place twenty-four hours a day.

Gunnar's grin had me snarling at him. We'd been best friends forever but there were times he needed to show the proper respect to me, as his sergeant at arms. Shoving off the counter, I left the room, gritting my teeth while their laughter followed me.

I heard a pair of boots on the stairs behind me and huffed out an annoyed breath when I looked back and saw my brother following me. I ignored him at first, but I knew he wasn't going to leave me alone. It was rare that Riggs wanted to have a serious talk, but when he did, he always said what he needed to.

"What?"

"Who is she?"

I grunted a non-committal answer. I reached the door to my room within the clubhouse and tried to shut it in my brother's face, but he just propped a massive shoulder on the frame. Riggs crossed his arms over his chest and waited.

"Just some girl I met yesterday morning."

He cocked a brow at me, but said nothing. He knew if he cracked a joke right now, I'd slam the door on him.

I wasn't sure how to explain why this particular girl was stuck in my head and was creating such a restless, predatory feeling inside of me. All I knew was that when she'd been running away yesterday something inside of me had been triggered and I'd wanted to chase her, toss her down, and fuck her. More than that, I knew once I caught her, I wouldn't let her go.

"What Cade said…"

"He was fucking with you."

"Still, let the others know that she's mine. Anyone puts their hands on her, and I'll cut them off."

Our eyes locked. "Fuck." Riggs rubbed his hand over the stubble that lined his jaw. "Yeah alright, little brother. I'll make sure the guys understand."

We nodded at each other and he pushed off the door frame and walked down the hall as I went inside. I'd just told him, without as many words, that I was claiming this woman as my own. A woman I knew nothing about. It didn't matter because I now knew the only thing I needed to. It'd been nagging me since yesterday, but hadn't clicked until Cade had goaded me and until my brother had prodded me into admitting it.

Whoever she was, she belonged to me.

CHAPTER 7

Remi

I dropped my bag at the door of our house and walked over to flop onto the couch on my back. Today had been busy, but had gone smoothly. It'd been hard to concentrate, knowing that tonight we were supposed to be meeting up with the bikers from yesterday. I still had plans to try to talk some sense into Bridget, but I wanted to grab a shower, then settle in to work on my homework.

Bridget jogged down the stairs. "Hey! I'm glad you're home! Now, you have a few hours at least, to shower and change." Bridget looked at me expectantly.

I frowned at her. "What?"

"The party. It starts at ten." She glanced at the clock.

I gave her an incredulous look. "Seriously, Bridget? What makes you think it's a good idea to go to a party at their place? Those guys are dangerous."

She laughed. "Of course, they are. They're one-percenters."

I frowned at her in confusion. "What does that mean?"

"It means their club is part of the one-percent who delve into illegal shit. Most MCs are just guys who want to ride bikes. The one-percenters live a whole different lifestyle."

"Was that guy you dated in high school, Todd? Travis? Tim? Whatever, was he in one of those one-percent clubs?" I asked her in shock. Her dad had thrown a conniption fit when she'd brought the guy home, but consorting with a known felon? It literally would have put her politically-minded father in the grave.

"Todd. No, he was way too strait-laced to ever be involved in anything illegal." She laughed and pulled out a compact with a mirror to check her makeup.

"Look." She set it down. "Just come with me tonight. If we don't have fun, I'll never ask you to do anything like this again."

I narrowed my eyes at her. "Bullshit, you'll ask again." She blinked at me with an innocent look on her fast. I sighed, but knew I'd already lost.

"Bridge, I really, really don't think this a good idea."

"Noted. Now, let's go find you something to wear so that you can get ready."

"It's four-thirty, Bridget." I stared at her in disbelief. "It's not going to take me five and a half hours to get ready."

She wrinkled her nose at me, managing to look like an adorable bunny. "Maybe if you took five and a half hours, you'd be able to keep a guy around."

I threw my hands up in the air. "For fuck's sake. Yes, because that's what's important to me right now. I'm a twenty-one-year-old in danger of becoming a cat lady because I don't have a boyfriend." I glowered at her. "I am taking more than a full load of classes this semester, so I can hopefully graduate a year early. Not to mention, I have Mackenzie's to deal with. I don't have time for a guy."

Bridget winced at the mention of my dad's company. I sighed as the ache started up in my chest. I'd lost him almost a year ago, and I still felt like I was drowning. Sure, I had my uncle, but it wasn't the same without my dad. He'd always been my rock. He'd been so proud when I'd gotten into the University of Texas. That pride, and the love he had for Mackenzie's, were the only things that finally made me pull myself out of the deep well of despair I'd found myself in and kept me moving forward.

Uncle Caleb was ready for me to fully take over, he'd been showing me the ropes along the way. But I wanted to finish my business degree. Dad had wanted that, too. Besides, a twenty-one-year-old kid in charge of a multi-million-dollar company? It was ridiculous. But it was my life and now it was up to me to keep Dad's business running. I'd need to work hard to impress the truckers who drove for us.

I was hoping since Uncle Caleb was staying on as the manager, even after I started running the show full time, that the transition would go smoothly. I'd known these truckers for most of my life. I hoped they weren't going to object to me being their new boss.

"I'll help you pick out what to wear tonight." Bridget's eyes brightened.

Hell no! The last time I fell for that, she'd had me in a skirt and three-inch heels. I almost broke my neck.

"I can dress myself."

Bridget rolled her eyes. "Will you please make an effort?"

"They're bikers, Bridge. I doubt there will be anyone there in Louis Vuitton." Bridget's love of fashion had rubbed off on me enough to pull that brand name out of my head. The girl had so many designer names in her closet, even I knew who some of them were. She sighed but gave up, wandering into the kitchen for a drink. I grabbed my bag and escaped up the stairs and into my room before she realized I left.

CHAPTER 8

Remi

I tossed my bag onto my bed. Glancing at the clock, I let my gaze bounce between my bed and the bathroom.

Shower or homework first? Shower, I decided.

Shucking off my clothes, I crossed the room. Leaving the trail of clothes from my room to my attached bathroom, I turned on the water to a blistering temperature.

Hopping into the shower, I soaped up my hair and thought back to yesterday. The biker with the gray eyes was downright frightening, but he was incredibly sexy, too. It was a lethal combination. He wasn't as pretty as the guy Bridget was into, but the rough and rugged look worked for him. I wasn't one to get rattled easily, but I'd never been around guys like that. He worried me even more than Gunnar, and I couldn't quite figure out why. It's not like I expected these guys to attack us. They were just unsettling. Maybe that's why he was so appealing.

I let the hot water pound over my body and leaned my head to the side to rest it on the tiled wall. Things had changed so much in the past year. I was just trying to keep up. I wanted to bail on tonight, but if I did Bridget would still go. I couldn't let her go by herself. I shut off the water and dried off and got dressed. I sat down to get as much homework done as I could before Bridget dragged me off to this party.

* * *

I PULLED my car into the dirt lot and shut it off. "We're going to die," I said, only half-joking, as I stared out the window. The complex was lit up. There was an enormous building sitting off to our left. The fence line went on forever and past the building was a dark forest.

"Shut up. You're being dramatic." She rolled her eyes at me. "This is going to be fun!" She hopped out of the car.

So much fun, I mouthed sarcastically as I slowly got out of the driver's side.

A long, low whistle drew my attention as a guy walked up. He had to be around our age, maybe a year or two older. He had on black jeans, a black t-shirt, and a black leather vest that had a patch on it that said prospect. I knew from Bridget — she had gone over some of her knowledge of MCs with me on the way over — that it meant he was trying to become a part of the club.

"Nice ride. I'm Bass." He eyed my car appreciatively as he introduced himself. His name made sense. His voice was deep and vibrated like the bass that was coming out of the speakers currently screaming from inside the clubhouse. The guy should have his own radio show with a sexy voice like that. It wrapped around a girl and made her think naughty thoughts. His handsome face helped with that, too.

The cherry red 1969 Camaro Z28 pretty much always got this reaction from guys. Not that the reaction was the reason I would forever keep it, or why I drove it. It was my dad's car. He bought it when I was fourteen and he'd been desperate to connect with his increasingly independent teenage daughter. We'd restored it together and had so much fun doing it.

"Thanks," I told him. I watched as a few other men passed by and eyeballed my car before their gazes raked up and down me and Bridget. "I'm Remi," I said, holding my hand out to him.

He grinned and gripped my hand. He had dark brown hair, blue eyes, and an easy smile. I was really surprised that Bridget was still scanning the crowd instead of taking notice of the hottie in front of us. I liked how at ease I felt around him.

"You two meeting someone here?" He looked between us curiously. I caught a spark of interest in his blue eyes when he looked at Bridget, but she was restlessly scanning the crowd, looking for Gunnar.

"Yeah, we're…" I broke off when Bridget about yanked my arm from its socket.

"Let's go!" Bridget pulled me along with her.

"Sorry!" I shouted back at him as we moved away far quicker than I thought she could in heels.

"Jesus, Bridge. You really have forgotten all those fancy etiquette classes your mom made you take, haven't you?" I laughed when she snorted at me. But then I glanced back at my car warily as we walked away. "You don't think anyone is going to steal the Camaro, do you?"

She didn't bother to answer. She hurried forward and pushed through a throng of bikers who were standing around in a circle. They were all yelling and whooping at whatever they were watching. Bridget shoved forward and disappeared into the crowd, leaving me on the outside.

"Um, excuse me," I yelled and tapped a man's shoulder. The nearest three bikers pinned me with irritated looks at first once they noticed me. When they realized it was a female talking to them, they moved aside with filthy grins. I hurried past, but not before someone grabbed my ass. "Gross," I muttered and pushed through until I found Bridget.

We were standing at the edge of a circle that'd been drawn in the dirt. I watched in shock as the two guys in the ring beat the hell out of each other. They didn't have gloves or shirts on, just jeans and boots. The bigger fighter caught the smaller guy in the face and blood sprayed across the dirt. His eyes rolled back into his head and he crumpled into a heap on the ground.

Everyone around us was either cheering or booing, depending on who they'd bet on. Bridget's wide eyes met mine, and she opened her mouth. Before she could say anything, an arm went around each of our shoulders. I cringed at the tall blond guy who tucked me up under his arm and started toward the clubhouse.

"Hey, baby. Let's head inside." He didn't give me a chance to respond, he just started pulling me along with him. The guy's breath wafted into my face and my eyes stung. The fumes coming off him were enough to get me drunk.

I looked over and saw Bridget stumble a little in the dirt. The red-headed guy walking with her caught her and kept moving, propelling her forward. Those high heels were giving her problems out here. I'd been wrong earlier, there was someone at this party with Louis Vuitton's on.

I shook my head at Bridget's expensive shoes and her short skirt. Bridget didn't sleep around; she didn't need to. She was gorgeous, rich, and popular — the men waited for her. But she did enjoy showing off her...assets. I tried to pull away from the biker, but his arm just tightened until he almost had me in a headlock. I decided it would just be better to go along. The crowd that'd been watching the fight was filing back into the building.

As we approached, I let out a strangled noise when I noticed what was happening on the porch. Bridget let out a high-pitched, nervous giggle, and the guys 'escorting' us gave us lecherous grins. Sitting halfway out of the shadows, a guy was on a long bench with a woman kneeling between his legs, giving him a blow job. The guy looked over at us and raised his beer in a salute. Everyone around us laughed and went inside.

Well, fuck me, I thought and was dragged inside by a tattooed arm.

CHAPTER 9

Remi

The blare of the music made my ears ring. It poured out of a stereo sitting along a wall near a table that had bottles of hard alcohol on it. Next to those were rows of coolers. Bodies were pressed together and gyrated on the makeshift dance floor. A couch had been shoved into a corner, and a bunch of chairs and stools formed a U around the dancers.

Men in cuts walked past, talking, drinking, and eyeballing the women. Most of the women had skirts on as short, or shorter, than Bridget's and bras were being worn in lieu of shirts.

Oops, I guess I'm overdressed.

I had on my typical jean shorts, tank, and white Adidas. It didn't matter though. I didn't want to dress up for these guys anyway, and I wouldn't be caught dead in any of the outfits the women wore.

I was tired of being dragged along by this guy. We were moving toward a set of stairs that headed to the next floor.

That can't be good. I caught Bridget's eye and made a motion. She nodded, and we both heaved our elbows back as hard as we could into the guys' stomachs. I was instantly grateful for Sergio and those self-defense classes we were taking. This was the exact move Sergio showed our group last night. As soon as they doubled over, we bolted.

Well, I ran. Bridget clip-clopped her way across the floor in her heels. I looked back at her and couldn't help but laugh. She looked ridiculous.

Behind her I saw the guys coming after us, their faces thunderous. My gaze shot back to her face when her blue eyes widened. I didn't have time to wonder what the problem was because I plowed directly into a heavily muscled body. Strong hands caught my shoulders as I rebounded backward off the guy. I would have landed on my ass if he hadn't grabbed me.

Bridget tried to stop but the bottoms of her heels slid as she put on the brakes. She crashed into me, shoving me into him further.

His body was like concrete. Bridget was bent over, gripping my hips, and had all her weight on me. I was pinned. My face was dangerously close to his neck, if I stuck my tongue out, I'd be licking that deliciously tanned skin. Not that I wanted to do that. I closed my eyes and inhaled the smell of motor oil combined with something citrusy before I yanked my head back and looked up. A cold feeling settled in my stomach as gray eyes glared down at me. It was the second biker from yesterday. I glanced over and watched as the two guys we'd elbowed caught up and started yelling, or slurring since most of their words were running together.

Finally, Bridget's weight was off of me and I stumbled backward, away from the guy I'd just run into. My backward momentum was halted when he wrapped a hand around my wrist. I looked up at his face, but he was looking over at the drunks. I tugged my arm, trying to break his grip, but he just tightened it without even looking at me.

Following his gaze, I saw Gunnar had gotten into the face of the guy who had been walking Bridget inside. Between the music and the voices of the people gathering around us to watch, I couldn't hear what they were saying. Their body language was telling a pretty good story, though. They looked like they were about to come to blows.

Sure enough, Gunnar cracked his knuckles right into the guy's jaw. My gasp was swallowed up by the roar of the crowd. The guy who had been pulling me along had gotten smart and backed off. He was standing with the spectators, but when I met his gaze, his eyes flashed furiously at me. I swallowed; my mouth had gone dry because the look he shot me was filled with hate.

Someone crashed into my shoulder hard enough that I almost lost my balance. The hand holding my wrist tightened again and gray eyes reeled me in toward his body. His arm moved from my wrist and wrapped over my shoulder and down across my back, his hand ending up on my left hip as he tucked me up against his side. He took a drink from a beer bottle as he continued to watch the fight.

What the hell is wrong with these people?

Furiously, I flattened my left hand against his side and tried to push away from him. The look he shot at me as he, once again, tightened his arm, made every bit of moisture flee my mouth. He glared down at me, his eyes flashing dangerously. It was a warning to stay put.

I considered my options. I could elbow this guy, like I had the last, and run, but that would mean leaving Bridget. I couldn't even find her in the crowd of tall bikers. The crowd cheered as the two men went down on the floor and they started wrestling for the best position. I went back to my plans. I could stand here and let this guy manhandle me, or I could do something about it.

Nope, not an option, I thought grimly. I settled for plan C.

I snuck a sideways glance at his face. He was back to watching the fight. The sound of bone hitting bone and grunts of pain filled the air when the crowd wasn't cheering. Someone had turned the music off when the fight started.

"Hey Steel!" Someone called and gray eyes looked over and focused on someone across the room. Steel? Why did bikers always have oddball names?

He raised his other arm, signaling to two guys who started pushing their way to where the fighters were still pummeling each other. I couldn't tell if Gunnar was drunk too, but even drunk, both of these guys could fight. They seemed pretty evenly matched.

As the guys rushed the ring, I realized they were about to break the fight up. That meant my window of opportunity to get away from Steel was closing fast. His thickly muscled bicep was heavy around my shoulder and despite liking how he smelled I wasn't about to hang around here for another minute.

As he watched the others, I quickly ducked, bending almost all the way forward. Once his hand had slipped off my hip, I stepped back and then to the side, accidentally hitting the top of my head on his side as I ducked the rest of the way under his arm. I didn't hesitate for a minute. Once I'd cleared his body, I ran.

I didn't hear him over the noise, but I knew he was coming after me. My heart pounding, I darted around the outside of the circle, trying to find Bridget. I caught a flash of pink out of the corner of my eye and slowed for a fraction of a second. That was all it took. A freight train rammed into me from behind. Two muscular arms wrapped around me, one under my breasts, the other over my hips, and Steel picked me up. I dangled there as he took a few more steps. He'd been trying to stop. Rather than run me over, he'd just brought me along with him.

Once he set me back on my feet, I started struggling again. There was no way I was going to stand here and wait to be dragged upstairs. I yelped in surprise when Steel whipped me around to face him. Stormy gray eyes searched mine for a heartbeat. Before I knew what was happening my world turned upside down. He'd thrown me over his shoulder.

Oh. My. God. I was fuming. I didn't think guys did this kind of shit anymore. I pounded my fists on his back.

"Put me down, you fucking asshole!"

CHAPTER 10

Steel

The brunette was a wildcat. She was punching my back as hard as she could. They weren't dainty little slaps either. The girl could throw fists. Luckily, since she was currently draped over my shoulder, there wasn't any real power behind her hits. Not that it would have stopped me either way. I slapped my free hand across her ass. Chuckling at her yelp, I listened to her cuss me out, but it made her stop hitting me.

Gunnar and I had just walked into the clubhouse when we saw our girls being led across the floor towards the stairs going up to the bedrooms. We'd run over to Cade's house and had missed their arrival. Normally, that wouldn't have been a big deal, but an hour earlier five of our MC's nomads had shown up unexpectedly. That was why we were at Cade's in the first place. These guys traveled around to the different chapters in our MC. We had chapters all over the country and they stuck around for a while until they moved on again, never staying in one place for long.

All our brothers who were here permanently had been warned not to touch the two girls Gunnar and I had invited tonight. That message hadn't been passed on to these assholes. Two of them were good guys. The other three, well, there was a reason they didn't belong anywhere.

I carried her all the way to Cade's house. Striding up the porch steps, I was about to open the door when it opened. I might have laughed at the look on Cade's face as he saw us there in the doorway if the girl hadn't started struggling again. An impressive string of profanity spewed out of her mouth. I could see my president trying not to laugh as he stepped aside to let me into his house.

We had fifteen acres that the clubhouse sat on. We'd built homes for the president and VP. Once the rest of the officers, myself included, got sick of living in the dorm-style rooms that sat on the top floor of the clubhouse, we'd build homes for ourselves as well. Usually, the guys moved out once they got married and started having kids. Cade and Riggs just liked having their own space. I found it easier to stay in the clubhouse so I could keep an eye on things.

Cade strode out of the house, shutting the door behind him without saying anything. I heard her make a sound of frustration. "I'm getting a headache. Put me down. Now."

I smirked at the authority in her voice. She wasn't in any position to be making demands. But I didn't plan on carrying her over my shoulder all night. I swung her down and set her on her feet. She swayed as all the blood rushed back to her head, so I held onto her shoulder to steady her.

She stepped back, swatting at my hand on her shoulder, and her eyes darted around the house. She was looking for the exit points.

"I need you to stay here for a bit." I tried not to growl, but my deep voice didn't sound reassuring at the best of times. It certainly didn't now, judging by the look on her face. Seeing Ty with his hands on her had sent rage rocketing through me. I was still riding the high. I sighed when she flinched.

"Look, just have a seat." I gestured to the couch behind her. "I'm not going to do anything to you. Those guys you were with aren't usually here, and they didn't know that you and your friend were off-limits." Her gorgeous eyes flashed up to mine. "Gunnar is giving them the message."

CHAPTER 11

Remi

"Off-limits? Why would you have to tell them that people are off-limits? I'm pretty sure anyone with a brain knows you don't fucking touch without consent." Except the guys hadn't bothered with that. I'd like to give them the benefit of the doubt and say that they would have stopped to talk to us, but his next words sent an icy dread swirling through my stomach.

"These aren't frat parties. There's a different set of rules here." He ran a hand over his short, dark hair. "If a woman isn't someone's old lady, kid, or isn't claimed, it's assumed they're a club bunny." My brows drew together in confusion.

"A club bunny?"

"Women who specifically come to these parties to get drunk and fuck. Most of the time no one bothers asking because they're fully aware of what they're here for."

My mouth dropped open. Women wanted that? I mean, yeah, a lot of the guys here were gorgeous, so I guess I couldn't fully blame them.

"Those guys thought we were here to…" I trailed off, realizing that I was sitting in a random house, alone, with this guy. My eyes slid to the front door.

"Do. Not. Run," he growled out between gritted teeth. He must have read my expression. "Until we get shit straightened up out there, it's not safe for you to be running around. A couple of those nomads aren't known for being gentlemen."

I scoffed. Like any of these guys were even close to the realm of gentlemen. But I got what he was saying. They were worse than bad. A thought occurred to me. "Bridget!"

"She's fine. Trip was hanging onto her until Gunnar finished pounding the message into Red's face." He crossed those huge arms over his chest.

I took this completely inappropriate time to study his tattoos. It was hard not to notice the one across the front of his throat. I peeked at his left arm and could tell by the pattern that it continued up under his shirt. I wondered how far up his shoulder it went.

"Look, if you promise not to take off, I'll go grab you a drink." I nodded my assent. He gave me a hard look before he went through the doorway, leaving me to think about the life choices that had landed me here.

I was like Alice in Wonderland. Bridget said these guys lived a different lifestyle, but I hadn't realized what she'd meant until now. My thoughts were a complete jumble. I guess Steel had just been trying to help me. But I still didn't trust him as far as I could throw him. Eyeballing his huge frame standing in the kitchen, I estimated that was about zero feet.

I was also still worried about Bridget. At the same time, I'd been mentally throwing every curse word in the book at her since I was first slung over Steel's shoulder. I would say I couldn't believe that she got us into this mess, but really, I could. The situations she'd managed to get us into hadn't been this bad in a while.

The last time was in the funhouse with that clown... I shuddered at the memory but shook the thoughts away when Steel walked back in with two glasses.

He handed one to me, then pulled the coffee table backward, one-handed. He sat down on it, facing me. I glanced down into my glass and tried to figure out what I was about to drink. Drinking wasn't something I indulged in often, but if it could chase away the cold in the pit of my stomach that flared up anytime I thought about what could have happened, then I'd happily drink a whole bottle.

Steel took a long swallow of his and I lifted my glass. Something occurred to me and I quickly dropped it back down. Steel's eyebrows rose as he studied my face. A look of recognition appeared on his face and then he rolled his eyes at me. He leaned forward and snatched the glass out of my hand. He drank a small amount out of my glass and then handed it back to me. He must have been able to see the conflict on my face.

It was unnerving how well this man could read me. I'd never really considered whether I was easily readable before now. I wondered if I was or if he was just good at it?

"Hey." He waited until my eyes met his. "I won't rape you. I won't drug you. I won't hurt you. I would never do anything like that to any woman. But I especially wouldn't do anything to you." His tone was so starkly honest that it left no doubt in my mind that he was telling the truth.

His declaration eased some of the indecision warring in my brain. I took a swallow of what turned out to be whiskey. I coughed into my hand. I hated whiskey.

Steel smirked, then stretched his long legs out in front of him. His boots were now sitting next to me in front of the couch. "What's your name?"

I responded without thinking about it. "Remi." As soon as it was out of my mouth, I wondered if I should have told him that.

Oh well, at least he doesn't know my last name.

"Steel."

I nodded. "I know."

Something I couldn't read flashed in his eyes. "How do you know my name?" His voice was deadly calm, emphasis on the deadly.

"Oh, I heard someone at the fight call for you. You answered it, so I figured that was you," I finished lamely as he just watched me quietly. I'd never been around a guy who made me this nervous. He reminded me of a predator. He said he wouldn't hurt me, and I believed him. But when he went still and intense like that, it was like he was a big cat, like a tiger.

I took another sip of my drink, then licked the whiskey off my lips. He relaxed when I reminded him that someone had used his name. His gaze dropped to my mouth and held there so long that I finally cleared my throat. He looked back up and focused on my eyes. Maybe that wasn't a good idea. I'd never seen eyes the color of his before, a pale gray with the barest hint of blue. They were beautiful and hypnotizing. I broke the contact.

Rolling the glass between my palms, I wondered how I was supposed to feel about what happened tonight. Maybe it was an unintentional fuck up that happened because of a miscommunication and lack of knowledge of the rules. How was I supposed to feel about Bridget potentially dating Gunnar? Knowing that these are the kinds of situations she could be in on any given day? I peeked up and saw Steel still watching me.

How should I feel about that? He wasn't watching me with friendly concern.

Despite my lack of dating for the past year, I wasn't a nun. I knew when a man was interested in me. I couldn't lie to myself either, I was sexually interested in him.

God, I hope it's only sexual. Who wouldn't be attracted to this guy? I thought as I eyed him as discreetly as I could. But something told me this man only did things on his terms, and I would need things to happen my way right now.

There were so many things that were a night and day difference between his world and mine that even if I had the time, I wasn't sure I could give myself over to him. The way he was looking at me had my brain, heart, and libido going to war with each other. I was getting tied up in knots and he was sitting there looking completely calm.

"If you think any harder, your brain will stall." I looked up and gave him a soft laugh.

"I've been known to overanalyze occasionally." That was putting it mildly. I mentally shrugged. I didn't consider it to be an overly negative trait. In relationships, it sure was. But in other areas of my life? Examining a problem from every angle often helped me see the best course of action without having to fail first.

"What would make you feel better?" I blinked and asked myself the same question. "Would it help if I answered some questions? About myself. Maybe a little about the club, although there isn't much I can tell you there."

I nodded with a small smile. I was surprised he was willing to tell me anything. I wondered if this was the first time he'd offered to talk with someone. I hadn't been around him long, but it seemed like he wasn't much of a talker. Steel made a 'go-ahead' gesture.

"Steel. Metal or action?"

He gave me a strange look, but answered, "Metal."

"Uh-huh and is that your real name or nickname?"

"It's my road name." He said without elaborating. I chuckled to myself with how brisk and short his answers were.

"What's the difference between a road name and a nickname? One sounds tougher?" He glowered at me and crossed his muscular arms but didn't answer. I decided I should probably stop teasing the guy who could drag me out back and kill me without anyone knowing.

I looked down at the tattoos on his arm. They went all the way up from his wrist to disappear beneath the sleeve of his t-shirt. I wonder how many more he had? A naughty voice whispered in my head and asked where else he had them. I felt my face heat up. The ringtone on my phone blared into the silence, making me jump.

I pulled my phone out and groaned when Uncle Caleb's name showed up. I started to answer, but before I could, Steel's hand shot out and gripped my wrist, pulling it toward him. I looked at him incredulously and tried to pull my hand, with my phone in it, back toward me.

He tightened his grip, and it felt like he was seconds away from grinding the bone in my arm down to powder. Fury flashed in his eyes.

"What the hell, Steel?"

"Boyfriend?" his accusation came out short and choppy.

I was so confused I gave in and let him pull my hand close enough that he could read it.

He frowned when he saw **Uncle Caleb** on the screen. "Don't tell him where you are." He released my wrist, and I answered the phone while staring at him like he'd grown another head. I don't know why he cared if it was a boyfriend calling.

"Hey, Uncle Caleb, is everything okay?"

I heard him pause before answering. "Where are you?"

"I'm at a party with Bridget." I shifted in my seat. I didn't like lying to him, but then again, it wasn't really a lie.

Steel hadn't stopped doing that intense stare thing. *Stop it,* I mouthed at him.

His eyebrows shot up almost to his hairline and though he looked amused at my demand he didn't stop what he was doing.

I gave him a frustrated look. Maybe he didn't realize he was constantly giving me a broody stare?

"Seriously, Remi? You're out partying when you know we have a lot to do tomorrow?"

I sighed at the disappointment in his tone. "I'll be in tomorrow, Uncle Caleb. I promise. I just needed to blow off a little steam."

His silence stretched out longer than was comfortable. "You should be focusing on school. You should be focusing on the company. What you shouldn't be doing is partying." He snapped.

I closed my eyes and tried to take steadying breaths.

I am not going to lose my cool, I chanted in my head, *I am not going to lose my cool, I am not going...*

"Your father would be heartbroken to see you throwing his company away so you can go get wasted."

That fucking did it. "You know what, Uncle Caleb?" I shouted into the phone, too pissed off to notice the dangerous look Steel shot me.

"Maybe Dad would be fucking disappointed that his lazy-ass brother is pressuring his twenty-one-year-old daughter into killing herself trying to finish school and graduate early so that she can run his company. The company that you promised him, on his fucking death bed, that you would run for the next three years so that I could get my degree and learn the ropes."

Tears of frustration and exhaustion stung my eyes. The tension was so thick I could feel it across the connection. It had been a hell of a night so far, and I was close to my breaking point. Honestly, with how hard it'd been since Dad died; I've been at my breaking point for months.

"You know what, Remi?" I flinched at his cold tone and the way he threw my words back in my face. "Why don't you take the weekend off? I'll deal with the vendors tomorrow and I'll see you Monday night." The connection cut off.

He wasn't being nice, giving me the weekend off. No, that was a punishment. A fuck you, I don't want to see your face for a few days.

I loved my uncle; I really did, but the stress of Dad's death and running the company had us at each other's throats more days than not. It felt like he was constantly pushing me to hurry up. Finish school faster. Learn the business faster. Do everything better. Sometimes it felt like he wanted me to quit. Only he always insisted he didn't want Mackenzie's.

I was looking forward to taking over completely so that I could have my fun-loving uncle back. He hadn't wanted to be in charge, but he was the only one who could be once the cancer had taken over. It had happened so quickly Dad hadn't been able to teach me anything or hire anyone else. I let out a shaky breath and tapped the edge of the phone against my forehead.

I couldn't believe I just had that argument in front of a stranger. It was embarrassing and slightly pathetic. A strangled sound left my throat when Steel ripped my phone out of my hand. I blinked at him as he shut the ringer off, then shoved it in his back pocket.

That made me nervous. "Am I a prisoner here or something?" I tried to say it jokingly, but it must have sounded a bit desperate because his face softened ever so slightly.

CHAPTER 12

Steel

I listened as she spoke with her uncle. One nice thing about all these new smartphones, the speakers were amazing. I could hear everything coming through from the man on the other end. One side of my mouth twisted with humor when she blew up and chewed him out. She had a temper on her.

I raked my gaze over her body while her uncle responded. I saw her jerk slightly at what he said. I'd been thinking about what I wanted to do with that body while listening to her family drama. I watched as she thunked the phone against her forehead. She looked exhausted and by the sound of it; she was. I leaned forward and grabbed her phone. Turning the ringer off, I looked back up at her while I put it in my back pocket. She needed a night off and her uncle struck me as the kind of guy who'd keep hounding her all night.

A flicker of fear crossed her face. "Am I a prisoner here or something?" She might have pulled off the nonchalant tone if her voice hadn't cracked on the last word. She'd set her drink down while we were playing tug o' war over her phone, so I picked it up and thrust it back at her. She stared at it then took it from me.

"No, I just thought you wanted to blow off some steam?" Her head shot up when I repeated what she'd told her uncle. There was a hint of challenge in my voice. Her eyes narrowed.

Gotcha.

This girl was competitive. Now I knew how to work around her fear and uncertainty. Remi knocked back the rest of the whiskey and I grinned at her.

"I didn't know you could do that."

I raised a brow, a silent question.

"Smile," she clarified.

I just shook my head as she started to joke around again. I didn't smile often but seeing that flash of fire in her eyes as she silently accepted my challenge and slammed the rest of the liquor amused me.

"What are you in school for?" I asked her.

"A business degree. My dad was planning on leaving me his company in the future, so I thought it would be helpful." A sad look flitted over her face. The need to erase it rose sharply, surprising me.

"I guess that happened faster than any of us thought it would." She looked down at her glass.

"What happened?" I was a dick for asking, but I was curious.

"Cancer."

I nodded and changed the subject.

"What's the deal with you and Bridget?"

A big grin split her face and relief ran through me to see it. "We've been friends forever. Somehow, whenever we're together, we always manage to find trouble."

I smirked at her, "I believe it."

She gave me a look that said she was far from impressed and tapped a finger against her bottom lip. I thought about sucking that lip into my mouth. I'd offered to answer her questions for two reasons. One, so that she could get to know me more. I already knew a foolproof way of gathering information about her. Two, it passed the time without her going over every worst-case scenario in that overly active brain.

"How old are you?"

Eyes still on her mouth, I let my filthy thoughts run through my head. "Twenty-eight. You?"

"Twenty-one."

I got up to pour us another drink. Her voice called out from the living room. "What do you do?"

I waited until I was sitting again, and she'd taken her glass before I answered. "Mechanic." I didn't mention that my brother Riggs and I owned the garage we worked at, or my club job as sergeant at arms.

"What kind of hobbies are you into?" she'd asked before I could ask what kind of business she now owned.

I paused at her question. I wasn't sure how to answer. There wasn't much I did other than work and handle club business. "Bikes and engines." She tipped her head, trying to figure out what else to ask.

"What are your hobbies?" Since I'd first seen her yesterday morning, I'd been wanting to know more about her. Once I'd claimed her to the club she'd become a fucking compulsion for me. I had already texted Rat with her name during one of my trips to the kitchen. If anyone could dig up information on her for me, he could. When I saw Ty with his hands on Remi earlier tonight, fury had flooded me. Ty would be dealt with later. No one touched what was mine. She didn't know she belonged to me yet, but she'd figure it out soon enough.

"I don't really have time for hobbies anymore between school and work." She'd just about finished her second drink when Gunnar flung the front door open. Remi jumped about a foot in the air and I couldn't help but chuckle. She shot me a dirty look.

"Coast is clear, bro." He pulled Bridget into the room and shut the door. His lip was split, and he had a nasty bruise forming on one side of his face. I just settled back, putting my hands behind me on the table, and leaned back on them.

Bridget ran over to Remi and hugged her. Remi handed her friend the whiskey, and she downed the remainder in a couple of swallows. Gunnar chuckled as he carried the bottle and two more glasses out of the kitchen. "Does Cade know you opened this?" I shrugged. "He's going to kick your ass."

I smiled grimly. I looked forward to that. Cade, Riggs, Gunnar, and I sparred together regularly. There were never any gloves or rules. It kept us sharp.

Gunnar filled a glass and handed it to Remi and then filled the rest of ours. "Sorry for all the trouble, ladies." Gunnar considered himself a ladies' man most days. He always poured on the charm.

"It was kind of exciting," Bridget chirped.

Remi looked over at her, astonished. I covered my laugh by drinking. Those were the types of women who dated men like us — the kind who were excited by the danger. I glanced over at Remi and wondered how long it would take for her to get used to my world.

"We should get home." Remi set the glass of whiskey down, gave Bridget an insistent look, and stood up. Bridget hesitated, but then sighed in acceptance.

"Yeah, fine." She smiled at Gunnar when he took the spot Remi vacated.

"We'll see you out at the car." I took Remi's hand, interlaced our fingers, and all but dragged her out the door. She looked like she was going to insist Bridget come now. I turned to shut the door and saw that Gunnar already had his tongue down Bridget's throat.

We walked over to the parking lot and my eyebrows shot up when she walked up to an older Camaro. I may not like to drive anything but a bike but that didn't mean I didn't appreciate a fine machine. Riggs would get a hard-on for this car. Remi stepped up and unlocked it. I rubbed the back of my neck. She peered back toward the shadow of the house.

"Let them say goodnight. You need to relax."

She shot me a glare. "I am relaxed."

She was standing there stiffly, arms crossed over her chest, one sneaker tapping the ground. *If that was relaxed, then I was a God-fearing man.*

"I'm going to let you go home." Her eyebrows shot up, and she got this half offended, half defiant look on her face. I continued before she could respond. "But you're going to give me a kiss before you go."

Remi's face went red with embarrassment and indignation, and she sputtered. "Oh, really?" The defiant look deepened. "And what if I say no? Are you going to stop me from leaving?"

"No, I wouldn't stop you if you said no." She blinked at me in confusion. I stepped a little closer to her, lowering my voice. It sounded husky, gravely even to me. "But you're not going to say no." Her mouth dropped open in shock. "Because you want to kiss me." My grin was slow, challenging. "Go ahead, Remi. Tell me no."

I stepped forward and used my body to bump her off balance. Her butt and lower back hit the car, and I put my hands on either side of her, caging her in. She looked up at me in surprise. Indecision played across her face and one of her hands shot out to my chest as I swayed toward her. She didn't shove me back, or say no, so I kissed her.

She didn't move, not pushing me away, but not joining in. She seemed to be frozen. I looked into her eyes when I kissed her, and I saw desire there, but maybe a little fear, too.

I couldn't see her getting past that indecision in the next few minutes, and I wanted to feel her mouth moving against mine. So, I'd taken the initial choice out of her hands. But she could've stopped me at any time, and I would've let her go.

Biting her bottom lip hard, I groaned when she gasped at the combined feeling of pleasure and pain. As soon as her mouth opened, I plunged my tongue in and played with hers. I pressed my body against hers, pinning her against the car, and tangled my hand into her hair. Cupping the back of her head, I deepened the kiss.

I could taste the whiskey on her, and I swear it tasted better than the stuff had in my glass. My opposite hand slid down her body and cupped her ass. Jerking her hips forward, I shoved one of my thighs between hers. I groaned again when I felt her heat on my leg. She made a little noise in the back of her throat and hesitantly her tongue brushed mine.

Fucking finally.

I slowed the kiss so she could take it at her pace, as long as she didn't stop. Now that her sweet lips were moving over mine, I never wanted her to stop. Her movements were getting more confident now, a little more frantic.

CHAPTER 13

Remi

I couldn't believe his arrogance when he said I was going to kiss him. What pissed me off and confused me even more, was that I wanted to. I shouldn't be this attracted to him. But then Anna and Bridget had always claimed that bad boys were the most attractive. Maybe they were right, and we just had a natural affinity toward a dangerous man. It seemed like I might.

I could feel my face heating and my words seemed to trip on my tongue. He'd caught me off guard and now he was just standing there smiling smugly. "Oh, really?" My voice rose in pitch a bit and I fought for control over my temper. Fear was a tiny flame in the back of my mind. "And what if I say no? Are you going to stop me from leaving?"

"No, I wouldn't stop you if you said no." I blinked at that. Something tightened in my stomach with his admission. Then he stepped closer and his voice was deep, smokey, and so sexy my whole body was tingling.

"But you're not going to say no." I couldn't help it. My mouth dropped open and now my face wasn't flushed due to embarrassment but because he'd turned me on. "Because you want to kiss me." Then he gave me a smile that shot straight between my legs. "Go ahead, Remi. Tell me no."

When Steel pinned my body between his and the car I was surprised. He started to move in and reflexively I put a hand on his chest. I could feel his muscles rippling under my palms and the heavy, fast beating of his heart belied the calm demeanor that he outwardly showed.

Even I didn't know if I was pushing him away or trying to get closer. That voice in my head told me that if I wanted to say no, now was the time to do it. I trusted that if I said it, he would honor it. But he was right. I wanted him to kiss me. I needed to know how his lips felt against mine. How would his neatly trimmed beard feel rubbing against my skin as his lips fused with mine?

After what he'd said earlier about never hurting me, a lot of the fear I had of him had disappeared. I was still uneasy about the club and its rules. The reason I let him explore my lips was knowing and believing that this man wouldn't hurt me. The fact that all I had to do was say stop, and he would? That was the reason I joined in on the kiss. This man read my body perfectly.

He molded our mouths together and pressed his thigh between my legs. The hair on his face rasped against my skin and sent a shiver skating down my spine. My pussy was pressed against those hard muscles and I dizzily wondered if I was going to cum with just that touch and the buzz of anticipation heating my blood. If these delicious feelings weren't enough to make me lose my mind what he did next ensured that I would.

Steel used both hands this time and palmed my ass, his fingers digging in. The pleasure-pain combination had me moaning. Then he dragged my body up close to his, rubbing my pussy up along his thigh. My clit gave a hard throb, my pussy clamped down, feeling too empty, and the breath shuddered out of me.

Steel allowed my body to slide back down his leg before quickly repeating the motion all over again. I was going to cum. There was no way I was going to be able to hold back when he was putting all this amazing pressure directly onto my clit. I was panting into his mouth, beyond caring about anything around us. Bridget's giggle made my eyes snap open. I jerked my head back and stared at Steel in shock. We were both breathing raggedly, and he looked like he was seconds away from continuing, despite our audience. His intensity was sexier than anything I'd ever seen.

My body was throbbing, and I couldn't believe we'd just been doing that right out in the open. People were milling around outside, and worse, Gunnar and Bridget had just walked up and had seen everything. I knew my face was turning red. I don't know how, but this man played my body like a fiddle. I knew I was going to have to tread carefully.

Bridget climbed into the passenger seat of the car, giving me space to disentangle myself from Steel. This time I pushed against his chest and he instantly let me go. Stepping back, he pulled both of our phones out of his pocket and I watched quietly as he put my number into his.

Steel opened my car door, and I slid inside. He crouched down next to me and gave me a long, quiet look. He was a pro at those looks, and if he hadn't already turned my insides liquid, that would have done it.

"Steel…"

He quickly wove his fingers through my hair and yanked my head to his, crashing our lips together. I moaned; I couldn't help it. This guy knew how to break down every barrier I built, however big or small. If any other guy had tried that he'd get a swift knee to the balls. He broke the kiss off with a nip to my bottom lip.

"Night, Remi." He handed me my phone then stood and shut the door as I sat there, trying to get my remaining brain cells to work well enough to get us home.

Pulling out of the parking lot so we could head back into the city, I watched as Gunnar strode up and rested his hand on Steel's shoulder. They both stood watching us leave. Finally, I couldn't see them anymore and I focused on the road ahead of me.

"Okay, that looked so hot." Bridget was smiling at me, eyes gleaming. I just shook my head. I was slightly numb. I couldn't believe I'd let Steel kiss me, or that I'd kissed him back. Even worse. Better? Either way, I couldn't believe I'd basically been humping his leg and in public. I groaned in embarrassment, but a sharp spike of heat made my clit throb, too.

"Not hot, Bridget. This isn't good. What the hell happened tonight?" My thoughts were completely jumbled together. I knew that tonight topped our extensive list of 'nights that weird shit happened'. This had been so much worse than the funhouse clown.

The guys had technically saved us. But it was their party that got us into trouble to begin with. Then there was that kiss. Before that, I had a mild attraction to him. He was gorgeous after all. But too much had happened for my brain to take it there. Until he'd kissed me. Now I wondered if I'd get to do it again.

I argued with myself during the thirty-minute drive back into the city. Bridget had fallen asleep in the passenger seat and I shot her a bitter look. She was sleeping like a baby. So, obviously, her mind wasn't conflicted about this. By the time we pulled up in front of our house, I'd decided that it had been a crazy night. I'd gotten a deliciously filthy make-out session out of it with a hot guy. But I'd never have to see that hot guy again, so there was no need to worry. Right?

CHAPTER 14

Steel

It was Monday morning, and I thought of Remi all weekend. It had been such a long time since I'd been this into a woman. I shook off my thoughts and smiled when Rat handed me the background check I'd asked for. We tapped knuckles, and he didn't say anything else as he quickly left the room. The kid was a genius with a computer, but extremely shy. He wasn't our normal type of recruit, but was another example of Cade's genius.

Cade and Riggs had found Rat years ago. They'd been working a job for our president at the time. Gunnar and I had only been prospects and had been pissed that we hadn't been allowed to go on that assignment. Dagger had sent Cade and Riggs to go gather some intel on a few cops who were working with one of the Dons of the Italian Mafia. He'd been trying to get these cops in his pocket, but it was suspected they were loyal to Don Angelo Accardo at the time. The Italians had a new Don these days. Angelo hadn't lasted very long in his position, only a few short years, but long enough to cause trouble for our club. The new Don was too busy fighting with the Russians to bother us and that's how we liked it.

The guys had only told a few of us about Rat's story out of respect for him but Gunnar and I knew what there was to know. Sadly, it wasn't much. This homeless kid had approached Cade and Riggs and told them that he'd been watching them, as they'd been casing out two cops trying to catch them in the act of taking bribes. He'd offered to help them find out the information on the cops if they would accept him into the MC. When Riggs had laughed him off Rat had handed over their wallets and keys. They hadn't even felt the kid lift the items from their pockets. That had shut Riggs up quickly enough and he helped convince Cade to bring the kid home.

Cade hadn't needed much convincing, he knew then and there that there was a place for Rat and his skills in the MC. He managed to convince Dagger to give him a place to live, which got him away from the corrupt piece of shit who collected homeless children and used them to hustle money for him, and the club gained a valuable asset.

It hadn't been easy convincing Dagger to bring on a scrawny twelve-year-old. He hadn't been able to see how Rat's tech skills would be able to help us until he'd found the information needed to blackmail the officers, forcing them to turn from helping the Italian Mafia and instead begin being loyal to our MC.

Unfortunately, that hadn't gone over well with the Don and the officers had been killed, in the line of duty of course. Anyone in the life knew that wasn't the case but that was what was fed to the press. Rat was skilled enough to keep our MCs name out of it, though. Not long after the death of those officers the war between the Italian Mafia and Bratva sparked up, taking the heat completely off us and we steered clear. Rat's been a brother to us ever since. He was twenty-two now and his talent had grown beyond anything I could hope to understand.

Just by giving the kid Remi's first name, he'd managed to find five pages' worth of information on her. I now had her birthdate, home address, work address. I paused and reread the last line, stating her ownership of Mackenzie's Trucking. We'd been considering switching over from our current shipping company to using theirs.

We'd been using Harris's Shipping for the last year, but more than once now they'd fucked up on our shipments. We traded back and forth with our chapter in Long Beach, California. We stole vehicles and bikes here in Texas and broke them down into parts and frames. After grinding down and then etching in new serial numbers, we then shipped them over to Cali. Al and his boys had a chop shop over there and did the same, then sent them our way. That way both chapters could resell the vehicles in different states without having as much suspicion thrown our way.

Any time Harris's messed up, the likelihood that we'd be caught went up. I smiled grimly and told myself to remember to talk to Cade and get approval to make the switch. The garage may be half mine, but we shared everything with the club. So, we always got club approval before any large changes.

I sat at the island in the clubhouse, reading through the papers, and I marveled at the details Rat had managed to get about her life. Gunnar flopped down on the stool next to me. He glanced over and tried to snatch the papers from me. I shifted them to my left hand and used my right to slam a fist into his side, just below his ribs.

Gunnar grunted, then glowered at me and flipped me off. The look I shot him had him muttering under his breath. Gunnar got up and poured two cups of coffee and set one next to me. "You going into the garage today?"

I shook my head and drank from the cup. I'd tried to call Remi Sunday afternoon. She hadn't answered and hadn't bothered to call back. Clearly, she thought that she could shut me out. She was very wrong; I covered my grim smile with another long swallow of coffee. "I have some stuff to take care of today." My eyes strayed to the paper where Remi's entire school schedule was laid out, thanks to Rat.

Gunnar just shrugged and hung his head while he nursed his coffee. He wasn't a morning person.

Soon we parted ways, and I headed into the city on my bike. I pulled into an empty spot in one of the parking garages on the university's campus. I strolled across a large grassy area and smirked when I saw more than one of the women watching me walk. Pulling the ladies had never been an issue for me. Typically, I chose not to deal with them. I enjoyed sex, but other than the club bunnies, I usually didn't waste my time. At least, until that morning last week when I'd seen Remi. Since then, she'd been the only thought in my mind.

I found the building I'd been looking for and followed the numbered rooms until I found one-twelve. Leaning against the wall opposite the door, I folded my arms and waited. Shouldn't be too much longer now. A faculty member walked by and she paused as she caught sight of me.

Her eyes trailed down my tattoos, looked at my vest, then at my face. I gave her a slow smile. She blushed straight to the roots of her mousy brown hair and hurried down the hallway without saying anything to me.

Keeping my eyes on the door in front of me, I watched as students began to exit the room. As soon as I saw her come out, my dick hardened. Seeing her had that effect on me. She was laughing, looking over at an Asian girl. Remi was involved in whatever the conversation was, so she hadn't seen me. Her friend spotted me immediately, and she said something I couldn't hear over the noise in the hallway. She grabbed Remi's arm, then jerked her head in my direction.

Remi's whiskey-colored eyes met mine, and she looked stunned. The hallway began to clear out as the two girls just stood there and watched me warily. I waited for the kids from her class to move and took a few minutes to run my eyes over her. She was in jeans today and a university t-shirt that she'd tied in a knot at her lower back so that the end of it stopped at the beginning of her jeans. She wore a pair of white and orange sneakers that matched her shirt. Her dark hair was loose, and it was hanging down her back.

My eyes shifted to the girl next to her. She looked tiny next to Remi. Not delicate, but much shorter. She had long, black hair and eyes so dark they looked black from across the hall. She had a pretty face which had a pinched, worried look on it. It was obvious that they were friends since she hadn't left when it became clear I was waiting to speak with Remi. She also knew who I was.

From the minute she'd seen me, there'd been recognition on her face. I couldn't stop the rush of satisfaction at knowing she'd told her friends about me. She'd told them enough that this girl, without ever having seen me before, knew exactly who I was in a crowded hallway. Well, not so crowded anymore. Finally, it thinned out, and I made my way over to where they were standing. "Ladies."

I read the suspicion on Remi's face. She'd had time to get over her surprise at seeing me, but now I could tell she was riding on anger, suspicion, and curiosity. I wondered which was going to win out. Anger, I hoped. I liked seeing her all fired up.

"What are you doing here Steel?" She hissed at me, clearly wondering how I'd managed to track her down. She looked around and saw a few people that had stopped in the hall to watch us curiously.

"I came to see you. Let's talk." I motioned for her to walk ahead of me. She shook her head, then she and her friend shared a silent look.

"Uh, hi. I'm Julie." She held out her hand. I stared at it for a minute, then took it. It was tiny in my huge grip. "We have to get to our next class so…" She started to shift as though to walk away, and Remi went to follow.

My arm shot out and I put my palm on the wall next to Remi's head, preventing her from following Julie. "You go right ahead, Julie. Remi will catch up to you later." I spoke the words to the other girl, but I kept my eyes on Remi's. Hers widened slightly, and then she licked her lips. I narrowed my eyes as I watched that pretty pink tongue moisten her plump lips. I imagined what they'd look like wrapped around my cock.

Neither girl said anything. I could see out of my peripheral that Julie was glancing back and forth between Remi and me, unsure of what to do. "Rem?" Her tone was hesitant.

"It's okay, Julie," Remi finally said, her eyes breaking from mine to smile at her friend. "I'll catch up in a few minutes." Julie still hesitated, but when I turned my head to stare at her, she seemed to lose her nerve. She murmured her agreement then hurried down the hallway, away from us.

CHAPTER 15

Remi

He was here. Steel was standing directly in front of me, entirely too close for comfort, since we were in public. I saw a group of girls come around the corner and stop, shock on their faces when they spotted him. I knew exactly what they were seeing, a sexy, huge, rough-looking biker. He was wearing a black t-shirt under his cut, blue jeans, and a pair of black combat boots.

If the girls stared much longer, they were going to start drooling. I wasn't entirely trusting myself not to either. The girl in front flicked her eyes over and they met mine. I may not be claiming Steel as mine, but that didn't mean I was going to sit here while this girl eye fucked him in front of me either. I shot her a dirty look that finally got her moving.

Steel hadn't seemed to notice. He was staring at me again. That intense, pale gaze set me on edge.

"Seriously, Steel. Why are you here?"

He took my hand and started leading me out of the building. I let him just pull me along in his wake. He crossed the courtyard and found a shady spot under a tree. Releasing my hand, he leaned against the trunk and folded his arms over that huge chest. I refused to look down at it. If I did, I'd start picturing him naked. There had been a lot of that over the last few days. But I'd been firm with myself, and I hadn't answered when he'd called. I wasn't going to get tangled up with this guy, physically or emotionally. That traitorous voice in my head whispered, *'liar'*. I ignored it.

"You didn't answer your phone."

My eyebrows shot up. "Contrary to what you must think, my life doesn't revolve around you. Nor is my phone on me every minute of every day." I was proud of myself for how calm I sounded. His arrogance was infuriating.

"Why didn't you call me back?"

I was shocked. This guy had come to my campus in the middle of the day, found my classroom, all because I hadn't returned his call? My eyes narrowed when the thought hit me again.

"How did you know where to find me?" I had only told him my first name at the party, and he hadn't gotten many other details that night. I certainly hadn't told him anything that should have allowed him to track me down.

He just shrugged. "I have my ways."

I looked at him in amazement. "Does anyone ever tell you no?"

Now he grinned. It was shockingly charming. I blinked and then wished for the cold, gruff guy back. It was easier to keep my distance from him. The man standing in front of me, smiling at me like that, wouldn't be as easy to avoid.

"Rarely."

That didn't surprise me in the least. He had a confident air of authority. He moved like he expected everyone to get out of his way. He spoke like I'd obey his every command. My eyes narrowed. Well, obeying demands wasn't something I usually did. I didn't rebel much as a kid, but Dad figured out pretty quickly that if he didn't want me to do something, forbidding it was the worst thing he could do. It just ensured I would go ahead and do it.

HEART OF STEEL

The thought of my father had sadness jolting through me. This was how it went. In the weeks and few months that followed his death, I'd been dragged under the surface of my grief and sadness. I'd stayed there, never coming up for air. Now, I lived back on the surface, above those emotions. But every once in a while, a wave would come out of nowhere, a memory, and break over my head, shoving me back under until I struggled long enough to break to the surface again.

Steel shoved up from the tree and closed the distance between us. His brows were pulled together and there was something in his eyes. Was that…concern? He cupped my cheek, swiping his thumb over my skin, sending flutters from where he touched me down to my stomach. "What just happened?"

I stared at him blankly. It was taking all of my strength not to lean into his caress.

Damn it, Remi, I berated myself. *You're not supposed to be seeing or talking with him. You certainly aren't supposed to be letting him touch you. Remember what happened last time?* I asked myself. *'Oh boy, do I remember,'* the voice responded wickedly.

I cleared my throat. "I don't know what you mean? You were asking me why I hadn't called you back," I started to answer, but he cut me off.

"Right, and I was enjoying watching you get all fired up. You're sexy when you're pissed, Remi." I blushed. His compliments were so blatant and hot. "Then, it was gone." He searched my eyes. He didn't need to say it, he'd seen the sadness. When it overwhelmed me, there was no way for me to avoid showing it to those around me.

Stupid expressive eyes.

"It's nothing." I sighed. "Look, Steel. I'm sorry I didn't call you back. That was pretty shitty of me. But this," I motioned back and forth between us, "isn't something I can do."

He cocked his head and somehow, he managed to look adorable, like a puppy. Okay, he looked like a fierce Rottweiler puppy. He dropped his hand, then shoved them both into the pockets of his jeans. He pinned me with a flat look.

Uh oh, I thought, *the adorable puppy has left the building.*

"You can't do what? Exactly?"

"This." I motioned again, but he just raised his brows and waited. "I have too much going on for a relationship." His brows remained up.

Shit. "Not that I'm saying that's what you were going for, but you called me for a reason." When a slow smirk spread across his face, I hurried on. "And I don't do the one-night thing. If that's what you're looking for, I suggest you go elsewhere." His silence was starting to unnerve me. I knew I was babbling, but it was far too late to stop myself. "Not that I want you to stay even if it wasn't a one-night thing because I don't have time for…"

"This." He interrupted me; the smirk still pinned to his face. The ass. He was enjoying this.

"Exactly," I said. I was irritated that he was getting enjoyment from my discomfort. How was I supposed to be comfortable around him? My head kept screaming at me to run in the opposite direction. My body kept trying to get me to lean into him so that I could smell the distinct smell of oil and citrus. Who would have known that combination would smell so good?

He just shook his head at me, but he shot me a full-blown smile at the same time. I wished it would disappear. I couldn't think straight with those white teeth flashing at me. His eyes were slightly crinkled at the corners and his beard just lent itself to the whole 'tough guy' look. I wanted to feel it scratching me again as we kissed. Trailing down my body and rubbing on all my tender spots.

Whoa, girl. I mentally slapped myself and stepped back a tiny bit. I needed distance from him.

As soon as I focused back on his eyes, I knew that step backward had been a huge mistake. The smile was gone instantly.

Wish granted, yay…

But the look that replaced the smile was far more dangerous. He looked hungry. Those gray eyes were boring into mine. It was the same look he had given me when I first saw him, the look of a predator. The realization hit me like a bucket of icy water.

Vaguely, I remembered what our girl scout leader had told us when we were young girls. She'd said that if we ran into any wolves or bears on our nature walks that we should stand our ground, make ourselves look as big as we could, and yell at them to go away. Something told me that wouldn't work on Steel. I'd just inadvertently triggered his prey drive. He looked like he wanted to chase me down, tackle me, and have his way with me.

Swallowing hard, I noticed that his eyes dropped as he tracked the movement. I opened my mouth to say something, anything, to get him to go back to the smiling man from a few minutes ago. I'd been very wrong. This look, the one that said he wanted to devour me, this was the most dangerous look he had, that I'd seen so far anyway. If I wasn't lying to myself, I'd admit that I wanted to see more.

The shrill sound of the bell made me jump, and I took another few steps back. When he followed me at a much faster pace, I cursed myself.

Steel slid his left arm under mine and splayed his hand across my lower back, pulling me into the heat of his body. Everywhere we touched, all I could feel was hard muscle. The thought had me getting a bit lightheaded. His right hand went under my hair to surround the back of my neck. He'd immobilized me. I watched him with wide eyes, wondering if he was going to…

"Miss Mackenzie!" I jerked again, although I couldn't move much, thanks to Steel's hands on my body. I looked over, then groaned when I saw Mr. Richards moving toward us. He kept shooting Steel worried glances but by the time his gaze would land on me he'd look irritated and angry again.

Just great. This was exactly what this tense situation needed right now.

Mr. Richards had stopped next to us. He cleared his throat and pointedly looked where Steel was holding me. Steel didn't seem inclined to let me go and I wasn't going to be able to move unless he let me.

Steel turned that piercing stare onto Mr. Richards. The way the man paled told me that Steel was looking at him in a very threatening manner. Mr. Richard's mouth opened and closed, closely resembling a fish. I was trying to hold in my laughter, and I didn't realize my shoulders were shaking with it until Steel shot me an amused glance.

"Miss Mackenzie." Richards' voice cracked. "Don't you have a class you should be in?" His resolve was admirable. I wasn't sure I'd have had the balls to stand here with Steel looking like he might murder me any second, let alone ask questions.

"I was just about to head that way," I murmured. I experimentally tried to pull out of Steel's hands. It worked pretty much the same way it had at the party. He tightened his grip on me then reeled me into his body. Tucking me under his arm, he pressed me up against his side. Steel turned us to face Richards.

"Leave."

I almost choked on my shock. Steel did have an impressive hold on that authoritative attitude.

He probably would have made a good cop. Well, except for that whole criminal thing. Mr. Richards's face screwed up in disgust.

"You'll need to be the one to leave Mr...?" When Steel didn't bother to give a name, Richards continued, "You'll not be allowed to remain here to harass students."

"Oh, he's not harassing me." I was more than a little surprised that I was defending him. But it was technically the truth. He hadn't been threatening. Once again, I knew that if I had refused to come out here with him, he wouldn't have pressed the issue. I'd chosen to come out here. I couldn't wrap my mind around how my common sense seemed to leave me whenever this biker was around.

"Be that as it may, you have a class to get to and he needs to leave the premises. I trust that you'll make smarter decisions, concerning those you spend time with, in the future, Miss Mackenzie," he said with a sniff, his face pinched like there was an unpleasant smell in the air.

I looked over at Steel. He was standing there with that calm façade. But most of my body was plastered up against his right now, so I could feel how tense he was. If Richards' words affected him, he didn't let it show, but he was ready for any action that needed to be taken.

"It's none of your business who I spend time with," I said in a clipped tone, and Richards' eyes widened. Since the lunchroom incident, I had been extra nice to this man, trying to win him and some of the other faculty back onto my side. But I wasn't going to stand here and let Richards insult him. He didn't even know Steel. "It also doesn't matter to me what your opinion is of me, or my decisions. Come on, let's go."

I didn't bother to look back, but I could feel Richards' stare as we walked across campus. Finally, we turned a corner and were out of his line of sight. We'd been walking exactly as we'd been standing, with his arm around my shoulders. When I shifted, he removed it but placed his hand over mine, interlacing our fingers, and wouldn't let go of me as he led me into a parking garage.

"Uh, where are we going?"

He stopped next to a large black and chrome motorcycle. The same one he'd been on the first day I'd seen him. It said Harley Davidson on the front part of the bike. I'd heard of the brand before. Some of the guys around campus even wore some of their shirts. None of those guys looked anything like the one in front of me though. He flipped down pegs on the side of the bike and took a helmet out of a compartment.

Handy.

Turning back to me Steel put the helmet on my head then tightened the chin strap. His calloused fingers lightly ran down the skin of my neck.

"No way." I shook my head. "I'm not getting on that."

He smirked. "Scared?"

I glared at him. "No, smart-ass. Do you know how many people get into motorcycle accidents every year?" He watched me impassively, not bothering to answer. "And out of that number how many end up dying?"

I didn't give the numbers because I couldn't remember them off the top of my head. I'd researched the topic in middle school when Dad had come home with a motorcycle. I'd been terrified he was going to wreck it and die. When I'd spouted off the statistics, the look on his face looked a lot like the one on Steel's now. Sort of a resigned acceptance resided on that ruggedly handsome face. As though he knew it was pointless to interrupt me while I was on a roll.

Once I stopped, he just turned and mounted the bike, kicked up the kickstand, balancing the machine between those strong thighs. I let my eyes trail up to his waist and I wondered if he had a six-pack. My eyes shot to his biceps.

He absolutely has a six-pack. No way a guy has arms like that, but doesn't bother with the rest of his body. I felt his gaze on me and mine shot up guiltily. That hungry look was back on his face. I started to back up from the bike when he grabbed my wrist. He said nothing, just waited, not letting me go. I knew what he was doing. I had two choices, verbally tell him no, or get on the bike.

"I've never ridden on one." He gave a light tug on my arm and I walked forward.

"It's easy. Put your feet on the pegs back here," He motioned to them. "Hold on to me and just lean when I do."

I eyed the seat behind him, then his face. It was too late to make my class, but I still had two more before I was done for the day. I looked back toward the opening of the garage. I debated with myself internally. It drove me crazy that Steel made me make these decisions instead of just taking them out of my hands and doing whatever he wanted.

Well, no, that *I appreciated.* I hated that each time he challenged me to tell him no, I've done exactly what he'd said I'd do. How did he know what effect he would have on me?

I took a deep breath, adjusted my backpack straps, so it was fitted tightly to me, then climbed on the bike. I slid forward a bit until my legs bracketed his and put my feet on the pegs. He started the engine, and the bike roared to life, then began to purr as it and the man waited for me to be ready. I chewed my bottom lip. I was nervous, and my hands were starting to shake. I reached out to his body just to get them to stop trembling. I placed my arms around his waist and locked my hands together. They brushed his stomach, and I felt the hard planes.

Definitely has a six-pack, I thought, my blood heating in my veins.

Grabbing his waist was clearly his cue that I was ready, so he walked the bike backward then shot forward so fast I yelped. I slapped my body against him so fast I bumped his shoulders with my helmet and my arms tightened around him in a death grip. I could feel the vibrations of his laughter where my breasts were squished against the hard planes of his back.

He slowed as we approached the exit, and I saw Anna's car pulling in. She was heading into her afternoon class. Our gazes clashed and her mouth dropped open in shock. I gave her a small smile and a shrug. Her eyes slid down as she eye fucked Steel. I wasn't upset by the look from her like I had been by the other girl doing it. Anna would never go after any of our guys.

Wait, I thought frantically, *not mine, not mine, not... shit.* The bike took off again, and I had to close my eyes so I didn't see the asphalt whipping past us as Steel accelerated and left campus.

CHAPTER 16

Remi

There was no way for us to talk once the bike got up to speed, so I just let Steel take us wherever he wanted. We left town and ended up on a road that curved and twisted up into the mountains. After the first twenty minutes, I finally calmed down and started enjoying the ride.

It sure as hell beats my statistics course.

Steel handled the bike with power and, surprisingly, grace. Even with an inexperienced rider on it, he didn't seem fazed at all. But I certainly was. His presence had this unexpected effect on me. It had since the first morning I saw him sitting on his motorcycle on campus.

Even the beauty surrounding me was only a brief distraction. The forest was dense. As we kept going a rock wall appeared on our right-hand side and I watched in pleasure as we passed a small waterfall spilling down the rock face. We began passing more of them and I eagerly began looking for them.

Finally, the wall receded, and Steel pointed to something on our left. I sucked in a breath as the trees thinned out and I could see down the embankment to a large lake, glistening in the sunlight. It was breathtaking.

Other than the roar of his engine, there didn't seem to be any other man-made sounds around. I watched as a deer stepped from the tree line, then cautiously waited as she spotted us. Deciding we were too far away to be a threat she continued out to the water's edge to drink. I made a high-pitched squeaking noise when two babies followed her out slowly. I don't know if Steel heard the embarrassing noise I made at the sight of the cute deer or if I'd tightened up, but I could feel the rumble of his laugh.

He'd slowed down as we'd passed the lake so that I could get a longer look. A few miles down the road there was a fork, and he took a tight left turn onto a new road.

As much as I was enjoying this, being out of the city, seeing the lake, being able to relax, I was also becoming a growing bundle of nerves with every passing mile. It was getting hard having my body slathered against his and smelling his unique scent. I liked having my arms wrapped around him, having my hands resting on all that muscle. Then there was the bike itself. I swallowed and subtly tried to shift. I didn't want to shift so much that it threw us off balance, but Steel had me on edge and turned on before the ride and now the vibrations of the bike were compounding that issue.

There wasn't any other option than just to deal with the fact that my sensitive nipples were scraping against his back and with every purr of the bike my pussy fluttered back. So, for miles, I gritted my teeth and tried to distract myself with the scenery. When I shifted again Steel shot me a look over his shoulder.

"Almost there!" He shouted at me and I saw that we'd looped around and were heading back into the city. I didn't necessarily want the ride to be over because it felt really freeing, with the wind whipping past. It was almost like none of my worries could catch up with us. But my libido was becoming hard to ignore. Because of that, I sighed with relief when we pulled up in front of the house I shared with the girls.

Once Steel cut the engine I hopped off and took off the helmet. I dropped my bag on the ground next to me. I watched as Steel got off the bike. It was amazing how seamlessly he moved for such a big man.

"So… What did you think of your first ride?"

"It was awesome!" I grinned at him. "Once I got over being terrified of being smeared into the pavement, it was easy to relax and enjoy it."

He chuckled. "It can get addicting. Just wait, soon enough you won't want to ride on anything else." Before I could respond to him and tell him that learning to drive a motorcycle wasn't in my plans anytime soon, he stepped closer to me and brushed a piece of hair off my face. He started to lean down, and I knew he was going to kiss me. Frantic, I glanced around.

I saw Mrs. Crawford pretending to dig in her flower bed across the street, but her eyes were very obviously locked on us. I took a small step back. A few of my neighbors knew my uncle. This neighborhood wasn't too far from the one I grew up in, and Uncle Caleb had a house in this area up until a few years ago when he'd moved.

"I really appreciate the ride." His brows pinched together as he straightened back up. "Sorry, you don't know my neighbors though. They can be super nosey and most of them are old so they're pretty old-fashioned." He didn't look like he gave a shit what my neighbors thought. Suddenly something occurred to me.

"Wait a minute." I looked over my shoulder at my house and then narrowed my eyes on his face. "How did you know where I lived?"

Steel's face shut down surprisingly fast. He took a step back and just shrugged but didn't say anything. I watched him curiously, but he just stared back at me impassively, shoving his hands in the pockets of his jeans.

"You're not going to tell me?" I wondered if maybe Bridget had told Gunnar and he'd passed it on? It was the only thing that I could think of. But then, how had he known what classroom I would be in today? I started to open my mouth to ask again when he stepped forward and pressed a brief, light kiss to my lips.

"I'll call you." With that, he turned, got on his bike, and drove off. I lifted my fingers to my lips and wondered if I was ever going to understand that guy. My gaze was drawn to Mrs. Crawford as she stood up and put her hands on her hips, staring at me.

As I turned to head back into the house it was as though all my responsibilities came crashing back. The fact that Steel somehow knew my class schedule and where I lived told me I was dealing with someone far outside of the usual realm of guys I typically dated. This was a man. One who took control over the things in his life and he wasn't afraid of doing whatever was necessary to make things go his way. I sighed and tried to toughen my resolve. It didn't matter that a part of me really liked him. We were too different and I didn't know how to bridge that gap. When it came to Steel, I needed to take a firm stand. With that echoing in my head, I went to catch up on schoolwork.

CHAPTER 17

Steel

Over the next couple weeks, I took any spare time I had to drop into places that Remi visited frequently. The shocked look on her face almost made me laugh when I stopped into On the Mats, a boxing gym that one of the guys I used to know from high school owned.

Rat's information mentioned that Remi and her friends were signed up to take one of Sergio's self-defense courses. I liked the idea that she was learning how to protect herself. It also explained the moves that she and Bridget had used on the nomads at the party a couple weeks ago.

I wandered into the gym and quietly watched as Serg ran the group of women through some boxing drills. My eyes quickly found Remi and the corner of my mouth tipped up when she punched the focus mitts that Bridget held. Each strike had the smaller blonde's elbows buckling until finally, she held a mitt up, silently asking for a break.

Looking back toward the front of the room I caught Sergio's gaze. His eyes widened in recognition and a huge smile split his face. Gunnar and I had been pretty friendly with Sergio in school. His dad had owned this gym before Serg and we'd end up here most afternoons, along with Riggs and Cade.

"Look what the cat dragged in," Sergio said as he approached and we clasped hands then patted each other on the backs in a side hug. "It's been a long time, amigo."

I grinned at him. "Too long. Just wanted to stop by and see if the place was still standing." Sergio laughed good-naturedly. I'd heard his dad had passed away five years ago, and he'd taken over the business. We had a fully functional gym at the clubhouse though, so none of us had been back here for some time.

"It's going pretty well actually. I got away from only training the serious fighters, although I still train them as well. I opened it up to women and fitness classes. It's brought a lot of steady business in."

I nodded, looking around. "The place looks great." We chatted for a few more minutes before he left to keep teaching his class. Once I'd gotten involved with the Vikings, old friendships that didn't include the club had faded away. I was surprisingly happy to see that Serg didn't seem to hold that against me.

I glanced back up at the class and whiskey-colored eyes clashed with mine. Her brows were pulled low over her eyes. She'd been watching Serio and me, but I'd refused to look her way until now. I let a slow smile stretch over my face and I jerked my head at her, in a nod of greeting, before I turned and walked out.

The sound of the door opening behind me and her voice calling my name had a satisfied smirk playing on my lips. I wondered if she realized what I was doing yet. I'd figured out fairly quickly that I'd need to slowly integrate myself into Remi's life, making it harder and harder for her to avoid me. I slowed and watched as she caught up to me.

Remi was wearing short compression shorts that molded to that sexy ass and nothing but a sports bra on top. Her signature Adidas were on her feet. It felt like my tongue was glued to the roof of my mouth as I watched her tits bounce as she ran up.

"What are you doing here Steel?" She frowned at me. She was clearly suspicious of why I was here.

She should be. But I wasn't about to tell her that. I'd come with the express purpose of her seeing me, another thing I wasn't going to mention. We'd had enough small, and some slightly longer, encounters in the two weeks since I'd met her outside her class, that I was sure she was catching onto the game.

I shrugged nonchalantly. "I needed to drop something off to Sergio." Her frown deepened. Despite watching us and seeing that we knew each other, she wasn't buying it. I'd tried calling her again last night and when she'd, once again, not answered and not returned the call, I'd decided that it was time to put an end to this. I had too much business to take care of tonight, but tomorrow I'd be paying her another visit. She was going to find out that avoiding me didn't work.

"Did you know I was going to be here?" I gave her a bored stare and raised a brow.

"As I said, I needed to drop something off." I pulled out my phone to check the time. "I'm running behind. I'll see you later, wildcat." I leaned in and dropped a kiss on her lips. They parted in surprise and I wanted to deepen the kiss, sweep my tongue between those lips. Instead, I shoved my hands in my pockets and strolled over to my bike. Before I pulled out, I looked back and saw her standing there watching me. I drove out of the parking lot and headed back to the clubhouse for church.

CHAPTER 18

Steel

The next morning, I was in the garage, working on rebuilding an engine when my ringtone sounded. I checked the caller ID and swallowed the irritation when I realized it wasn't Remi returning my call. The screen flashed Axel's name. He was the club's road captain, and I had assigned him a set of roads to patrol that we'd been previously ignoring. We still hadn't seen any sign of the Lycans since that first day, so I had started expanding the areas we were looking in. I answered and after a minute motioned to Riggs. He came over and we both listened intently to Axel's report.

It didn't take me long to get on the road after I hung up. I turned onto a road downtown and checked the address that he'd given me twenty minutes earlier. Luck had finally turned our way, and he'd found some Lycans dealing in our area. He'd called for backup since he only had Scout with him, who was still a prospect. I'd told them to sit tight and wait for us. I called my enforcers and set out to meet up with everyone. Riggs stayed behind at the shop.

Ten minutes later, we rolled up on the location. I pulled up next to Axel, who looked over and grinned. "Check it out." He handed me a pair of binoculars and I watched as a Lycan passed over a baggie to someone in an alley and palmed some cash. I put them down and looked over at my guys.

"Alright. Trip, Drew, Deuce, and Scout, you guys go hit the road north of the alley. Let them see you riding in. It'll funnel them to Gunnar, Axel, and I on the south road. Give us about five minutes to get into position, then go." They nodded as Axel led the way, heading to where the alley let out.

We pulled up and threw the bikes into neutral to walk them close to where we'd park them. You wouldn't hear the idling with the city's background noise. The revving as the bike shifted was what people picked up on.

I didn't want us getting in any collisions with the guys, so we lined them up, stacked one next to the other off the left side of the wall. They extended out, making the wall longer on that side. We walked further into the alley and stood, guns in hand, blocking the exit. The sound of motorcycles revving hit our ears. "Here we go. Don't flag each other and definitely don't shoot each other." The guys grinned, we all lived for these confrontations.

"Remember our other four are likely going to be chasing them down the alley so make sure you either hit what you aim at or don't shoot at all." They nodded. We caught sight of the first Lycan about the same time he noticed us. He gunned it and poured on more speed. The other three were still a ways away, meaning our guys were even further behind. I aimed and pulled the trigger a few times. The rounds hit him dead center in the chest. The guy toppled off his bike and sent it skidding our way.

Shit. My eyes widened when I realized the bike was still flying forward toward us. I dove out of the way, taking Axel down with me, and felt the air move behind me as the bike shot past. We were about thirty feet up the alley, but the bike kept sailing until it exited and hit a parked car. The momentum made the bike careen backward, where it finally stopped near the entrance. I was just glad it had been going straight. If it had veered at all, it would have hit one of our bikes. I cursed when the three other bikes shot past us, as Axel and I tried to scramble to our feet.

The front two Lycans fanned out, driving around the wrecked bike, but the guy on the left had to slow down because of where we'd parked ours. It created a narrow opening to squeeze through on the left side. The right side was wide open and the Lycan who drove that way took off down the street. Unfortunately for the guy at the back, he couldn't see that, and he swerved left, hot on his buddies' heels.

When the first guy slowed so he didn't crash through our bikes and chance wrecking, the second rider had to make a quick decision. He was either going to slam into the back of his brother, or he would have to go over the tail end of the bike laying in his path. These big bikes couldn't jump shit, so the guy bailed off the bike and let it crash into the wrecked bike.

Gunnar ran up and grabbed the rider by the back of the cut. The Lycan started fighting but Trip, Drew, Scout, and Deuce had pulled up and were already helping Gunnar out. Axel pulled out his phone and called Riggs to have him bring us a truck. Luckily, we kept a few at our garage for situations like this, so we wouldn't have to wait thirty minutes for someone to get here. It was only a seven-minute drive from the garage to this alley.

People would have heard the gunshots and the crash, so we didn't have long before the cops got here. Especially since the wrecked bikes had slid out of the alley onto the sidewalk. Stepping forward, I glanced at the patches on the Lycan's cut. He wasn't an officer, but I was relieved that he wasn't a prospect. I didn't want to fight a young kid who wasn't even in the club yet.

I glanced up at the guy's face. *He was somewhere between his thirties and forties*, I estimated. I didn't bother to talk to him. I just searched all his pockets. I slid the drugs and money he had on him into my own. I walked away and did the same to his dead friend. I tensed up as a vehicle pulled up but luckily it was Riggs. Right behind him was another of our guys with a tow truck.

I walked over to Axel while Riggs and Gunner tossed the body into the back of the truck and bungee corded a tarp over the bed. Drew and Deuce had taken over the live Lycan and shoved him in the back seat. Scout and Axel were busy dumping bleach over the spot where the Lycan had bled out. I grabbed a gallon and helped. One of our brothers who came with Riggs was loading the wrecked bikes onto the tow truck so we could get them back to the shop. Once the blood was diluted, and everything was cleaned up, we all hopped onto our bikes and followed the trucks back to the garage.

Drew, Trip, and Deuce tossed some shovels, more bleach, and some other equipment into the back seat and immediately took off to dispose of the body. Axel and Scout transferred the Lycan to a new truck. They were going to drive him back to the clubhouse. They pulled up beside me. "Axel. Could you call Rat and have him check to make sure there weren't any cameras in that alley? Or on any of the businesses on the other side of the street. Have him fuck with the traffic cameras, too, for both the north and south sides of the alley."

"You got it."

They headed out and I stepped inside Valhalla Choppers to check-in. One of our employees was manning the desk and looked up when I walked in. "Hey, boss." My eyes swept the waiting room. No one was here.

"Anything on the schedule for the day?"

The club brother shook his head. "All clear. There is one service appointment for tomorrow at two p.m. but that's it for tomorrow too."

I nodded. "Great. Riggs and I are going to take off. If anyone comes in just set them up for an appointment tomorrow."

"No problem. You guys have a good night."

"Thanks. You have a good one too." Riggs acknowledged the guy as he left.

I sat on my bike. "Did you call Cade yet?" My brother shook his head and lit up a cigarette. I did the same then dialed our president. After a quick update, we headed back to the clubhouse. We'd be spending the rest of the night questioning the Lycan and planning.

CHAPTER 19

Steel

Cade walked into the kitchen the next morning and sat at the head of the table. "Okay, let's do this." He cleared his throat and his gaze fell on me. "The nomads have been here for a little over the two-week trial period that's required." The men had never been to our club with our new leadership. Anytime they wanted to visit a new club and potentially add it to their list of places they were welcome, they had to stay for two weeks. This let our club judge whether they'd be a good fit and the same for them.

"They've officially asked to have our club added to their list. They'd also like permission to remain here for an undetermined amount of time. Three to four months is the plan for now, but they said it could be shorter or longer." I clenched my jaw to keep myself from saying anything. Gunnar had been staring down at the tabletop but with Cade's announcement, his head shot up. He wasn't happy either.

I knew Cade could read the fury and frustration in my eyes. "Steel, you already took care of that situation. So did Gunnar." As soon as Remi's taillights had disappeared, I'd tracked down Ty, the nomad who had touched her. The fight had been quick but bloody, well bloody for Ty.

"None of the guys have stepped out of line since that night. Everyone has chalked it up to a misunderstanding, and they accepted their punishment for putting hands on your women. The rules of our club and our chapter say we should give them this chance."

I turned my head and looked over at Gunnar. The table was silent now, every eye on us. Cade was giving us the respect of making this decision since it had affected our girls. If we said we didn't want them here, Cade would respect it and make them leave. But he was right. According to the rules, we should give them another shot. Had anything more happened between them and the women, especially without consent, they would have been booted out of the MC immediately.

They wouldn't have had the chance to strip them of their rank, I thought, *because they both would have been dead and buried*. I read the reluctant acceptance in Gunnar's face. I nodded once at Cade. It was all he needed.

"If they step one ass hair out of line, they're fucking gone. Got it?" It was a promise for us, but it was also a warning for the rest of the officers to keep an eye on them. Everyone nodded in agreement.

As church continued, we went through the plan for the Lycans. The fucker we'd caught yesterday had tried to hold out. He'd kept his cool for most of the night but once we brought Axel in, he'd spilled everything. Axel had a very special talent for getting men to talk. It rarely went well for them if they tried to refuse.

According to their member, the Lycans were dealing drugs laced with fentanyl in our area. They wanted heavy casualties so that we'd be tied up with the authorities and the community while they continued with their plans for attacking us. I sighed in aggravation. The Lycan we'd caught was too low down on the totem pole to know much more.

He didn't know where his club was getting the drugs; he didn't know what the next steps were or how Blaze, the Lycan President, was planning on striking out against us. He had been able to tell us that they were recruiting in high numbers and not being very selective of who they were taking in at the moment. *Amassing an army*, I thought grimly. They'd be fucking stupid to try to take us on, but it didn't surprise me that Blaze was doing it.

"Alright, anything else to report?" We'd already gone over the information we'd gotten from the Lycan. We'd come up with the perfect way to get a little more information. There was no way we were going to be caught unaware. But in order to protect our club and our territory, we needed more information.

Cade nodded to me and I stood up. Walking to the kitchen door, I popped my head out and found Bass standing there. "Come on in, kid."

Returning to my stool, I watched as Bass nervously entered the kitchen. I didn't blame him, he'd never been in church before, none of the members came in for these meetings, only the senior officers. He stood awkwardly near the end of the table, waiting for someone to tell him why he was here.

"Bass, thanks for coming in." He nodded at Cade but remained silent. "We have a job for you." A wary but determined look crossed the kid's face.

"What can I do, Prez?"

"You've been with us the longest out of our new prospects. You're at the point where we will be patching you in." Bass's eyes widened and a slow smile spread across his face. "We'd rather wait to do that until this job is done, however." Bass nodded in understanding.

"The only prospect that we're sure the Lycans know about is Scout. But you're the only one we'd trust with this. The Lycans are bringing on a lot of prospects right now, according to our sources, trying to build up their manpower before they come after us. We're a step behind at this point so we need you to go get picked up to prospect for them." Bass looked surprised but then nodded slowly. "You'd still belong here, but we need you to feed information back to us."

Finally, Bass grinned. "I can do that, Prez."

"This isn't a game, Bass," Cade warned. "If they figure out that you're connected to us, they'll kill you. And it won't be a pleasant way to go."

"I get it. I won't fuck up, promise."

I felt pride for the kid. He'd taken his prospecting duties seriously since day one. He wanted to be here, to be accepted, and once he finished this assignment, he'd be promoted to a fully patched brother.

"Steel, get him squared away on what we'll need and go over the rest of the plan with him after church." I nodded and led Bass out of the room.

"Wait for me out here. We'll go over everything in a bit." Bass agreed, then sat down on the back-porch steps and pulled out a cigarette.

"Alright, other business?" Cade asked as I stepped back into the kitchen.

I jerked my chin at him, and he gestured for me to speak. "Al called yesterday. There was a delay in the last shipment." Al owned the garage in Long Beach, CA, and was the president for the LB chapter of the Vikings.

Cade leaned forward and rested his forearms on the island. "It was Harris shipping that messed up." They dropped the shipment of bike parts off at the wrong location. Again. This was how you got the attention of the Feds. Harris was the shipper we'd been using for the last year. "Since this is the second time in two months that they've dropped the ball, I'd like to use someone else."

Cade nodded. "Do you think they figured out why we were shipping parts and frames?"

I shook my head. We'd never clued the shipping company in since the business wasn't owned by club members. As far as they knew we had two shops and just supplied both out of our Austin location. "No, they're just fucking incompetent."

"I agree. Do you have someone else in mind?"

"Mackenzie's Trucking. I was planning on heading over there after church if the suggestion passed."

"Perfect. Do it." I nodded and rapped my knuckles on the table. Remi didn't know it yet, but she'd be seeing me soon.

Cade adjourned the meeting not long after, and I glanced at my watch. Ten-thirty a.m. Perfect. That gave me time to fill Bass in on what we needed. I watched an hour later as the kid rode out to one of the locations that the Lycan member had mentioned they were recruiting from. He'd left his cut with me and I ran up and stored it in my room before I also headed out.

The ride over was short, and I was walking through the double doors of Mackenzie's by eleven-fifty. An older guy was sitting at the service counter, head down, scribbling something on a piece of paper. I walked up and leaned my forearms on the countertop.

He glanced up when I did and gave me a tight smile, his eyes staring cautiously at the patches on my cut. Professionalism won out. "Hello, how may I help you today?"

"I'm here to have something shipped." If I had to guess, I would say this was Remi's uncle. They looked enough alike that it was a high likelihood.

"Great, will it be a one-time shipment, or will you need a commercial account?"

"Commercial."

The guy scribbled something down, then gave that same pained smile again. "Okay, I'll be right back, and I'll have someone out here to help you shortly." He walked to the hallway that must lead to offices in the back. He paused and looked back at me over his shoulder. "It will just be a moment. Don't… go anywhere." He disappeared down the hall.

I gave a humorless laugh. 'Don't go anywhere' meant 'stay where the cameras can see you'. Or 'if anything goes missing, we'll blame you'.

CHAPTER 20

Remi

I looked up as Uncle Caleb popped his head in my office. "Hey, Rem. There's a guy out front who needs to set up a commercial account. I need to go next door to straighten out a mix-up in the warehouse." I frowned, he sounded hesitant about wanting to leave. He'd told me this morning that he'd have to head over and speak with the loaders and truckers.

Mackenzie's was a large operation. We had three adjacent warehouses. One, Dad had renovated into our front area where the customers could come in if they chose, offices, and meeting rooms in the back. Directly next door were our loading bays. For most jobs, we went to the client to pick up, however, occasionally we had to bring the shipments back here to load up with other deliveries going the same direction. Why waste the space when two shipments are headed to the same location?

Everyone except our office staff and mechanics worked next door. The truckers would get their schedules and pick the trucks up from there before heading out. The third building was our service garage.

Dad had always insisted on hiring our own mechanics for our trucks. It was hard to find reliable mechanics that could work on big rigs and he'd never wanted to have to wait in line to get something fixed. It had been a huge expense but had saved our bacon more than once when we had problems with the vehicles.

"No problem. I'll head out front right now." He hesitated again and shot a glance toward the front. "Janet is going to be back from lunch any minute," I reminded him when he still hesitated. "We'll be fine." Uncle Caleb nodded and left out the back entrance. I shook my head; he was clearly worried about my ability to run the front counter alone.

Pulling my heels out from under the desk I slid them on. I stopped in front of the full-length mirror I had. Mackenzie's was the only place that I dressed up for. I turned and looked over my shoulder to make sure nothing was on my butt. All clear. I faced the mirror again and smoothed my hands down the tight, gray striped, dress pants.

Tugging on the matching vest to settle it into place I took in my reflection. The vest by itself would be way too scandalous for an office. The lowest button stopped above my navel and the top button stopped at the bottom of my breasts. I'd paired it with a long-sleeved, silk blouse to make it office chic.

I poked at my hair; it was pulled up, clipped, and spilled curls everywhere. Bridget had insisted on doing it this morning. I'd put my foot down on the makeup though. I never wore it and she always tried to put too much on me. I grabbed the stack of order sheets, invoices, and other random paperwork. As I stepped out of my office, I met Janet as she came back from lunch and we walked out front together. "Did you have a good lunch?"

She smiled. "Yeah, you have to try the new Mexican place off of..." We'd stepped out into the front and she stopped mid-sentence. I looked over and sucked in a sharp breath.

"Wow." There was awe in her voice. "He is... wow." Standing in the middle of Mackenzie's was Steel.

Shit.

"Do you want me to go help him?" Janet's voice was excitedly hopeful.

"Thanks, but I've got it." She kept an eye on him as she walked behind the counter, and I grimaced when she smacked into a cabinet because she wasn't watching where she was going. I peeked over at him. His pale gray eyes were fixed on me. I licked my lips, tipped my chin up, and strode over to him.

"Hello, you needed something shipped?"

A large, amused grin split his face when I pretended not to know him. It was all for Janet's sake. She was a nice lady but could gossip with the best of them. I didn't need Uncle Caleb to find out I knew him. I didn't want him jumping down my throat any more than he already did. It annoyed me how much he tried to dictate my life, but he was the only family I had left, besides the girls. I wasn't in a space to be pushing anyone away. Plus, I wasn't sure the truckers wouldn't mutiny without Uncle Caleb there to run that side of things, for now.

"Yup."

I narrowed my eyes at him and glanced over at Janet who was watching us with rapt attention.

"Great, if you'd like to follow me back to our meeting room, I can get you taken care of." The grin only grew bigger. His eyes trailed lazily down my body, paused at my heels then flicked back up to my face. I kept the tight smile in place.

"Lead the way."

I clenched my teeth and spun on my heel, heading for the back. Steel hadn't been subtle whatsoever about checking me out so when I looked over at Janet her eyes were bugging out of her head. "I'll be in a meeting. If any calls come in could you…?

She waved a hand at me to keep moving. "Absolutely, Remi. I'll take care of it." She smiled. I glanced back one more time before we went down the hall. Steel's back was to her and she held out two thumbs up. I stifled a groan.

I entered the meeting room and waited for Steel to pass before I shut the door. Turning, I stared grimly at him. "What are you doing here?"

"I need to set up a commercial shipping account." His voice was infuriatingly calm at a time when my heart was pounding against my rib cage, trying to break free. Seeing him standing in my shop was so unnerving. Not because I was scared of him. I'd taken a lot of time, over the last two weeks, to think about his role in what had happened the night of the party.

He'd done everything he could to get me to safety and then make me comfortable until it was safe to go home. Not that I was under any illusion that he wasn't a dangerous man. I just didn't think he was dangerous to me. At least, not that night and not right now.

Blowing out a breath, I motioned for him to take a seat at the table. I settled in next to him and spread out the papers I'd need to fill out. Later I'd be putting them into the computer system. It drove me nuts to have to take the time to duplicate the work when I could just use the laptop I kept in here and get it done in one go. But both Dad and Uncle Caleb hated computers. There hadn't even been a computer system until I'd started taking over.

Uncle Caleb still refused to learn how to use the program so Janet, Anna, Julie, or I entered his orders. He always complained and said the paper system had been working fine for years. Eventually, I'd be getting rid of that paper system completely.

I looked up and my mouth dried as I found him quietly staring at me. Why did he have to do everything with such intensity? It always threw me off my game instantly.

"To set up a commercial account, I'll need an employer identification number for your business." I folded my hands in front of me. This was a test to see if he was seriously interested in working with me or if he'd just come here to see me. I shoved back the insecurity that flared at my assumption that he'd taken the time out of his day to come here specifically for me.

Steel rattled off the number and I quickly picked up a pen to fill out the form. *Alright*, I conceded. He'd really come here for business. My stomach settled a little. Business, I could do. I carefully guided him through the process, making sure I didn't miss anything that would make it hard for my guys to complete the shipment.

"Just a few more things. What is it you're shipping?" I didn't look up from the paper because I was still filling out the answer to the previous question.

"Various vehicle parts and frames."

I nodded, filling out the new line. "Where will we be picking them up from?"

"The garage address."

I flicked my eyes up and then back down as I copied the address that I'd already printed at the top of the page. Once I'd finished, I set my pen down. "You're set to have your merchandise picked up by nine a.m. tomorrow and it's guaranteed to make it to your ending destination by the following day at or before three p.m."

I pursed my lips, trying to think of anything I'd forgotten. I'd gotten all the information, accepted the payment, and reiterated the guarantee. I was really starting to get the hang of this, and it almost felt second nature. I slid a paper over to him and held out a pen. "Sign here, please."

Steel had been leaned back in his chair, legs sprawled out, arms crossed behind his head as he watched me. Now he leaned forward, and his fingers brushed mine as he took the pen, sending a pleasant jolt through me. I tried not to suck in a breath and alert him to my reaction at the feel of his skin touching mine. Not once had I ever felt like this with any of my boyfriends from the past.

Once he'd signed, I stood, prompting him to follow me. "That's it. This was the hard part. Next time you need a shipment, you can either call or set it up online through our website." I smiled at him as I began to open the door of the meeting room. I was mentally congratulating myself on remaining professional and composed. It hadn't been easy. I wasn't used to the way he affected me. The loss of control over my body was irritating.

"So business is over?"

I frowned at the odd phrasing. "Yes, I have everything I need. You are free to go." I said the last line teasingly but felt lame as soon as the words left my mouth.

"Good, that means we can discuss the other thing."

"Other…"

I couldn't finish my question because he'd pinned me against the door and his tongue was already sliding smoothly against mine.

"Mmmppphhmm." I tried to shove at his chest, but he just caught my wrists and jerked them up over my head. He was well aware that I wanted him. The way he handled me threatened to have my resistance melt. He held me immobile between him and the door, and his mouth was wreaking havoc on my senses.

I couldn't start anything with this intimidating, sexy biker. My life was a constant shit sandwich right now. Not to mention Uncle Caleb would have an aneurysm if he found out. But my body seemed to forget that any time he came near me. My brain usually wasn't far behind in forgetting. My eyes fluttered closed, and I gave in to temptation. The inner voice whispered that it was a bad idea to encourage him if I wasn't planning on having it go anywhere.

We're both adults, I told the inner voice. A few kisses weren't a commitment to anything. If they were, Bridget would have a whole harem.

Work and school had kept me running, but each time Steel had shown up over the last few weeks I'd been impulsive and dropped what I was doing to either go with him or to sit and talk. He had me on edge, wondering where he was going to show up next. After each time, I'd reprimanded myself and promised I would avoid him from that point on. His phone call was the only thing I'd managed to keep that promise with. When he was standing in front of me, he was too hard to resist.

I pulled at his grip on my hands and his kisses paused before he released them. He hadn't taken his lips off mine, but he was only brushing light kisses, gentle flicks of his tongue against my lips, as he waited to see what I would do. I brought both of my hands down to his chest. The heat of his skin through his t-shirt would have burnt if I wasn't already on fire.

I slid my hands over his chest, under his cut, then down his sides, feeling all the ridges of muscles along the way. The sound he made was somewhere between a growl and a purr. I let my hands stop just above his hips. When I didn't try to move away, he attacked my mouth with a new intensity. Despite the warning sounding in my head, I joined in.

I'd ignored his call the other day. I knew that meant he would just show up somewhere unexpected, but he was doing that anyway. I wasn't trying to string him along. I hadn't contacted him or sought him out. But I also hadn't insisted he leave me alone. The night of the party was supposed to be a one time, unplanned, totally spontaneous make-out session. He'd ruined that by randomly popping up.

I still couldn't figure out how he knew where I was at any given time. It was making me a little paranoid. Bridget had adamantly insisted she hadn't told him or Gunnar anything when I'd asked her. I knew Bridget and Gunnar had been hanging out, but I didn't think she'd ever tell them anything about my schedule. If she had, she wouldn't lie to me about it once I'd confronted her. No, he was getting his information from somewhere else. Once again, the thought that he would make an excellent cop flitted through my head.

Despite the thrill I got every time I saw him, I just couldn't figure out how I was going to fit anything else into my life at this point. Also, how would he and I work? I was a responsible, hardworking, rule follower. Honestly, I didn't know exactly what he was. That voice was back telling me that's because I hadn't given him a chance to show me. I couldn't tell whose side my conscience was on.

Then there was the whole criminal thing. The thoughts exploded in my head when his lips dropped to my neck and I felt his tongue lap the side of my neck before gently sucking. His beard was scraping my sensitive skin, adding to the feelings his lips and tongue were creating, heightening my pleasure.

Holy shit. My head dropped back against the door, eyes closed, and my pussy throbbed to the same rhythm in which he sucked on my neck.

"Open your eyes Remi." They fluttered open at his husky demand. I met his darkened gray gaze. "I want you to remember who's making you feel this way." He dipped his head and his breath feathered over my ear. "Then maybe next time you'll return my call. Maybe I won't have to find you at work. I won't have to get you alone in a meeting room. I won't need to mark you so anyone who sees you knows you're mine." His words penetrated my lust hazed mind. I frowned. "Yours?" He reared back his head, and we locked gazes. "Mine." He growled it before his lips crashed down on mine.

A knock on the door penetrated my lust-filled thoughts and made me jump, simultaneously. "Sorry, Remi." Janet's voice came through the door. "I just need to know where Mr. Felix's paperwork is?"

"Just a sec and I'll give them to you." Steel had paused with his lips on mine when Janet had knocked. He'd moved his head back to the side of my neck so he could rub his lips over the soft skin where my neck and ear met. I didn't know how I managed to speak without stuttering. I lightly pushed back on him and he reluctantly let me go, stepping back, but only a few steps.

I jerked my head, indicating I wanted him to move back further into the room. His eyebrows shot up and he just slid his hands into the pockets of his jeans. Otherwise, he didn't move. I huffed in aggravation but hurried to the table and rifled through the documents there. I breathed a sigh of relief when I found them quickly. I headed to the door and opened it. "Here you go, Janet." I smiled and handed her the paperwork.

Janet frowned, and her eyes dropped down to the side of my neck. The side of my neck that Steel had just been sucking on. I felt a flush creep into my face as I remembered the words that he'd said. "Marked me." They hadn't penetrated at the time.

Not much did when his hands were on me, I thought wryly.

Her gaze slid over my shoulder to him, but she didn't say anything. Janet murmured 'thanks' and scurried back to the front. I shut the door and turned to face him, slapping a hand to the offending area. "Please, tell me you didn't give me a hickey?" The victory in the amused look on his face told me he had. I groaned. "What the hell, Steel? How am I going to hide that?"

Steel shrugged nonchalantly. "I don't care if you don't." I glowered at him, but everything I wanted to say died in my throat when I heard Uncle Caleb's voice coming down the hallway. My eyes widened and Steel just went along in amusement as I quickly shoved him out of the room, through the building, and out into the parking lot as quickly as I could, before my uncle could see that he was still here.

Outside, I watched as he straddled his bike. He was as graceful as a big cat. Images of tigers stalking prey in tall grass flashed through my mind until his voice broke through my thoughts. "It's rude not to call people back, Remi."

Here was this biker, who I was almost one hundred percent sure was a criminal, lecturing me on social etiquette. It was absurd.

But he wasn't wrong. Guilt was thick inside my chest. It didn't matter that I didn't know him well, I still felt bad for blowing him off.

"Don't make me have to come find you again." Heat spread through my body and I watched as he drove off. I glanced back at the warehouses and grimaced when I saw one of the guys who worked in the loading dock slowly walking toward the building. He was rubbernecking it and had been watching Steel and me.

I waved a greeting at him and he called out a hello before booking it inside. I pulled my phone out of the pocket of my pants and opened a group chat with my housemates.

Remi: SOS, house meeting needed ASAP.

The responding texts from my friends flooded in as I walked back into Mackenzie's.

CHAPTER 21

Remi

I dropped the bags of chips onto the coffee table next to the cans of soda and the rest of the junk food. House rule: she who calls the meeting, provides the snacks. I pulled the large whiteboard and easel over to sit in front of the TV. Ming had insisted we use it for our meetings. After the initial groaning, we had all conceded that it was a good idea.

We had house meetings for all types of reasons. Actual issues in the house were the most common. Man trouble was the second biggest reason. With five young women living together, it didn't take long for someone's drama to appear. It was nice to have Ming and Julie's organization and my good girl ways to balance out the wild natures of Bridget and Anna.

Unfortunately, Ming texted and said she was on rounds at the hospital, so I'd have to fill her in later. I was disappointed but understood. She basically lived at the hospital right now, only coming home to occasionally sleep. Getting out to our classes with Sergio was the only time we were able to see her.

The door flew open, and my three roommates piled in, chattering. I'd managed to get out of Mackenzie's not long after Steel left, citing homework as the reason for leaving. Thank God Uncle Caleb had been distracted. Otherwise, he would have noticed that I'd kept a hand to the side of my neck anytime we spoke. That fact hadn't escaped Janet's keen eye. Luckily, she hadn't mentioned it and I just prayed she didn't say anything to my uncle.

"We're dying, Rem! What's with the meeting?!" Bridget flopped down in a chair, her eyes blazing with curiosity. The other girls followed suit, sitting on the couches and chairs, eager to participate. I recounted what had happened at Mackenzie's and they all looked stunned. Both Julie and Anna had met Steel at one point or another over the last few weeks. Ming was the only one who had yet to meet him. They were as stunned as Bridget and me that he'd somehow figured out my schedule and was showing up wherever I was.

"He said I was his." I shook my head in confusion. "I don't even know what that means."

Bridget gave me a patronizing look. "Exactly what he said. He considers you his already. Obviously, since he's been showing up all over, he's trying to pursue you."

I gave her an irritated look. "I know what he meant. What I don't get is, why? We don't even really know each other." Sure, that was because I hadn't really given him a chance to know me, but that was beside the point.

Anna shrugged and chugged from a soda can before speaking. "Some guys are like that, Rem. It's like they still live in the stone ages. It's kind of sexy." She smiled wickedly.

"But is it, really?" I asked. "I don't know if I want a guy who is that intense and possessive. Plus, all the other reasons we've gone over about why it's a terrible idea for me and him to spend any time together."

"Are you worried about the fact that you want to throw him down and fuck him? Or the fact that your uncle would flip his ever-loving shit if he found out?" Bridget asked. The twist of her lips gave away her amusement for my predicament.

"Yes." I sighed, indicating that both were accurate and worrisome. The first thing she mentioned kept making me forget why I should be running in the opposite direction from Steel.

Julie clapped her hands, drawing our attention. "You know what this needs?" She took our curious looks as confirmation to continue. "A pros and cons list." She grinned, happily. Her dark brown eyes were sparkling. There was nothing that made Julie happier than a good list. We all groaned.

Julie mapped out almost every decision in her life with the damn things. "You can't pro and con sexual attraction, Julie," Bridget said, horror etched in her face.

Julie thinned her lips primly. "Yes, you can. I've done it many times." Anna snickered and made some comment about Julie scheduling blow jobs. Julie flipped her off but stood up and picked up a marker. She made the headers on the whiteboard.

"Okay, let's start with pros. That should be easy. One, he's sexy." Julie wrote that down under the pro side of the board.

Anna nodded and piped in, tapping a finger on her full bottom lip. "He's possessive." She fanned herself as though the idea were going to make her burst into flames.

"Wait a minute, isn't that a con?" I asked her.

She looked at me as though I'd lost my mind. "You're telling me you don't find it hot as fuck when your guy is protective of you?"

Well sure, it was. "I don't think protective and possessive are the same thing," I said sarcastically.

"They absolutely are," Bridget argued. She shot me a heated look.

Julie shushed us and wrote the word on both sides of the board, effectively ending the debate. "What else?"

"Oh! He's not after you for your money." Bridget said smugly. We'd all had too many encounters with gold diggers of the male variety. All of our families were fairly wealthy. It was another reason we'd all banded together. Everyone who found out we had money usually just assumed we were a bunch of stuck-up snobs.

I looked at Bridget curiously. "How do you know that?"

She gave a dramatic sigh as if it was all so romantic. "Gunnar never lets me pay for a thing when we go out." They'd had two dates since the party. I wasn't sure if that gave her the authority to mark gold digger off the checklist yet, but they tended to make themselves known pretty quickly, so I trusted her. I was happy for her, if not a little worried that she was in a similar situation since both of the men were equally dangerous. Bridget, of course, wasn't worried in the slightest.

"It's a point of pride for all those guys. They won't let their women, or even just a date, pay. Plus, Gunnar mentioned that Steel and his brother own a business." My brows shot up. That surprised me. He'd come in to do the shipping for a garage, but I'd just assumed he was a manager. Now, I wondered if the mechanic shop he'd given me the information for was his, and he wasn't just an employee.

"That goes in the plus column." Julie chirped. At our looks, she shrugged. "What? I love when men are gentlemen and do stuff like pay, pull out your chair, open doors for you…" I swear her eyes glazed over and she had little hearts floating over her head. She was such a romantic. "Plus, we can add a business owner to the plus column as well." She scribbled furiously on the board.

An hour, and much arguing, later we all stared at the disaster that was the whiteboard. There were so many things written in both columns that Julie had to start writing really tiny halfway down in order to fit it all. The living room didn't fare much better. Soda cans, empty chip bags, and chocolate wrappers littered the coffee table and floor. We were all finally silent, just staring at the board. I didn't feel any less confused about what I should do.

Finally, Bridget spoke. "I didn't know you had all of this bouncing around in your head, Remi." She gestured at the whiteboard as she searched my face. "I think I would go crazy if I had to consider all of that before I hung out with a guy I liked." I nodded miserably. I wish I could let go the way Bridget and Anna did. I saw an empathetic look on Julie's face. This was the way she operated too, so she at least understood it.

"Okay." Bridget leaned forward and rested her hands in her chin as she glanced at the whiteboard. "I don't think any of us knows whether the pros won or if the cons did." We nodded in agreement. That board was a mess. "So, let me ask you a question." Her gaze zeroed in on me. "Do you like him?"

"I don't really know him."

"But what you have seen so far. Do you think you could like him? We know you're attracted to him, so that's a huge plus."

I thought about the ride he'd taken me on past the lake. I'm sure he didn't realize it, but I'd felt freer and more alive in that short hour than I had in the last year. He took me away from the craziness that was my life and showed me how to enjoy the moment. I wasn't sure if I wanted to admit that yeah, in a way, I did like him. "I think I'm most worried that the attraction is making me think that I do. That it will blow up later."

"I think you're not telling the whole truth." I stared in shock when Julie spilled the worries that most deeply plagued me. "I think you know it'd be easy to fall in love with him." I felt my face pale.

"Loving him scares the shit out of you because his lifestyle is so far out of the realm of what you know. You know your family is going to lose it when they find out, and you've already lost the most important person in your life. You may also be scared of getting close to him because you might lose him too. He does dangerous things daily. That makes it way more likely he could get hurt."

We were all silent, looking at Julie in shock. "Pssfftt, psychology majors. Am I right?" Bridget grinned at all of us. Julie blushed, but we all knew she was going to be an amazing therapist one day. No wonder she'd been acing all her psych classes. I made a mental note to have her help me out when I had to take the basic course that was required for any degree from the university.

"Now that we know what the problem is. I think I have a solution." This came from Anna. She looked between me and Bridget. "Bridget has been seeing Gunnar, right?" At our nods, she continued. "She's not worried about any claims he thinks he has on her, future commitments, or whether he could die tomorrow. I think you need to live in the moment, Remi, and give the guy a chance. Hang out with him, without worrying about future consequences, and see if he really is someone you may like."

Not worry about future consequences? I grimaced. I wasn't sure if I could do that. My entire life, but especially the last year, has been about taking the right action so that there weren't any negative side effects from my choices. But they had a point. If I gave Steel a chance, what's the worst that could happen? He breaks my heart? Broken hearts and college kids go together hand in hand. If he didn't, someone else probably would. His claims that I was his aside, we weren't talking about getting married. We'd have a few dates and maybe see what happened from there.

I looked up and saw Bridget's hopeful look. She'd been wanting me and Steel to double date with her and Gunnar. She squealed when I sighed in defeat. I shook my head but grinned. "I can't promise you guys this will work. But I'll try to give him a chance."

"You know that means you have to answer his calls, right?" Anna said patronizingly. I rolled my eyes at her and nodded. They all knew I'd been ducking Steel's phone calls. "Good, you can start now." She held out my phone, which I had set down somewhere once the meeting had started. I'd turned my ringer off, but she must have noticed the buzzing.

I hesitated, then looked around at all the garbage in the living room desperately, hoping to use it as a distraction. "Remi, no." Julie glared at me. "You just said you were going to try to give him a chance. Answer the phone. We'll clean this up."

Anna shoved the phone in my hand, and everyone stood to start cleaning as I went up the stairs toward my room. I answered at the top of the stairs and I heard mutters of 'finally', 'thank God', and 'hallelujah' coming from downstairs. I turned and flipped them all off.

"Hello?" I said as I walked into my room, shutting my bedroom door behind me.

"Good girl."

I sat down on my bed. "What?" I asked in confusion, but my belly fluttered at hearing his deep voice uttering that phrase.

"For answering." His voice sounded amused.

Rolling my eyes at his arrogance, I kicked my heels off, aiming toward my closet. "What do you want, Steel?"

"You." I clenched my thighs together as the tone of his voice and meaning sent a flash of heat straight between my thighs. "I'm off on Sunday. I'll be there at six p.m., to pick you up."

I hesitated, my silence stretching out over the connection as I decided if I was going to do this. *What's the worst that could happen, remember?* That little voice reminded me inside my head. Plus, I'd promised the girls. "Fine." I finally said. A heavy sense of finality settled over me.

"Good," His voice rumbled in my ear and I tried to ignore the way my pulse picked up as I thought about spending uninterrupted time with him.

CHAPTER 22

Steel

I glanced around as I got off my bike but didn't notice anyone loitering who shouldn't be. I walked over and leaned against the wall, smoking a cigarette outside the coffee house where Bass and I had agreed to meet. We weren't taking the chance of talking on the phone about anything he'd seen since he'd started prospecting with the Lycans.

They really must be desperate because they'd taken Bass in immediately. Typically, a guy would have to hang around a while before a club would consider allowing him to prospect. He'd come to the parties, functions, and events the club put on, and once everyone began getting to know each other, then they would let him prospect. The Lycans had cut that part out and immediately taken him in.

Finishing, I flicked my cigarette across the sidewalk and ignored the nasty look a woman with green hair and a nose ring gave me. *Like she was a pillar of morality.*

Inside, I found Bass and sat down. I'd ridden my motorcycle but had taken my cut off and worn a baseball cap and shades for this meeting. I didn't want to risk anyone recognizing me while I was with him. It was unlikely that the Lycans were this far into our territory, they'd mostly been sticking to the borders, with the exception of getting their drugs onto campus.

"Stacey?" I arched my brow at him. When he'd called me earlier that morning to see if we could meet, he'd pretended to be setting up a date with Stacey. He laughed and showed me his phone. Under my contact information was the name Stacey Wales and a picture of a stacked blonde.

"Hey, I gotta keep up pretenses, man." He sniggered at the look on my face.

"How's it going over there?" I asked, and he sobered up.

"Good. They don't have any idea who I am."

"Good. They treating you alright?" All of us guys felt bad using such a new guy to do this, but we didn't have any choice. Anyone else would have been recognized.

Bass's lips twisted ruefully. "They're dicks. They're nothing like our club, but otherwise yeah, it's fine. Blaze is a real nasty fucker. Most of the guys are terrified of him." I made a sound of agreement. We'd known Blaze and Reaper, his VP, since we'd all been kids. They'd always been sadistic assholes. You didn't want your club members dissatisfied, and you didn't want them afraid of you. Both types would turn on you in a heartbeat.

"I know it's only been a couple of days, Bass. But have you found anything out?"

"Oh right, I called because of what happened last night." He leaned forward so he could talk a little lower and I did the same. "We were at a drop…" He shrugged at the look on my face. They were letting day old prospects go on drops with them?

How fucking stupid were these guys?

"I know, I know… anyway, the other weird part was Blaze himself went on this drop with us." I couldn't figure out what game the Lycans were playing. It's highly unusual for a club president to go on any drops unless the club was expecting trouble. "Then, right before the buyers get there, this woman comes in. Waltzes right in, like she owns the place. Blaze wasn't surprised to see her though."

Bass leans back in his chair, looking as confused as I felt. "They just started going at it, yelling at each other in front of everyone. Blaze told her she needed to go get the money early. Chick kept insisting that it wasn't very long until she'd go pick it up. He'd grabbed her and yanked her to the back of the warehouse by that point. So, I didn't hear any more from them."

"Some of the other guys were talking, though. I guess Blaze's been stockpiling weapons and ammo and is tapping the club dry. One of the guys said his side piece went once a year and got a big payday. She usually splits it with the MC according to them, but they said she and Blaze have been fighting for weeks about it. He wants the full amount now, but she wants to wait to get it when she normally does."

I absorbed everything he was telling me and wondered who the woman was that was helping fund the Lycan MC. Everyone knew Blaze was married, but now he had this new woman hanging around? "Do you know how long she's been giving them money?"

"The guys weren't sure, but one of them has been in the club for five years and he said she was there before he got there. She's never around when Blaze's wife is, of course," Bass smirked.

So, this was a permanent arrangement. It wasn't unusual that we didn't have too much information on an old lady. Most MCs had a strict rule, you didn't involve women and children. It kept everyone's families safe, knowing that other clubs weren't going to target guys' wives and kids.

There wasn't much else for Bass to report yet, so we took off, each heading in different directions. I was heading back to the clubhouse to report in with Cade. As I passed by the college campus, I couldn't stop the grin from forming on my face. Tomorrow was Sunday.

CHAPTER 23

Remi

After finally making the decision last night, to give Steel a chance and go out with him, I'd slept like a baby. After weeks of indecision, it felt good to make a choice and just go with it.

A noise of aggravation came from my closet and I sighed. With my hands on my hips, I stared down at the floor of my room in dismay. It looked like a small tornado had ransacked my closet, spilling and flinging clothes everywhere. That tornado had a name… Bridget. I sidestepped when she chucked a pair of shorts over her shoulder. She'd come close to nailing me. Her aim had always impressed me.

Bridget was on her hands and knees in my closet, head down, ass up. "Don't you have anything, ANYTHING, other than jeans, jean shorts, tank tops, t-shirts, or work clothes?" She turned around and glared at me, as though my breathing was an affront to her world.

"Ummm…"

"Oh. My. God, Remi!" She shouted at me.

Damn.

She whipped back around and continued scrounging, muttering under her breath. I stood there, unsure of whether she wanted my help or for me to get out of the way. I stumbled back when she shoved to her feet and charged at me. The crazy gleam in her eyes made me nervous.

"What if you wear something of mine?" A laugh busted out of me. I smothered it with a cough when her look threatened to kill me.

"I wouldn't be able to fit into anything of yours." I was seven inches taller and built very differently from her. I eyed her pert, little breasts. I've always wanted to switch with her. Mine were too big to hide and only got in the way, most of the time.

"A skirt?" She asked hopefully.

"Absolutely not. Even your longest skirt would have my ass hanging out." She smirked at me. "No, that is not the message I want to send." I sat down on my bed and chewed my bottom lip.

"You need to lighten up and go have some fun. Stop worrying about whether you made the right choice in agreeing to go out with him and just relax." She knew me too well. That is exactly what I'd just been doing.

"Seriously girl, if you don't go unwind you are going to crack and kill someone. Don't make us lock you out and refuse to let you back into the house." When I met her blue eyes, she pursed her lips. She read the nerves on my face.

"You're not backing out. You will go. You will have fun. Hell, have sex with him if it'll help you unwind." My mouth fell open. Miss never give it up until you've got him in a committed relationship — was telling me to go for it?

"What?" I sputtered, laughing.

She rolled her eyes. "Normally, I wouldn't advocate sex on a first date." She had a prim and proper look on her face. Bridget had a strict code that she stuck by. She wouldn't sleep with a guy until he'd committed to her. That didn't mean she wouldn't do anything else, but typically sex was off the table. "But if anyone deserves an orgasm, it's you."

"Jesus, Bridge. Can we not talk about my orgasms, please?"

"You mean your lack of them?" She smiled smugly at me and crossed her arms under her breasts.

I shot her a glare. But she wasn't wrong. Most nights I was too tired to do anything to myself other than fall into bed and go right to sleep. I waved at her, motioning for her to leave. "Go. I'll dress myself."

Bridget's face fell with dismay. "No. Please, I can help. I'll go ask one of the other girls…."

"OUT." She sighed at my order and left. I eyed the disaster that was now my room. Once Bridget left, I squeezed into the very darkest corner of my closet and pulled out the one sundress that I owned. I put it on and slid on my white and red striped Adidas, and stood in front of the mirror.

The dress was red with little cap sleeves that left my shoulders bare. The sweetheart neckline showed the swells of my breasts without me having to worry all night that they'd fall out. I smoothed my hands down the form-fitting dress to where it stopped mid-thigh. The shoes were going to drive Bridget insane, but I was hoping the fact that I was wearing a dress would shock her into silence.

I put a white jacket on over the dress and picked up my cigarette case, which acted as my wallet, and shoved it, keys, and my phone into the pockets of the jacket. I was nervous, and I wanted to look nice for him. I was trying to figure out if I should do something more with my stick straight hair when the doorbell rang.

I walked out of my room right as Bridget walked out of hers. The happy, almost manic, look in her eyes at the sight of my dress, turned sour as soon as she saw my sneakers. "Seriously?" Her blue eyes met mine. "You're wearing Adidas with a sundress?" She whispered in horror. I nodded slowly, afraid to make any sudden movements. The doorbell peeled again.

"They match," I said, as if that was all that mattered. To me, it was. But to Bridget, the fashion major, my wardrobe was an atrocity.

"Got it!" One of the girls downstairs called. Bridget was still staring me down.

"Oh, honey. No. How about a pair of heels? You can't wear sneakers. Not for a date, Rem." Her eyes pleaded with me.

"Rem. Your sexy biker is here." Anna grinned at me and waggled her brows as she came up the stairs. Jesus, they all seem to think I was going to jump him immediately. I mean, sure, we'd shared some hot kisses. Okay, they were a bit more than that. But that still didn't mean I was going to throw myself at the guy.

"Thanks. Um, maybe you can keep Bridget company for a bit after I leave?" Anna looked at Bridget in confusion. As I walked past, I whispered to her, "Take anything sharp away, and get her shoelaces from her too."

"Remi!" I hadn't heard Bridget yell like that in a long time. I knew she wanted to drag me into her room to try to make me change my shoes, so I raced down the stairs. I glanced up and laughed when I saw Bridget standing at the top glaring at me.

One minute I was moving down the stairs, the next I was propelled backward. The wind was knocked out of my lungs. I would have ended up on my ass if Steel hadn't wrapped his hands around my shoulders and pulled me forward after I bounced off his chest. He crushed me in his arms, steadying me. I was finally still, while my stunned brain tried to process what had happened. I heard Anna and Bridget giggling at the top of the stairs.

I glanced up, aware that this was the second time I'd slammed into Steel and ended up plastered against his chest in the short time we'd known each other. The scent of motor oil and citrus hit me. Jesus, why did he always smell so good? I cleared my throat and stepped back, my face heating up. He let me back up and just shook his head at me.

"You ready?" His gaze flicked between me and Bridget, who was motioning, still trying to get me to reconsider changing. He nodded at Bridget and Anna, a typical Steel greeting. They both smiled and waved at him.

"You two have fun." Anna grinned as she said it, but then she pulled Bridget away. I mouthed 'thank you' at her as she strong-armed the blonde down the hall.

I looked back at Steel and noticed his eyes were slowly perusing my body. I fought the urge to fidget. But then his eyes met mine and heat pooled low in my belly at the look he gave me. Honestly, the girls may have been right to assume I'd jump him. I wasn't sure I'd be able to stop myself if he kept looking at me like he wanted to eat me.

"Yup. Let's go."

CHAPTER 24

Steel

I took Remi's hand and led her out to where my bike was parked in front of her house. I couldn't say I minded how often she ended up bumping into me. Anything to get her body against mine. I glanced over at her. I'd about swallowed my tongue when I saw her standing there in that tiny little red dress. It hugged all her curves perfectly. I couldn't wait to see her without the little coat she had on over the top. It wasn't buttoned, so I already had a great view of her tits, but I still wanted it off of her. Hell, I wanted the dress off her too, if that was an option.

I looked down at her feet and laughed silently to myself. Wearing her Adidas seemed to be her trademark. Although I wasn't sure if she did it to make some kind of statement or if she just really liked the shoes. The only time I'd seen her in anything else had been at her office. Remembering what we'd gotten up to in that office had the little bit of blood that was left in my head flowing south.

As we stopped at the bike, I saw her look at it apprehensively, then back at the house. "Maybe I should go change."

I frowned. "Why?"

She looked at me like I was an idiot. "A dress isn't the best thing to wear when riding a bike. I'm going to end up flashing my ass at someone." I couldn't help but grin at the thought.

She started to go back toward the house until I caught her hand and stopped her. I stepped in close to her, enjoying the way she softly sucked in her breath and held it. It was nice to know I wasn't the only one affected by whatever this was between us. I tucked a piece of her dark hair behind her ear.

"Don't change. That dress looks sexy on you." I let my eyes roam appreciatively. When I looked back at her face, it amused me to see the way it had pinkened slightly. "Let's go." I moved away and pulled out the helmet. Remi put it on as I straddled my bike. She shot a quick look around before she quickly clambered on the bike behind me. I waited while she adjusted her dress so that she was sitting on the back of it securely.

After driving across town, I pulled into the parking lot of Lock, Stock, and Barrel, the local bar that the club owned. Technically Cade owned it, but he felt the same as Riggs and me; what we owned, the club owned. Just as my brother and I had the guys in the club working for us in the garage, Cade employed only club members. It made it easier whenever things went down. In our line of work, things were always going down. Making up excuses for people outside of the club was more trouble than it was worth.

As Remi and I entered the building, I saw Trip working behind the bar. His girl Amy was running drinks to the few customers here tonight. It was Sunday evening, so it was quiet. I didn't mind. I didn't feel like sharing Remi, and if a bunch of my brothers were around, they'd all want to meet her. I jerked my chin at Trip in greeting. I ignored him when he grinned, wiggling his brows, looking between me and Remi.

We settled near the pool tables in the back, and I shrugged off my leather coat and draped it over the back of a chair. I grinned smugly when I saw her eye me appreciatively. I was wearing my usual jeans, t-shirt, cut, and boots, but luckily for me, that seemed to do it for her. We both looked up as Amy came over.

"Hey Steel." She looked over at Remi curiously. "Hi, I'm Amy."

"Hey, I'm Remi." Both girls smiled warmly at each other.

"Amy." I acknowledged her.

"What can I get you two?" I could tell she was dying to ask about Remi, but she wouldn't with her sitting there. Thankfully, Amy hadn't been at that party the first night and Trip obviously hadn't mentioned that I had a new girl. I knew the next family barbeque there'd be no getting around explaining who Remi was, though. I liked Amy a lot, despite her nosey nature. It was all done with the best intentions. She was a really good girl and great for Trip.

"I'll take a beer. Trip will know which kind." Amy nodded, and we both looked over at Remi. She blinked at us for a second before she responded.

"Can I get a Long Island Iced Tea?"

"Sure, sweetie. I'll be right back." Amy hurried back to the bar and both Remi and I watched in amusement as Amy lit into Trip, motioning back toward us.

Giving him an earful for not keeping her up on club gossip, I thought to myself. The women that our members dated were no different than most other women. They loved to know what was going on with those closest to them. Most of the wives and girlfriends of our guys got along, although there were a few who didn't. We were lucky that our club members and their families were all pretty close. It was one of the things that was important to Cade. He wanted us all to be a family.

I nodded over to the pool table. "Want to play?" I laughed at the mischievous look that spread across Remi's face.

"You're on."

"Have you played before?" I asked, wondering if I was about to have my ass handed to me. I saw a few of our members scattered around the bar, along with a few of our locals that weren't part of the club but were permanent fixtures here. The club members were watching us. I knew bringing her here would get a lot of attention, but I wasn't about to bring her anywhere else to drink. Besides, the more the guys saw her with me, the more likely they'd be to remember to keep their hands off when they saw her at any future events.

"Maybe," she said. "I have to warn you." She shot me a grin that was cute and mischievous. I mentally shook my head, wondering what it was about this girl that got to me so easily. I liked everything about her, and that was rare. "I'm extremely competitive."

"Good, so am I," I laughed.

Her eyes flashed at me in challenge. "Good, I hate it when guys try to let girls win."

"There's no danger of that happening. In fact," I said tilting my head while looking at her. "Why don't we bet on it?" I dared her. Her smile got bigger.

"Okay. What are the stakes?" Amy came back and set our drinks at our table. Remi called a thank you as Amy scurried off quickly, trying to give us privacy.

"Best two out of three. If I win, you kiss me." She narrowed her eyes at me but then nodded.

"If I win…" She glanced around, then shot me a smug smile. "You dance with me." She jerked her head over to the jukebox, which was currently playing a low, slow song.

"Deal," I said immediately. "Do you want to rack or break?" I smiled at the indecisive look on her face.

"I'll rack. I'm not sure I'll break very well." She walked over to our table and stripped off her jacket.

"Jesus, fuck," I muttered and rubbed a hand over the back of my neck when she turned around. She was going to fucking kill me. The dress was sexy. Her body was even better.

"What?" She smiled at me innocently, but I thought I caught a gleam in her eye. I just shook my head, grabbed my beer, and took a long swallow. As she started racking up the balls, I glanced over at the bar and found Trip grinning at Remi like an idiot. I narrowed my eyes at him until he focused on me. He snapped up and got busy mixing a drink for a woman sitting alone at the bar.

I leaned over the table with my cue and lined up the shot. I saw Remi studying my actions out of the corner of my eye. The balls scattered as the cue ball struck the triangle. Two stripes landed in separate pockets. I gave Remi a smug look and lined up my next shot.

"So, how does a twenty-one-year-old end up with a company like Mackenzie's?" I watched as the ball landed lightly in the pocket, then looked over at her. I instantly noticed the stricken look on her face and cursed myself for being a moron. "I'm sorry. I know it's because of your dad…" I rubbed the back of my neck and tried to salvage the situation. "I just meant; I'm surprised it didn't go to your mom? Your uncle? A grandparent?"

Thankfully, she seemed to have pulled herself together, and I hoped I hadn't just hurt her too badly. Clearly, her father's death was still a very difficult topic for her. For some reason, the thought of her in pain brought out every protective instinct inside of me.

"My mom… isn't in the picture." She let her gaze skip from mine, and it landed on my pool cue, which I was leaning on. "Uncle Caleb doesn't want it." She looked back up at my face and laughed at the look of disbelief she saw there. "No, really. Money and power don't motivate him." I narrowed my eyes at her and shook my head, dismissing that idea.

"Money and power motivate every man," I stated matter-of-factly.

She frowned at me, then just shrugged. "Well, as far as I can tell, he doesn't care about either. It's too much work for him. He wants enough to be comfortable but not so much that it eats into his home life. He's a really good manager, He understands the truckers and mechanics, but… he's not good with the higher levels of stress. Being the acting owner is more than he can handle."

I still didn't get that, but she'd gotten a little defensive before when I'd mentioned that her uncle may not be as disinterested in taking over Mackenzie's as she thought, so I didn't comment.

"My grandparents are gone. I have no other family. But even if I did, Dad wanted me to have his company."

I didn't miss the fact that she called the business his. I searched her face. "And do you?" She looked at me in confusion. "Want it," I elaborated. She blinked slowly at me as though she hadn't expected the question.

CHAPTER 25

Remi

Not once, from the time my dad had gotten sick, and certainly not since his death, had anyone asked me what I wanted. Dad and Uncle Caleb decided the whole way through what I would do. The only thing I put my foot down on was selling the home I grew up in. Uncle Caleb insisted it was pointless to hold on to it. I refused to sell it. I wasn't willing to part with anything that was once my father's and was now mine.

Somehow Steel saw through all the bullshit and knew what to ask, even though I didn't fully know the answer. "I don't know." It came out as more of a whisper than I'd meant. He just sat there silently staring at me, waiting for me to continue. "Yes, because I don't want to disappoint him," I said finally, firmly.

Steel watched me longer than was comfortable before he spoke. "I doubt you could do anything that would disappoint him." He reached past me and picked up his beer with his free hand, drinking before setting it back down. "Something tells me you were more important to him than a company."

"Now, your uncle? It wouldn't surprise me if he'd be pissed if you sold. Or maybe that's exactly what he's hoping for so that he can buy it from you. All while having it be your idea." At my surprised look, he shrugged. "Sorry wildcat, in my world men don't pass over the opportunity to gain more money or power, let alone both."

I glared at him. "You don't even know Uncle Caleb." But his words sparked doubt inside of me. Was Uncle Caleb only saying he didn't want Dad's company while secretly waiting for me to break down and give up on it and sell to him? That would explain why it felt like he was constantly pushing me past my breaking point with both school and taking over within the business. Steel's next words broke me out of my somber thoughts.

"You're right. I don't." His tone was anything but reassuring though. "So, are you going to keep it?"

I had been staring down at his boots, considering his previous words, when he asked the next question. I met his curious eyes. Determination swirled through my stomach. At that moment, I made a decision on something I hadn't even known I'd been wrestling with for the last year.

"Yes. I am."

The corner of his lips tipped upwards before he turned back to the pool table.

I watched as Steel made shot after shot as we talked. We'd lightened the mood considerably from the beginning of the conversation. We talked about school and how it was going. I found out his favorite color was forest green, which was weird since he only wore black or white. We told each other a few stories from our childhoods, although I could tell he wasn't sharing much on that front. I didn't want the conversation going back down such a serious path though, so I didn't push for more information.

Suddenly I realized how few balls he had left on the table. *Uh oh*, I thought as I took a drink of my Long Island. He was going to run the table if I didn't do anything.

Trailing my fingers along the side of the pool table, I strolled over toward him, hips swaying. He was leaning down, but his eyes were no longer on the ball in front of him. I angled myself so I was directly in the path of his gaze, bending down to study his shot. I knew I was playing dirty, giving him a great view of my breasts, but a girl had to do what a girl had to do.

I tilted my head enough to draw Steel's gaze up to my face, and I smiled innocently at him. The look on his face would have worried me only a few short weeks ago. He looked intense, a frown pulling his eyebrows low over those gorgeous eyes. But I was beginning to figure him out. The look in his eyes was pure lust.

I couldn't keep the innocence in my smile when I saw how he was looking at me. He narrowed those gray eyes at me before he focused back on the table. He knew exactly what I was doing. He drew back his cue, and I ran my hand up and down my own as he brought his forward. It was enough to draw his attention at the last minute, and his ball tapped the outside of the pocket before spinning away.

"Aw, nice shooting though." I sauntered away, heartily enjoying myself. I hadn't let loose and flirted with anyone for far too long. I bent down to line up my shot and flicked my eyes up. There was no doubt he was enjoying the view as he sat drinking his beer. I grinned to myself and sunk my first ball.

I managed to put two more solids into the pockets before I missed. Steel prowled around the pool table, searching for the best shot. I leaned back against the table and took slow sips of my drink. I wasn't planning on getting drunk tonight. I needed to stay sharp to keep up with this guy and not just in pool. He had a way of getting under my skin that made me feel nervous, but also excited.

Finally, Steel leaned down for his shot. My eyebrows rose because it was directly in front of me and I watched as his jeans molded to his ass. He sunk the ball and went back to his restless stalking. It was like he was a big cat in the jungle going after prey, not a guy in a bar playing pool. I wasn't even paying attention to how many balls were left on the table anymore. I only had eyes for the way the muscles rippled in his back. The way his biceps tightened and flexed as he made his final shots.

Steel turned around and gave me a satisfied smirk. It was at that point I realized he'd just won the first game. I set my empty glass down and felt my head spin lightly as I headed for the table.

Shit, I shouldn't have drunk that so fast. I wasn't drunk, but I had a slight buzz going. Now, I was really going to have to pay attention if I wanted to win. It was rare for me to not be ultra-focused when playing for stakes.

He set the balls back up, and it was my turn to break. I leaned over the table, and I was very conscious of him standing behind me.

Please don't let my dress have ridden up too high, I thought with a blush. I took the shot and frowned when only three balls broke off the triangle in the middle of the table. I'd over-embellished a little when I made it seem like I'd even played pool a few times. I'd played twice. Enough to know the rules, but never enough to have gotten good.

Strong hands slid down my biceps to my forearms as I felt the heat of his body close to mine seconds before I felt him from chest to thigh against my back. He directed my hands back into position and I fought to breathe as he leaned us over the table to set me back up to re-break.

"Tighten this hand." His breath tickled my ear, and I tried to suppress a shudder. His deep voice in my ear had my nipples hardening. Licking my lips, I tightened the hand that he tapped. Then he moved his hand and placed it on my hip.

Oh, good Lord. Even the slightest touch from him was turning me on. He was going to melt me into a puddle. There was certainly puddle action beginning to happen somewhere.

"Now, loosen your grip on the front hand just a little." He kicked my right foot slightly, forcing my stance wider, and shoving my ass directly into his thigh.

Oh, maybe that wasn't his thigh. I suppressed a nervous laugh when I realized I was breathing a little quicker. Fighting to calm myself, I took a deep breath so I didn't sound like a hyperventilating, horny rabbit.

"Pull back, then really drive it home. Don't manhandle the shit out of the front of the stick though." He reminded me as I started to do just that.

Steel moved to my left side, just enough that I wouldn't hit him with the cue when I made the shot. I laughed in triumph when all but two of the balls scattered and I pocketed a stripe. I turned and smiled at him in triumph.

The smile slipped off my face as desire hit me straight in the stomach. We were standing so close I had to tip my face up to look at him. Steel's eyes dropped to my lips, and I leaned in toward him as his hands settled on my hips.

"Hey!" A big, brown-haired, green-eyed guy slapped Steel on the shoulder and made both of us jolt. I swear Steel let out an actual growl of frustration. I wouldn't know what else to call the sound. He glared over his shoulder at the guy but didn't drop his hands from my hips. Stepping away, I ducked my head and went over to search for my next shot, giving them some space and taking a little for myself as well.

Amy set a refill down on the table for me before I could tell her I didn't need another. She came over to me and shot the guys, who were now talking, a look before smiling at me. "How long have you and Steel been seeing each other?"

"This is our first date," I said nonchalantly. She just gave me a wide grin. "What?" I asked in confusion.

"Trip," She jerked a thumb over her shoulder at the guy behind the bar, "mentioned you were at one of the parties a few weeks ago." I looked over at the blonde who was pouring shots and tried to remember if I'd seen him there. For the life of me, I couldn't remember. It had been a bit of a hectic night. But he obviously knew me.

"Yeah, a friend and I went. Are they always so…" I tried to find a polite description.

"Wild? Absolutely." She laughed.

"Hey, Remi." We both glanced over and found both guys watching us. Amy murmured something and took off back toward the bar. Bringing my drink, I walked back over to the men and tried not to fidget under their intense gazes. "Remi, this is Cade. Cade…" Steel motioned at me. We shook hands, and I remembered back to the first day when I'd seen Steel and a bunch of the guys sitting on their bikes in front of the school. I'd been right then; all of these guys were huge. Cade was as tall as Steel, a little less bulky, but still muscular. I wonder what they put in their water?

"Nice to meet you." I smiled, and he returned it. Then just did the nod thing that Steel usually did. Cade clapped Steel on the shoulder again and said something about heading back.

As he strode toward the door, he hesitated then looked at me over his shoulder. "Hope we'll see you at the barbeque next weekend, Remi." He shot Steel an amused look, then left before I could respond. I looked over at Steel but couldn't read the expression on his face.

CHAPTER 26

Steel

We both watched as Cade left. He thought he was making me uncomfortable by inviting Remi to next weekend's family event. It didn't bother me as much as I would have thought.

Cade had been in his back office finishing up the paperwork for the night when he'd spotted us. Like a dick, he'd broken us up, right as I was about to kiss Remi. I liked that she was being more receptive to me now. I hadn't missed how she'd leaned into me or the way she'd been looking at me.

"Want to finish?" She asked as she went back to the pool table and I went back to watching her. She clearly hadn't played much pool before, but I liked the fact that she accepted a challenge even when it wasn't something she was good at. When she missed the next shot, I stepped up to the table. I was on a mission now. I wanted to win this game and finish what we'd just about started before we got interrupted.

I went back and looked down at the table. "So how about you?" My gaze left the shot I was considering and found hers at her question.

"What about me?" I asked.

"What's your story?" She took a slow sip from her drink, her lips wrapped around the straw. I watched her throat as she swallowed and had to adjust my stance as my pants got too tight in the front. I met her eyes again and silently watched her, considering how to answer her question. She shifted, but I couldn't tell if she was uncomfortable or turned on.

Remi wiped one of her hands on her dress. "Uh, how did you and Riggs end up in the MC?" She rephrased the question.

I went back to the pool table. If we were going to talk about me, I needed to do something with my hands. "Our dad left us when we were young. Mom worked all the time. Riggs and I pretty much grew up with Cade and Gunnar. My brother and Cade decided they were going to join the Marines once they graduated," I saw her shift a little and interest flared in her eyes, "but that didn't work out. They got into some trouble and one of the guys in the club helped them out. They showed up the next day to prospect. Gunnar and I had to wait two more years, but then we did the same as soon as we could."

I missed my shot and watched as she settled in to take hers. Her dress rose as she stretched, revealing more of those gorgeous, toned legs. Watching her flatten over the table was fucking with me. I reached down and adjusted my dick, so it wasn't tenting my jeans out.

I looked back at the bar and Trip held up a beer and pointed to both of us. I subtly shook my head, then went back to the game. I needed to be able to drive and wanted her to be able to ride after this. She sank three more balls. This was a tighter game than I was expecting it to be. I only had one more shot then the eight ball, she had three then the eight. She hissed in frustration when she missed the next shot.

She hadn't been kidding about being competitive. I chuckled, and she shot me a glare. The smile slipped off my lips though, when that look turned calculating and she walked closer to me. She was back to trying to cheat by distracting me. I certainly didn't mind that. I looked down at her as she stopped directly in front of me. Remi dragged her finger down my chest and wet her lips as she watched me.

Two can play this game, wildcat.

I gave her a wicked smile, enjoying it when hers slipped slightly. I grabbed her wrist and watched those delicious lips part. Bringing her hand up, I brought it to my lips and nipped the tip of her finger before I pulled it fully into my mouth and sucked firmly. Her gasp had my cock jumping in my pants.

I released her suddenly and watched as she tried to compose herself. Now that she was suitably distracted, I returned to the table and finished out the game. It wasn't easy to tamp down my raging hard-on, but I wasn't going to lose. I hadn't been kidding about being competitive either.

"Well, you won," she said it in a grumpy voice, but her eyes were teasing. "Would you show me how to play better?"

"Sure." I racked the balls up and we spent the next hour or so practicing shots and learning more about each other. Technically, she practiced shots, while I ran my hands all over her. She didn't seem to mind. But now I was at the point where I needed a little more. I had wanted it earlier but wasn't about to deny her request.

Taking her hand, I led her into the back hallway, bypassing the bathrooms. When we got to the back, I punched in the code to the lock on Cade's office door. As we stepped through, I saw her look between me and the lock with a questioning glance. "Cade owns the bar."

With a non-committal sound, Remi pulled her hand from mine and went to look at some of the stuff Cade had hanging on the walls. She ignored the desk, which I appreciated since he had piles of paperwork scattered on it. Who knew what she might see if she were to look through those? But she was just waiting for me to shut the door. As soon as I did, she turned and watched me quietly.

Striding forward, I wasted no time. I slipped my left hand into her hair and cupped the back of her head, and my right went to her hip. She sucked in her breath and looked up at me. Her eyes dropped to my mouth. "Well…" My lips quirked when she looked up at me.

"What?" Her voice was husky.

"I won. You owe me a kiss."

She frowned, then understanding dawned that I wanted her to initiate. Her cheeks pinkened, but she stood up on her toes slightly to close the gap. Her lips brushed mine, and I had to fight myself to keep from taking over. I wanted her to control this, for now. Her fingers came up slowly and brushed over my throat, grazing my tattoo as her lips moved softly on mine.

I squeezed her hip, fighting for control. That encouraged her because that sexy little tongue licked along my bottom lip. She broke hers from mine and trailed them down to where her fingers had been. Her tongue licked my throat, lips whispering over my skin. That snapped my control.

With a groan, I pulled her up against me and kissed her again, thrusting my tongue into her mouth. Her answering moan had me backing her up until the back of her thighs hit Cade's desk. I dropped my hand from her hair to her other hip. Picking her up, I set her on top of the paperwork on the desk. She let out a startled squeak, but it was muffled as I stroked my tongue against hers.

I bumped her legs apart and stepped in between them. With my hands still on her hips, I slid her forward, so that we were pressed together. The motion hiked her dress up so that nothing except her panties were in my way. Her arms had wrapped around my neck when I'd picked her up, and now her hands slid down my chest. I ran my fingers down the tops of her thighs and then felt her shudder when I ran them back up the insides of them, stopping short of the one area where she wanted to be touched.

She squirmed a little on the desk, trying to get me to move my hands further, but I just pushed down on her thighs, stilling her. I dropped my lips to the side of her neck and licked and sucked my way down toward her shoulder. Her head fell to the side, and she made little encouraging sounds. Now that she was sitting still, focused on my lips which had moved onto the spot where her neck and shoulder met, I let my hands creep up her body to her waist. As they kept rising, she tried to pull my hand up higher, so I nipped that sensitive spot on her neck. She gave a sharp hiss, then moaned on the exhale.

Remi was going to figure out quickly that she wasn't in control of this anymore, despite her giving that first kiss. I sucked on the spot, swiping my tongue over it to ease the sting from my teeth. She'd end up with a hickey, but I didn't care. I loved marking her, seeing the proof on her skin that I'd been there. I switched to the right side of her neck and trailed my lips up until I sucked her earlobe into my mouth. Scraping it lightly with my teeth I gave her one of the things she'd been asking for, I palmed her tit. Fuck, she felt good. Touching her body forced me to shift slightly so I could relieve the pressure of my jeans against my hard-on.

Remi groaned and arched against me, thrusting into my hand. I easily slid my hand beneath the top of her dress and had to grit my teeth as she rubbed her body against mine. She wasn't wearing a bra, so I ran my thumb over her nipple and felt it pucker. Remi wrapped her arms around my waist, trying to tug me closer as she started lightly rocking against me.

My breath caught, and it felt like my heart was going to beat its way out of my chest. The little sounds she was making were setting my blood on fire, and I was close to fucking her here on the desk. I ground back into her and plucked her nipple, swallowing her gasp with my mouth, when suddenly the door swung open behind us.

We froze, and she looked up at me with wide eyes, her cheeks turning red. I glared over my shoulder and saw my asshole brother leaning against the doorframe with a shit-eating grin on his face.

"Get the fuck out." I removed my hand and made sure Remi's dress was covering her, even though my body blocked Riggs's view of her.

"Sorry, little brother." His tone and the laugh told me he was anything but sorry. He was enjoying this. "Cade needed me to pick up something he forgot." Staring at Riggs at least had the benefit of making my dick go soft. It was obvious that I wasn't going to be able to continue this with her here. Not that I had planned to fuck her for the first time in Cade's office, although if we hadn't been interrupted it could have happened with how quickly she made me lose control.

"Fine, get it, and get the fuck out."

Riggs cleared his throat and motioned toward where Remi was sitting on the desk.

"For fuck's sake," I growled and picked Remi up off the desk and gently set her on her feet. I moved her away, and we started toward the door as Riggs moved into the office and began sorting through papers on the desk.

Once in the hall, I took Remi's hand and walked directly through the bar, grabbed our coats, and strode out to my bike. I hadn't bothered introducing her to my brother since I figured she'd been embarrassed enough. They'd meet at some other time. I handed her the helmet.

"Uh, Steel?"

I looked over at her as I was shrugging my jacket on.

"Was that your brother?" The pink had faded from her cheeks and she looked less embarrassed now. I felt the tension seep from my body, my annoyance, and aggravation at my brother falling off as I looked down at her. My mood started shifting back as I focused on her once again.

"Yeah, unfortunately." I straddled the bike and waited for her to get on. "I'll introduce you to him some other time." Remi nodded and straddled the bike behind me.

"What's it going to be?" I gave her a heated look over my shoulder.

Confusion flitted over her features. "Am I taking you home? Or am I taking you... home?" I emphasized the last word. Between that and the look in my eyes, she caught my meaning pretty quickly. Her tongue darted out to wet her lips, and I wanted to drag her into my lap and claim her mouth.

CHAPTER 27

Remi

"Am I taking you home? Or am I taking you… home?" There was no mistaking his meaning. I shifted slightly on the seat as my pussy throbbed. I probably should have him drop me off at my house and call it a night, but I didn't want to. I especially didn't want to after kissing him inside.

Fuck it. I wanted him and I was going to throw caution to the wind and have fun tonight. "Take me… home." I put the same emphasis on the word that he had. His eyes widened slightly then narrowed, almost as if he'd been expecting me to ask to be taken to my house. I'd surprised him. Good, he'd been keeping me off balance since the day I met him. It was only fair that I do the same to him every once in a while. Steel turned around and we pulled away from the parking lot.

I laid my head to the side on Steel's back. I couldn't believe his brother had just walked in on us. I was so embarrassed. Now that I had decided to give him a chance, I was surprised at how well we got along.

Even when we weren't making out. Although, that was a lot of fun too. He'd been teasing me, and we'd joked and laughed during the time he taught me to play pool. I'd gotten a chance to see that intense nature of his melt away for a little bit. It hadn't left for long, but it was nice to see he had a sense of humor, too.

It didn't feel like it was very long before we pulled into the parking lot of the clubhouse and I felt a little sense of trepidation. Considering what had happened the first time, I wasn't sure if I'd ever feel comfortable here or not. I studied the building as Steel put the helmet away. It certainly looked different on a Sunday night. There were hardly any bikes parked in the lot, no music was playing and only a few people were scattered around outside.

Everyone ignored us as Steel once again took my hand and led me inside. It made me smile; I loved the way he always either held my hand or put his on the small of my back to help lead me. We went through the building and directly upstairs. I had only paused slightly when we'd gotten to the landing of those stairs, but when he'd looked back at me, I'd given him a small smile and followed him.

Upstairs, we walked down a long hallway that had rows of doors along both walls. *It's like a dorm,* I thought, looking around. We walked to the end and Steel opened the door that was on the back wall before tugging me inside.

I glanced around curiously, standing just inside the door as he moved away and shrugged off his jacket, dropping it onto the back of a couch in a small living room area. It was bigger than I thought it would be. The space between all the doors in the hallway told me that those rooms were a lot smaller than his.

"Does everyone in your club live here?"

He looked up at me. "Cade and Riggs have their own houses on the property." He walked over to the fridge in the kitchen. Nothing was separating it from the living room and he pulled out two beers. He opened them, then handed me one. "I have this apartment and Axel has the matching one on the other side of the building. We're remodeling and a third larger apartment is being built. That will be Gunnar's once it's finished."

He jerked a thumb at the living room wall where a big flat screen TV sat. "The rest of the guys have the rooms you saw in the hall. The set up is the same across the way. Some live here full time. Others only use their rooms when the parties run too late or they're too drunk to drive home."

I nodded absently, even though I didn't know who Axel was, and took a drink of the beer. I figured if I hung around long enough, I'd learn who everyone was. I discreetly looked around. Other than the furniture, TV, and gaming consoles, there wasn't a lot in here. I glanced at the closed door, adjacent to the door that led to the hall, assuming that went to the bedroom. His gaze followed mine. Steel walked up and took my beer from me and set both down on the island in the kitchen. I swallowed at the look in his eyes as he stalked back towards me. Nerves and excitement fluttered in my stomach.

Steel's hands slid under my jacket and stroked over my arms before sliding it down them. I wiggled and helped get out of it. Tossing it aside, he threw it onto the back of the couch. He stepped toward me and I moved a step back automatically. His eyes narrowed. Steel tightened his grip on my upper arms and moved toward me again, preventing me from moving away. Not that I did this time. I hadn't meant to the first time; it'd just been a reflex.

Using his hands on me and pushing his body into mine, Steel nudged me backward until I felt the bedroom door against my back. As soon as I felt the press of the wood, Steel's lips were on mine. My hands lifted to his biceps. To steady myself? Just to touch? I didn't really know, but he moved closer to my touch and flattened our bodies together. My moan was muffled as our lips moved together.

Steel didn't waste time. His hand slid down and pushed the sleeve of my dress down. First on one side, then the other, until it pooled at my waist and my breasts were bare. When he tore his lips from mine and wrapped them around my nipple, I tossed my head back, hitting the door a little harder than I'd meant to. I wasn't sure if the lights behind my now closed eyes were from the scrape of his teeth or because I'd bashed my skull into the wood. Either way, it didn't matter. My breath hitched when he switched to the other side and bit down, almost harder than was comfortable, before he soothed it with his tongue. My knees trembled and now my hands on him were there to help hold me up.

I let him keep playing for a few minutes because every nip, lick, and teasing suck was sending sparks straight down between my thighs, but the tremble had become a quake and I was worried I wasn't going to be able to keep standing. I slid my hand over his head. His dark hair was trimmed close, slightly longer on top, but not enough for me to grab. He released my nipple with a wet pop and my thighs clenched at the sound. He looked up at me and those eyes were a dark gray.

"Steel." I tried to push him back a little bit. He grabbed the wrist of my hand that was in his hair and pinned it against the door, above my head. He lowered his face, lips skimming my jaw as he grabbed my other hand and pinned it down against the door near my hip. I loved the way his beard rasped against my skin whenever he kissed me.

"I'm not done." His throaty growl had heat pooling low in my belly. I couldn't hold back the little moan his words pulled out of me. He leaned harder into me and released my lower wrist so he could pick up my thigh and wrap it around his waist. I gasped and closed my eyes, his dick pressing into me. It'd been too long since I'd felt like this. Hell, it'd been too long since I'd even taken care of my own needs, let alone anyone else's. His low chuckle in my ear had a shiver skating down my spine. "I'm going to fuck you hard, Remi," he said into my ear, rubbing his cheek against mine. His filthy words tore another groan out of me and that seemed to spur him on.

Steel banded one strong arm around my waist and yanked me up against his body, then moved us backward. It was strangely sexy how easily he was able to move me around. He opened the door we'd been leaning on and then let me slide down his body, slowly. The feel of his muscles sliding against my skin had tingles shooting across every nerve ending in my body. Steel walked me backward until my knees hit the bed and with a grin, he tumbled me back onto it. I scooted back, making room, and watched as he reached behind him, caught his shirt, and ripped it off over his head in one smooth movement. The breath caught in my throat.

Holy muscles, Batman. My eyes scoured over his chest.

He had tattoos running from his left shoulder down his arm and over the back of his hand. I licked my lips. I hadn't thought about tattoos one way or another before, just like I hadn't thought about large muscles, and now I was thinking I'd been missing out. My two prior boyfriends certainly hadn't been built like this. I eyed his body, taking in his six-pack, all the way down to where his low-slung jeans showed off that sexy vee of muscle that led down underneath his waistband.

He knelt on the bed, then crawled across it toward me, and all the thoughts scattered out of my head. His large hand wrapped around my left ankle and my eyes widened when I realized what he was about to do, just before he yanked me back across the bed toward him. I laughed when he pounced on me and buried his face between my breasts.

The laugh choked off and I nearly swallowed my tongue as he went back to tormenting my nipples with his teeth. At the same time, his hand slid down my body and I felt him cup my pussy through my panties. My hips arched involuntarily as the heat of his hand made contact. I keened, irritated that the scrap of fabric was in the way. I felt the rumble of his chest more than heard his chuckle.

CHAPTER 28

Steel

I couldn't help but laugh as I heard Remi's frustrated noise. I knew how she felt, but now that I finally had her here and alone, where no one could interrupt us, I was going to take my time. Swirling my tongue around her nipple, I slid my finger under the side of her lace underwear. Her hips moved restlessly, so I threw a thigh over hers to pin her in place.

I ran my fingers over the top of her thighs, then slowly moved them down to that spot between her legs. Watching her face, I felt my breathing deepen as Remi held my gaze while I inched my hand higher. When I parted her folds and lightly circled her clit with the pad of my finger, she let her head drop back. I gave a quick flick over her sensitive flesh. She gasped and tried to lift her hips to increase the pressure of my finger. My thigh prevented that, and I grinned when she lifted her head and frowned down at me.

Remi was panting hard and that, plus the other sounds she was making, was really testing the limits of my control. She was so fucking sexy. I grabbed her panties and ripped them off of her, watching in satisfaction as her pupils dilated at the action. I skated both hands from her hips up to her ribs, then back down as I backed myself down her body. I closed my eyes and rubbed my face on her thigh as I moved.

Her silky skin made mine feel more sensitive. She was so smooth everywhere and I just wanted to grab handfuls of her and taste her all night. Remi started to reach for me as I withdrew from her, but I pinned her closest wrist down to the bed and used my other hand to open her thighs enough to settle my wide shoulders between them. Understanding dawned and her eyes widened, but I didn't give her more time to react.

Lowering my head, I moved one hand to her inner thigh, using it and my shoulders to hold them open, and took a long slow lick from the bottom of her slit all the way to her clit. Her cry and the way her one free hand flew to my hair, clenching there, had me desperately reining in my control again. No other woman had ever tested my patience the way she did. She tasted too sweet to stop now though. I used my tongue, lips, and even a light scrape of teeth to see how many sounds I could draw out of her. She was writhing below me; I'd had to lay an arm over her hips to hold her in place. I could tell she was close, and I wanted to make her cum on my tongue before I fucked her. Circling her clit with my tongue I slid a finger inside her and grinned to myself at her breathy moan.

There'd be no quiet sex with my girl. That thought had my dick pulsing harder. Remi was soaking wet. I slid my finger in and out of her tight pussy. Curling my finger, I hit her g-spot, and she bucked her hips. Adding a second finger, I sped up the rhythm of my tongue as I felt her contracting around me.

I kept up the motion with my hand while I brought her clit fully into my mouth and sucked hard. She screamed and her muscles bore down on my fingers hard as her orgasm shattered her.

Fuck yes. I sucked on her through the waves of pleasure. Finally, her eyes opened, and I released her clit and slid my fingers out. Swiping my tongue up and down a few times, I licked up all her sweetness before sticking my fingers into my mouth and cleaning them off. Her eyes widened as she watched me, and her cheeks went pink.

"You taste fucking delicious." Her cheeks went from pink to red, her mouth opened in shock. I covered it with mine and groaned when her tongue swept in to tangle with mine. I quickly stood up and shucked my boots, then jeans off.

When I looked back at her, I saw the huge grin on her face. "What?"

"You go commando?" She asked teasingly.

I chuckled. "Most of the time, yeah." I rolled on a condom and crawled back onto the bed, covering her body with mine.

Palming the base of my cock, my breath hissed out when her hand settled around me, right above my hand. I gripped her wrist and shook my head when she looked at me questioningly.

"Not this time." There was no way I was going to be able to last long enough to make this good for her if she started touching me. Not this first time. The evil smile that crossed her face told me she wasn't going to listen to me, so I grabbed both her wrists and pinned them above her head. Shifting both to one hand, I reached down and palmed my dick as I pushed forward slowly into her.

We both groaned as I slowly filled her. Fuck, this was torture. I wanted to thrust forward and bury my cock in her, but I didn't want to hurt her either. So, inch by inch, I slid into her heat as she gripped me. Gritting my teeth, I held still once I finally bottomed out. Our ragged breathing was the only sound as I gave her a chance to get used to my size.

"Steel." I looked down into those whiskey-colored eyes. "Fuck me. Please." She begged and it tore the last of my patience to shreds. I withdrew only to thrust back in, and we both groaned in pleasure. I set a fast, demanding pace, and the friction grew, pulling us both higher. It felt like I couldn't get deep enough inside of her wet heat to satisfy myself. Reaching between us, I used my thumb to circle her clit while I kept pounding into her. Remi's breathing got choppier and choppier as she moved against me.

Dropping my head to her neck, I nipped her delicate skin and enjoyed the way her pussy fluttered around me. I wasn't going to finish until she came at least once more. Luckily for me, I could tell she was, once again, right there. "Come all over my dick, Rem," I growled into her ear as I plowed into her hard, paused, then ground in a circle, rubbing against her g-spot at the same time as I pushed down hard against her clit. She came with a shrill scream. Her body shuddered, and I resumed thrusting, drawing out her orgasm.

As soon as Remi started to come down from the high, I gripped both of her hips and focused on chasing my own pleasure. It hit me like a freight train, and I felt Remi wrap her legs around my hips and tighten her inner muscles, which pulled a low groan from my chest. Her convulsions milked every drop of cum out of me.

I rolled over to avoid crushing her and dragged her half on top of my body. I pulled her dress off, it had gotten shoved down around her waist and I'd been in too much of a hurry to fully remove it. Tossing it onto the floor and disposing of the condom, I pulled so she was once again laying half on top of me. We were both still breathing hard.

I trailed my fingers up and down her spine while I lay with my eyes closed, trying to remember the last time I'd been this fucking relaxed. Remi made a little noise that almost sounded like a purr as she shifted into a more comfortable position. I couldn't help but grin in satisfaction. I smoothed my hand over her hair, then went back to trailing my fingers over her back.

Moving wasn't in my plans for the next hour, at least. Then maybe we'd do that again. I opened my eyes when I felt her breathing even out and glanced down. Her cheek was flat against my chest, arm wrapped around my waist, and she'd fallen asleep. I watched her quietly for a minute before I reached over and hit both switches on the lamp next to the bed, which turned off both the overhead light and the lamp. It only took a few minutes before I drifted off with her in my arms.

CHAPTER 29

Remi

Sunlight stabbed my eyes, and I cracked them open, then closed them with a groan. I always closed my blackout curtains at night before going to bed. Why hadn't I last night? As my brain woke up slowly, I realized there was a heavy arm over my hip and a hard erection digging into my ass. I glanced over my shoulder and grinned. Steel was snoring softly. His hard body was curled up behind me and he was putting off so much heat I almost didn't need any covers.

I pulled the blankets off and started to slide out of bed when his arm tightened around me and he hauled me back against him. The snoring had stopped, but he was still asleep. I huffed out a laugh and tried again.

"Go back to sleep," Steel mumbled as he kept me pressed up against him.

"Steel. I have to go to the bathroom." He sighed but rolled over onto his back and flung the back of his arm over his face. I stood up and smiled down at him. The blankets were pooled low over his hips and I stared down at his gorgeous body. Nature pulled me away, though.

A few minutes later when I came out of the bathroom, I slowly walked up to the bed and stopped, staring down at him again. Steel had rolled onto his stomach, his cheek pillowed on his arm. The muscles in his back were impressive. Hell, all of him was impressive. I pulled the blankets down lower to get a better look and shamelessly ogled his ass.

Trailing a finger down the length of his back, I smiled when he let out a soft huff of breath. I moved my finger lower then let out a yelp when he flipped around, grabbed my wrist, and yanked me down on the bed. One minute I was standing there; the next I was lying under him.

"Morning." He grinned; those flinty eyes were sleepy but mischievous. Before I could respond he was kissing me. I moaned and wrapped my arms around his neck. Arching my back, I rubbed my breasts against his chest.

I wouldn't mind a replay of last night. Before we could go any further, my phone's ringtone went off in the living room. We broke apart, and I looked over at the nightstand and gasped. It was nine a.m. *Shit.* I'd missed my first class of the morning.

Steel stood and helped me up before disappearing into the bathroom. I ran into the room and found my phone. The display flashed Bridget's name before I answered. She'd tried texting multiple times before she'd given in and called.

"Hey Bridge."

"Hey, Rem. You must have had a good night." I frowned. She had a teasing sound in her voice, but she also sounded odd. Almost like she'd been crying.

"Yeah." I glanced up as Steel walked out, naked. I looked down when his gaze raked down my body and I realized I was also standing there naked. I grabbed his leather coat off the couch and put it on. It hung down to mid-thigh on me and I narrowed my eyes at him. He just smirked at me before disappearing into the bedroom again.

"Is everything ok, Bridget?" I thought I heard her breath shudder.

"Of course. I just wanted to check in on you. No one saw you come home last night, and Julie said you weren't in your first class this morning."

I grinned. "Yeah... I'll tell you later," I muttered as Steel walked out, with only those low-slung jeans on, and over to the kitchen where he started making breakfast.

"Why aren't you in class?"

She paused. "I had dinner with my parents last night. It was a last-minute thing, and I didn't feel like going to classes today."

Okay. Something was wrong. I glanced over at Steel and found him watching me.

"Okay, well, I'm going to be home in a while. Then we're going to talk about it." Her sigh told me she knew I didn't buy that she was telling me the truth, or at least not all of it.

"Fine. But don't hurry home for me. I'll be here all day and I don't want to ruin the rest of your date." Now her voice sounded smug.

"Love you." I hung up after she reciprocated.

"Everything alright?" Steel was turned back toward the stove, scrambling eggs, but he shot me a look of concern.

"Yeah, I think so." I walked up and slid my arms around his waist from behind, pressing my breasts against his back. He stiffened slightly, and I was about to pull away, thinking I'd overstepped somehow when he turned with a growl and used the edges of his coat to tug me against him. He kissed me hard, his tongue sliding into my mouth as he backed me against the island.

"I can't fucking get enough of you," He muttered against my lips. I pulled his head down so that his mouth crushed into mine harder, deepening the kiss. Before his hands could start wandering, I slid out from between him and the counter and darted away when he lunged for me.

I laughed at the look on his face. "I'm hungry. Is any of that for me?" I nodded at the eggs. He grumbled but finished cooking them and handed me a plate after dishing them. "Thank you." I met his eyes and smiled at him.

We ate while standing at the island. We were quiet, but it was a comfortable, companionable silence. When I was finished, I put my dishes in the sink and pushed the sleeves of his jacket up to wash up.

"Leave them." I glanced over my shoulder when he said it. "I'll do them later." He left his on the island and started stalking toward me, unblinkingly. I swallowed. His eyes roamed down between my breasts and down my stomach, the trail of flesh that was left bare where his jacket fell apart. He reached for me and pulled me against him.

A loud knock on the door made me jolt in his arms and yelp. I lifted a hand over my mouth, embarrassed by the sound. He looked torn between amusement at my reaction and irritation at whoever was disturbing us. I pulled out of his arms and went back into the bedroom, grabbing my jacket as I went.

I laid his jacket on the bed and pulled my dress over my head. It felt weird to not be wearing a bra or panties underneath, but I'd found the scrap of lace, and Steel had destroyed those last night. I felt myself getting wet and clenched my thighs together.

Get it together, Remi. I pulled on my socks, shoes, then jacket and listened at the door. Their voices were a low murmur that I couldn't quite make out. Whoever Steel was talking to was still there, so I sat on his bed and waited.

A little while later he came into the room and held out his hands to pull me up. Once on my feet, he tugged me into his arms. He smelled so good. "Hey, I have to head into the garage. Something… came up and I have to go deal with it."

I nodded, my head bumping against where his chin was resting on it. Steel fisted his hand in my hair and tugged my head backward, laying his lips on mine, and kissed me softly. "No problem. I should be getting home anyway." We quickly finished up and left the clubhouse behind, heading toward the city.

CHAPTER 30

Remi

Steel dropped me off in front of my house and kissed me again. "I'll call you later." His voice was low. I smiled at him and nodded. I walked up the path to my house and turned to watch as he took off down the street. Two houses over, Mr. Rechinich scowled at the bike as it drove by and then over at me. I smiled pleasantly at him and waved. He blinked owlishly at me and went inside his house.

Nosey old fart.

"Bridget?!" I called as I walked into the house. I glanced around. She wasn't in the kitchen or living room. The house was quiet. I trotted upstairs and lightly tapped on her closed bedroom door. I heard her sniff inside.

Uh oh.

Opening the door, I peeked my head in. Bridget was lying on her side, facing away from the door. Her shoulders were shaking, almost silently. I hurried over to her and laid down behind her on the bed, wrapping my arms around her.

"What happened, Bridge?" She started sobbing openly. I laid there quietly, letting her get it all out.

Once Bridget's sobs died down, I leaned over and grabbed a box of tissues. I dried off her eyes and handed her some so she could blow her nose. She did, then sighed. We settled back down, me behind her, arms wrapped around her again.

"Someone saw me with Gunnar and told my mom and dad."

Oh shit.

"They told me to come over for dinner last night after you left. Then they ambushed me about him." I tightened my embrace, silently showing support.

"Dad was such an asshole." She said quietly. "He wouldn't listen. He just kept saying Gunnar was a piece of shit and that he was using me."

"God, I'm sorry Bridge." I felt awful for her. I knew if Uncle Caleb ever found out about Steel, he'd be saying the same things, so I was outraged for her. "Why does everyone judge people before they get to know them?" Bridget shrugged and wiped the back of her hand over her eyes.

"I thought Mom would at least have my back. But she just sat there. She just fucking sat there while Dad told me I couldn't see Gunnar again."

I took a deep breath, wondering how to help make this better for her. I'd figured that was how Mr. Jordan would react, but it still sucked. Bridget was an adult and could technically see who she wanted. "How are they going to keep you from seeing him?" I asked dryly.

Her voice cracked as she answered. "He threatened to have Gunnar arrested if I see him again."

I frowned. "He can't do that! Can he?" I leaned over and looked down into her watery blue eyes.

"My godfather is the Chief of Police, Remi. If Daddy asks him to look into Gunnar's background and dig something up, he'll do it."

"Shit."

"Yeah," She said miserably.

"What are you going to do?" She and Gunnar had been getting

along great. Bridget had been deliriously happy for weeks. Where I had been indecisive and hesitant, Bridget had moved forward full throttle. It had been so nice seeing her so in love because whether she'd admit it or not, she was in love with Gunnar.

"I broke up with him last night."

I sucked in a breath and sat up on the bed. She sat up too, and we faced each other. "How did he take it?"

She grimaced. "Not well. He was pissed."

"Well, it's just for a little while, right? Until you guys can figure out what to do about your dad?" She shook her head, sadly.

"He wouldn't even let me explain. I tried, and he just exploded. He started yelling at me about being a princess and a coward and then left." A tear dripped down her face. "He thought I was worried about Dad disowning me or something, even though I never said anything about that."

"So, he had no idea it's because you're worried about the whole Austin Police Force coming after him?" She shook her head. I sighed. "Jesus, why do guys always refuse to communicate?"

Bridget looked up and smirked at me through her tears. "This coming from the queen of putting her head under the covers?" I grimaced. She had a point. As a kid, whenever they'd try to talk to me about something that made me mad, I'd stuffed my head under the covers and put my fingers in my ears. I may not do that anymore, but I still had an unhealthy habit of bottling stuff up until it was either ready to explode or I did.

"Good point. I have no room to talk." But Bridget was a great communicator. This must be killing her, to not be able to explain to him what had happened. "What are you going to do?"

She shrugged. "Let him cool off, then try talking to him again."

"Will you get back together with him?"

The heartbreak on her face was agony for me. I wished I could fix it. I pulled her into a hug. "Any way I can help, just let me know." She nodded, and we sat there silently for a while.

CHAPTER 31

Steel

I watched with interest as Remi stretched. She was wearing yoga pants. She insisted they were leggings, but I didn't care what the difference was, just that they hugged her ass. She bent over and touched her toes. I grinned and silently thanked whoever had created them. She straightened up and looked at me over her shoulder with a smirk.

"It's not healthy to work out without stretching."

I shrugged. "Conflicting information. Some experts say you shouldn't stretch cold." Her eyebrows went up, and she laughed. She went back to her stretches. The door to our clubhouse gym opened and Rat froze when he saw I was in here with Remi.

"Sorry, Steel. Uh… I'll come back." He was already trying to back out the door.

"Get back in here, Rat." I motioned over to the treadmills. "You won't bother us." Rat never lifted or sparred. He was a thin, pale kid and could use some serious muscle building, but he wouldn't ever let us work out with him. The kid could run fucking circles around us and never break a sweat, despite smoking a pack a day.

Running seemed to be an escape for him. I knew it had a lot to do with his childhood and growing up on the streets. We were pretty close with Rat but there was only so much he'd tell us about the time before we'd found him, or rather, he'd found us. Cade and Riggs knew everything he knew about his past, which sadly wasn't much. They knew about every member of our chapter, but no one was forced to share it with anyone else.

"Hi!"

I couldn't help the grin that spread over my face. Remi was a naturally outgoing, friendly person and her overly enthusiastic greeting just made Rat's face go even paler. I didn't think it was possible for skin tone to go translucent, but it just had. He mumbled something and hurried over to the treadmill, shooting Remi quick glances over his shoulder. Remi gave me a confused look, and I just shook my head, indicating that she should drop it.

It had taken most of us years to get Rat to relax long enough to stay in the same room with us, let alone talk or touch us in the simplest of ways. You'd think that a kid that started out in a biker club at twelve years old would be a cocky shit, but Rat was the exact opposite. With his skills and smarts he had every right to be an arrogant asshole too, but he never was. It was one of the reasons the rest of us were so protective of him.

Remi just shrugged and pulled an arm over her chest, using her other arm to stretch out her shoulder. The little tank top she had on covered all but a small section of her stomach. With Rat in here, I was going to have to focus more on the sparring session than what I'd originally had in mind when she'd pranced in with those clothes on. I'd tried to get her to come out to the clubhouse and stay the night with me last night, but she'd had to work at Mackenzie's and didn't want to drive out afterward. I think she was just trying to create a little space, something I wasn't about to give her.

Yesterday had been the day after our date, so it would have been back-to-back nights of her spending time at my place. She was making me work for this, but I was enjoying it. I'd convinced her to meet me this morning, to work out together. There wasn't much going on at the shop today and Riggs said I wasn't needed. He preferred being there alone as much as possible anyway, besides having one of the guys in to run the front counter. If my brother didn't have to answer phones, that was best for everyone, especially our customers. Riggs wasn't known for his tact and customer service.

Remi turned and placed her hands on her hips, eyeballing me as hard as I was her. The sexual tension was thick. It was going to be hard not to cut this lesson short and just toss her over my shoulder and bring her upstairs. I could hear the rhythmic pounding of Rat's feet across the room. My eyes swept down her body before meeting her eyes. She slowly let hers do the same, then met mine in challenge. I folded my arms over my chest, a smug sense of satisfaction filling me when her eyes instantly dropped to them.

I was wearing a t-shirt with the sleeves cut off and basketball shorts. I hadn't missed the looks she'd been giving me when she thought I wasn't looking. But I had a purpose for this training session today and needed to stay on track. I knew she and her friends had been training with Sergio in self-defense. I'd called him a few days ago to check in and see what they'd gone over so far. I needed my girl to be able to take care of herself. My life was dangerous and as much as we all tried to keep club life from spilling over onto our families, sometimes it did.

It was important to me that she knew at least the basics on how to throw a punch, kick, how to do a little ground wrestling, and a few moves to get out of holds. I would teach her as much as she'd be willing to learn. She had an athletic body and seemed game for it, so I was hoping over the years we'd get her to a place where she'd be a threat to anyone who'd try to take her on.

"Show me what you've learned with Sergio so far."

Her eyebrows pulled together. I walked over to the side of the room and tossed her some MMA gloves. They were lighter than boxing gloves but didn't provide as much padding while punching. That was fine, in the real world if you hit someone there wasn't any padding, I'd rather she get used to fighting with less than more. She pulled the gloves on but just waited. I raised a brow and waited as well.

"Aren't you going to get some focus mitts?" She asked.

"No, just hit me. Show me what he's taught you."

She looked at me like I was crazy, and I couldn't help but chuckle. She'd probably be horrified if she saw any of the sparring sessions between me, Cade, Riggs, and Gunnar.

"You can't expect me to just hit you." Those fists went back to her hips.

"I expect you to hit anyone who attacks you." The humor was gone. The idea of someone coming after her filling me with a cold fury.

"Well, you haven't…" She broke off with a squeal when I lunged at her. I didn't go full speed but put enough in the movement to make her work for it. She was quick and managed to dart to the side and out of my grasp.

"I wasn't ready." She huffed as I lunged at her again, and she had to sidestep to avoid me. She'd just barely managed to get out of the way.

"You think someone coming after you is going to wait while you set up?"

I circled her, and she narrowed her eyes. I was satisfied to see her drop into a fighting stance as she circled me, though. Once her brain clicked into fight mode, it came to her naturally. She bent her knees slightly, her weight on the balls of her feet, arms raised, fists in front of her face. She glared at me but didn't respond. She was focused now.

Feigning to the right, I jabbed lightly but quickly with my left, toward her. She blocked the light punch with her right forearm and returned her own jab. It was too soft. I would never punch her at even one-quarter of my strength, but I didn't want her holding back during our sessions.

"Don't hold back, hit me. You won't hurt me. The guys and I spar at full strength a few times every other week." I saw the surprise on her face. A look of determination crossed her face and her fist shot out in a surprisingly strong right hook. I laughed and rubbed my chin where her glove had landed. She laughed with me, but we kept circling, looking for openings.

For the next thirty minutes, we exchanged punches and a few kicks. I noted the areas she needed to work on for her boxing, but for the most part, I was happy with where she was at.

Now for the fun part.

"Alright. We're going to work on getting out of some holds and then work on your ground game a little." She had a light layer of sweat shining on her skin and it was sexy as hell. I couldn't wait to get my hands on her. All in the name of self-defense, of course.

CHAPTER 32

Remi

"What would you do if someone grabbed you from behind? Like this?" One of Steel's thick arms slid around my waist, while the other came around my neck. He gently tugged me back against his body. He didn't tighten his hold to where I couldn't breathe, but it took the barest shifting for me to realize he wasn't going to let me go anywhere. I could feel the heat of his body seeping into mine and every muscle from chest to thigh. Seriously, it should be a crime for a guy to be this ripped.

Shit.

I struggled but quickly stopped when his hold tightened more. If he were a bad guy that would just get my air cut off. I couldn't throw an elbow because the band of his arm wasn't only around my waist, but had my arms pinned to my sides as well. I crunched my foot down on the top of his as hard as I could and was rewarded with a grunt of pain as he released his hold on my arms. It was satisfying, but he didn't release me. I didn't even have enough leverage to throw my head back at him so I could headbutt him.

"I don't know," I muttered, irritated with myself. That feeling fled quickly when his lips came down and brushed my temple, running down the side of my face until he was nibbling on my jaw under my ear.

Who knew that spot was so sensitive...? Or could get that reaction by kissing there, my inner voice added with a sigh. Liquid heat pooled low in my belly as Steel flicked his tongue over the lobe of my ear. I shuddered, and he chuckled softly at my reaction.

"So, you're going to raise onto your toes. At the same time, you're going to want to slide your hands between your neck and my forearm. Raising up is going to create enough space to get them in there." He was still speaking low into my ear, and I was having a really hard time concentrating on what he was saying because I just wanted to rub backward against him.

"Then you'll squat a little and turn. You're going to want to get your hip anywhere into me that you can. Using your legs, you're going to be able to lift a bigger guy like me, especially since you'll be doing this all in one motion so the momentum will help." He waited until I'd gotten my grip and stance right before he continued.

"Once you've got my feet unbalanced, you're going to lean forward, drop the shoulder that is closest to me, and shove. This will send whoever is behind you flying or sprawling to the ground, depending on their weight. Here is the important part." He shifted so that our eyes met. His gray eyes were serious and intense. "Don't fuck around. Don't check to see how they are. You run. Got it?"

I nodded. I wasn't sure why he'd gotten so serious all of a sudden, but I wanted to lighten the mood, so I leaned forward and brushed my lips over his. He froze for a moment, so I took the opportunity to explore the silky-smooth texture of his lips. Turning in his suddenly loose arms, I wrapped mine around his neck and slipped my tongue into his mouth. He groaned but didn't take over the kiss. I unwrapped my arms and slid my hands down his chest, then over his sides, feeling all the bulges that attested to many hours spent in this room.

Speaking of bulges...

Wickedly, I thrust my hips forward, grinding against him. He bit my bottom lip, and I sucked in a breath. Steel's hands came up to my shoulders, and he shocked me when he suddenly spun me around and jerked me back and up against him. We were back in the position we'd started in, both breathing hard. I could feel his hard dick against my ass and I pushed back against him. He was breathing hard, but he laughed then nipped my shoulder.

"Let's practice this move. Then we'll finish what you just started." His voice was husky, and it turned me on to hear how obviously hot my kiss had made him. I felt him shift, so I looked up at him. He was looking over at the corner of the room and I glanced over and felt my face flood with heat.

Fuck. I'd forgotten the other guy was in here. He was looking down at his treadmill; it told me there was no way he'd missed what we were doing. I wasn't really into voyeurism, so I appreciated that Steel seemed to have kept his wits about him a bit better than I had. We practiced and about the time I was getting very irritated and wanted nothing more than to move the party along upstairs, Steel finally seemed satisfied with my progress.

Seriously, I didn't think he was actually going to hold out until I was a pro at the move.

Rat had left somewhere in the middle of one of the times that I'd tossed Steel to the floor. Well, tossed wasn't the right word. He was really heavy. But I'd managed to break his hold and get him off of me, anyway. It was just me and him alone in the gym again. Steel stood up, a dangerous look in his eyes. It triggered some kind of instinctual reflex in me because my eyes darted around as I looked for a way to escape. It was weird how he could bring that feeling out in me. Like I needed to run away, in more ways than one. It was hard to explain.

I tried to dart around him and reach the door that led upstairs. I didn't make it more than three steps before he tackled me from behind. Steel twisted as we fell, and I landed on top of him. Before I could even catch my breath or figure out what had happened, he rolled and pinned me to the mats. The smug tilt of his lips had me glaring at him. That was another thing he excelled at. He made me want to kiss him and throttle him, often at the same time. His lips attacked mine as though I was the last sip of water in a desert, on a hot day.

Those huge hands were roaming everywhere along my body, making my breath hitch. Steel nibbled lightly at my lower lip and shifted his hips until he was lying between my thighs. When he ground himself forward all I could do was gasp and move with him. One of his hands tangled in my hair and pulled my head back and to the side so he could lick his way across my neck.

"Ew. Steel, I'm all sweaty."

"Mmmm," He growled and just kept tasting my skin. It was strangely arousing. Suddenly, Steel disentangled himself from me and stood. I lay there, panting, staring up at him in surprise. He held a hand out to me and pulled me to my feet when I accepted it. I expected him to take me upstairs, but he pulled me through a door at the opposite end of the room.

It was a locker room. I laughed and shoved him. "What are we doing here?" He pulled his shirt off and the smile fell from my face.

Holy— my thought was interrupted when he jerked me back against him again and kissed me hard. Somehow, we managed to strip in between kisses. That's tough when you didn't want to take your lips off each other. I watched his bare ass as he walked over and turned one of the showers on.

I walked over to him and slid my arms around him from behind, pushing my breasts into his back. Letting my palms slide up and down his chest I rested my cheek on his back. I loved his body; it was so sexy. My hands trailed lower, and his body tensed. The shower was starting to put steam out into the air. I wrapped my hand around his cock and his head dropped forward. Moving my palm from base to tip, I experimented with my grip and pace before I stroked my thumb over the tip.

Steel's hand covered mine, as though to stop me. I bit one of the muscles on his back, hard and he snarled at the sting. Shooting me a glare over his shoulder he dropped his hand from mine. I continued playing with him, inching my body closer so I could drop my hand lower and fondle his balls for a moment before I returned my attention higher up once more. When I let him go, I felt him relax slightly but I quickly moved around him and dropped to my knees. My lips were wrapped around his cock before he could stop me.

"Remi," My name broke on his lips, his gruff cry one of pleasure. I wanted him to feel as good as he'd made me feel. I wrapped my right hand around him again when I went to work with both it and my mouth on his shaft. When he shifted, to lean against the wall of the shower, I went with him, not giving him a moment of reprieve from my hand, lips, and tongue. I wanted to drive him wild. One of those large hands tangled in my hair and I could feel him put slight pressure on my head. Enough that he was helping me move on him, but not so much that he was dictating the speed or depth. He let that be my choice.

Glancing up at him, I found those piercing eyes watching me hungrily and it made me groan. He echoed the sound as the vibrations surrounded him. I found my clit with my free hand and began rubbing myself. It was so hot, having him under my control like this. I heard Steel mutter a curse and met his gaze again.

"Jesus, fuck. Remi." He sounded tortured. His eyes were glued on my hand, where I was pleasuring myself. His hand tightened, painfully, in my hair and I had no choice but to let his dick pop wetly from my mouth and rise to my feet as he tugged me up. He kissed me hard, tongue punishing. I could tell he was holding onto his control by a thread. Walking me backward, Steel propelled us under the spray of the shower. The hot water felt amazing as it pounded down on me.

He kept us moving though, and I gasped when my back hit the cold tile. There was no sympathy from Steel, I'd pushed him past that. All he could think about was fucking, and that made my core clench. I wanted that too. It's all I'd been thinking about for the last hour while he'd made me train the same move over and over again.

Payback's a bitch, I thought with a grin.

He paused long enough to pull a condom out of one of the lockers nearby and roll it on. I decided not to think too hard about why they'd had those stashed all over their clubhouse, it would just ruin the mood. Despite the fact that we hadn't made any promises to each other, we'd have to have a talk later about being exclusive, at least in the sex department. I didn't sleep with men who fucked around on me.

Steel lifted me by the thighs and hiked me up until my legs were around his waist and he rested between them, pulling my attention fully back onto him. It was amazing how easily he could pick me up. Every thought in my mind was obliterated when, with one thrust, Steel lodged himself as deeply inside of me as he could. I screamed in pleasure. He started up a pounding rhythm, and I scored my nails down his back as I matched his pace. His hands went to my hips, helping to push and pull me. It was brutal, the sound of slapping flesh loudly echoing throughout the locker room, mixed with his grunts and my moans.

When my climax hit, I swear I thought I was going to pass out. I had never orgasmed that hard in my life. I slumped in his arms while he rode out his release. Afterward, we leaned there, attempting to breathe, and I nuzzled into his neck. Even after sweating for an hour and a round of hot, rough sex, he smelled like sin.

"Fuck. Did I hurt you?" He pulled back enough so that he could look at me. I gave him a satisfied smile.

"If you did, I liked it." The look on his face at that answer was priceless. A moment of silence passed, and I started laughing. I'd shocked him speechless. I didn't know that was possible. Finally, he just shook his head and chuckled as he let me slide down his body. I could feel the aches and pains now but some could have easily been from the sparring session.

"Come here." My eyebrows rose at his tone of voice and the look in his eyes. I wasn't sure I had the endurance for the round two his eyes were promising. We spent the next half hour, soaping each other up, scrubbing each other down, and playing in the water. Who knew this big, bad biker could be so playful? I grinned at him. Something told me not many people got to see this side of Steel. It made me feel all warm and fuzzy that, for now, this side of him was reserved for me.

CHAPTER 33

Remi

I walked through the door to our house on cloud nine that night. Sure, I'd skipped another day of school to hang out with Steel, but it felt so good, and not just the orgasms. I thought back to the round two that we eventually got around to and smiled.

I paused when I saw Ming, Julie, Anna, and Bridget all sitting in the living room. It was unusual to have us all home on a Tuesday night, I glanced at my phone, ten p.m.

"Hey, guys." I looked around and they all smiled at me.

"Hey," they all chorused back.

"Now that we're all here." Ming met each of our gazes and then got a stern look on her face. She and Julie shared a knowing look and Anna looked a bit guilty. I glanced over at Bridget, she looked as confused as I felt.

"Bridget, Remi, we've been wanting to talk to you both."

Uh oh.

"Bridget. We're starting with you," Ming said firmly and folded her arms over her chest. I dropped down into a chair. We were going to be here for a while. "What's going on? You've been depressed and not like yourself at all." Bridget shot me a desperate look, but I just grimaced. No way was she going to get out of telling them about Gunnar. Ming could be like a hound dog on a scent once she figured out one of her girls was in trouble.

"It's nothing, really." The other three girls managed to look both unimpressed and unconvinced, all at the same time. I plucked an imaginary piece of lint off my leggings.

"I broke up with Gunnar." When they all started firing questions at her rapidly, she finally broke down and told them what had happened.

"So, how is that going?" That came from Anna and she sounded dubious.

Bridget shrugged. "He's pissed and I'm confused. I'm supposed to stay away from him. But I don't want to and I don't want him to be mad at me. I also don't want him to get into trouble because of me. I'm not sure what to do." We sat quietly for a minute.

"Are you still seeing him?" Ming asked.

Bridget shook her head. "We haven't seen each other since I told him we had to break up. But we've talked on the phone and texted a bunch since."

"So, he doesn't want to be finished?" I asked. I hadn't asked Steel about Gunnar at all. It wasn't fair to put him in the middle of it, especially since he wasn't pressuring me and asking me about Bridget. Honestly, I wasn't even sure if he knew that Gunnar and Bridget were having issues. Talking wasn't exactly his strong suit and I couldn't picture him and Gunnar sitting down to share their feelings. The mental image almost made me giggle out loud.

"No. He wants me to tell my father to fuck off. But I haven't told him everything either."

"Why not? You can't have a relationship with him if you won't be honest." Bridget rolled her eyes at Julie, but then nodded because she knew that Julie was right and just trying to help.

"I know. I'm just scared that if he finds out how...connected my family is, he'll be the one to leave. You know?" She whispered the last part. We did know. Gunnar had no idea who Bridget's family was. But we did. We knew how much trouble they could cause for the MC and Gunnar. Bridget was her daddy's princess. Brent Jordan would burn down the city for his daughter, whether she wanted him to or not, and as the former Mayor, he still had a lot of pull.

"Sweetie. You're going to have to tell him. You'll be worth the risk for him," Ming said matter-of-factly. She may be going into medicine, but she was the romantic while Julie was the practical sister.

"I know. I will," Bridget whispered. Ming turned her gaze on me, and I gulped. She was done with Bridget, recognizing that was as far as she'd get with her tonight. It was my turn now.

What had I done wrong? Trying to think of why Ming might be looking at me so disapprovingly.

"Now Remi. What is this I hear about you missing classes?"

I hissed out a breath and glared at the other three girls. They all studied either the ceiling or the floor, avoiding my hard stare. I flicked my eyes back to Ming.

"I'm just a bit burnt out," I muttered. I looked down when she sighed.

"Look, Remi. I know you've had a lot going on with your dad's death and your company. I'd love for you to finish college but," she paused until I looked up at her again, "if you don't, it's not the end of the world." My mouth dropped open in shock. I hadn't been expecting that. She was going to be a doctor. They had to devote so much time to school and studying, I figured she would expect everyone else to as well.

"You own a business that has made you independently wealthy. You'll work hard for it, but you don't need that college degree. Most people get it so that they can get the job. You have the job. If it's too much, you can always learn the business now then finish the degree later." She narrowed her eyes at me speculatively.

"Although, don't think I haven't noticed that you only started missing classes once you and Steel met." She dropped the tough girl look and grinned. "But honestly? I think it's good for you. He's good for you. You were working yourself into the ground, and mostly because your uncle was pushing you to do it. You need to take some time for yourself. Trust me, I know." With that, she stood up. "I'm going to bed. I have rounds at six a.m. tomorrow."

Ming paused at the foot of the stairs and held each of us in a look for a heartbeat. "I love you all. I'm always here if you need me. Well, I'm always around if you need me, if not specifically here." She called a good night as she slowly walked up the stairs. I huffed out a breath and looked around at the other girls.

"She's right. For both of you." Julie and Anna came over and gave both me and Bridget hugs. We spent the rest of the night talking, laughing, and eating junk food. Despite all of us having either early classes or work the next morning, we didn't regret the time spent together.

CHAPTER 34

Remi

I'd decided that Ming was right. College wasn't life or death right now, so I decided to take the week off of classes. I spent extra time at Mackenzie's, picking up more of the work. Strangely, I couldn't tell if Uncle Caleb was happy about that or not. It was almost as though he was irritated that I was there so much. When I questioned him about it he'd just lectured me about missing classes, which made sense. Adults got super weird about wanting you to get a college degree. But I couldn't get Steel's skepticism about Uncle Caleb not wanting the company out of my head.

The discussion with Uncle Caleb about me being at Mackenzie's more had dissolved quickly into an argument, so we'd parted ways and neither of us had brought it up again. When Steel and I weren't working, we'd been spending as much time together as possible. It was really nice how easily we clicked. We didn't have to try to get along or enjoy each other, we just did.

Finally, it was Friday night and after finding out Steel had club stuff to do tonight, I got the girls together and talked them into hanging out. Then Bridget had talked us all into going to a party on campus.

We piled out of her BMW and I grinned as I looked up at the fraternity house. There were football players in various stages of undress, playing a drunken game of touch football on the front lawn. Half-naked sorority girls cheered them on. Music poured from the house. Anna and Bridget towed Julie and me toward the house. We hadn't been to a campus party together in a long time.

Inside we wound our way through the throngs of partygoers toward the keg. Bridget quickly filled cups and handed us the alcohol. I surveyed the room. Anna was waving at a few girls she knew, and a group of guys had already come up and started talking with Bridget, who was still standing next to the keg. Even Julie wandered off to say hi to a few of the girls I recognized from her study groups. I knew quite a few people at the party as well, and I was about to start up a conversation with a girl from one of my business classes when I caught a familiar face in the crowd.

Frowning, I followed the girl. What would Amy be doing at a college party? I'd seen her at the clubhouse a few times over the past week, after having met her on my first date with Steel, and we got along great. The crowd finally parted, and I saw her standing with a petite strawberry blonde girl near the stairs.

"Amy!" I had to shout to be heard over the music. Her head snapped over in my direction, eyes wary. They warmed as soon as she saw me. The girl next to her was still on guard though. I saw her take my measure, but I couldn't figure out why.

"Hey, Remi!" We gave each other an awkward hug. You know, one of those hugs that says, 'I know you well enough to greet you intimately in some way but I'm not sure if this is too much?'

"This is Delia." She gestured to her friend when we finally broke apart and I shook her hand. The girl's shake was limp, and she quickly looked away once I'd let go.

Oookay, I thought, *I guess I'm not wanted.* I smiled at Amy.

"Well, I just wanted to say hi. I'm here with some friends." I jerked my thumb over my shoulder toward where I'd come from. Amy's gaze followed the movement, and she nodded.

"If you get bored or need anything come on over," I said with a smile, despite Delia's suspicious look. We said goodbye, and I made my way back. I sat chatting with a few people I knew and noticed a lot of different kids approaching Delia. She had that shifty look every time someone approached her so maybe it wasn't just me. Some people just weren't good in crowds. I made a mental note to try to get to know her better in the future, if I ever had the opportunity to see her in a less crowded place.

"Remi! They're going to play our song!" Bridget's face was flushed and glowing. I groaned because I knew what was coming next. We'd gone through a shuffle dancing period in high school. I knew what song was about to come on and what dance she wanted us to do. The music starting up just confirmed it. Anna and Julie laughed as the shuffle dance version of Rihanna's Umbrella came on. I shook my head at them but as they started dancing, I joined in. People stopped what they were doing and moved, giving us room and creating a circle around the dance floor.

We were all grinning like maniacs as we danced around the small area. For those who have never seen shuffle dancing, it's like mixing the running man, hip hop dancing, and a fish flopping out of the water all mixed together. There are certain choreographed moves you can learn and do together or you can pretty much just do whatever you want and fling your arms and legs around. Either way, it ends up looking like you're doing it on purpose. A few people at the party started joining in with us, dancing to their own moves.

Soon enough the song ended, but I declined dancing to another. The other three kept going, and I went in search of another beer. Whoever was in charge of the music kept the style up since they'd finally gotten people interested in dancing to it. The dance floor was packed now.

Sipping my new beer, I turned and watched everyone on the dance floor. Some were still shuffling, others were grinding, but everyone was having a great time. The hair on the back of my neck stood on end right before a voice spoke directly into my ear from behind me.

"Hey, Rem."

I couldn't hold back the groan, but I was pretty sure the loud music covered it. I pasted a fake smile on my face and turned.

"Hey, Scott." Scott Reynolds. We'd dated my sophomore year of college and to say I regretted it would be downplaying it. He was a douchebag. Dad had always hated him and now I could easily see why.

At the time his blonde hair, blue eyes, and Adonis good looks had made my heart flutter. Now I saw the smarmy look on his face and the slightly mean tilt to his smile. He had never treated me badly while we were together, and he'd have never dared to treat my friends badly, but I'd seen him treat so many others in a way I didn't like. It made me feel ashamed, even to this day, that it had taken me almost a year to see it and to stand up for those he picked on.

We'd ended things because I'd caught him dragging a young freshman guy into the girls' bathroom early one morning. That sort of thing was bad enough in high school but in college? No. He'd pulled the kid's pants down and was going to toss him in there while it was full of girls getting ready for the day. We'd had a huge screaming match in the middle of the hallway. For the remainder of the year, he'd made my life miserable. First, he'd try to get me back, then he'd try to embarrass me in one way or another. When Dad had died, he'd had the decency to drop off the face of the Earth and leave me alone.

Scott was staring at my tits. I sighed, and it brought his focus back to my face. His grin told me he didn't give a shit that he'd been caught. I was pretty sure he was already drunk. "Nice seeing you here, Rem. I haven't seen you around campus much this year."

I shrugged nonchalantly and took a sip of my beer. He reached out and put a hand on my arm. "I was so sorry to hear about your dad."

Swallowing hard, I smiled tightly at him. "Thank you, Scott. That's really sweet. It was tough but... things are getting better." I stopped, shocked. They really were starting to get better.

When had that happened?

I'd been wandering around with a weight on my chest for so long, but now it was hard to pinpoint when exactly that weight had started easing off. Before I could examine it too closely, I realized Scott was speaking.

"I'm sorry, what?" I asked when he looked at me expectantly.

He chuckled good-naturedly. He was being extremely laid back, especially considering how he'd acted after we'd broken up. Maybe he'd grown up and matured.

Lord knows I have.

"I asked if you maybe wanted to go outside? Get some fresh air? I've sort of been wanting to speak to you." I watched him suspiciously. It made him laugh again.

"I owe you an apology, Rem. I'm willing to do it here but I'd rather do it with fewer people around and somewhere I don't have to scream it."

A battle played out in my mind. I didn't really want to go with him. But it would be rude to refuse, especially since he and I had such a history together, and he was being the bigger man and apologizing for how he'd acted.

"Okay." He gestured toward the sliding door that led out to the backyard. I looked over my shoulder but didn't see any of my friends. They were swallowed up by dancers on the floor. As we moved toward the back of the house, I saw Amy and Delia. Catching Amy's eye, I smiled and waved at her but she just frowned at me and then gave Scott a hard look.

That was weird. The little voice in my head chimed in. *Oh, be quiet. She's probably just trying to figure out who he is. She was Steel's friend before she was mine, after all. I'd be curious too.* I mentally hissed at myself. But I was irritated. Amy didn't know me, but I'd never cheat on a guy. It wasn't my style.

Pushing those thoughts out of my head, I took a deep breath as we stepped outside. Scott led me over to a picnic table and we sat on top of it. I set my beer down next to me and leaned back on my hands looking up at the stars. It was still hot outside, even though the sun was down. We were getting into May and the summer heat could get brutal in Texas. I took another drink of my cold beer.

"What happened to us, Remi?"

I frowned and looked over at him. He was looking at me earnestly. That was a terrible way to start an apology. I sighed and had a feeling I was going to regret coming out here.

"We've gone over this many times, Scott."

"Humor me."

I rolled my eyes but focused on the dark sky above me again. "I didn't like what you were becoming… or always were? Once I'd finally seen it, I couldn't keep going like nothing was wrong."

"That's bullshit." His tone was dark. I shot him a quick look, but he was looking at the grass.

"I never acted any different than when we first got together."

"Maybe, maybe not, but I didn't like how you were treating people, Scott. You were being a dick, all the time. Never to me," I amended when his furious gaze met mine, "but to a lot of other people. I don't like bullies." He was quiet for so long I started to get nervous.

"Can we start over? I've changed." His voice was gentler, but there was still something in it that made me nervous.

"Sorry Scott. I'm seeing someone." A loud crashing noise made me jump. It took me a minute to realize he'd hit the tabletop.

What the fuck? I stared at him in shock.

"Fuck you Remi!" He yelled in my face. He'd turned so that he was facing me. I scooted back a little bit, trying to get some distance. The way his body tensed told me if I tried to leave I'd set him off, so I stayed sitting. "I waited for you. I gave you space after your dad…" He was breathing hard, glaring at me. "I waited."

"I never asked you to do that, Scott. In fact, I told you, explicitly, that we were over and not to do that."

"I love you, Remi."

I stared at him in disbelief. "No, Scott, you don't. We haven't been together for over a year. Even when we were together, you didn't love me."

"Don't tell me how I feel!" He screamed in my face again.

Okaaay, stop pissing off the drunk, angry guy, Remi.

"Okay, I'm sorry. You're right. But Scott, it's been so long and we've both changed."

"Then give me another chance. We were good together. I can be good for you."

"Scott," I said his name quietly. "I told you, I'm with somebody else."

"Dump him." He scooted closer and put his hand on my cheek. But it wasn't until he leaned in to kiss me that I lost my temper.

"Knock it off, Scott. We're not together anymore. I don't love you; I never did. I love Steel…" I froze, my eyes widening at what I'd just said. Did I really? I hadn't meant to blurt it out, but since I had I realized that it felt right. Scott reared back as though I'd slapped him.

"I'm sorry but we're finished and I'm going back inside now." I eyed him warily as I slowly stood and started to edge around him to go back inside. His arm shot out and he grabbed my wrist. When I pulled it, trying to break his hold he twisted it painfully. I hissed at the pinching sensation, distracted enough that I didn't realize he'd stood and gotten in my face.

"We're not…"

"Take your fucking hands off her."

Oh shit.

I looked over, wide-eyed, and saw Steel heading our way. His stride was so large he was clearing the length of the backyard in an impressive amount of time, but it didn't look like he was in a hurry. Scott yanked on my arm again and I gritted my teeth as it twinged my wrist a second time.

What was Steel doing here? Not that I wasn't thrilled to see him. Especially considering… I glanced at Scott.

Scott was glaring at Steel, but his face had paled. Scott was a fairly big guy, about six-two, but he wasn't as tall nor as large framed as Steel. Scott was always one of the biggest guys at our school, besides the jocks, and it's probably why he felt comfortable beating up kids smaller than him.

CHAPTER 35

Steel

I'd just sat down to meet with Bass when I'd gotten a text from Trip. Apparently, Amy and Delia were at a campus party tonight, dealing for the club, and they'd spotted Remi and her friends. I didn't like the idea of her being there with a bunch of drunk frat guys, but I'd head over once we were done.

Then Trip had texted again that Remi was leaving with some guy. All it had taken was seeing the look on my face and Bass insisted on knowing what was going on. Then he was riding with me to the address that Trip sent over.

We'd easily found Amy inside the party and she'd pointed me in the direction that Remi had gone. She'd been worried about Remi, the guy she was leaving with didn't have the best reputation for treating women very well.

"Want me to go with you?" Bass asked in a low voice. I could hear him despite the loud music. I saw Remi's friends heading in our direction.

"No, I'll handle it. Thanks though." I shot him an appreciative look.

"Hey, Steel!" The girls all said in unison as they walked up. They eyed Bass curiously as they waited for introductions and to see why we were here.

"Bass," I pointed to him; it was as much an introduction as I was going to give. I noticed him watching Julie with interest. "Where's Remi?" I was done with the small talk. I just wanted to find my girl.

"Uhhh…" Julie looked around in alarm. She was just now realizing she hadn't seen her in a while. It had taken us about fifteen minutes from the time we'd gotten Trip's first text until the time we'd gotten here.

"A friend of ours said she saw her leave with a blonde kid, tall, looked like an asshole." I crossed my arms over my chest.

All three girls sucked in their breathes at the same time. "Scott," Anna spat the name out. The other two nodded in agreement. "Remi's ex. Your friend was right, he's an asshole."

"Stay here," I muttered at Bass and gave him a look, indicating I wanted him to keep the girls inside. He grinned and hooked an arm around both Anna and Julie. Anna laughed up at him, but Julie just gave him a disgusted look. I turned and headed for the back of the house.

As soon as I stepped outside, I saw them across the yard. I also saw that Scott had his hands on Remi. "Take your fucking hands off her." I reached them quickly and wasted no time. He hadn't let her go by the time I'd gotten to them.

"Steel… what are you… oh my God!" Remi gasped when my fist collided with Scott's face. He didn't say much of anything, just gave a grunt of pain and surprise, but he did let her go so he could cover his broken nose. He looked up at me in shock as blood spilled through his hands.

"You broke my damn nose!"

"You ever touch her again. Fuck, you ever speak to her again, and I'll break more than that," I growled at him. I gently tugged Remi to me and she came along willingly. I looked her over, silently. Once, I was satisfied that she wasn't hurt, we went back inside to find the others.

The girls ran up to Remi when we approached, and I gave Bass a nod when his look asked if I'd handled it. Keeping an eye on the back door I spoke to Bass, "I'm taking Remi home." He nodded, and I grabbed Remi by the hand and led her outside. I saw Bass explaining to the girls as we were leaving, although I was pretty sure they could guess what was happening.

Bass managed to con Julie into a dance before we even made it outside. "Thanks for coming to get me." She frowned and tilted her head up so that she could look at me as I led her toward my bike. "How did you know I was here?"

I just shrugged and when she frowned and started to ask again, I stopped and kissed her. That only gave me a short reprieve though. "Steel," She said warningly.

"Amy. She was worried about you leaving with that guy."

Remi's eyes narrowed but before she could respond my phone went off.

"Shit. I have to take this." I kissed her, and we walked the rest of the way to my bike. I straddled it and Remi climbed on behind me. I listened to Cade's update on a drop that Riggs was taking care of tonight. Something had come up.

"I'll be there in twenty minutes. I had something come up with Remi. I need to drop her at home." I hung up.

"Let's go."

"I came with the girls. I'll catch a ride home with them." She started to scramble off the back of my bike. I reached back and pinned a heavy hand on her thigh.

"No, I'm taking you home." When she glared, I went on. "I'm not taking the chance that I'll leave, and that guy will come back." I released her and folded my arms over my chest.

"There are plenty of people here Steel. I'll be fine. Besides, I doubt he's coming back."

"Remi," I growled her name in warning. I didn't plan on letting her put herself in danger and that guy hadn't been about to take no for an answer. I was going to be tied up for the rest of the night. The only place I was leaving her was at home.

She put her hands on her hips and gave me a stubborn look. I settled the matter by starting up my bike. She was forced to hang onto me as I pulled away from the curb. Not that I would have taken off before she was ready, I just wanted her to think the decision was out of her hands.

As we headed toward her house, I felt her shift closer toward me and felt my heart pulse in my chest. Seeing her with that asshole tonight had nearly made me lose my shit. He was lucky he hadn't hurt her, or I'd have pulled him apart with my bare hands.

CHAPTER 36

Remi

We pulled up in front of my house and I dropped my forehead onto Steel's back. This wasn't my night. Uncle Caleb was sitting on the porch and he looked pissed. I felt Steel tense up once he saw my uncle too.

I rolled my eyes. "Well, this should be fun." I got off the bike and gave Steel what I hoped passed for a reassuring smile.

Steel grabbed my hand and started walking with me. I looked up at him in surprise. "I know you have to go. You don't have to stay." His gaze met mine.

"I have a few minutes."

We stopped in front of Uncle Caleb. He was looking at Steel like he was a piece of dog shit smeared on the bottom of his shoe. "Uncle Caleb, I..."

"What the hell are you doing Remi?" He all but spat the words at me. I was shocked into silence. Uncle Caleb's gaze went to where our hands were joined. Steel's fingers tightened around mine. I wasn't sure if it was to comfort me or so that he didn't punch my uncle. "You're with this... biker?" He sneered that at Steel.

"Yes," I said while lifting my chin. "Steel and I are dating."

Oh yeah, and I just figured out I've fallen in love with him at some point within the last month. I hadn't been able to pinpoint exactly when that had happened. Not that I'd had a chance to sit down and think about it, what with everything going on.

"No. You're not." My mouth dropped open when he said that.

"What?"

"My niece is not getting involved with a biker." Uncle Caleb glared at Steel. Both men were having a stare down.

"You don't get to make that decision, Uncle Caleb," I said through gritted teeth. I'd had enough of guys telling me what to do or not to do tonight. "I will date whoever I feel like dating."

"Your father..."

"Isn't here," I finished, in a cold but firm tone. My uncle's eyes met mine, finally. "And even if he was, he wouldn't get to make this decision either. Dad didn't approve of either of my previous boyfriends. But I still dated both of them. You don't get to tell me what I do with my life or who I spend my time with."

He narrowed his eyes at me and started to speak but I cut him off. "Go home, Uncle Caleb. I don't want you here tonight." He was furious. He stood there, fists clenching and unclenching while he tried to decide what to do. I wasn't going to let him win this though. I was an adult and I wouldn't cater to him any longer. Not with the business, not with school, and certainly not with my love life.

"You heard her."

Steel's voice was deep and commanding. I was glad he never used that tone on me. Uncle Caleb let out a huff and stormed off around us. We both watched as he got into his car and left. I sighed and looked at Steel.

"Sorry about him."

His eyes met mine, and he shrugged. "I'm used to it."

"Oh yeah? I can see that. I bet you're used to a lot of dads and uncles trying to run you off." I teased. We'd walked up and were standing next to my front door.

"Tons," He deadpanned. I smacked his chest.

"Jerk." He kissed me, swallowing whatever else I was going to say. He could completely erase every thought in my head. Soon he left, and I wandered around the house, waiting for the girls to get home.

CHAPTER 37

Steel

A couple weeks had passed since the party and Remi and I saw each other almost every day. Much to the club members' wives and girlfriends' dismay, the club barbecue had been canceled. Cade didn't want to give the Lycans a target to hit since they were continuing to come into our club's territory. It just gave me more time alone with Remi before I had to introduce her to everyone, officially. I knew the women were dying to meet her, but I didn't feel like sharing yet.

It amazed me how much I liked the girl. Between Remi, the club, and the garage, I was keeping busy. A good thing, because despite checking in with Bass every few days we were at a standstill with the Lycans. Everyone was on edge. We were all waiting for the other shoe to drop. Bass kept saying the woman associated with the Lycans kept talking about a specific date where she'd be able to get the money they'd need to get the remainder of the weapons for their war with us.

Then we'd finally have some action. We were all ready for it, anything for a break in this waiting game.

I glanced over as Gunnar walked into the kitchen and poured himself a cup of coffee. It was Monday morning, and I had to head into the garage later. I had an appointment for a custom build coming in that afternoon. Leaning against the kitchen island, I drank my coffee and watched Gunnar. Something had been bothering him for the last few weeks, but I hadn't been able to pry it out of him yet. He'd been pissy as fuck. If he kept it up, I was going to give him the fight he was looking for, if nothing else, just to get him to talk.

"Morning."

He looked up and grunted at me in response before sitting on a stool. Before I could say more Ty and Red walked in and nudged each other when they saw Gunnar. My eyes narrowed. They were standing at Gunnar's back, so he hadn't seen them yet.

"Hey there, Gunnar." He looked back over his shoulder, but just nodded at them and turned back around.

Red gave me a shit-eating grin before focusing on the back of Gunnar's head. "Well now, I heard a rumor about you and that stuck up little bitch you've been seeing." Both men chuckled. I saw Gunnar stiffen, and I straightened up warily. "I heard that she dropped your worthless ass…" Before he could continue Gunnar had jerked out of his chair and lunged at both nomads, taking them down.

"Shit." I came around the island, Gunnar was on top of Red, but Ty was behind him trying to get him in a chokehold. I ripped Ty off Gunnar and heard the sickening thud of bone on bone. There was no time to see who had thrown the punch though because Ty was up and advancing toward me.

The door to the kitchen was thrown open so hard that when it hit the wall, the glass panes shattered, showering glass all over the men on the floor at Cade's feet.

"What the fuck is going on?!" He roared as he pulled Gunnar and Red up and apart. Gunnar instantly stopped fighting, but the nomad kept struggling against our president's grip. I stopped as well and had let my guard down, expecting Ty to give Cade the same respect, but he kept coming and sucker-punched me when I started to move back toward the group at the door.

The sound of the slide of a gun being racked had us all freezing. Riggs stood in the doorway that split the common room and the kitchen. His gun was pointed directly at Ty's head. He didn't say a word, but neither nomad moved again.

"Steel." I looked over at Cade. "Take Gunnar over to my place. We'll handle this." I looked back over at the nomads, to my brother, then back at Cade. I didn't want to leave, but I wasn't going to disobey his order. Nodding I walked over and shoved Gunnar out the door when he tried to resist going.

Once we were out in the yard, he rounded on me. "Get the fuck off me. I can fucking handle myself."

"Sure, looks like you can," I said, folding my arms over my chest, raising a brow at the temper tantrum he was throwing.

"Fuck you, Steel."

I narrowed my eyes and took in the look on his face. He looked fucking miserable. He might be drunk. I looked at my watch, seven a.m. I looked back at his face and saw fury overshadowing everything now. I shrugged out of my cut and laid it over the porch railing of the clubhouse. He watched me intently. Reaching behind me I pulled my t-shirt off over my head, tossed it onto the porch, and faced him.

Gunnar glared at me for a minute then his face relaxed slightly before he followed suit and took off his cut and shirt. We moved further away from the porch.

"Do you want to talk about it?"

"Fuck no."

"Is what he said true?"

Gunnar grunted then lunged.

Fifteen minutes later when the President and VP stepped out of the clubhouse, they both stopped short on the porch and stared.

Gunnar and I lay in the dirt on our backs, breathing hard, bleeding just as hard from various cuts. Gunnar already had a black eye. The sneaky fucker had busted my lip. Neither of us had a set of knuckles whose skin hadn't split open.

"Jesus, Steel. I told you to get him out of there, not beat the shit out of each other." Gunnar and I shifted in the dirt so we could see each other and grinned. Then we shot those grins at the guys on the porch. Both men shook their heads and stalked off, Cade mumbling under his breath.

I stood up and held out a hand to help Gunnar up. "Feel better?" He just grunted. I nodded and slapped him on the back.

CHAPTER 38

Steel

I looked up from the carburetor I was working on when Cade walked into the garage. He walked over to where I was crouched next to an old Corvette. "Hey." It was rare for Cade to be anywhere but working at the bar on a Wednesday morning.

"Hey Steel." He nodded over toward Riggs's office and I followed him in. My brother was out on an errand and the other guys were either working the front desk or working on other cars or bikes, so we mostly had the place to ourselves.

"What's up boss?"

"I just got off the phone with Al." I stiffened. Typically, Al went through Riggs or me for business, since we owned the chop shop here and Al owned the one in California. If he was going through Cade, it meant something was wrong or it was a different type of club business.

"They were loading up a shipment to send back our way when the feds raided their shop. The Mackenzie's Trucking driver was still there, so they seized everything."

"Fuck."

"Yeah." He ran a hand through his hair. "Al wasn't sure who tipped off the feds. Unfortunately, I think I know who did." I gave him a curious look, but he shook his head. "I've got Riggs on that already. I need you to take Gunnar, Trip, Axel, and Drew and ride out to California and give Al a hand wherever you can."

I nodded and then grimaced. "Shit, do you think they've talked to Remi or her uncle yet?"

"Honestly, I don't know. But I need you to head out to California first thing. We can handle that when you get back, alright?"

I didn't like it, but I nodded. Cade was right. We had to get out there and take over Al's shop, see what needed to be done, bail them out of jail, and handle any of the loose ends for now. Al would do it for us. I'd have to wait to explain to Remi. I knew the feds would speak with her but maybe I'd have some time since they were busy over in California.

"I'll go grab the guys now and we'll head out."

Cade and I shook hands before he left. I pulled out my phone and dialed Remi. Glancing at the time I realized she should be in class so I left her a voicemail letting her know I had to go out of town and should be back in a few days. I shot a group text to the guys, letting them know we were heading out, so they'd have time to get ready while I rode back to the clubhouse.

CHAPTER 39

Remi

I groaned as I woke up Sunday morning. I was not a morning person. I glanced at my phone. I hadn't heard from Steel since Wednesday morning when he'd left a voicemail saying he had to leave town. It was obviously an emergency, so I had only texted him once, later that day, to tell him I'd gotten the message and to be safe. I didn't want to bother him while he was dealing with whatever, besides I had more than enough problems of my own to deal with. Especially today.

My door burst open, and I yipped in surprise. Ming, Bridget, Anna, and Julie danced in, carrying a huge cake singing, awfully might I add, Happy Birthday at the top of their lungs. I couldn't help but smile at them.

"Blow out the candle." Ming smiled softly at me. I complied and returned the smile. I looked down at the cake and felt tears well up in my eyes. Ming had been making our birthday cakes for years. They weren't lavish, professionally done, or even the most beautiful. But early on the morning of each of our birthdays, she would bake the cake, gather all of us together, and deliver the cake in bed. The four of us always baked her cake on her birthday as well, although hers usually tasted better than ours. They all came from boxes so we couldn't figure out why hers were better.

"Thanks, guys." They all gave me hugs and set the cake on the bed. "I thought we agreed to wait on all of this?"

"We'll wait on the celebration," Bridget said, folding her arms in disapproval. "But there's no waiting on cake. Now, let's go. We're having it for breakfast."

I knew we were all going to end up feeling sick, but followed them down to the kitchen. We spent an hour stuffing ourselves with cake and ice cream at eight a.m. After we all felt sufficiently full and slightly queasy, we split ways to get ready for the day. Bridget hesitated by her door.

"Are you sure you don't want me to come with you today?" Her eyes searched my face. My love for her, and the others, about split my heart open.

"I'm okay, Bridge. I just want to be alone."

She sighed but nodded. Hesitating for a second longer, she finally went into her room and shut the door. I went into mine and got ready for the one day I wished I could fast forward through.

Two hours later I parked in front of the older two-story home. I sighed and walked up to the front door to let myself inside. Standing just inside the door, I felt my heart shred as memories poured through me. Sunday morning breakfasts with my dad, always waffles with strawberries and whipped cream, before we'd go spend the day fishing on the lake. Him coming to watch my basketball games. Yelling at the five of us girls to turn the lights out during one of our sleepovers.

Leaning back against the front door I slid down until my butt hit the ground and I leaned my forehead on my bent knees. The memory of the day before he'd died flashed through my mind. He'd been laying in that hospital bed. I'd been so angry at him. He had been trying to go through everything he wanted to be done for the funeral, for the company, laying out how everything would happen once he was gone.

He'd given up, and I could see it. I had just wanted him to keep fighting, for me, if not for himself. I knew now that it was selfish on my part. He was tired, in pain, and he couldn't fight anymore. I think the only reason he held on as long as he did was because he wanted to celebrate one more birthday with me.

I sniffed and wiped my face as I realized tears and, gross, snot was running down my face. I stood up and stumbled upstairs. I went into Dad's room and laid down on his bed, burying my face in his pillows. His scent had long since fled. I'd spent a lot of time here the months after his death. I swear his scent was the only thing that had grounded me in this reality during that time. I'd scared the shit out of my friends and Uncle Caleb. In fact, the only reason any of them agreed to leave me alone today was because I insisted that I would be safe. I'd never tried to actively harm myself; I'd never do that. But falling into despair to where you won't eat or shower or take care of yourself can be pretty detrimental too, I'd learned.

I didn't know how long I laid there, lost in memories, mostly good, some shattering. But suddenly I realized the doorbell was ringing. I looked at the clock and realized it was four p.m. I'd been dozing and zoned out for six hours. It wasn't surprising. That was what my life had been after Dad's death. The doorbell was still ringing insistently, so I wiped my face and hurried down the stairs. Opening the door, I started to greet whoever was there, but it never made it out of my throat. Standing on the porch was my mother.

CHAPTER 40

Remi

We stared at each other silently for a few heartbeats. *She looks like shit.* Her hair was greasy and short, curly like it had always been but dull and lifeless. She had on skintight jeans, a midriff-baring tank top, and leather high-heeled boots. She was too skinny and the way she was fidgeting I wondered if she was on drugs. I racked my brain and tried to remember if Dad ever mentioned her being a junkie. He never spoke about her much so I couldn't remember.

"Remi. Baby, it's so good to see you." Her eyes looked at me speculatively.

"Hey, Rhonda." I stepped out onto the porch and shut the door behind me. I wasn't letting her into our home. I saw her expression tighten but then the look wiped off her face as though it had never been there. She looked around and slid her palms down the thighs of her jeans.

When she didn't say anything, just looked around nervously, I lost my patience. "What do you want?"

She looked up at me. "I was hoping to talk to your dad." She took a slight step back at the look on my face. I don't know if it was fury or grief that had shown through more. Since she moved backward, I would guess fury.

"No one told you?"

She just blinked at me and I laughed humorlessly at her. "Dad died a year ago today, Rhonda." I waited to see if the significance of the date would sink in for her.

She sucked in a breath and I was surprised that she remembered my birthday. Then it was taken away when all she said was, "Darren died?" She sounded horrified, so that was something at least.

I just nodded. She looked back towards the street and I followed her gaze but didn't see anything. Frowning, I wondered how she'd gotten here. Only my car sat at the curb. That thought left my head with her next words.

"Could I… come in?" I looked at her incredulously. This was the most I'd spoken to her since I was ten years old and stupidly had given her a second chance. That had lasted a week, then she'd stolen money from my piggy bank, and I'd refused to ever speak to her again. I'd never told Dad why, but he'd never forced me to try again with her. Even as a kid I'd known she was a loser.

"Please, Remi. I… I didn't know about your dad." I sighed. I was under no illusions that she still loved my father. But I knew they still saw each other once or twice a year. I owed it to him to help her through this and then I'd never have to see her again. I opened the door and motioned for her to go inside. She glanced toward the road again and then went in. I followed her, closing the door behind me.

We settled on the couch. She was perched on the edge like she would jump off any second and dart out the door.

I'd be totally fine with that.

"How…" She licked her lips. "How did he die?"

"Cancer," My voice cracked and her eyes shot up to mine. I avoided them and stared at the wall past her head. I didn't like being vulnerable in front of this woman, even if she was the woman who had given birth to me. She'd never been my mother. She'd left when I was a baby. There wasn't a maternal bone in her body.

"Did your dad…" She paused and picked at her jeans, staring at her lap. I finally focused on her again. "Did he ever tell you why we met every year?"

"No."

Her hands shook. "We always met around this time."

Because it's my birthday and he was probably hoping you'd remember, I thought bitterly. Something told me she never had. I wondered how much disappointment she'd caused him over the years. I watched her and wondered how much of her I had in me? The thought sickened me.

"Darren helped me out." Now she met my gaze steadily.

I frowned. "Helped you out?" She nodded, still holding my stare. "What do you mean?"

"He helped me every year." She insisted, as if I should understand what that meant. I just shook my head in confusion.

"He left you money? In his will?" Rhonda asked, barely able to contain her eagerness.

It dawned on me. "He gave you money," I said dully. It wasn't a question. She nodded and looked at me expectantly. "You came here every year, around this time of year," I sneered, "to take money from him." She frowned and shook her head.

"He owed me." She dropped all of the previous pretenses.

I stared at her in shock. The look on her face was ugly now.

"He'd want you to take care of your mother, Remi." She had seen the look on my face and realized she'd fucked up when she'd said that. Now she was trying to manipulate me in a different way.

"Get the fuck out of my house," I said with such a venomous tone that she stared at me in shock before fury overrode her features.

"We had a deal. Your dad and me. You're going to need to uphold that deal or we're going to have problems. I can bring a lot of problems down on you and the company, Remi." She smiled at me as though she held all the cards.

"What was your deal, exactly?"

"A hundred thousand dollars."

My mouth dropped open. "Dad paid you one hundred thousand a year?" She smiled smugly "Why would he do that, Rhonda?" Her lips twisted into a pout as if she didn't like me using her name. That was tough shit because I certainly wasn't going to call her mom.

She shrugged. "He was a smart man, Remi. He knows that my boyfriend is powerful and that it was better to stay on our good side. You need to realize that, too." She frowned at the defiant look on my face and grabbed my wrist. "It's not like you can't afford it. He had plenty of money."

"Get. Out." I wrenched my arm from her grip.

Standing, I walked over and flung the door open. I had to cross my arms over my chest, so I didn't deck her when she sauntered past. I never wanted to hit anyone so badly in my entire life. Of all the fucked-up days to show up and do this.

"You have three days Remi." She held out a piece of paper. I just stared at it, making no move to take it. She let it drop. "Text me when you're ready to give me the money." She started to walk down the steps. Halfway down she stopped and looked back at me.

"You'd better make the right choice, honey." I gritted my teeth at the hollow term of endearment.

"You don't know what we're capable of." She fluffed her greasy hair then wandered down the path and up the road. I watched for a few minutes, to make sure she wouldn't double back, before I picked up the paper and went back inside.

CHAPTER 41

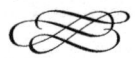

Remi

I paced back and forth in front of the door a few times, fuming. How dare that bitch come here, to my home, and try to blackmail me? I paused.

Oh, Dad, I thought sadly, *why did you give her money? Who was her boyfriend?* Not that it mattered. I wasn't scared of either of them. I crumpled up the paper with her number on it and threw it to the side of the room. The fury bubbling up in my chest made me want to scream. I was pissed at everything. At God, if I even believed, for taking Dad. At Dad, for dying. At Rhonda, for being a shit person and pulling this bullshit.

Not knowing what to do with all the anger and hatred in me, I did something really stupid. I punched the wall next to the door. Pain flooded through me, drowning out the anger. I grasped my hand and gasped in pain.

Okay, note to self: never ever do that again.

I'd seen guys do that a lot and it always seemed to make them feel better. I didn't feel better, I felt worse and now I wondered if I'd broken my hand.

Walking into the kitchen, clutching my hand to my chest I went and searched through drawers until I found some ibuprofen. I poked around in some cabinets and paused when I found Dad's stash of liquor. I looked around as though he were going to walk in and catch me. Shaking my head, I grabbed a bottle of vodka, there was only about a quarter of the bottle left.

I unscrewed the lid and took the pills with a shot. It was probably a terrible idea but at this point, I didn't care anymore. I took the bottle with me and after locking the front door I climbed the stairs. Laying back down on Dad's bed I proceeded to drink and look at photos and videos I had of us for the next four hours.

It was eight p.m., almost dark, the vodka was gone, and I was buzzed. Okay, maybe I was a little drunk. Enough that it seemed like a good idea to go get more vodka. There wasn't anymore in the house and I didn't like any of the other stuff Dad had here. My hand was still throbbing a bit, and I hadn't been able to chase away all the ghosts just yet. I stumbled out of the house, remembering to lock up. I wandered up to my car and frowned.

No drinking and driving, I giggled to myself.

I ordered an Uber and waited on the porch. It felt like an eternity before it pulled up.

"Hey lady." The kid popped his gum. "Where to?"

I blinked. "Is there a liquor store near here?" I couldn't seem to remember what was around here. I hadn't spent my childhood frequenting liquor stores anyway.

He turned around in his seat and looked at me. "No. But there's a bar just a few miles up the road. Want me to take you there?"

I nodded, and he pulled out onto the road. I leaned my head on the headrest in the back seat and closed my eyes. The car jerked to a stop, startling me and I blinked at the driver. I must have dozed, although it felt like I had only closed my eyes for a minute.

"Alright, here you go." I could tell he wanted me out of the car. I thanked him and got out. Watching as he drove off, I shoved my hands in my jean short pockets then winced and touched the tender, split knuckles on my right fist. I sighed and decided another drink would fix that.

Turning, I looked at the bar then groaned. I glanced back to where the driver had left and wondered if I could get him to come back. Probably not, he hadn't seemed thrilled to have me in his car, he could probably smell the alcohol on me.

I turned back around and stared at Lock, Stock, and Barrel. I hadn't realized when Steel had taken me here that it had been so close to my old house.

No helping it now, I thought and walked through the door. *Maybe no one would recognize me.* It was Sunday night again and last time it had seemed slow, plus it was relatively early. I kept my head down as I walked up to the bar and I was glad to see I didn't recognize the bartender.

"Hey, Darlin'," The guy said, smiling at me and I returned it. The name on his cut said, Hush. "What can I get ya?"

"Rum and coke and two shots of vodka, please?" His eyebrows went up, and I inwardly groaned thinking maybe I shouldn't have ordered them all at once. He just shrugged and moved away to get my drinks. I sighed and pulled my phone out as it dinged. Ming, Bridget, Anna, and Julie had all been checking in. The last was from Uncle Caleb. I quickly checked in with everyone. Rather I quickly punched in a bunch of typos and gibberish. Slowly, I went back and corrected everything before sending out the texts, then I put my phone down on the bar.

The guy brought my drinks over and I waited for him to turn around before I downed both shots of vodka. I drummed the fingers of my left hand on the bar and wondered what I was going to do about Rhonda. *Should I tell Uncle Caleb? Could the cops do anything about someone trying to get money from you? It was technically blackmail, right? Or coercion?* I picked up the rum and coke and drank thoughtfully. The alcohol was finally dulling enough of the pain in my hand and my head.

I looked down at the glass. *Happy fucking birthday,* I thought bitterly. Dad's voice saying that phrase, albeit without the cussing, drifted through my head. He'd say it while waking me up by tickling me and then taking me on birthday adventures throughout the years.

The memories had me knocking back the rest of the drink in a couple of swallows. My phone buzzed again. Sighing, I picked it up. If I didn't respond to the girls, they'd just try to come find me. I saw the text was from Steel.

Steel: Back in town. Can we meet tomorrow?

I frowned at the phone. I was excited to see him but now that I'd decided my course of action tonight was to drink my sorrows away, I decided to wait until tomorrow to text him back. I set the phone down. Tonight, I was going to drink, figure out what to do about my loser mother, and try to forget everything else.

My mouth went dry. Why had Dad given her so much money? *Every year he gave her a hundred thousand dollars?* My head spun. I wasn't sure if that was the amount or the drinks. Maybe Rhonda was lying. I brightened at that. If Dad was paying her off, there should be some kind of record for it.

I was going to visit Mr. Jeffries down at the bank. He was the sweet old man who had helped me get all of the business and Dad's personal bank accounts straightened out after his death. Smartly, Dad had put me on the accounts before he'd died, otherwise, I wouldn't have had any access to them. Since he had, I'd never switched over to new accounts. So, the old transactions should still be there. I'd be able to verify if Rhonda was lying about the amount. Or even if he was ever paying her at all. Maybe she was lying about everything.

The bartender leaned on the bar in front of me and I jumped. I'd been so caught up in my plan I hadn't noticed he'd come back. "Another round?" He raised his brows and looked pointedly at my empty glasses. I glanced around, luckily Amy didn't seem to be working tonight and I saw no one else here that I recognized.

"Uh... Sure. Why not?" The guy nodded and swiped the glasses out from in front of me. I avoided looking at him and picked up my phone. I flicked through TikTok, just to give myself something to do. If this was any other bar, I wouldn't be nervous. But the last thing I needed was to see any of the guys I'd met through Steel. Or Steel himself, since I'd just found out he was back in town. I didn't want any company tonight. The bartender set the drinks down in front of me.

I pulled up my email and typed out a request to meet with Mr. Jeffries, the manager at our bank, at his earliest convenience. Tuesday, if possible. I hit send and realized that a different man had replaced the first guy behind the bar.

Huh, he must have gotten off shift. I picked up the first shot of vodka and tossed it back. I was beyond buzzed at this point. I'd had to close one eye to type out that email. I just prayed it made sense when the man went to read it.

Tossing back the second shot I pulled up the Uber app and checked for any cars in the area. Nothing.

Damn. Oh well, I'd finish my drink and check again. I could always try Lyft or even call a taxi. I picked up the rum and coke but before I could lift it for a drink someone grabbed my wrist, spilling it all over my hand. I hissed in pain as the alcohol spilled over my split and bruised knuckles. I glared up into green eyes.

Uh oh. Busted. Fuck... my drunk brain stammered, *what was his name?* For some reason he wasn't wearing his cut, so I couldn't cheat.

"Remi." He was still holding onto my wrist. His eyes narrowed on my bleary ones then looked down at my busted knuckles before returning to my face. I couldn't decide if the way he said my name was a greeting or a warning.

I cleared my throat. "Hey. Uh, how's it going?" *Smooth,* I groaned to myself. "Nice seeing you again. I was just about to pay and head home." I tried to tug my arm away from him, sloshing more of the drink over my hand and making me wince again. He snatched the drink out of my grip, without letting me go.

"How about you stick around." It wasn't a request.

"That's sweet. Really. But I was just heading out." I smiled at him.

Fuck. What was his damn name? I dug into my pocket with my opposite hand and pulled out some cash. I tossed some twenties on the top of the bar and slid off the stool. Those green eyes narrowed on me. He didn't look happy. *What was his problem?*

"You can let go of me now." I looked down at his hand on me then back up at him with impatience.

"No."

My mouth dropped open. *What the hell?*

"I don't appreciate you touching me." Okay, even I heard the slur in my voice on that one. He just tugged me closer to him. We were playing tug o' war with my arm, but I didn't have any hope in hell of winning when I was sober, let alone drunk. Before I could go off on him the door to the bar slammed open. Everyone inside went silent.

The look on green eyes' face turned smug when he looked from the door to me.

Uh oh. I glanced over my shoulder. Steel was striding across the bar and he looked pissed. This time when I tugged my arm away the guy let it go. I glared at him, snatched my phone off the bar, and tried to dart around Steel toward the door. He just snaked out an arm and wrapped it around my waist, reeling me in.

"Thanks, Cade."

Cade. That was his name, I remembered finally.

Steel nodded at him then at the original bartender who had finally come out from the back hallway. I glared at both of them.

"Tattletale," I muttered at them. The bartender looked surprised that I was calling him names, but Cade just looked amused. He crossed his arms over his chest and grinned at me.

Steel ignored that and turned us around, heading for the door. I stumbled a bit, but he caught me and marched me right out into the parking lot. He opened the door of a large pickup truck and I frowned in confusion.

"Where's your bike?" He just stared down at me then picked me up by the waist and all but tossed me into the truck. I was fuming by the time he climbed into the driver's side. If he was going to ignore me, two could play that game. I leaned my head against the headrest. The truck had a smooth ride. I closed my eyes.

CHAPTER 42

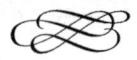

Steel

I looked over to where Remi was sleeping across from me and clenched my jaw. I had been at the garage trying to finish up a few things before heading home for the night, when Cade called. We'd just pulled back into town about forty-five minutes earlier and I'd texted her as soon as I'd gotten in. I hadn't thought anything about it when she didn't respond.

Then Cade had called and said she was sitting at his bar, drunk, and looked like she'd gotten into a fight. I glanced over at her hand. Her knuckles were swollen, the skin split and bloodied. When I'd walked in, she'd been trying to leave, and Cade had clearly been keeping her there. I definitely owed him and Hush, the new club bartender who had originally recognized her and told Cade she was there.

I let her sleep the whole drive back to the clubhouse. I'd left my bike at the garage since she was plastered, and I needed to get her home. I'd borrowed one of our cage rides. Pulling into the lot I groaned when I saw my brother strolling up. I swear he and Cade were like an old married couple. What one knew, the other did. I parked and got out of the truck. Riggs leaned on the bed of the truck looking in the window at Remi.

"She alright?"

I shrugged. "She passed out as soon as I got her in the truck." He chuckled.

"Need any help?" I shook my head, and he slapped me on the shoulder before he headed to his house.

I opened the door and pulled Remi out into my arms. She mumbled something and snuggled into my chest. Kicking the truck door closed, I walked across the parking lot. I entered the clubhouse through the front door and paused when about twelve sets of eyes zeroed in on us as I stepped through the door. Damn, there wasn't usually this many people around on a Sunday. There were a lot of raised eyebrows.

Gunnar walked up and frowned down at Remi. "Shit, what happened?"

"Don't know yet."

"Should I call Bridget?"

"Sure, just let her know she's here." Gunnar nodded and went up the stairs ahead of me. He walked down the hallway first and opened the door to my apartment.

"Night."

"Thanks, Gunnar." He grinned at me as he closed the door behind us. Setting Remi down on my bed I stripped off her shoes, socks, and shorts then slid her under the covers. I walked into the bathroom and grabbed the first aid kit and brought it back to the bed. I stroked a thumb over her cheek.

"Remi." I lightly patted her cheek. When she didn't wake up, I let her sleep.

Digging through the kit, I used an antiseptic wipe on her knuckles. She woke with a gasp, jerked her hand away, glaring blearily at me. Grabbing her hand again I went to keep cleaning it, but she put her other hand over mine. "That hurts."

"I'm surprised you can feel anything with how much you drank."

She glared. "I can drink if I want to. I'm an adult."

I set the wipe down and ran my thumb over her fingers, careful not to hit her knuckles. "Why were you at the bar?"

"The stupid Uber driver didn't tell me it was that bar," She muttered. I frowned.

"Why did you take an Uber across town to go to Cade's bar?"

"I didn't. I was only a couple of miles away. I didn't realize that was the closest bar until the guy had already left or I would have gone somewhere else. He wouldn't come back for me though 'cause I was already buzzed." Her eyes fluttered closed. I was trying to piece together what was going on. The girls' house was across town from Cade's bar.

"Why were you only a few miles away?"

"I was at Dad's house."

I hadn't realized she still had her dad's house. "Why were you already buzzed?" I figured out that short questions were easier right now.

"My hand hurt. And she made me so mad."

I shook my head. What was she talking about?

"What happened to your hand, Remi?"

"Punched a wall." She was falling back asleep. She'd punched a wall?

Remi's phone started ringing, so I picked it up. Bridget's name flashed.

"Hey, Bridget."

"Steel. Hey," she said, sounding surprised. "I didn't realize you were back in town until Gunnar texted."

"Yeah, we just got back a bit ago."

"Remi's with you? She's… okay?" I frowned at the hesitation.

"She got drunk at our club bar, apparently punched a wall, and is passed out here at the clubhouse. But otherwise, yeah she's fine." Bridget sucked in a loud breath. "What's going on Bridget?"

"She didn't tell you anything?"

"That's pretty much all I got out of her."

She sighed. "Steel. It's Remi's twenty-second birthday today." I glanced down at her and frowned. I wondered why she hadn't told me that? "It's also the first anniversary of her dad's death." I rubbed a hand over my forehead. That would be why she hadn't mentioned it. Jesus, she was stubborn.

"Thanks for telling me, Bridget. I'll take care of her."

"Thanks, Steel. She wouldn't let any of us stay with her today. She doesn't like to lean on anyone when she's hurting. Anyway, have her call me tomorrow."

We said goodbye. I finished cleaning up Remi's hand, grateful that she didn't wake up this time. Cleaning up, I stripped, climbed in bed, and pulled Remi in close to me before turning off the lights. We'd be hashing this out in the morning, but there was nothing to do but sleep it off tonight.

Remi's moan woke me the next morning. She shifted against me and put a hand up to her head. I'm sure it was torturing her for her decisions last night. I slipped out of bed and went into the bathroom. Flicking on the light, ignoring her hiss of pain as it spread across the bed, I rummaged around in the medicine cabinet and found some Tylenol, and grabbed a cool glass of water for her.

I sat next to her on the bed as she slowly sat up, and handed the pills and the water to her.

"Thanks," She murmured.

"Feeling pretty shitty?" She just nodded and sipped the water. I glanced over at the clock. It was eight a.m. but I had closed the blinds so the sunlight wouldn't wake us up too early. I wanted her to be able to sleep off some of her hangover.

"Think you could eat?" She shook her head, then winced. I got up and went out into the kitchen. Popping some bread into the toaster, I grabbed eggs from the fridge for myself. I needed to get something into her because, whether she was hungover or not, we had a few things we needed to discuss. What happened last night was one. The other was what had sent me to California for the better part of last week.

Glancing over, I watched as she slowly walked into the kitchen and sat on a stool at the island, silently watching me. She looked like hell and I watched as she rubbed her knuckles. They didn't look much better this morning. Her hangover seemed to take precedence over them, though. I was impressed that she hadn't thrown up yet, but she was looking a little green. The toast popped up, and I slid it onto a plate and set it down in front of her. She stared down at it. I filled a glass with ice then water and set that in front of her as well.

"You should try to eat."

Her eyes met mine then she picked up the toast and nibbled on it. Satisfied I turned around and stirred my eggs. When they were finished, I sat across from her and started eating.

"How did Cade know I was at the bar last night?"

I paused, fork halfway to my mouth, and looked at her. She looked curious but not angry like she had been last night.

"Hush recognized you."

She frowned. "Who is Hush?"

"One of the new nomads who came into town. He was working the bar."

"How do these guys know who I am when I don't know them?"

"They know who you are because you're mine."

She narrowed her eyes at me and started to speak but her phone started ringing and cut her off. She flinched at the sound but answered it after checking the caller ID.

"Hello?"

I ate my breakfast, listening to her half of the conversation.

"Yes, this is she." She paused, a frown marring her face.

"Yes, that's correct. What is this concerning?"

I grinned at her formal, boardroom voice. Who knew I'd find that hot?

"I can meet you there at ten a.m." She listened as the other person spoke. "Well, I understand that, but I will not be able to meet you before then. So, you can either meet me at Mackenzie's at ten a.m. this morning, or I won't meet you at all and you can feel free to track me down and arrest me if that's how you'd like to play it."

I froze and looked up at her. *Fuck.* Her voice was ice cold, and she didn't sound nervous, but her hand was shaking as she listened again.

"Wonderful. Ten a.m., it is. I'll see you then Special Agent Flynn."

God damn it. My time to warn her had run out. She ended the call, and I started to speak but she'd already dialed another number.

"Preston. Sorry for the unexpected call, but I just got a call from the FBI. Apparently, something happened, and they want to meet me at Mackenzie's at ten. Could you meet me there? Absolutely. Thanks, Preston." She sighed as she hung up and she furiously typed away on her phone.

"Hey, about that…" She looked up at me.

"Thank you for taking me home last night, Steel. I have no idea what's going on, but I need to get back into town, get my car, get home, so I can go meet this Agent. Could you drive me back to my dad's house?"

I swallowed; my mouth was dry because I needed to tell her what I knew. "Listen we should talk."

She sighed. "I know. I'll explain what happened last night, but I don't have time right now. Could you please take me back?"

I nodded and like a fucking coward I took her back to her car and didn't tell her why I'd gone to California. I knew it was going to bite me in the ass later but there was no way I'd have time to properly explain it to her on the thirty-minute drive into town. I'd have to take my chances and make her hear me out later.

CHAPTER 43

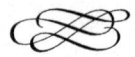

Remi

At nine forty-five, I walked into Mackenzie's and let out a sigh of relief when I saw both Preston and Uncle Caleb standing there. I'd texted Uncle Caleb after I'd gotten off the phone. I hadn't had the patience to go over it again with him, plus my head had been killing me. After the bombshell Rhonda had dropped on me and the hangover this morning, this was the worst morning for something like this to be happening.

The blistering hot shower had made me feel somewhat human and the suit and skyscraper heels exuded power, Bridget and Julie had assured me. I'd filled them in this morning before I'd rushed out the door. Anna had already left for classes. I grimaced. I'd been missing so many classes lately, for one reason or another, there was no way I was going to end up graduating early. Uncle Caleb was going to be furious.

But that was another problem for a different day. Things still weren't right between us since he'd found out about Steel. It seemed like I was hiding more and more things from him.

"Preston." I shook my lawyer's hand. He smiled at me and his other hand went over the top of mine in our shake. His gray eyebrows were low over his brown eyes. The man had been Dad's lawyer forever and now was mine. I remember being a kid when Dad was just starting the business; Preston would sneak me candy when Dad wasn't looking.

"What the hell is going on Remi?" Uncle Caleb looked furious. "Why is the FBI wanting to meet?"

"I'm not sure Uncle Caleb. The lady wouldn't say a whole lot, just that we needed to talk and that if I wasn't willing to voluntarily meet with her, then they'd pick me up and make me speak with them down at the nearest local Austin Police Station." Uncle Caleb huffed out a breath.

"I'm sure it'll be fine." Preston let go of my hand, but his tone was soothing. He was trying to calm both of us, but he gave my uncle a hard look. It settled Uncle Caleb down a little. Before we could discuss anything more, the front door opened and a woman and man in black suits walked through the door.

They look straight out of the movie Men in Black.

They walked forward towards us and all five of us eyed each other up. "Ms. Mackenzie?" I nodded and held my hand out to shake Agent Flynn's. She was clearly the one in charge. "I'm Special Agent Flynn and this is my partner Special Agent Ramirez."

I shook Ramirez's hand and gestured to the men behind me. "This is my Uncle Caleb, my manager, and Preston Durston, my lawyer." All four exchanged handshakes. Uncle Caleb excused himself and went back to get Janet from the back so that she could watch the front. Her eyes widened when she came out and saw the FBI Agents standing in the lobby, but she didn't say a word.

"If you'll follow us?" I led the way back to the meeting room. Once we'd all settled in, I shot a glance at Preston and he gave me a slight nod. I took a breath. "So, Agent Flynn. Agent Ramirez. What can I help you with?"

Flynn looked at me in what could only be called a calculating manner. I decided immediately that I didn't like her. She was looking at me as though I was scum. It surprised me. It was rare for me to make snap decisions about disliking a person.

"Five days ago, Wednesday morning, the Commercial Crimes Division of the Long Beach California Police Department raided a local vehicle repair shop. They'd received an anonymous tip that the business was a front for an illegal chop shop that was importing and exporting stolen merchandise out of state."

"We know they are working with someone here in Texas, but the manifest was destroyed on the scene before our teams could confiscate it and track who the second shop is. We have our suspicions, of course." She looked back and forth between the three of us. I saw Uncle Caleb stiffen next to me and Preston sighed and rubbed his fingers over the crease between his brows.

Agent Flynn continued, almost gleefully. I tried to keep my expression neutral even though I didn't understand what was happening yet. "We seized everything within the shop and everything that was set to be shipped that morning, including the Mackenzie's Trucking semi that the stolen vehicle parts were loaded on." I froze in shock.

What the fuck?

"One of our trucks was at the shop?" She nodded in confirmation at my question. I looked at Agent Ramirez. He had yet to speak, and I was pretty sure his facial expression hadn't changed once. I was beginning to suspect he was a robot.

"And it had illegal vehicles in it?" This came from Preston.

"They were disassembled, but yes. The original serial numbers had been ground down and new numbers had been assigned."

I blinked. "Why are we only finding out about this five days later?" I looked over at Uncle Caleb. He had a pinched look on his face. "Uncle Caleb, did you know about this?"

He grimaced. "I knew Fred had gotten held up in California. He called me Wednesday afternoon. He wasn't able to give me any specifics though. I was going to follow up this morning if I hadn't heard from him by Friday." I gaped at him.

"Why the hell didn't you tell me that?" I tried to keep my voice calm, since both of the FBI Agents were listening closely to everything we said.

"Because dealing with the truckers is my job, Remi." He glared at me.

"I think if a trucker and one of my trucks goes missing, that warrants me being told about it."

Preston cleared his throat and gave us pointed looks. We could speak about this later, his message came through loud and clear. I shut my mouth but not before I gave Uncle Caleb a death glare. I looked back at Agent Flynn.

"Okay, so now what?"

"We will be prosecuting Mackenzie's Trucking, and you as the owner, Ms. Mackenzie, with 18 U.S.C. 2314, Transportation of Stolen Goods. Transporting stolen goods across state lines is a federal offense and falls under our jurisdiction. We will also be adding 18 U.S.C. Chapter 113, Criminal Possession of Stolen Property to those charges as well." The smug way she said it sent my temper through the roof.

"What the fuck are you talking about?!" I looked at her incredulously while simultaneously yelling. Preston placed a hand on my shoulder, but I shrugged it off and leaned closer to Agent Flynn.

"I didn't steal shit. I had no idea that I was in possession of stolen shit. I had no idea that I was transporting stolen shit. And I had no idea that my company was doing any of these things either." I folded my arms over my chest. "I may not be a cop or have gone to law school, but I'm pretty sure you're going to have to prove that I had knowledge of these things to make those charges stick."

I glanced over at Preston. He didn't look thrilled at my delivery, but he nodded in the affirmative. I glared back at Agent Flynn and she raised a blonde eyebrow. Her matching blonde hair was neatly coiffed up on top of her head, not one hair out of place. She calmly interlaced her fingers, and I noticed her nails were done with a French manicure. Bridget would have been impressed with her. She was cool, calm, and collected, all while I felt like a steaming pile of shit.

"You, yourself said that the serial numbers had been ground down then new ones put on. If they had numbers on there, and those numbers matched the numbers on the manifests, how would I, or any of my people know if they were incorrect?" I leaned back in my chair. Flynn didn't look smug any longer, but she didn't look worried either and that worried me.

"We have all types of ways of proving when someone has been an accomplice in a crime, Ms. Mackenzie."

I looked at her patronizingly. "So, am I an accomplice, or am I in criminal possession of stolen goods?" I sneered at her. Giving her attitude probably wasn't smart, but it was the only shred of control I had over all of this.

"Yes," She said smugly, indicating that both were accurate.

I threw up my hands. "Okay, I'll bite. Who am I in cahoots with?"

Agent Flynn tossed a file down in front of me. "Ever heard of the Vikings MC?" My stomach felt like I'd ridden an elevator to the hundredth floor, and it had dropped unexpectedly into a free fall. I opened the file and flipped through the pages. Looking out from those pages was Cade, Riggs, Steel, Gunnar, and then a few other people I didn't recognize.

"Not really, no. Should I have?" I looked up at her and quirked a brow. I wasn't going to give this bitch anything. Not that I'd ever had a problem with the cops or the law, but I didn't like how this lady had immediately stepped into my business and started treating me like the bad guy.

Agent Flynn leaned forward and flicked back to Steel's picture. "You don't recognize this man?" I felt Uncle Caleb stiffen next to me. I studied Steel's photo. It wasn't a mug shot but more like a surveillance photo. He was walking across a road, looking around as though he could feel eyes on him. He had sunglasses on and was dressed in his usual jeans, t-shirt, and cut. Next to the photo was a quick rundown.

Logan "Steel" Steele
Twenty-eight years old
SGT at Arms with the Vikings MC

It went on to list suspected criminal activity and a few other things.

Shit. His name was Logan? He had said Steel was a nickname. Well, clearly it was his last name as well. He'd had me so distracted and nervous the day he'd filled out the paperwork, I hadn't paid any attention. It seemed weird now, that I'd been so intimate with him but hadn't even known his real name. Then I wondered if this was the right time to get hung up on that? I shrugged nonchalantly.

"I'm not sure. He might look familiar?" I slid the file back over to Flynn and tried to ignore the glare that my uncle was aiming in my direction. Preston cleared his throat and gave me a pointed look. I shot him an apologetic look and sat quietly.

"We have the paperwork," she slid over the official paperwork that Steel and I had filled out that first time he'd come into the office a month ago, "Showing that he was here." She tapped the papers with one perfect nail. I looked in shock at the paper she slid toward me. It was a copy of the original. Who had made a copy for her? I side-eyed my uncle and Preston.

"Where did you receive this document from?" I was thankful that Preston had stepped in and voiced my question, especially since he'd basically told me to stop talking with his last look.

Agent Flynn's eyes flashed over to Uncle Caleb for a moment before fixing themselves on Preston. With almost a bored look she replied, "It was in the file when it was handed to me. I'm not sure who obtained it or from where." Preston looked unconvinced.

"Doesn't that mean..." I started but stopped once I caught Preston's glare. Agent Flynn's attention returned to me.

"Does this jog your memory at all?"

I shrugged again. "I suppose that might be why he looks familiar."

Clearing his throat, Preston addressed the Agent but I could tell he was getting impatient with me. "My clients have a lot of commercial accounts, Agent Flynn. They also have multiple employees. It is illogical to assume Remi would remember every client she signs up, off the top of her head. She did her due diligence and ran the background check on both him and his business before Mackenzie's entered into business with this gentleman." Preston glanced at me and I nodded in affirmation.

He interlaced his fingers in front of him on the desk. "Now, are those the only charges you'll be bringing against my client?"

Agent Flynn nodded, her blue eyes focusing on my lawyer. "For now. We have a warrant to search both the premise and Ms. Mackenzie's home at 215 N. Hursh Rd." I kept my face neutral. They didn't mention Dad's house. They may not know about it yet.

"At this time, we won't be taking Ms. Mackenzie into custody, but if she attempts to flee or do anything unadvisable that will change quickly." She shot me a dark look. I leveled the same look at her, unwilling to back down an inch. If she thought I was scared of her, she didn't know who she was dealing with.

"You can't officially arrest me, anyway. You have no proof that I've done anything wrong. So, you can take your warning and shove it up your..."

"Remi!" Both my uncle and Preston interrupted me, but I continued to glare at the Agent and she just smiled grimly at me. I wanted to knock her pearly white teeth down her throat. I'd always had a temper; I'd gotten it from Dad. But I idly wondered if it had gotten worse since I'd met Steel?

"We'll be spending the day here, going through the offices. We have a team that will be at your home in the next twenty minutes. You'll be welcome to be present at either location." She handed Preston a copy of the search warrants. I folded my arms over my chest and gave her my best 'eat shit and die' look.

"Ms. Mackenzie, if I might have a word... alone?" Agent Flynn gave me a challenging smile. Both Uncle Caleb and Preston started sputtering, clearly not wanting me to be alone with this woman. Agent Ramirez left quietly.

Jesus. Could my life get any worse right now? I looked over at Uncle Caleb, who was white as a sheet, and Preston, who looked grim.

"It's fine. Just give us a minute," I said, and Preston sighed.

"Don't answer any other questions," he muttered. To Agent Flynn, he said, "Anything she answers will be off the record." He waited for her to agree before he walked out.

"We'll be right outside." Uncle Caleb followed, closing the door behind him.

I met Agent Flynn's gaze. Curiosity and judgment were shining in it. "I was just wondering…" She paused as though searching for the right words. "Why?"

My brows pulled together. "Why what?"

"Why would you risk all of this?" She motioned around her. "Everything you have. For a guy like Logan Steele. A criminal? We've spent the last few days looking into this case, Remi." She walked back over to the table and sat, crossing her long legs. "You don't mind if I call you Remi, do you?" I wrinkled my nose. She was beautiful and looked elegant in the suit but there was a toughness about her too. Something that said it'd be a bad idea to fuck with her. I didn't answer her question.

"What makes you think I am risking anything for him? I told you I don't even know him." I maintained eye contact when Flynn stared at me without blinking for a moment.

"What is it about him, I wonder?" She mused, continuing on as though I hadn't asked her anything. She tapped a nail against her cheek. "He's sexy, there's no denying that." Her laugh was husky, but I didn't feel any jealousy at her admission. Steel wouldn't be interested in this cop. Her eyes skated down my body and I fought the urge to fidget under her intense stare.

"Not going to tell me?" I remained stubbornly mute. If she wasn't going to answer any of my questions, I wasn't going to give her the satisfaction. I needed to find out how she knew about me and Steel, and how she'd gotten paperwork from within Mackenzie's though.

Her next words jerked me back to the conversation. "Pity… but it doesn't matter. He'll move on once you're in prison." I sucked in a breath. She stood up and stopped directly in front of me, slightly too close for comfort. When she spoke next her breath fanned across my cheek.

"The women are going to love you in prison. You're gorgeous." She stepped around me and opened the door. "Have a nice day, Ms. Mackenzie." She called as she walked down the hall. I stared at the door in confusion.

Had she just hit on me? Or was she just trying to scare me? I sat there speechless until my uncle and Preston came back into the room.

"What am I going to do?" I asked them. I mentally reminded myself to tell Preston about this conversation and ask him how she had all of this information.

Preston started gathering up the files and papers the Agent had given him. "Go home. I'll start working on this. Remi, don't go anywhere." He cautioned. "This isn't my normal area of expertise. I need to talk to my partners who specialize in criminal prosecutions. We'll sort this out. I'll call later today, and set up a meeting to go over everything you know, okay?" I nodded. Preston and Uncle Caleb walked out of the meeting room together again.

I sat there, stunned. *What the hell was going on?* I looked over and noticed a company laptop sitting at the end of the table. Someone had destroyed the physical manifest at the pickup location.

That's what Agent ass face had said. I leaned forward and peered down the hallway.

Standing, I leaned out the door and saw the Agents speaking with a team of about ten people, explaining where they wanted them to start the search. Uncle Caleb was still speaking with Preston by the front door. I didn't know what was happening yet, and I didn't know how or if it connected to Steel or the Vikings, but I know that the feds were at least trying to pin some of this on me. If there wasn't a manifest to find, that was going to be very hard to do.

I had already shredded the physical copy of the manifest when I'd entered it into the system. The only other copy had gone with the trucker. I quickly sat down and pulled the laptop over to me.

A voice in my head started singing *you're going to prison; you're going to prison.* I shoved the voice out and typed in the password to the generic admin user account. I thanked every possible higher power that Uncle Caleb had been so ornery about technology. Because of it, we had one generic account that everyone at the company used instead of individualized accounts. It was a logistical nightmare.

This was one time that the nightmare might work in my favor. I pulled up our tracking system and quickly, and permanently, erased every manifest that had anything to do with the Vikings or Long Beach. Logging back out I shut the laptop and loped over to my office.

I quickly searched through and made sure there were no surviving hard copies of the previous manifests floating around. I was pretty diligent about shredding them once I'd inputted them, but the other girls may not have been. I didn't find any. Grabbing my keys, I turned and jolted.

"What are you doing in here?" Agent Flynn glared at me suspiciously. I walked up and twirled my keys in her face.

"Getting my keys so I can go home." I gave her my best haughty look, walked past her, and sailed out the door. I ignored my uncle's calls behind me.

I had to fight to drive home at the speed limit. The last thing I needed was to get pulled over. By the time I got home, there were marked and unmarked police cars all over our street. I puffed out an irritated breath and sat in the quiet of my car for a minute. I wanted to scream. I wanted to cry. I wanted to hit someone, preferably Special Agent Flynn.

Instead, I got out of my car and met my frantic roommates inside the house. I yanked them into my room and explained everything that had happened, both with the cops and with my mom. Their eyes were as big as saucers by the time I was done.

"Jesus, Remi," Julie breathed. "What are you going to do?" I shrugged, trying not to break down and have a pity party.

"I guess the first thing I need to do is talk to Steel." They nodded in agreement.

"What are you going to do about Rhonda?" That came from Bridget. They knew just how awful my mother was. I'd never hidden anything from them. I'd never told Dad the things Rhonda had done to me because I hadn't wanted to hurt him, but the girls knew. They hated her as much as I did.

"I honestly don't know. I guess one good thing about going to prison. If I am there, she can't get to me." I laughed, slightly manically. The girls grimaced at my joke. "And if they've frozen all of my accounts, there's no money to pay her."

"Okay, that's enough, Rem." Anna glared at me. "You're not going to jail. You're not losing the company. And no one is paying that bitch any money." All three nodded. I sighed and leaned in, pulling them all into a group hug.

"I don't know what I'd do without you guys. You are the only family I have left. I love you; you know?" They all mumbled it back.

A knock on the door had us looking over. A younger woman was standing there, smacking gum, staring at us. "Gotta check the computers in here." She was eyeballing us cynically. I rolled my eyes and changed into jeans, a tank, and sneakers.

"It's all yours," I said to the Agent then looked at the girls. "I need to go." They all knew who I was seeing if not where I was going.

"We'll take care of everything here, don't worry." Anna glared at the woman as she stepped into my room.

I looked at her then at my friends. "Make sure she doesn't root around in my underwear. I don't need these freaks sniffing them." The Agent looked at me in disgust, but I just sneered at her as I left.

Hopping in my car I texted Steel.

Remi: SOS. Meet at Dads ASAP

I was thankful he'd dropped me off there this morning, so I didn't have to give the address. Who knew if they'd tapped my phone? That was something the cops did, right? Especially the feds? I shook my head and wondered how far down the conspiracy theory hole I needed to go. The drive to Dad's house was quick, and I sat on the couch and waited for Steel to show, wondering how my life had gotten flushed down the shitter so quickly.

CHAPTER 44

Remi

As soon as Steel walked through the door I was up off the couch and pacing. He eyed me warily, standing with his hands in his pockets. The look on his face was all I needed to see in order to know he had an idea about why I'd had him come over.

"Why were you in California last week, Steel?" I snapped. I tried to keep the anger out of my voice, but it was hard. He'd knowingly fucked with my dad's company. There was no way he was clueless about what was going on.

"The feds raided the Long Beach chapter of our MC." He said it flat out. I paused, staring at him incredulously. I had kind of expected him to deny it or beat around the bush.

"Did you know they seized one of my trucks?"

He nodded, still quietly watching me.

I shook my head in disbelief. "You didn't think that was worth mentioning to me?"

"I had to get down there and take care of everything as quickly as I could. I thought I'd have time to get back and give you a head's up."

I sank onto the couch in defeat. A wary look passed over his face.

"So… let me get this straight. You pursue me." I narrow my eyes at him. "Sign up your business to work with mine, knowing that you're getting me involved in illegal shit, without telling me that part. Still, you move forward with having us unknowingly do illegal things for your club all while knowing that this company is the last remaining thing I have of my dad."

His face had gone stone-cold at this point, but I was on a roll. "You find out that the other half of your operation has gotten caught by the feds and choose to run down and take care of them while leaving my ass to hang in the wind?"

Now his face wasn't cold, it was hot with fury.

"Do I have that about right, *Logan*?"

Shock filtered through the rage on his face at my use of his name, but he didn't reply.

"Because what it's looking like to me… is you decided you wanted me and put on a big show to "claim me". Once you had me, you chose your club's wants over mine, by choosing your business over mine. Then, rather than tell me, you just hide in your club like a coward. Once again you helped them instead of me. Correct?"

"No." His jaw was clenching. It looked like he was going to crack his teeth if he ground them together any harder. I didn't feel sorry for him in the least though. I was too pissed and way too hurt. I'd had plenty of time to think and come to these conclusions while I'd been sitting here waiting for him, replaying the day and what the Agent had told me. I'd been right to be wary of him. Instead, I'd let my guard down and he'd crushed me.

"No? No?! I'm not right?" I glared at him. "What am I not right about, Logan?" I stood up and crossed my arms over my chest. He ran his hand over his head. I could tell he was frustrated but didn't know how to fix what he'd done.

"You come first."

I laughed in disbelief. "Well, you sure as fuck could have fooled me there. When did you put me first in any of those situations?"

"Okay, I fucked up. I'm not used to juggling the club and someone else. I should have used a different company and not gotten you involved. I messed up there. But as far as going to California, I had to do that. Cade asked me to, and I had…" His words were sharp, clipped barks. He was so pissed he could barely speak. I wasn't sure if he was more pissed at me, himself, or the situation we found ourselves in.

"And whatever Cade wants, he gets. Right?" I strode forward and poked Steel in the chest. In the back of my head, I realized it was a bad idea to literally be poking a pissed-off bear, but I was so mad I couldn't help it. "I'll always come second to the club. To Cade. To Gunnar. To the members." He grabbed my wrist to stop my finger from pile driving every point into his chest.

"I can understand you putting Riggs first. He is your actual brother. Hell, you know what?" I laughed without an ounce of humor. "I guess I can understand you putting the club and Cade first too. They've been your family forever. I'm just some girl you talked into bed. I get it, Steel. I fully get where I stand with you." He frowned at me, shook his head, and started to speak.

"No!" I yelled at him. "I don't want to hear it. You just ruined my dad's company. I'm probably going to jail." His mouth fell open in shock.

"Oh yeah, they're charging me with 189 USAC blah blah blah… whatever it was, multiple counts of felonies for stealing and transporting stolen shit, Steel. I'm going to lose everything I have, all because you couldn't be bothered to warn me. The fucking lady cop basically told me that the women were going to have fun fucking me in prison." I couldn't help the humorless laugh that spilled out. I was so beyond stressed by this point.

"But I guess a lot of this is my fault too. I knew what I was doing. I knew you were into illegal shit and I still got involved with you." I shook my head, angry at myself when a tear spilled down my cheek. I didn't want to cry over him. I certainly didn't want him to see it. I yanked my hand out of his grip and moved back across the room before he could stop me.

"You accused my uncle of wanting to steal my business from me, but it turns out you're no different. You just wanted to use me. Soon, I'll be in jail and you'll be shipping parts through someone else."

He stepped forward, but I kept moving backward. "Don't touch me. Don't call me. You can report back to Cade that I erased the manifests off of our computers before the feds could execute their search warrants, so I'm sure you guys will be fine." I wrapped my arms around my waist. I was so tired. The last two days were bearing down on me. Grief, anger, and overwhelming sadness were crashing over me in waves.

"Get out."

"No." Steel glared at me. "You had your chance to get it all out. Now it's my turn."

I shook my head. "No, Steel. You had your chance, five days ago. You had your chance up until I got that phone call this morning." I took a few more steps back when he growled and started moving toward me again.

"Get the fuck out. I don't want to see you anymore."

Steel took a page out of my book. He turned and slammed his fist into the wall. Unlike when I did it, his fist plowed straight through the drywall. I hadn't even made a dent.

He lunged for me and I wasn't fast enough, he caged me between the wall and his body. His hand, the one he'd put through the wall, yanked my hair, forcing my head to tilt back. Our eyes clashed. "I'm not going anywhere, Remi. You're mine."

"Fuck you, Steel," my voice cracked. "You don't get to screw me over and then claim me." He growled at me in frustration. I couldn't help it, I laughed. "Did you seriously just growl at me? Do people actually do that?" My anger was turning into pure condescension.

He must have realized he wasn't going to get through my anger with words because his mouth crashed down on mine. I had to fight to bite back the moan. It didn't matter if I was pissed off at him. Hell, the added emotions almost made the vicious kiss hotter. But I wasn't going to give in. It was a savage struggle between my mind and my body as I let Steel kiss me while I tried to regain control.

Finally, once I had, I shoved him as hard as I could. It only rocked him backward the barest amount. But it was enough. His lips left mine, and he stared down at me, breathing hard. His eyes were piercing. Steel was as angry and hurt as I was.

What did he have to be hurt about? I'd been nothing but loyal to him. I saw some sort of decision flash in his eyes and his head started moving toward me again.

Oh no, I muttered to myself. I couldn't let him touch me. The spell he managed to weave over my body, my mind... *your heart,* that stupid inner voice whispered, was too encompassing when he touched me. It was too easy to lose myself in him and I'd just end up forgiving him. I quickly brought my knee up, and it connected hard and fast with his balls. He grunted in pain, the breath leaving his body as he cupped himself and leaned against the wall for support. I hadn't held back. I still only had a few minutes before he'd recover. I pushed past him and ran up the stairs.

Fuck. I could already hear him behind me. A man that big shouldn't be that fast. Racing into my father's bedroom, I thanked years of playing sports for my speed and coordination or there would be no way I'd have stayed ahead of him. I managed to get into the bathroom ahead of him and flipped the lock right before Steel slammed into the door. I stepped back a few steps.

"Remi! Let me in," he roared. I could hear him panting. Even now, with how pissed he was, I wasn't worried he would hurt me or retaliate for that knee to the junk. It wasn't the way he operated. Not physically anyway. He'd shredded my heart though. I cursed myself for a fool. I'd only known him for a little over a month. How had I let him so close to my heart in such a short amount of time? His fist slammed into the door and I had to bite back a yelp. I hoped the door would hold out.

"Go away and leave me alone, Steel."

"I'd never hurt you, Remi."

"You already have," I said quietly, but I knew he heard me.

"You're more than a girl I talked into bed..." When I didn't say anything, I heard him muttering. Then he said louder. "I'll fix this," he didn't shout it, he said it in a matter-of-fact tone, but his deep voice carried it through the door louder than any shout.

I heard him move away from the door and I let out the breath I was holding. The stress of my mother's visit, the knowledge that my father had been paying her off, the fact that my boyfriend had lied to me and used my company, and now having the FBI gunning for me was all too much for me to take. Breaking up with Steel was just the final straw. I slid down to the floor and finally let myself cry the tears I'd been holding in for the last two days.

CHAPTER 45

Remi

I woke up the next morning and frowned at the ceiling. Was that mine? I rolled over and groaned as I finally remembered the events from yesterday. The meeting with the FBI, the fight with Steel, crying my eyes out for most of the night before finally crawling into Dad's bed in our old house. I grabbed my phone to check my messages. Three emails on the University's email server from different professors. I ignored them.

I'd already figured out that I was close to failing one of my courses, even if I aced the final. That was all going to have to get put on hold until I figured out everything with Rhonda and the FBI. If it meant I had to retake the course, then so be it. With that grim thought, I ignored the texts and missed calls from Steel and opened an email from Mr. Jeffries.

"Shit!" I jumped off the bed and started searching for my keys. He'd responded that he could meet this morning at eleven a.m., and it was already nine-thirty. I needed to get home, shower, change, eat, and get over to the bank so I could figure out if Dad really had been paying Rhonda. I wouldn't put it past my sleazy mother to be lying.

Finally, I found my keys laying near the sofa downstairs. After locking up the house I looked around the quiet neighborhood before driving home. I had an uneasy feeling that the next few days were going to be the second-worst of my life. What could be worse than the death of my father, after all? Jail, blackmail, and heartbreak definitely didn't compare.

I walked through our front door and tossed my keys on the counter. "Anyone home?"

Anna's head popped up from the couch in the living room.

"Hey, Rem!" She looked me up and down. I'm sure I looked like hell since I'd been crying for hours the night before, then slept in my clothes. "How did your talk with Steel go?" The way she said it and the hesitant tone of voice told me she already knew it went badly.

"I broke up with him." I walked up and crossed my arms over my stomach, a gesture that Julie would have loved to point out was a defensive, protective one, even if unconscious. Her psychologist's brain would have wanted to pick apart why my mind and body were obviously at war with the act of breaking up with the man that I had been falling in love with. *Was already in love with*, whispered the annoying little voice in my head.

"Back off, bitch," I muttered.

"What?" Anna's eyes were huge as she stared at me in shock.

"Sorry, not you."

She blinked a few times then stood up and felt my forehead as though checking for a fever. "Remi, I'm worried about you." I slapped her hand away. "No, really. We're all worried about you. About all of this. What can we do to help?"

I pulled Anna into an abrupt hug. She yelped at the sudden movement but then relaxed into it after a moment.

"You guys are the best friends I could ever hope for. More than friends really, sisters. I don't know if there is anything that can be done right now. But if there is, I'll let you know. Okay?"

She nodded, chin bumping my shoulder as we clung to each other. I broke away reluctantly.

"I have to shower. I need to go meet Mr. Jeffries down at the bank." I shook my head at her questioning look. "I'll tell you guys about it later but I'm going to be late if I don't get moving. I have to go talk to Uncle Caleb after that, so I need to shower and change, badly." We parted ways as I trotted up the stairs and down the hall to get ready for my meeting. All through the next hour, I tried to come up with a game plan in my head for how I was going to handle the next few meetings in my day.

My game plan was failing massively. The first bullet point had been to find out that my mother was lying, and Dad hadn't been paying her off. Okay, maybe that wasn't realistic? But was it realistic to just believe it when your loser mother shows up in your life and tells you a crazy story like that? I sighed and looked down at the printout that Mr. Jeffries had handed me. Rhonda had lied, sort of. Last year was one hundred thousand. Before that Dad had paid her eighty thousand, the very first year had only been ten thousand. Each year the business got bigger and she had been paid more.

There was no way Dad could have easily afforded that amount in the first few years of business. Businesses were rarely profitable in the first three years after starting up. That's why the payments in the first years were so small. Rhonda was greedy but seemed smart enough to demand what the business could afford.

I could thank my college classes for teaching me something. So why was he paying her?

This was the first time since his death that I wished I could speak to him more than just to hear his voice. I felt tears pricking at my eyes. I missed him so much and I wondered if he was watching the mess my life had become and was disappointed? I hoped not, because I was doing my best. I took a deep breath and met Mr. Jeffries's curious gaze.

"Is there a memo on any of these? To say what the payments were for?"

"I'm sorry Ms. Mackenzie there isn't."

I nodded. I didn't figure he'd have put down 'for blackmailer' in the memo but I was curious. I made a mental note to contact Mrs. Clarence, my accountant, to see what these payments were being placed under.

"Thank you very much for all your help today, Mr. Jeffries." We made pleasant, if brief, small talk before I hightailed it out of there. I wasn't looking forward to speaking with my uncle, but it needed to happen. He was beyond pissed at me for continuing to see Steel after he told me I had to break it off. Then I had blown him off after the FBI came yesterday. Yeah, it was going to be an uncomfortable day.

That was pretty much the only kind of day I had any more.

We needed to figure out what we were going to do about the FBI, and what needed to be done to get our truck back. The missing driver had come back a few hours after my fight with Steel. I'd paused my crying jag long enough to answer Uncle Caleb's call and set up a meeting for this afternoon. I pulled into the lot at Mackenzie's Trucking and just sat looking at the storefront. I was so proud of this company and not only because it was Dad's place. I loved it as my own too, so much that it added a whole other level of terror when I thought of losing it.

So, I was doubly petrified of messing up. It was like a self-fulfilling prophecy, though. Worried about destroying that which I loved so much that I destroyed that which I loved. I slammed a hand down on the wheel of the Camaro.

Enough Rem. It was time to stop feeling sorry for myself and just do what needed to be done to fix it. It would take time, but I was willing to put in the work and money.

I was fairly proud of myself when I only cringed a little when I met Uncle Caleb's disapproving and pissed off look. I was absolutely going to get an ass chewing. I knew he loved me, but I also knew he was angry and frustrated that I was 'mixed up' with Steel, as he so aptly put it. It drove me nuts when he treated me like I was still a kid. I might be young, but he was trusting me enough to put an entire company on my shoulders.

He should trust me with my own love life too. I followed him into the back with all the enthusiasm of a prisoner walking toward the gallows.

CHAPTER 46

Steel

The banging on my door made my head throb, and I groaned. Flipping onto my stomach I stuffed my pillows over my head to drown out the sound. I was in the middle of wishing whichever asshole had woken me up a quick and untimely death when they started yelling on top of the banging.

"Steel!"

Shit. That was Riggs yelling, but I could hear both Cade and Gunnar arguing with him in the hall about just busting in the door. I pulled my head out from under the pillows and looked at the clock. Six-thirty a.m. *Wednesday? Did that say Wednesday? What happened to Tuesday?*

I was pretty sure I was still drunk from the bender I went on after I left Remi's place. I rolled out of bed and cursed when I didn't catch myself in time and landed on my ass next to the bed.

I managed to stagger to my feet and pull on jeans and padded to the door, bare-chested and barefoot. Whipping open the door I glared at my three best friends. I ignored the looks I got from them. There was no need to look in the mirror to know I looked fucking rough; I felt it.

"Fuck off." I started to shut the door, only for it to catch on the boot that Riggs stuck through at the last moment.

God damn it. I just wanted to be left alone so I could go back to sleep. My brother wrenched the door out of my hands and opened it, letting the other two stroll in. I growled and went to check the coffee maker. I always had it set to be ready by six-thirty. If I was going to have to listen to these assholes this early in the morning, I was going to need caffeine.

All three sat at the island and watched quietly as I fixed my first cup. Finally, I turned around and returned their stares. I didn't offer them any. They were family, if they wanted it, they could get some themselves. I wasn't feeling nice enough to wait on them.

"What the fuck do you want?"

"You look rough, bro." I rolled my eyes at Cade's brilliant deduction.

"What happened?" That came from Gunnar. I narrowed my eyes at him. I'd only gotten the barest story out of him in California, about what had happened with him and Bridget and that was only because of the fucking nomads, to begin with. I didn't feel like fucking discussing my feelings.

Although, I did need to tell them about the FBI going after Mackenzie's. It didn't have to be right this minute though. I remained stubbornly mute and crossed an arm over my bare chest and lifted my cup to take a long drink from it.

"Logan."

Fuck. My brother never used my given name anymore. Unless he wasn't messing around. I met his gaze.

"We didn't have time to catch up when you got back into town between you picking Remi up, meeting Bass, and then disappearing again." I nodded. After I'd dropped Remi off, I'd gotten a text from

Bass, saying we needed to meet. He hadn't had a lot of concrete evidence, but he'd found out that somehow the Lycans had known about our Long Beach chapter getting busted by the FBI, and which of our members had left town to deal with it.

Bass had still been trying to figure out how they knew what our club was up to, but he had wanted to inform me right away that we had a snitch. I'd been able to pass it on to Cade before I'd gotten the text to meet Remi. Fuck, Monday had been a shitty day. The idea that one of our brothers had betrayed us made me feel sick. Having the FBI sniffing around Remi pissed me off. Remi trying to break shit off with me made me want to find out who caused all of this and take out all of this anger and frustration on them. All in all, I was in a pretty foul mood.

"We figured out who was giving information to the Lycans." I straightened up and waited for Cade to continue. "It was Red and Ty."

"I'll fucking kill them." I slammed my coffee cup on the island.

All three men were shaking their heads. "We haven't found them yet." I frowned at that.

"We got that out of Rhett, yesterday." Ty and Red had been kicked out of the Vikings after they started that fight with Gunnar before we left for California. We hadn't considered it was them leaking information because they were already gone before we'd left. But Rhett hadn't been a part of that fight, so he hadn't been ejected with them, even though the nomad brother had shown up at the same time as the others.

"Where is Rhett?"

"We got everything out of him we could, then we took care of him." Riggs picked up the coffee cup I had set down and finished it off.

"And we still don't know where the other two are?"

"No, but once we find them, we'll kill them." Cade gave me a dark look, and it calmed me a little. "We looked for them yesterday and last night. Anyone who wasn't looking last night is out looking now." I grimaced because I was drinking myself stupid yesterday and last night and I wasn't out helping right now. Cade caught the look.

"Obviously, you have something going on Steel." They all looked at me expectantly.

I scrubbed my hands through my hair. "One of Al's guys managed to get rid of the manifest before the FBI made that raid." They all nodded, that wasn't news to them. "Since everything was on the Mackenzie truck already, they weren't going to be able to pin anything solid on our club, so now they're going after Remi personally, and her company." All three cursed.

"Two Agents met with her Monday and listed off a few different charges they were coming after her with and it freaked her out pretty badly. They were stupid enough to leave her alone for a few minutes though, and she deleted the manifest from the company records. She doesn't keep hard copies except for what she sends with the truckers. So, there is nothing to link us with the crime. But that puts her holding all of the stolen property."

I put my hands on the edge of the island and leaned all of my weight on them and looked up at the ceiling instead of meeting the guilty and angry looks of my brothers. "We had a pretty big blow-up about it. She's convinced we're done and that she's going to prison."

They all started talking and arguing at once and I couldn't help but laugh. The outside world may think we're just a bunch of criminals but if you fuck with our families, we fight hard to protect our own, and Remi was ours now. Sure, she thought she was done with me. Done with us. She was wrong.

"You know we won't let her, or Mackenzie's take that fall," Cade promised, and I nodded at him, in thanks.

"As far as her being done, I assume that's bullshit?"

"Who knows?" I muttered darkly.

My brother snorted. I shot him a glare. "Grow some balls, Steel. Or is Remi carrying them around in her purse?" I clenched my fists. I wasn't in the mood for his version of humor.

"Fuck you, Riggs…"

He cut me off. "No, if you're going to be a pussy and let her get away because of something small like this, then fuck you." He stood up, came around the island and got in my face. "And fuck her if she is going to treat you..." My temper snapped. I grabbed my brother by the shirt and spun us around, slamming him into the fridge.

"Don't fucking talk about her like that," I snarled in his face.

"Oh yeah, why not?" He taunted.

"Because I'll kick the shit out of you. No one talks about the woman I love..." I stopped mid-sentence. My shocked brain missed the smug grin on Riggs's face. I noticed it once he spoke again though.

"Yeah, that's what we figured." He shot a look over my shoulder at the others. I plowed my fist into his jaw. The crunch was satisfying, even as the pain washed over my knuckles. My brother's cursing was even more so.

"Seriously Steel, you can't let her back off," Gunnar said quietly, but it calmed Riggs and me down instantly. Cade gazed quietly at Gunnar. We all knew he was hurting over Bridget, but he wouldn't let any of us in to help. It wasn't going to be as easy as them helping me with Remi. Before I could say anything in response, my phone rang. The readout told me Bass was calling. I shot Cade and Riggs a look and answered.

"Yeah." I put it on speaker.

"Hey. I don't have time. Ty and Red just showed up where I am." Bass was talking in low tones, which meant the rest of the Lycans were around. It also meant it wasn't safe for him to be making this call.

"Have Rat trace my cell and get over here as soon as you can." The call disconnected. Gunnar had already run off to wake up Rat. I ran into my room and pulled on a t-shirt, socks, boots, and my cut. I smelled like a booze factory but there was no helping that. I grabbed my wallet, gun, and keys and we all ran down the hall to Rat's room.

I waited impatiently while Rat pulled up the location of Bass's phone through the find my-Apple app. Gunnar seemed to have some idea of what he was doing but that technology bullshit was so far outside of the scope of what I was capable of it wasn't even funny. Instead, I just bided my time, imagining what I was going to do once I got my hands on our former nomad brothers.

"There. It stopped at that warehouse."

We all leaned in and looked at the map that he had pulled up on his computer.

"Let's go." We were all running for the parking lot before I realized I had left my damn phone. Cade and Riggs made the calls to get as many of our brothers to meet us there with as many guns as possible. There was no telling how many Lycans were going to be there or what we'd be walking in on.

CHAPTER 47

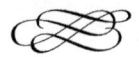

Remi

Groaning, I rolled over and smacked my phone as it happily started chirping at five a.m. I'd stayed the night at my dad's place again. My life was a tornado right now and being here was helping to ground me. I had an early morning meeting with Uncle Caleb and Preston this morning to go over a preliminary game plan for what to do about the FBI Agents. Preston spent all day yesterday going over the case notes he'd gotten and the charges they planned to bring against me.

I showered and got ready for the day as quickly as I could. By five forty-five, I stepped outside and turned to lock the door. I took a deep breath of the clean, crisp air. I may not be a morning person but there was something about the cool air right as the sun was starting to rise, which made you feel alive.

That's when cold, hard hands wrapped around my head and face and I sucked in a breath to scream.

"Scream and I'll stab you."

The sound strangled in my throat. The guy's rank breath tickled my cheek, and I froze. Was I seriously being kidnapped in front of my house in broad daylight?

Well, in early morning daylight.

Suddenly Steel's deep voice rumbled in my ear and I remembered our sparring lesson from a few weeks ago.

"What would you do if I grabbed you like this?" One of his arms had snaked around my waist and the other had gone around my neck.

This guy had both arms around my neck, but I think the principal would be the same.

Better than not fighting. I had to take the chance that the guy would be caught off guard and wouldn't have time to make good on his threat to stab me if he did have a knife. Steel always seemed to have multiple knives and guns on him, so I doubted this guy was any different.

I quickly raised onto my tiptoes then brought my hands up between his arm and my neck. I quickly gripped his wrist, dropped my shoulder, and sent the asshole sailing over my shoulder and onto his back. I gave him three or four hard, sharp kicks to the chest and ribs. Sergio would have been proud.

I broke into a run, sprinting toward my car. If it had just been him, or I hadn't wasted time with kicking him, I would have made it. *But they were such good kicks.* I saw a dark blur racing toward me out of the corner of my eye. I was embarrassed to admit I squealed as I tried to dodge the second guy who was running toward me. He tackled me, sending us sprawling to the ground. I groaned when his weight came crashing down on me. Then, I couldn't even do that because he knocked the wind out of me.

Worse than that the asshole had flung a leg over me and was now straddling my chest as I wheezed and struggled to breathe. He had something in his hand, and I realized it was a cloth that he was pouring something on.

Fuck. Darkness was creeping in from the edges of my vision. He wasn't going to need to use that on me if he didn't let me breathe soon. I didn't know if he was actually cutting off my air or if I was panicking but either way I started scratching and punching at the man as hard as I could.

I felt some smug satisfaction when one of my punches connected with his crotch and he grunted in pain. Unfortunately, from underneath him, I had no power behind my hits and as soon as that cloth touched my nose and mouth it was lights out.

CHAPTER 48

Remi

"Remi... Remi!"

I groaned; my head was throbbing.

"Remi, wake the fuck up."

I huffed and pried an eye open. That was a really sweet way to wake a girl up. Both eyes snapped open as I looked at the guy sitting in front of me. I gasped. He was tied to a chair. I looked down. Well fuck. I was also tied to a chair, and we were facing each other. I looked back up at him and winced. I sure hoped I didn't look like him though.

Bass grinned at me and his lip split open wider, sending blood trickling down his chin. "You alright?"

I eyed him. "Better than you... I think?" I thought about it but other than a little soreness from being tackled I didn't feel like I'd had my face pulverized.

Bass, on the other hand, had two black eyes, a split lip, and more bruises than I wanted to count and that was just from what I could see on his face. Normally he was a gorgeous guy. Not so much right now. "What happened to you?"

"Lycans."

"Huh?" I looked around. Was he talking about werewolves? Maybe he had a concussion? I remember Julie's sister, Ming, saying that people with really bad concussions could hallucinate.

"The Lycans. They are a rival MC."

Oh, okay, that made more sense than werewolves.

"Why are you here?"

"I was working undercover. Cover got blown," he said.

Something told me there was more to it than that, but I didn't bother to ask more questions. There had been more than one phone call that Steel had taken in private and he never discussed club stuff with me. Well, except for what had happened in California. But that had directly involved both me and Dad's company. My face must have darkened because Bass's brows shot up.

"Any idea why I am here?"

"Because I warned you that you had three days to get me my money." I groaned when Rhonda's nasally voice came from somewhere behind me. I met Bass's gaze.

"Is there a skinny, ugly, coke head looking woman standing behind me? Probably five-sixish? Dark, greasy, short hair? Wearing jeans that are too tight and a shirt that is too short?"

Bass snickered at my description of Rhonda, then winced when his lip split further.

"Your girl sure has a mouth on her, Rhonda." A man stepped into my view and I sneered. He was probably about thirty and younger than my mom by at least ten years.

Gross. Mom had been a young mother and my dad had been quite a bit older than her. But if this guy was her boyfriend? She'd gone the opposite direction after leaving my dad and robbed the cradle. I eyed the patches on his vest that said Lycans, President, and Blaze.

Blaze grabbed my face roughly in his hand and turned it this way, then that, studying it. "It's a pretty mouth, I'll give you that though."

He said it low but the pinched look on my mom's face when she stepped into view told me she'd heard it.

"She looks like her father, Blaze," She sneered at him. He just raised a brow but didn't take his eyes off me.

"Handsome man then." He grinned. The way he was looking at me made my skin crawl. Finally, he moved away from me and pulled my mother up against him, and kissed her. With tongue. *Gag.*

"Where's my money, Remi?" She sounded breathless once they finally broke off the kiss.

I glared at the woman who I was unlucky enough to have to call my mother. "I'm not giving you shit. I'll die before I give you anything."

"That can be arranged," she snarled, stepping forward threateningly. I raised my chin. It wasn't much of a defiant gesture since I was still tied tight to this stupid chair, but it was all I had.

"Now, now ladies. Let's take a breath. Luckily, I thought ahead. We have some visitors who should be here soon."

I frowned at Blaze.

"Did you two idiots deliver the message?"

I saw Bass stiffen and craned my neck around, trying to see who he was looking at. It was really hard to do when I was stuck in this chair and they were standing behind me, but I saw enough to have my blood run cold. It was the guys from that first party at the Viking's clubhouse. The ones who had been dragging Bridget and me upstairs. They sauntered closer and smiled at me.

"Sure did boss. Told them to be here by eight." The taller one licked his lips as he eyeballed me. So much grossness was happening in this warehouse this morning. I assumed it was a warehouse. It was a cold, steel building. There was nothing in it but rows of wooden crates and cargo containers stacked along the walls and throughout, creating a maze in the large space. It was hard to tell just how big the place was because everything was sectioned off by these containers. There were no sounds of traffic nearby. *Definitely a warehouse.*

I glanced back over and saw more men in leather cuts wandering in from behind me where a lonely row of wooden crates was all that separated us from the metal door. All around us to the sides and in front, the shipping containers created pathways through the building. If we were going to get out of here and had to go through those paths, it'd be like mice in a maze. The men all gathered around us. I knew from their cuts they were all Lycans, except for the two Vikings. I glanced at Bass and saw the grim look on his face. This wasn't good.

"Fucking traitors," Bass growled at the Vikings. They both grinned at him, completely amused at both his anger and at seeing him sitting there tied up. Another man, built like the Rock, walked up and punched Bass directly in the face. His head snapped back so hard I thought it would break his spine.

"Leave him alone!" I glared at the guy when he turned around and narrowed his eyes at me. They dragged up and down my body, but I held his gaze when it settled on mine.

"So, you're Steel's little piece of ass, huh?" If looks could murder, the guy would fall dead at my feet but I didn't bother to respond to him.

"Might have to keep you for myself once I kill him." I sucked in a breath at the nauseating thought of that. I looked down at his vest to the patch with his name, Reaper. *Great.* According to the other patch, he was the Vice President of this MC. I looked over at Bass. His poor face couldn't take much more today. The visitors they had coming today had to be the Vikings. Who else would come here for us?

CHAPTER 49

Remi

I had my answer entirely too soon for my liking. A shrill voice cut through the men's low murmuring and I groaned. I'd know that voice anywhere. What the fuck was she doing here?

Scratch that, I thought as I looked on in horror, *what the fuck were they doing here?*

Bridget, Anna, Julie, and Uncle Caleb all walked into the warehouse. Uncle Caleb was the only one who had the good sense to look scared. The girls looked beyond pissed. This was my worst nightmare. All they needed to do was add Ming and Steel and every last person I cared about on this planet would be here, in danger.

"Rhonda!" Bridget called again. "You sent your scraggly ass bikers to our home to tell us you had kidnapped your own daughter, and that you were ransoming her for money?" Bridget stopped in front of my mother and about ten of those 'scraggly ass bikers' and tapped her Jimmy Choos.

We're all going to die. Then I had to inwardly chuckle at how many times that thought had crossed my mind because of something Bridget had done or said in the past. The only upside was the look on everyone's face, including Bass's at Bridget's announcement.

Anna stepped forward and poked a finger into my mother's chest. "You have some serious mental issues, you know that? The fact that you would treat your own daughter this way?" Blaze stepped forward and shoved Anna backward, away from Rhonda. Before he could continue forward however Julie tossed a gym bag down in front of them.

"It's all there. We'll take them and be on our way now." She nodded at me and Bass. Ever the pragmatic one, Julie was trying to de-escalate the situation. Anna looked petrified, but she was still willing to harass my mother. Bridget didn't even have the good sense to look scared. The look Bass gave Julie had me grinning. If the night of the frat party hadn't convinced me he had a crush on her, I'd for sure know it now.

Blaze shook his head. "Only Rhonda's daughter is part of this exchange." He snapped his fingers and a couple of his guys jumped forward to grab the bag.

"Well, we're not leaving him." Julie crossed her arms over her chest and glared at the Lycan President.

"Then I guess none of you are leaving." That had come from Reaper. He pulled out a gun, and I saw my friends give each other a look. Now they all looked as scared as Uncle Caleb did.

"Put that away. We gave you what you wanted. We'll be taking my niece and leaving. You can have that guy." Uncle Caleb shot Bass a short look. I looked pleadingly at him and then at Bass who just shook his head.

"Go, Remi. I won't let any of you die for me."

"Change of plans." We all looked over at Blaze, who now held his own weapon. "Turns out Reaper has taken a fancy to her." Blaze gestured at me with the gun. "If you go now, the four of you can leave. But we'll be keeping her and the money."

The men in the warehouse chuckled. The girls and my uncle looked horrified, but I wasn't really surprised that they were pulling something like this. Why would they let me go when they could keep me and keep making these four give them a steady supply of money?

I met my uncle's gaze. "I'm so sorry Uncle Caleb. For everything. Just get them out of here." I looked into the eyes of each of the girls who could have been my sisters and tried to tell them, silently, what they meant to me. I had no idea what these guys would do to me but just in case I wanted some form of goodbye.

Reaper stepped over and shoved his gun in the back of his pants and pulled out a knife, flicking it open inches from my face. I couldn't help it, I yelped. Could you blame a girl? He chuckled then sawed through the ropes at my feet then hands. He hauled me up and against him before putting the knife away and pulling his gun back out. I tried to struggle, but he was built like a brick shit house and he ended up pointing the barrel of the gun at me. That had me stilling pretty quickly.

"You two. Untie him and bring him with us. If you kill him, I'll kill you. He's mine." Blaze ordered the nomads to handle Bass. Uncle Caleb and the girls were still standing in front of us hesitantly. My uncle was looking between us and the back door that led outside.

"Please, Uncle Caleb. Go."

We all paused. I saw a determination come into my uncle's eyes. Before I ever got the chance to figure out if he was going to leave or do something stupid though, all hell broke loose.

CHAPTER 50

Steel

Gunnar crept back toward us where we all waited by a back entrance to the warehouse.

"There's about twelve of them, all armed. Ty and Red have Bass. Reaper has Remi and I don't know why they are fucking here but Bridget, Anna, Julie, and Remi's Uncle Caleb are all in there too. There are a few rows of wooden boxes stacked along the back between us and them. All along the sides, there are huge rows of shipping containers."

"Wait. Who are Anna and Julie?" Riggs looked between Gunnar and me. Cade looked just as confused. They knew who Bridget was, and just saying Remi's uncle took care of who Caleb was but that left the other two as fair game.

"Remi and Bridget's best friends and roommates."

"Right." Our whole group looked grim. Instead of two of our people in there, we now had six. The odds of us getting in there and getting all of them out without anyone getting shot or killed was going down.

"We need to get in there. They're about to move," Axel hissed at us. He'd taken up the position by the window that Gunnar had vacated.

Unfortunately, we couldn't come in from different sides. We were going to have to funnel in from this one door. It was going to be dangerous, so we were going to have to move fast. We all crouched next to the door and Riggs counted us down. As soon as the countdown ended, I kicked in the door and Gunnar went in first, firing off a few rounds. He wasn't aiming at anything, in particular, just making noise to cover our entry and hopefully distract them as we fanned out across the aisles.

With Gunnar laying down cover fire, the rest of us got in the door and past the open area until we were behind the crates. Riggs went next, then me, Cade, and the rest of our crew scrambled in, all of us running for cover and firing off rounds as we could. Luckily, I saw that everyone dove for cover across the room. That was better than an unlucky shot taking out one of the girls or Bass. Remi's uncle, I wasn't as worried about. There wasn't any love lost between us, but I still didn't want him hurt, if only for her sake.

"Blaze!" Cade glanced over at me and nodded toward the left side of the room, indicating for me to split off to that side. I nodded and kept crouched down as I moved along the stack of wooden crates we were hiding behind, heading for an opening to a path between shipping containers. "Let our people go and maybe you'll get out of this alive."

Blaze's laugh bounced through the building. His crew echoed it like hyenas. "Not going to happen Cade. They're ours now and soon enough we'll be coming for the rest of your pathetic club."

I glanced to my right, Axel, Drew, and Trip were right on my ass, coming around the left side. I saw Riggs, Gunnar, and Scout going around the right. That left Cade and the remaining two of our guys to go straight down the middle. If you counted Bass, we were still a man down from the Lycans count, but these were the only men who'd been close enough to get here in time. It was possible some of our guys could ride in during the middle of the fight but for now, we'd have to make do.

"Try to take us on, and we'll wipe you off the map and take over your territory." An angry shout answered Cade's words. We were all listening intently. We didn't care what was being said. We were just trying to get a bead on where these guys were hiding. This warehouse was huge, and it had a lot of rows of boxes and shipping containers stacked around in it that were blocking our view but also distorting sound and making it hard to tell where anyone was.

Once we'd come into the building, they'd all scattered down pathways, disappearing into different sections of it. The Lycans, having spread out as we had, could be anywhere. Cade was trying to draw them out the best he could so we could pick them off.

I had my Glock in my right hand, and I reached down and grabbed my switchblade and palmed it in my left. We slowly snuck around the side of a shipping container and came upon two Lycans who were facing away from us, creeping toward the sound of Cade's voice where he was once again taunting Blaze. I quietly stuffed my gun into the back of my jeans and tossed my knife into my right hand. I saw Axel doing the same out of the corner of my eye.

He glanced at me and at my nod, we both lunged forward. He slit the throat of his target quickly and quietly. I didn't have the right angle for that so instead, I slid the tip of my knife into the side of his neck. My knife sliced through like butter. Both men bled out so quickly they didn't have time to make any noise. I'd grabbed onto the Lycan to prevent his body from hitting the ground and notifying anyone nearby of the struggle.

I quickly laid him down and glanced up as Drew and Trip continued moving forward ahead of us. I cleaned my blade on the Lycan's jeans then took his gun and shoved that into the pouch inside of my cut. Axel did the same before we moved on, following the direction the others had gone. That evened up our odds a little, I thought grimly.

By the time we caught up with them, they'd taken out another Lycan. I briefly wondered how my brother and Gunnar were doing going down the right-hand side. We kept moving forward until we reached the row of wooden crates at the very front of the warehouse. I realized that when we'd kept moving, we'd lost Drew and Trip. They must have turned down a different path. It was like one of those fun houses in here-the kind with the creepy clowns and mirrors?

A movement to the right of us had me and Axel freezing but then I relaxed slightly when I recognized Julie. I crept up behind her and clapped a hand over her mouth from behind, muffling her scream, as I wrapped my other arm around her.

"Shhhh, it's Steel." She instantly stopped struggling, relaxing in my arms. Still speaking softly, I turned to Axel. "Take Julie back the way we came and get them back to where Cade is at. If we can, we'll get her outside." Axel hesitated. He clearly didn't want to leave me alone. "I'll be fine. I'm going to look for Remi."

"No way. I'm going with you to go get Remi." Julie glared at me and crossed her arms over her chest. I shook my head at her in disbelief.

"Do you have a gun?" She shook her head. "If you had a gun would you know how to use it?" She hesitated but shook her head again. "If you had a gun and knew how to use it, would you be willing to kill somebody?" Julie's arms dropped in defeat.

"I'll go with him," She whispered and pointed at Axel. He didn't look any happier than Julie to be leaving but they did.

Once they'd taken the path to bring them back toward the front of the warehouse, I crept forward down a new aisle. Gunfire rang out, and I ran around the end of the box and burst out into an open area.

There were three people tangled up on the ground slugging it out and scrambling for a gun a few feet away. As I ran up, I saw Scout drag a Lycan back from the gun but that left the second Lycan open to scramble forward on his hands and knees to grab it. Just as he brought the weapon up, I aimed and pulled the trigger. Red bloomed across his chest. He looked down in surprise and then at me while he swung his arm toward me. I pulled the trigger three more times before the gun fell from his grip.

I heard the crack of flesh meeting flesh and looked behind me.

Scout was still fighting with the Lycan he'd dragged off. Two more Lycans, having heard the shots, came out from another pathway and ran toward me. I fired off a few rounds and managed to clip one of the men on the arm, but they tackled me.

I pulled my knife out prepared to fight both men laying on top of me, but someone dragged one of them off of me before the fight even started. I let out a sigh of relief when I saw my brother toss the guy like he was a scarecrow. I focused on the man in front of me. After a brief tussle, my knife found purchase. The Lycan lay writhing, with a knife in his chest. I heard Riggs let out a grunt of pain but after checking I saw that the Lycan wasn't long for this world. Riggs came and helped me up and Scout came over as we sat breathing hard, adrenaline surging.

After that quick breather, we continued. We cleared three more aisles without finding anyone. We'd heard five more gunshots and clear sounds of scuffles breaking out. We just hadn't been able to figure out where they'd been coming from. The next aisle we tried spit us out into a smaller squared-off area. In the middle, stood Reaper, Remi, Cade, Bass, and Ty. Red was lying dead, on the floor next to where Ty was standing. It looked like Cade had shot him.

Good, I thought grimly. Riggs, Scout, and I ran up. Five different paths opened up into this little room. I nodded at Riggs to try to cover the exit to our left then to Scout to take the one to our right. There was one directly behind me, the one we'd come out of. That only left one to the right of Reaper and one to the left of Ty. Cade was closer to that exit than Ty was but since he still had Bass as a hostage, I wasn't sure if Cade would be able to keep Ty from dragging him down the pathway.

I turned my attention to Remi. She didn't seem to be hurt, thankfully. She looked scared but there was a healthy dose of anger in her eyes too. We were all in a standoff.

"Back the fuck off Steel or I'll kill her." I gritted my teeth when Reaper ground the barrel of his gun into Remi's temple. My girl had massive balls though because she didn't make a sound. As much as Blaze had always hated Cade and Riggs, Reaper had always had a hard-on for me. It went back way before any of us were in charge of our prospective MCs. Our feuds would only die when we did.

"Let her go and we'll finish this now." I knew, even as I said it, he wouldn't. He was too cowardly to fight me without some kind of advantage. I saw Scout moving closer toward them out of the corner of my eye but so did Reaper.

"Stay the fuck back!" He took a jerky step back but didn't take the gun off of Remi's temple. Scout froze and then looked at me. I wasn't sure what to do. If he kept moving backward, he was going to go into the opening between the containers, and who knows if we'd find them again. I wasn't going to let this asshole take my girl. A movement behind Reaper made every Viking in the vicinity, who was facing that way, freeze. The unnatural stillness must have made Reaper nervous because he turned to look behind him right as Julie ran out from between two containers.

"Remi!" It was all the distraction I needed.

I leaped forward and grabbed his gun hand. Reaper and I fighting had thrown Remi off balance. She went flying into Scout and they landed in a heap on the ground. I was holding Reaper's arm into the air, but he started firing off rounds. Julie screamed and ran away from us as we both struggled to control the weapon.

I'd lost mine somewhere when I'd lunged at him. More gunshots came from the other side of the room, but I couldn't take my eyes off of Reaper long enough to figure out who they were coming from. We crashed to the ground, still struggling. Suddenly I remembered the second Lycan gun in my cut. I switched my grip on Reaper's wrist from my right hand to my left. I had to act fast. He was as big as I was and strong as a damn bull.

Quickly I reached into my cut with my right hand and pulled out the gun. Reaper's eyes were right next to mine when I fired into his chest, point-blank range. I watched as life left his eyes and tension left his body. Another gunshot rang out, and I cursed while looking over. The shots had brought even more people spilling into our little area. I watched as Blaze burst out of the aisle behind where Ty and Bass had been standing.

Somewhere along the line, Ty had gone down to the ground, dead, and Bass was leaning against the wall of containers. Blaze started firing. Riggs and Scout weren't able to return fire because too many people were between them and Blaze. Cade started running towards Julie, who had been moving toward Bass. Then he started firing toward Blaze trying to pin him down and get him to stop firing around the room.

Bass started running toward Julie, who was frozen, watching as Blaze's gun swung in her direction. She was crouched next to a wall of containers; the only place she could go once Reaper and I had started fighting. I watched in horror. I was too far away, and it was happening too fast for me to do anything to help.

A blur moved to my left and my arm snaked out as I grabbed Remi and pulled her against me. She wouldn't have been able to reach Julie in time, but I wasn't taking the chance that she'd catch a bullet. I pulled her into me and turned so that my body covered hers but I swung my head around and watched as Bass got to Julie just in time for one of Blaze's rounds to hit him right in the back.

Julie gasped and grabbed Bass but they both crashed down to the ground under his weight. Cade was returning fire, but Blaze used the chaos to run back up the aisle he'd come from. I couldn't tell if he'd gotten shot.

Shit. We ran over to where Julie and Bass were laying. Julie had already laid him out and was pulling off her shirt to put pressure on the wound. She didn't seem to care that it left her only in a bra. She was too worried about Bass to even notice. It looked like he'd gotten shot in the left shoulder, above the shoulder blade. Remi dropped to her knees next to them.

"What do we do Jules?"

Julie was crying.

I looked over at Cade.

"Fuck man. Should we get him to the hospital?"

"No hospital," Bass gasped it out between gritted teeth. All our crew in the area walked over and we all looked at each other grimly.

"Bass, if we don't get you there you could bleed out. We're not going to let you die." Cade put a hand on the side of Bass's head. He was lying on his stomach, cheek against the ground, eyes closed against the pain.

Remi shrugged out of her dress suit jacket and folded it before sliding it under Bass's cheek.

"No, hospital."

Fuck. Most of us refused to go to the hospital when we were hurt because of the questions it caused and law enforcement involvement but in situations like this, we couldn't patch ourselves up.

"Remi. Put pressure right here." Remi put pressure where Julie directed her to. Then Julie dug her phone out of her back pocket and dialed a number.

"Ming?"

Remi's head shot up and there was hope in her eyes. I had no idea who Ming was, but Remi did and she and Julie thought she could help.

"I need your help. I'm okay, sort of. A friend took a bullet for me and he's going to die if he doesn't get medical care, but we can't take him to the hospital." She stayed quiet for a moment, but we could all hear a frantic female voice on the other end.

Julie went off in a string of Chinese, speaking so fast my eyes nearly crossed. Whatever she said must have worked because she cut off the connection and looked at us.

"We need to get him somewhere safe. Can we get out of here?"

"Scout, Riggs, Steel go on ahead, find the other guys, and clear the building. I'm sure all the Lycans are gone but check, anyway," Cade barked orders at everyone.

We nodded, and I shot a look between Cade and Remi. "I'll have them help me get Bass up to the front. We need to make sure the way is clear and that no one else is hurt." Cade met my gaze, and that's all it took for me to get going.

CHAPTER 51

Remi

I felt so numb as I walked, Bass was hobbling between Cade and me, using us as support. Julie was walking behind him, keeping an eye on his wound. All of the Vikings met at the front. I looked around.

"My uncle?"

Gunnar grimaced. "Sorry, Remi. A couple of the guys saw him take off for the exit. We heard a car peeling out as the gunfire started."

I blinked. People had been shooting and Uncle Caleb had just left? I mean, I had originally told him to go, but that didn't add up. I'd find out more later. Julie and Bridget were still standing here. They hadn't run like my cowardly uncle. Bridget said she'd been stuck on the other side of the building and had been trying to find us when the shooting started.

"Where's Anna?" My voice cracked as I realized I hadn't spotted her. I looked around and saw nothing but blank faces.

"Let's head outside and see if she's out there." That came from

Steel's brother. He opened the man-sized door and stepped out, still looking over his shoulder as he was speaking to me. If he had been looking forward, he might have been able to sidestep. The look on my face as I saw the 2x4 swing toward his head was probably the only thing that saved him from being brained. Well, that and Anna's weak swing. But to be fair she gave it all she had.

Luckily, the wood bounced harmlessly off of Riggs's massive shoulder as he pivoted to try to avoid the blow at the last second. The look on Anna's face when she realized she'd just hit a friendly, would have been funny... I started laughing. Nope, it was funny, especially after the incredibly tense situation we'd just gotten out of. Riggs snatched the 2x4 out of her hands and it looked like a toothpick in his large, meaty paw. He was glaring at her, but his look didn't have the same heat that it usually did.

"I'm so sorry! I thought maybe you were one of those other assholes." Anna grimaced then gave Riggs a cute smile, trying to get out of trouble for having hit him. He just sighed and stalked off. He took the 2x4 with him though. Everyone was still laughing at Riggs when we all seemed to collectively remember our hurt friend.

"Where are we going to take Bass?" I looked at Julie.

"I'm supposed to call Ming back with a location as soon as these guys let me know. She is gathering everything she'll need. My sister is in her last year of residency to become an ER surgeon," Julie said to Cade.

Cade's eyebrows went up. He gave her the address to the clubhouse. Riggs and Steel loaded Bass into the back of Bridget's car while Julie called her sister back.

"You alright to ride back with me?" I looked over at Steel then nodded. There wouldn't be room to ride with Bridget and Julie. In fact, it looked like Riggs was loading Anna up on the back of his bike as well. She met my eyes, and I raised my brows and gave her an amused look. She flipped me off then blew me a kiss. No one wasted time, everyone mounted up and took off back toward the clubhouse. The only sign we'd been at the warehouse was empty shell casings and dead Lycan bodies.

We pulled into the clubhouse parking lot at the same time as Ming. She rushed over and pulled us into hugs, one right after another before laying into us in a slew of Chinese. We'd heard variations of this lecture before, we knew when we were getting cussed out. We'd heard it often enough growing up. The guys were smart and didn't stick around, instead, they opted to get Bass inside and settled into his room. Once Ming was satisfied we'd been scolded enough, she rushed after the guys and her patient.

Julie followed her sister up the stairs while Bridget, Anna, and I stopped in the kitchen and hugged each other. We'd just be in the way up there, so we decided to stay downstairs. We were all worried about Bass, but Ming had already given him a cursory exam in the parking lot, before laying into us, and said he would be okay. The bullet had hit him in the shoulder. He'd saved Julie's life though. He'd stepped in front of that round on purpose. We'd always owe him for saving our sister.

Hell, we owed all these men for saving all of our lives, countless times today. I had so many questions I wanted to ask. I glanced over at Bridget.

"What happened?"

She and Anna shot each other looks, as though they weren't sure how much to tell me. Finally, I could see she opted for the truth. I'd always been able to read Bridget like a book. "Those two guys showed up at the house this morning and said that your mom and their new club had you. Once I got them to explain who that was, they told me to bring a hundred and fifty thousand dollars to the warehouse by eight a.m. or they'd kill you." I cursed. They'd increased the amount.

"Where did you get the money?"

"Our dads," Anna spoke quietly, and I winced. She didn't have a good relationship with her parents. It couldn't have been easy for her to ask for such a large amount from them on such short notice. "It was easier to get them to give us each seventy-five thousand than to have one give the full amount."

"What did you tell them you needed it for?"

"We said you were in trouble."

"I'm shocked they didn't insist on more information or going with you," I said in surprise. Both girls looked uncomfortable.

"That's why we called your uncle. He came with us and smoothed it over with our dads. We still owe them an explanation, but they let us go since Caleb was going. And since time was short, they let us go without much of the story." It didn't surprise me. Anna's dad was a huge business mogul and at one time Bridget's dad was the mayor. He still ran in the political, high society scene. It wasn't surprising that both men would have that amount of money in a safe in their house.

"I'll go by both of your houses with you today and pay them back. We'll come up with a story that will keep you both out of trouble but will satisfy them as to why we needed the money on such short notice. Something to do with the FBI freezing my accounts but needing to pay a vendor or my lawyer should be a good front," I mused. They both looked up and happiness shot across their faces. The FBI was going to provide us a pretty good cover story for their families.

At least they're good for something. Despite everything that happened today I was still pissed off at what was happening with the FBI and Mackenzie's. I saw the girls exchange a relieved look. Trying to figure out a way to explain things to their dads, without bringing up the fact that they were caught between two warring motorcycle gangs, had been worrying them.

Well, it had been worrying them since we'd all figured out we weren't actually going to die in that warehouse. A chill shot down my spine. Once Blaze said they were keeping me I'd started fretting about all of us and what might happen. Then there was shooting and people dying. Luckily, none of ours had died.

"I'm not sure what's going to happen now," I said quietly, more thoughtful than anything. I couldn't think too hard on it right now or I'd lose my mind. So much happened in the last few weeks.

"We're here with you, Remi," Bridget said earnestly.

"No matter what. MCs, FBI, your uncle, our families, Mackenzie's. Whatever happens, we're family." Anna had tears in her eyes.

I blinked mine back and the three of us all but tackled each other in a group hug.

Gunnar, Riggs, and Steel came back downstairs, and we all stared awkwardly at each other for a moment, us girls from our huddle and the guys from the doorway.

"Uh, we can give you a few minutes." Gunnar rubbed a hand through his hair. All three of the men looked decidedly uncomfortable. Clearly, group hugs and tears weren't how they resolved things with each other. We looked at each other and snickered.

"No, we're done," I said and smiled at Steel as we disentangled ourselves.

Gunnar pulled Bridget into a hug and both Anna and I watched, grinning. We just sat there with stupid smiles on our faces as he tugged her out of the room and through the door that led to his half of the complex. Steel shoved his hands in the pockets of his jeans and stared between me, Anna, and his brother.

"What?" He looked at me then glanced curiously at the door that Gunnar and Bridget had disappeared through.

"Nothing, it's just nice seeing them with each other again." Steel just blinked at me then shot a glance at his brother. They shared a long look, some kind of secret, silent, communication thing between brothers. Something that they weren't going to share with us.

Riggs cleared his throat. "Anna, you want a beer?" Anna looked at him then gave me a calculating stare.

"Yeah, that'd be great."

"My house is over there." Riggs pointed at a white house sitting about two hundred yards to the south of the clubhouse. Anna gave me a quick hug and then they left. I stared at the back door in silence. It'd just hit me when Riggs and Anna had eyeballed us, that I had broken up with Steel.

I'd told him to fuck off, and that I didn't want to see him, and he'd come in, guns blazing, and rescued me from my insane mother and a biker gang. I frowned. I wondered if she'd lived?

"Do you know if my mom died?"

Steel looked at me in surprise. "Your mom?"

"Rhonda? I guess she's dating Blaze?"

Steel rubbed the back of his neck. "Your mom is the girlfriend? Shit. She's the one who's been funding the Lycans?"

"Funding them?" Understanding dawned. "Oh, man. That's what she was doing with the money?" He frowned at me. "I just found out, on my birthday actually, that my dad has been paying my mom a hundred thousand dollars for the past couple of years. He's been paying her however much he could though, every year on my birthday since he started Mackenzie's Trucking.

"Why would he start paying her?"

"She left right after I was born. I guess that's how she made ends meet after she left my dad."

"And your dad wanted to take care of her." It wasn't a question. It shouldn't surprise me that Steel just somehow picked up on the type of guy my dad was.

"I guess he saw it as his duty?" I answered anyway, and he nodded. She left him so I didn't understand it, but my dad had always been an honorable guy.

"Bass told us Blaze had hooked up with a new female who was going to give them money for a new shipment of weapons."

"So, they haven't been together long?" Steel shrugged at my question.

"He said the guys said they'd been together for a few years."

I nodded. It didn't surprise me. Once she started getting larger payments, she probably bought her way into a position of power.

"No one found your mom's body, so she must have made it out." He strode over to me and pulled me into a hug. I was surprised at the regret I felt. I wished she had been killed. Then I immediately hoped that didn't make me a horrible person.

"Is Bass going to be okay?" I nestled my face into the crook where Steel's shoulder and neck met and breathed in deep. It felt so soothing to be in his arms, a reminder that we were both alive.

"Ming was setting him up with an IV and getting everything ready to go in after the bullet when we came down. She said he'll be fine." He tightened his arms around me.

"We've already got Rat working on getting rid of the evidence against Mackenzie's Trucking. He's working it to make it look like the Lycans set you up. By the end of the week, the FBI won't have enough evidence left to bring any charges against you, Remi."

He leaned back and looked me in the eyes. Tears started welling up in mine. I refused to cry despite the relief I felt. I hadn't cried once all day, and I didn't want to start now. He brushed his lips over the corner of my eyes then over my lips. I tried to deepen the kiss. Steel may have gotten my company, and me, into trouble with the FBI but he was helping to get me out of it and he'd literally just risked his life to save mine. If a girl couldn't forgive a guy after those kinds of actions when could she forgive him?

When he didn't oblige me, I wrapped my arms around his neck and pulled him down toward me, and bit his bottom lip. Once his mouth slackened, I dipped my tongue in and rubbed it against his. Steel groaned and pulled me up against him.

There we go.

I moaned as he took control of the kiss, then shoved me back into the counter and ground his hips into mine. Someone clearing their throat had us pausing. Steel broke our lips apart but just rested his forehead on mine. After a minute we both looked over into Cade's grinning face.

"Ming got the bullet out. Luckily it didn't pass all the way through or it would have still hit Julie. She said Bass is going to be feeling it for a while but otherwise he'll be fine."

I sighed with relief and felt Steel relax slightly too. Cade looked pretty damn relieved as well. It hit me suddenly. These guys were family in the same way that Bridget, Anna, Julie, Ming, and I were.

Steel and I stepped apart and the three of us sat down at the island in the kitchen.

"Did Steel tell you we're working on the FBI problem?"

I nodded. "Yes, I really appreciate the help."

Cade watched me quietly before he finally spoke. "We got you into trouble in the first place and you did us a solid by getting rid of the paper trail linking us to the evidence the FBI had. Even if you hadn't, we'd have still helped you."

Cade gave me a long, serious look and then flicked his gaze over to Steel before settling back on me again. "You're a part of our family now, Remi. We take care of our own. I hope you know that." I blushed and watched as Cade got up and walked out the back door, heading toward his house.

I looked over at Steel. "Am I?"

He quirked a brow at me.

"Part of your family?"

"Seriously? You need me to tell you I love you, Remi? Throwing myself between you and a gun wasn't enough of a clue for you?" He grinned at me. I couldn't help but smile at him.

"A girl does like to hear it."

"I love you." He stood up and dragged me off the stool and into his arms. Lowering his lips to mine he said it again before he took my mouth in a searing kiss.

"I love you too, Logan." He grimaced and pulled back.

"I hate that name." I laughed and shook my head.

"Fine. I love you too, Steel."

"Better. So... What are we going to do about your uncle?"

I sighed. "I honestly have no clue. He's up to something. Why would he come to get me back and then take off as soon as the shooting started? If he had left with the girls, that would make sense. I told him to get them out of there. But he left them in that warehouse too. What do you think we should do?"

"For now? Don't let him think anything is wrong. We'll dig into it, see what's going on."

Steel suddenly grinned down at me. "But that can wait until tomorrow. I think we've earned the right to spend the rest of the day in bed... don't you?"

Steel laughed, picked me up, and tossed me over his shoulder. I yelped and pounded him on the back. I couldn't help but chuckle inwardly though, as I remembered the first time, he'd done this, in this very building. We'd come full circle. He took the stairs two at a time, heading for his room and I shrieked when the slap he laid across my ass echoed down the hallway.

I had a lot of things I was going to have to work on, fix, or cut off completely with Mackenzie's, the FBI, my mother, my uncle, this new relationship with Steel, and college. But like Steel said, that could all start tomorrow. I'd take it a day at a time, and I'd work it out, one way or another. I was looking forward to getting my life back on track.

I laughed as Steel dropped me on the bed. He stood staring down at me as he pulled his shirt off. Letting my eyes roam over him I couldn't believe how my life had changed in the last year. Some things had dropped me to my knees, to the point I thought I'd never recover. I'd thought I'd forevermore be walking around living a half-life. As Steel laid his body over mine, I realized he was a big reason that I was beginning to feel alive again.

CHAPTER 52

Remi

The next morning Steel brought me back into the city. I wasn't looking forward to meeting with my uncle, but it was something that had to be done. We pulled up in front of my house and I jumped off his bike and gave him a quick peck on the lips, mind already on what I needed to do today. "Thanks, I'll let you know how it goes." In my hurry, I missed the bemused expression on his face.

Quickly walking to the front door, I opened it but paused when I realized I didn't hear his bike start. Glancing over my shoulder I sucked in a startled breath when I found him directly behind me. "What are you doing?" I asked, turning around to face him.

"You think I'm letting you meet with that piece of shit alone?"

I frowned at him. "He's still my uncle, Steel. He's not going to hurt me." Steel folded his arms over his chest and raised a brow at me but remained otherwise silent. Not wanting to argue on my front porch I walked inside and grabbed one of those massive arms to pull him in behind me.

"He's not going to talk to me if you're sitting there. I need to figure out what's going on." We'd argued about this last night too. Steel didn't think Uncle Caleb was going to admit to anything and I thought I could at least get him to be honest with me about what happened at the warehouse.

"Something bigger is going on, Remi, and I know for a fact it has more to do than with just you and your uncle. But he is a part of it somehow."

"Well, how are we supposed to figure it out if I don't talk to him? He'll get suspicious if I come back and act like nothing's happened. So, I may as well try to get anything out of him that I can." I wasn't sure if Uncle Caleb was a part of everything going on, but Steel and the other guys seemed to think he was. It seemed strange to me that I now trusted Steel and his brothers more than the uncle I'd known for my entire life, but they had saved my life. They were also helping me take care of the issues I was having with the FBI.

I was reasonably sure that Preston would be able to keep me from going to jail, but how long would that take? And what kind of impact would it have on the business? I still hadn't been able to talk to Uncle Caleb about how the FBI had gotten paperwork that only an employee at Mackenzie's would have been able to access and hand over, or how the Agent knew I was dating Steel.

There were too many coincidences piling up and they were all pointing back to my uncle. He was the only one who had an issue with Steel and me and was the only one who stood to benefit from me being out of the picture.

"Fine. You can come, but I'm talking to him alone." That seemed to have pacified Steel slightly. I quickly got ready to head into Mackenzie's and tried to ignore him. That was hard to do since he was sticking to my side like a shadow. I knew he had a protective streak, but he was taking it a bit far since we were standing in my own home.

You were kidnapped outside your dad's house. On the front lawn of your childhood home, in broad daylight, the voice in my head helpfully reminded me. Suddenly, having Steel's bigger than life presence nearby felt comforting.

Soon we pulled into the parking lot at Mackenzie's. Uncle Caleb immediately rushed out the doors and wrapped me in a hug. He completely ignored Steel who was watching us intensely. "Thank God, Remi! I was so worried."

Pulling back, I searched Uncle Caleb's face. He didn't appear to be lying but I wasn't sure if it was because he wasn't, because he was good at it, or because I wasn't good at spotting it. "Really, Uncle Caleb? If you were so worried why did you run away from the warehouse?" Guilt washed over his features. "Why didn't you call me last night to check on me?" He held up his hands, stopping my questions.

"Let's go inside and talk about this. Not out here." He shot a disdainful look at Steel. "Thanks for bringing her home." Wrapping an arm around my shoulders he started to guide me inside. I dug my heels in, pulling us to a stop.

"Steel is coming with us." Uncle Caleb's eyes widened then narrowed. As his mouth opened Steel cut him off.

"I'm not letting Remi out of my sight." He moved up beside us and pulled me out from under my uncle's arm and against his side. My heart fluttered like a butterfly and I tried to shove the girly emotions aside. I could swoon about Steel's romantic, protective nature later but for now, I needed to concentrate. Uncle Caleb looked silently between us before he gave in.

"Fine, but we're still having this conversation inside." He led us back to the meeting room. After we'd settled down around the table Uncle Caleb sighed. "I'm so sorry, Remi." He dropped his head into his hands. Any other time I would think he was distraught. But I'd caught a look in his eyes before he'd covered them. The same look I'd seen when Agent Flynn had glanced at him, when I'd asked her how she'd gotten that paperwork. My uncle was having a harder time hiding whatever secrets he was holding.

"I was only concerned about getting you out of there, but then the shooting started and I... I panicked." He lifted his head and met my gaze. How had I never seen this? His eyes weren't devastated, like his tone of voice implied. Sure, they were crinkled around the corners and he had heavy wrinkles in his forehead, but the look in his eyes was cold, assessing. He was lying to me.

I glanced over at Steel but like usual, his face gave nothing away. I needed to play this smartly. It wouldn't help for Uncle Caleb to realize I suspected his involvement in any way. "It's okay, Uncle Caleb. I was terrified too. I don't blame you." I felt more than saw Steel tense up beside me. Ignoring him I continued. "Did you see anyone else leave… when you did?" I almost said 'when you ran away' but putting him on the defensive wasn't going to help.

"Your mother. She wasn't too far ahead of me. There was a car there waiting for her. She jumped in and it took off."

"Someone picked her up?" Uncle Caleb tensed at my question.

"I don't know. Yeah, I guess." He tried to evade. He hadn't meant to say that.

"Did you recognize them?"

He shook his head then reached forward to hold my hands between his. I had to repress a shudder. His eyes hadn't changed. Had they always been like this and I had never noticed? Or was he getting desperate? "I'm so glad you're okay. I was going to look for you this morning if you didn't come in."

It was eleven a.m.; he wasn't going to look for me. He hadn't even bothered to call and see if I was alive. "Thanks, Uncle Caleb," I choked the words out. They wanted to get stuck in my throat. "I'm glad you're okay too."

"I should probably get back to work." He dropped my hands and stood. "Take the day off. I can handle everything here today." Concern was shining on his face, but it still hadn't reached his eyes.

"I think I'll take you up on that," I replied even though I wanted to stay. I needed the time to figure out what was going on and I couldn't do that here. He gave me a smile before leaving. He'd ignored Steel the entire time.

"He's lying," I said as soon as he left the room. Steel glanced over at me in surprise.

"I'd say so too. Why do you think he is?"

I chewed on my bottom lip. How was I supposed to explain it? "I could see it in his eyes," I said lamely. "I know it sounds dumb, but I've known him my whole life. Something is different. The only real thing he said was about my mother."

"That was my impression too. Who do you think picked her up?"

I shrugged, "I have no clue. Do you think that there are surveillance cameras at that warehouse?" Steel's brows went up in surprise. He quickly pulled out his phone.

"Rat. Did you find anything on that footage from the warehouse?" He listened silently.

I guess they were already a few steps ahead of me. I wasn't used to having to cover up illegal activity, but these guys clearly excelled at it. The thought of that didn't make me as uncomfortable as it once had. It was working out to my benefit for now. *Did that make me a bad person?* I paused in my musings. *Did I care if it did?*

Steel hung up and grabbed my hand, pulling me up as he stood. "Rat has information and Cade wants us to head back to the clubhouse."

"Why didn't he just give you the information over the phone?" I asked, impatiently.

"Cade wants to talk in person."

I thought about arguing but finally conceded and left with him. I waved at Janet as we walked out the door. If I was going to be a part of Steel's life, the club was going to play a big role in mine. I was going to have to get used to doing things that benefited the group as a whole.

Climbing on Steel's bike I wrapped my arms around his waist and thought about that on the ride back to the clubhouse. Somewhere between dodging bullets yesterday and right now, I'd decided I was in this for the long haul. I wanted Steel and that meant accepting everything that came along with him.

CHAPTER 53

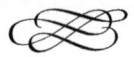

Steel

I strode into the clubhouse; Remi was close behind me. Sitting at the island in the kitchen were Cade, Riggs, Gunnar, Axel, and Rat. Everyone said hello to Remi as we sat down with them.

"Sorry to bring you all the way out here in the middle of the day," Cade said, looking at Remi, "but it's important."

She nodded and looked around at everyone. They were all staring at her expectantly. She shot me a deer in the headlights look before replying. "That's alright. What's going on?"

"Steel told you that we've had Rat digging into what happened with the Lycans and with the FBI?" Cade shot me a long look after Remi nodded. It was calculating and I knew exactly what he was asking without him needing to verbalize it. He was about to spill some pretty big club secrets in the next few minutes. He needed to know I was completely on board with Remi and that I was planning on making her my old lady. We didn't share anything with outsiders but the old ladies in the club knew exactly what was going on. It was rare to ask the brothers to keep them in the dark. They needed to know our business in order to keep themselves and our families safe.

I nodded at Cade, silently answering yes to his question. Remi glanced back and forth between us; her brows knitted together in confusion. Cade put his forearms on the island and leaned forward.

"We found out a little over a month ago that there were drugs being dealt in our territory."

Remi tore her questioning gaze from me and focused on Cade as he started speaking. I watched her out of the corner of my eye. I hadn't told her much of what the club was involved in yet and this would give me an opportunity to see how she reacted.

"After kids started getting hospitalized, we realized those drugs were being laced with Fentanyl. We also found out that it was the Lycans who were dealing them. They wanted to make it look like our club was responsible."

Remi absorbed that for a moment before she spoke. "So… you do deal drugs. Just not the drugs laced with Fentanyl?"

Cade grunted in affirmation. Riggs clarified, "We only sell clean drugs."

Remi pursed her lips and considered his words. "Okay. What does this have to do with me?"

This time it was Rat who spoke up. "While digging around, trying to figure out how to pin the stolen car parts on someone else, I found out that Mackenzie's has been sending a truck down to the Mexico/US border once a month. Of course, there is nothing on the official manifest about the shipments. Knowing our problems with the Lycans, and the fact that we still don't know where they're getting those drugs from, I took a guess. Sure enough, Mackenzie's Trucking has been transporting cocaine from Laredo for the Guzman Cartel and delivering it to the Lycans."

Remi gasped then clapped a hand over her mouth. She looked at me, eyes huge. "I had no idea."

"Of course you didn't, Rem," Riggs said soothingly before I could say anything. "None of us thought you had anything to do with it.

You're not exactly the criminal type." Everyone chuckled at that, including me.

Remi glared around the table. "Then who is involved? How long has this been happening? How could I not have known?" She groaned the last question and put her head in her hands. I put my hand on her back and rubbed comfortingly, motioning to Rat with the other, to answer her questions.

"It's been going on since your dad got sick," he said apologetically.

Remi's head shot up. "Uncle Caleb," she said, her voice was as dark as the look on her face.

"Yes, and a couple of your drivers."

"How did you find all of this out?"

Rat flinched, his mouth opened and closed a few times and he looked at me in a panic.

"He went through the electronic files at Mackenzie's," I answered for him. Remi looked shell shocked. I left out that he'd hacked the security cameras at the Laredo Port of Entry and the Homeland Security internal systems.

"But I have a firewall system, or something. I don't remember what the guy called it exactly."

I smiled reassuringly at her. "There isn't much that can keep Rat out." She looked over at him and he shrugged sheepishly.

She narrowed her eyes at him. "We'll talk about that later." I had to bite my lip to hold in my laughter. Rat's face went sheet white at her declaration. "How did my uncle get involved with a cartel?" I could hear the exhaustion in her voice. I was ready to have all of this be over and done with, for her sake. If anyone deserved a break, it was Remi.

"Actually, I think he's just a middleman," Rat's voice cracked and he cleared it before continuing. "I'm sure he's working with someone else. They're the person with the connections to the cartel and the Lycans. I haven't been able to figure out who though."

I sat up straighter at that and let my hand fall from Remi's back. If Rat wasn't able to find out who Caleb was working with, they had to have a lot of resources. Cade, Riggs, and I all exchanged glances. Every time we seemed to catch a break in this mystery, something else got thrown in and we had to start back at square one.

"That's not all…" Rat ran a hand down his face. Anyone could see he was miserable having to deliver this news to Remi. "Your uncle has been embezzling from your company, for years. Like, since before your dad died. Your accountant had to be covering it up for him. They would have known, having access to all your accounts."

Remi closed her eyes and her hands clenched into fists on top of the counter. "Thank you for telling me. All of it, thank you for everything, Rat." She shot him a warm smile. The depressed look melted off his face. "I'd rather know and fix it than be in the dark."

"There's good news too!" Now he was downright excited. Gunnar grinned at me from across the table.

This should be good if it's got both of them this excited. The look on Remi's face was pure resignation. I could tell she didn't want to hear much more news today.

"With everything I found I was able to link all the stolen car parts to the Lycans, and the shipping of them on your uncle," Rat quickly explained. "Hopefully you don't mind…" he hesitated. "I already set it up so that the FBI would 'find the evidence' themselves."

"Seriously?" My brows shot up. "None of it will blow back on Remi? Or the club?"

"Nope," Rat said smugly. "And I made it just hard enough to find that they won't suspect that the evidence was planted. The guy going through the files should find it somewhere between the next twenty-four to forty-eight hours." He met Remi's gaze again. "I won't be able to do anything about the embezzling issue. Bringing that up will cause too many questions with the FBI. It might make them take a closer look at you. So, I'm afraid those years of money are lost to you. But, if it's any consolation, your uncle and those drivers will be going to prison and they're going to have an MC and a cartel pissed off at them."

"I really don't know how to thank you all." Remi folded her hands together. "Not only for getting me out of trouble with the FBI…"

"Well, my idiot brother sort of got you into that, to begin with," Riggs joked and shot me a grin. I flipped him off.

Remi laughed and continued. "That's true. But still, it means a lot to me. Plus, you found out it was my uncle doing all of this and that he was stealing from my dad. I just…" Her voice sounded watery and now everyone looked distinctly uncomfortable. Luckily, she pulled herself together because Axel looked like he was about to throw himself out of the window to escape her tears. "It just means a lot that you went to so much trouble to help me."

"We're family. It's what we do for each other," Axel's voice was gruff, and he was looking at a spot above her head.

"You don't even know me."

Now he leveled a grim look at her. The other men at the table were looking at her in the same manner, even Rat. "We don't need to. He does." Axel nodded toward me and I gave him an appreciative look. It wouldn't matter how many times I explained this to Remi. She would understand it faster getting it straight from the guys. "You belong to him," Axel hurried on when Remi stiffened and opened her mouth like she was going to argue, "And he belongs to you." That settled her down. "He belongs to us, so you belong to us. It's really that simple. We protect our own."

"I couldn't have said it better myself," Cade said when Remi looked toward him. Everyone at the table nodded. "Every man in this club will tell you the same."

Remi took a shaky breath then smiled at us. "I appreciate that. With Uncle Caleb going to jail I'm getting really short on family unless you count my worthless mother. And trust me, I don't. All I've had for the last year has been him and the girls."

"Now you have us," Gunnar said with a smile and Remi returned it. Silence fell in the kitchen for a few beats and I could tell Remi was at a loss of what else to say so I took over.

"So, how are we going to figure out who Caleb was working with?" I looked between Cade and Rat.

"I could try talking to him?" Remi offered.

Cade shook his head but smiled at her. "I don't think he'll tell you anything."

"Plus, if you tip him off, he could bolt before the FBI has a chance to arrest him," Riggs added.

"I'll keep digging around. But I'm actually hoping the FBI will be able to find out more than I can. Then I can just hack their server and see what they know," Rat said, matter of factly.

Remi's mouth fell open. "You can hack into the government's computers?"

Rat laughed, "Yeah, it's no problem."

"Well, suddenly I don't feel bad about you getting into Mackenzie's information then," she grumbled.

"That can't be our only plan," I muttered and frowned at Cade. He just shrugged.

"What else can we do? Riggs's is right. If we talk to Caleb, he'll run. No one from the Lycans will talk to us if they even know who Caleb is working with. Blaze is probably the only one who has that information and he's not going to say anything."

"What about Rhonda?" Everyone looked over at Remi in surprise. "Do you think Blaze would have told her about any of it? Plus, my uncle said that she got into someone's car after the shootout. Blaze was still in the warehouse with us. She may know what's going on."

We all thought about that for a minute. "Maybe," Cade said hesitantly, "but even if she does, would she tell us anything?"

Remi shook her head, "No, but she might tell me."

"Rem. I don't know if she would. By your own admission, she's been a shitty mother," I started but Remi cut me off.

"Oh, trust me, I'm under no delusions that she would help out of concern for me. But maybe we can make it seem like Uncle Caleb is selling them out? She and Blaze? And if nothing else, I can just pay her off. Money talks with Rhonda."

At that point, I wished I had a camera. Every set of eyebrows at the table was up and some mouths were open. It was a damn good idea. I, however, didn't like it. "Not happening." Everyone looked at me. I saw understanding in all the men's stares, but Remi looked furious. "They fucking kidnapped you, Remi. I'm not letting you meet with her."

She threw up her hands and made a sound of disgust. "First, you don't get to tell me what I can or cannot do, *Logan*." Snorts of laughter followed that. I was going to kill that damn FBI Agent for telling her my name. "Second, it's a good plan." She looked around the table for back up but everyone except for Cade was busy looking somewhere else. They were smart enough not to get in the middle of it.

"She's got a point, Steel."

I glared at him before looking back at her. "No."

Remi laughed incredulously. "No? Seriously, no?!" She stood up so fast the stool she was sitting on shot out and hit the counter behind us. "Thanks again for your help guys." She smiled at each of them, then all but bared her teeth at me and stormed out the door.

Sighing, I stood up. I was trying to ignore all the chuckling that was happening at my expense. "She's right, Steel." I looked over at Cade. "It's a good plan. I know you don't like it, but I don't like waiting to see if the FBI finds anything out. They're useless. I'd rather go on the offensive." I held his gaze for a moment before I followed Remi out, without another word.

CHAPTER 54

Remi

Once I made it out to the parking lot, I realized I had ridden here with Steel on his bike. I hesitated for a moment before I began walking across the club lot and toward the road. My anger was riding so high I'd rather walk all the way back to the city than go back inside and ask for a ride.

My thoughts were ping-ponging around in my head. *Uncle Caleb had been stealing from Dad! He was still stealing from me. He was putting the business in jeopardy by transporting drugs. Drugs that were making kids sick, no less.*

Obviously, I knew drugs were dangerous, to begin with, but to knowingly sell them when they were laced with other potentially fatal substances was just disgusting. It was so hard for me to imagine my uncle mixed up in all of this. Then I remembered the look in his eyes this morning. I recalled his actions at the warehouse. *Something tells me I've never known the real Uncle Caleb.* The thought saddened me. I wondered if Dad had ever really known what his brother was like?

My thoughts shifted and relief poured through me. I was so thankful that I'd be off the hook for the stolen vehicle parts. A little piece of me felt guilty, placing the blame on Uncle Caleb, but then I remembered everything he'd been doing behind my back and it went away.

I don't care if Steel doesn't want me to do it. I'm going to speak with Rhonda. I need to find out who is involved in all of this. Anyone who was involved from Mackenzie's was going to be fired if they didn't get put into prison.

"Remi!"

I didn't bother to turn around when Steel called my name. I walked faster down the road. *He doesn't get to tell me what to do.*

Strong hands gripped my shoulders and spun me around. For such a big man he moved quietly. I shoved his chest, for all the good it did. He didn't move an inch.

"Leave me alone, Steel."

"Where are you going?" He sounded amused.

"Home."

Now he was grinning at me. It made me want to punch him in that pretty face. I tried to jerk out of his grip, but he tightened it then pulled me into a hug. "Look, I'm sorry." That had me stilling. "I just hate the idea of putting you into a dangerous situation the day after you nearly got killed."

"I don't think they were planning on killing me."

He gave me an exasperated look. "Maybe not at first but eventually it would have come around to that, Remi."

I just looped my arms around him and buried my face in his neck. "That doesn't change the fact that we need to find out what's going on. We need to make sure we get rid of everyone trying to take me out. And anyone trying to take out the club too," I said. I kissed the spot where his shoulder and neck met, and he sighed.

"Fine. But we're taking safety precautions."

I didn't know what he meant by that, but I looked at him and nodded in agreement. I could feel the smug smile on my face but couldn't wipe it off. He let out a frustrated grunt when he saw it. "Can we go back inside now?"

I eyed him suspiciously. I wouldn't put it past him to lull me into a false sense of security to get me back inside then try to cut me out of the plan all over again.

"We have to come up with an idea about how to get Rhonda to talk to you, don't we?" he asked in resignation. I happily agreed and walked with him back to the clubhouse.

CHAPTER 55

Remi

Internally, I groaned and muttered curses as I watched Rhonda plop a huge, bedazzled purse down on an empty chair. The bustling coffee shop was the perfect spot to meet my skeezy mother. The guys and I had finally gotten Steel to agree to let me meet with her as long as it was in a public place and as long as I had a few of the club members that Rhonda was unlikely to recognize there to help in case anything happened. I tried not to snicker when I saw Drew in the corner in a hat and sunglasses. He was trying to be inconspicuous, but the fact that these guys were all huge and gorgeous made them stand out.

"Good girl, you got the coffee I ordered." Rhonda slid into the seat across from me once she'd situated her huge bag. I gritted my teeth, biting back my scathing response instead, I smiled at her. I'd returned to my dad's house and tried to find the crumpled paper that had Rhonda's number on it, but it was nowhere to be found. Luckily, Rat had been able to track down her number so that I could get into contact with her.

Her eyes looked hollowed in and they darted nervously around the shop. I hoped whoever else Steel had watching us wasn't sitting too closely. I knew he was somewhere nearby too, but he wouldn't get spotted. He was too careful for that. "Thanks for meeting me, Rhonda."

She stopped perusing the room and her gaze snapped to mine. "You said you had a deal for me?"

I picked up my cup of coffee and slowly took a small sip. I willed my hands not to shake. This wasn't something I was used to, being an actor, not when so much was on the line. The nerves had my stomach clenching and palms sweating. I set my cup down and put my hands on my thighs under the table. I wiped them on my jeans once Rhonda couldn't see them anymore. "I do. Well, the club does."

Rhonda's eyes narrowed then she laughed mockingly. "You expect me to believe you speak for the Vikings?"

"Normally? No. But in this case, they thought you'd be more willing to work with me than anyone else. I will happily tell Cade that you weren't interested in his deal though." I started to stand up, as though I was going to leave. "I thought he was being far too lenient on you anyway…"

Rhonda's hand shot out and clamped around my forearm, nails digging into my skin, as she hissed at me, "Sit down. I'll listen to what you have to say." She looked around nervously again.

Cocking my head as I sank back into my seat, I studied her. She looked desperate. "It's simple. You give us all of the information you have on the drugs the Lycans are dealing. How they're getting them. Who they're working with. Any future plans they have for dealing in Viking territory. And we want to know who you left with that day at the warehouse."

Rhonda's eyes widened for a moment before her face relaxed. I kept mine impassive. I knew this wouldn't be easy. My mother wasn't stupid. If she was, she wouldn't have managed to align herself with people like Blaze and whoever else they were working with. She was shrewd, manipulative, and cunning. "That's a lot to ask. What would be in it for me?"

I unzipped my jacket and pulled a large manila envelope out of it. I passed it to her so she could read the printout. "Five hundred thousand dollars." It was every penny I had in savings. "It will be transferred directly to you." There was more if I dipped into the Mackenzie accounts, but I wasn't willing to do that for Rhonda. I'd give her only what I had. It would have been a bit more, but I'd paid back both Bridget and Anna's dads already.

Rhonda tossed the envelope back at me and scoffed. "That's not very much money for what you're asking me to do." My eyebrows shot up.

"It's half a million dollars, Rhonda." My voice was as dry as the stare I gave her. "It's also the only offer you're going to get." When she smirked at me, I reached over and pulled a laptop out of a bag on the seat next to me. She watched curiously as I tapped on the keys then set the machine on the table between us and swung it so we could both watch the live feed that Rat so generously put up onto the screen.

I watched Rhonda's face lose color out of the corner of my eye and my lips twitched. Biting back the smile I studied the Lycan's clubhouse property. There were police cars everywhere out front, flashing lights bouncing off the pavement and they already had a bunch of the members lined up on the ground, face down, hands on their heads. Local police and FBI milled around, some searching the bikers, others clearing vehicles and buildings on the property, and while the live feed was much clearer than I had expected it to be when we'd discussed the plan a few days ago, it wasn't clear enough to see if Blaze was in the group being arrested. The guys figured he wouldn't be.

They said Blaze and a few of his core group would have been paying off the local cops and probably took off before the raid happened. They wouldn't have been able to warn all of their guys though, without looking suspicious. I shut the laptop lid with a snap, making Rhonda jump slightly. We locked eyes and I could tell I'd unnerved her.

"We both know the Lycans aren't done. But it's going to take time for them to regroup. They're also going to be looking for whoever turned them over to the cops." I pursed my lips and trailed off. I didn't mention that law enforcement was there looking for stolen car parts and connections to the case that Mackenzie's was involved in. I purposely let her believe it was about the drugs.

"Well, it wasn't me!" Rhonda sounded downright offended at first. Then I saw doubt creep over her features.

"Will Blaze believe that?" I asked innocently. I looked down at my coffee cup as I picked it up and took another drink. Hers sat, untouched. When I looked back up Rhonda was worrying her bottom lip between her teeth. It sickened me to think of paying this woman more money. But, if it gave us the information we needed and got her out of my life permanently, I'd happily do it.

"Look, Rhonda. There are a few conditions I'm putting on this money, as well. On top of what the club wants." Her face clouded over with suspicion. I continued on before she could say anything. "If you take it, you'll never get another cent from me. If you contact me, I'll turn you over to the cops immediately. You'll leave Austin, and you won't come back." She started to speak, and I held up a hand, cutting her off. "You'll leave, I don't care where you go, but you won't come back here."

Her expression turned mutinous, but I didn't break eye contact with her. "And if I won't agree to your terms?" She all but spat at me.

"Then you can take your chances with Blaze and his bosses. I'm sure they'll be very understanding that it wasn't you who snitched to the cops about their drugs." I studied my nails, letting a bored expression flit across my face. That did the trick. Rhonda's face went bright red with rage before it leached of all color and stayed a bone white. She licked her lips and eyed my jacket where I'd placed the envelope.

"But if I tell your club what they want to know they'll let me leave?"

"Yes, if you tell us what you know, leave town, and never contact me again, I'll give you the money and you can disappear." I knew the minute she made up her mind, but I calmly waited until she agreed before pulling out my phone and sending a text.

"What now?" Rhonda asked nervously when I put my phone back into my pocket. I gave her a genuine smile and she blinked slowly at me in shock.

"Now, I'm finished with you, Rhonda." I stood up when I saw Cade walk through the door of the coffee shop. I paused next to her chair and looked down at her. I could forgive her for the things she'd done to me and I might have felt sorry for her as she sat there looking nervous and scared, except then I remembered all the things she'd done to my dad. I hardened my heart and walked away without another word or backward glance. I stopped next to Cade. "Have Rat send the money once you get the information you need."

Cade looked at me in surprise. "You don't want to wait until she is out of town to send it?"

"No, she'll need it right away to start over somewhere else."

"And you're sure you want to let her have the money?" he asked. "We could easily get it back from her."

I'd considered it. The last thing I wanted to do was give Rhonda more money. I shook my head at him. "Thanks, but let her keep it. Dad wouldn't have wanted her to be hurt," I added that because I knew if they took the money back Steel would make sure she never came around again, in the most permanent way possible. "This buys my freedom from her and it's worth every penny."

He nodded and stared at me thoughtfully. "I'll have a couple of guys follow her home and escort her out of town to make sure she doesn't get lost along the way."

I gave him a small smile. "Thanks, Cade."

"No, thank you. I know that wasn't easy. Offering to meet with her and to pay her off... We definitely owe you."

I cocked a brow at him. "It's what you do for family, right?"

"Right," he chuckled. "Well, you have somewhere else to be. Better go or you'll miss the show." With that, I hurried out of the coffee shop to find Steel and Gunnar.

CHAPTER 56

Remi

Everything was quiet when Gunnar, Steel, and I pulled into Mackenzie's parking lot. It was the end of the day and most of the employees had left for the day. Walking through the front door I waved at Janet, who was manning the front desk. She looked at us in surprise.

"Hi, Remi. I wasn't expecting to see you today." She gave me a warm smile. I'd always loved Janet. I was so happy to find out that the betrayal at my company was limited to my uncle, two truck drivers, and my accountant. No one else had known what Uncle Caleb had been up to.

Speak of the devil. Uncle Caleb walked into the front from the hallway and I pasted what I hoped passed for a genuine smile on my face. "Uncle Caleb." Now I was trying not to wince because my voice had come out far too high pitched and happy. Steel gave me a strange look. I ignored him and focused on my uncle, who seemed as surprised as Janet to see me.

"Remi." He gave the guys a dark look then turned back to me. "I wasn't expecting you." He gave me a smile I presumed was as fake as my own. I could only imagine how stiff and awkward we both looked. I snuck a peek at Janet and the confusion on her face confirmed that we weren't fooling anyone.

Luckily for me, Agent Flynn saved the day. That was probably the only time I would be happy to see her. She strolled through the front door casually with Agent Ramirez trailing behind her. Now, Uncle Caleb was looking between me and Flynn distrustfully.

"Agent Flynn, it's nice to see you again," he said charmingly and held out a hand for her to shake.

A slow, sultry smile spread across her face. "Is it?" She looked down at his hand then back up at him. Uncle Caleb dropped his hand when she refused to shake it. She stepped forward and slowly trailed a nail down the line of buttons on Uncle Caleb's dress shirt. I fought back a laugh. Now that I wasn't on the receiving end of her odd interrogation methods it was kind of fun to watch. Her weird way of flirting while questioning you was enough to throw the most seasoned criminals off track and Uncle Caleb had clearly not been in the game long.

Gunnar leaned over and whispered, "She's hot." I just rolled my eyes when Steel grunted in agreement. It didn't surprise me that the two men found the leggy, blonde cop attractive. Neither would ever go for her but that didn't stop them from admiring her while she continued to unnerve my uncle.

"What can we help you with?" Uncle Caleb looked nervous. He kept looking at me, and how calm I was, then back at the agent who was still standing awkwardly close to him.

"We're going to need you to come down to the station with us," she replied smoothly. When she motioned, without turning around, a local police officer came through the door to join them. I looked out front and saw at least four more police cruisers out there. My eyes widened and I bit the insides of my lips. It was probably awful of me that I was getting so much enjoyment out of this. Considering everything he'd done to me over the last year, I didn't care anymore though.

Folding my arms over my chest, I watched in amusement as Uncle Caleb angrily asked for an explanation. Steel stepped in behind me and wrapped his arms around me, enveloping me in his warmth and the unique smell that was his. It was amazing how I'd gone from feeling alone to having a family and feeling safe again in such a short time, all thanks to the man currently holding me in his arms. I leaned back against his chest as Agent Flynn read Uncle Caleb his rights.

He glared over at me. "This is bullshit!" I didn't know if he was talking to me or the agents. "You won't get away with this, Remi."

Oh, that answers that question, I guess.

"This is all your fault, you know!" The local cop turned him around and started patting him down, all while he was spewing nonsense at me.

"You didn't deserve this company! You never worked for a fucking thing in your life. Everything was just handed to you. I've spent years working and building this business. You and your father used me to make your money and now you think I'm going to take the fall for you? You fucking owe me!" His face was red as a tomato, spit was flying out of his mouth, but he finally stopped talking once those handcuffs snicked into place.

I stepped out of the protective circle of Steel's arms to face my lying, thieving, worthless uncle. "You stole from us," I said, my voice was dead calm and cold as ice. Uncle Caleb's mouth dropped open and he froze. Every eye in the room was on us now. I wasn't supposed to have said that, but I was too pissed to care. "You lied to us. You lied to Dad." His chin went up defiantly. I stepped in closer to him. I saw Steel and Gunnar both moving toward me from my peripheral, but Uncle Caleb had his hands cuffed behind his back and the cop had his hands on the cuffs, so I wasn't worried. I lowered my voice so only he and I could hear. "You transported drugs in my trucks."

Caleb's face drained of all color and his mouth opened and closed, like a fish. I stepped back. No longer would I think of him as family. "I know everything you did. Soon, we'll know everyone who was involved." I saw Agent Flynn give me a curious glance, but I avoided her gaze.

Turning my back on Caleb, I looked at Janet who was sitting there in stunned silence. "Janet?" Her glassy eyes met mine. "Could you close up for me?" She nodded and slowly returned the smile I gave her. The cops would be arresting the two truck drivers later tonight as well. I'd be firing the accountant tomorrow and the next week would be full of staff meetings, getting everyone used to the new way things would be run at Mackenzie's, but I would deal with all of that as it came. For now, I wanted to get back to the clubhouse and hear what Cade had learned from Rhonda.

My heart felt like it was racing Steel's motorcycle back to the clubhouse. I was flying high, so happy and free. I squeezed Steel's waist hard enough that I felt him grunt beneath me and couldn't help but grin. I had the man I loved, my company wasn't in danger anymore, my mother was out of my life and, hopefully, we were about to solve a huge problem for the club too.

When we parked Steel reached back and swung me around until I was straddling him. Laughing I looked down at him as Gunnar muttered something and wandered toward the clubhouse. "Thank you."

He cocked his head slightly. "For what?"

How could I explain it to him? I shook my head, suddenly overwhelmed with emotion, and unable to articulate what he'd given back to me. He leaned forward and crushed me in his arms.

"You've done that for me too." His voice was soft, almost a purr. He wouldn't let me pull back to see his face. I was too close to tears to speak so I made some sort of questioning noise. He understood me, as he always seemed to. "I may not have lost my family, or my purpose, like you did." He wasn't wrong with that assessment. "But having you has made what I had so much better."

Now I was beyond speechless. Steel wasn't the sweet words kind of guy. So, getting them now, when he knew I needed them most, tipped me over the edge. Tears spilled down my cheeks and suddenly he was wiping them gently away. Those rough fingers were caressing my skin, causing sparks to ignite wherever he touched. He kissed me gently, my tears wetting our lips, and I wondered how it would be possible to love this man more than I did at this moment?

"Would you two hurry the fuck up!" The yell had me jolting in Steel's arms and him cursing. Riggs chuckled from where he stood a few feet away. We'd been so wrapped up in each other we hadn't even heard him approach. "Cade needs to talk with you both."

Once again, we found ourselves sitting around the kitchen island. Once we'd gone through what had happened with Caleb it was Cade's turn. The grim set of his mouth told me it wasn't good news. "We found out who your uncle is working with…"

"Caleb," I interrupted him. Everyone looked at me curiously. "He's not my uncle anymore."

Cade nodded and continued. "We found out who Caleb's contact is for the Guzman Cartel."

My phone blared out the ringtone set for Bridget. The loud tone in the tense quiet of the room made me jump. "Sorry! I'll set it to silent." I pulled my phone out and stared at it for a second before I looked up at Cade. My stomach was in knots, Bridget never called first. She always texted; it was as though calling was an affront to her. He frowned at me, but I hit the answer button and held the phone up to my ear. "Bridge?"

"Ah, Señorita Mackenzie, si?" An unknown voice asked me. My gaze shot to Steel then to Gunnar. I silently put the phone on speaker.

"Yes, this is Remi Mackenzie. Who is this and why are you on Bridget's phone?" The guys around me had all stiffened but stayed quiet as we all waited on the answer.

"We'll need you to deliver Rhonda and Caleb to us by… eleven p.m., if you'd like to see your chiquita here alive again," came the reply.

The breath was trapped in my chest. I wanted to sit down and sob, but I didn't have the time or luxury. "How do I know you even have Bridget?"

I heard the muffled sound of someone speaking over the phone then the next voice had my heart clenching in my chest. "R… Remi?" Bridget's voice sounded watery and terrified. I looked over and saw

Gunnar's fists clenched so hard around the edge of the table top I was surprised he hadn't cracked it.

"Hey Bridge," I said softly, calmly. "I'm going to come get you, okay?"

I heard her breath shudder out over the line, and I knew she was crying. In my mind I could see the tears dripping down her face and it killed me knowing she was in danger. "Okay."

"Are you alright? Have they hurt you?"

"Fin. Enough!" There was a shuffling sound as I imagine the guy ripped the phone out of her hand. "She is fine, for now." He rattled off an address, which I saw Rat hurrying to put into his computer. "You will meet us there and we will exchange them for her. Come alone, just you and them or we will kill her." I heard someone nearby cry out at the man's announcement.

"That's not what we arranged, Miguel!"

I gasped. I knew that voice as well as I'd known my own father's. The sound of someone being hit echoed loudly over the phone.

"Daaaadddyy!" Bridget's scream had all the men around me stifling curses as they tried not to alert her captors that they were listening in on the conversation.

The man's voice came back on the line, slightly out of breath. "Bring Rhonda and Caleb tonight," he growled.

"Wait, was that Mr. Jordan?" I was desperately trying to piece together what was going on and stall for time. The click and dial tone told me he'd hung up on me.

"Fuck!" Gunnar slammed a fist on the table making me jolt.

"Caleb was the middleman between Brent Jordan and Miguel Guzman. That's what Rhonda told me after you left," Cade said grimly. "I had no idea they'd go after Bridget. I'm sorry man." He looked over at Gunnar. Gunnar looked miserable and I didn't blame him.

"So, Bridget's dad has been selling cocaine?" I asked, confused. "Why would he do that? He's a former mayor."

"No, he's been having the Lycans sell cocaine and taking a cut of the money. He gets money and has someone to do any of the dirty work he needs done." Cade explained.

"So why is Guzman here now?" Steel asked. "Why does he have Bridget and her dad and what does he want with Caleb and Rhonda?"

"He must have heard about the FBI raid and come to the same conclusion as Rhonda," I said dully. Cade and a few of the others nodded in agreement.

"They probably think they're going to rat them out," Axel added.

"Do you think they've heard about Caleb being arrested yet?" I asked. Anxiety was currently ripping my stomach apart. This had gone from a great plan to hell on Earth pretty quickly. I'd never meant for Bridget to get caught in the crossfire.

"It's unlikely," Steel said. "It just happened about an hour ago. I doubt anyone has heard yet."

"How am I supposed to find Rhonda and get Caleb out of FBI custody in," I glanced at my phone, "six hours?" Hopelessness seeped into every fiber of my being. Bridget was like a sister to me. I looked around the table at the grim faces around me and took a deep breath. It didn't matter. Bridget had come for me when I needed her, and I wasn't going to let her down.

"I'm going to need a gun." The horror on Steel's face at my announcement would have been funny if the situation wasn't so grave. He'd learn sooner rather than later that I'd walk through hell for my family. If that meant facing down a cartel to get one of them back, then so be it.

* * *

THANKS FOR READING!

Sign up for my newsletter to receive an extra chapter from Heart of Steel! https://www.cathleencolenovels.com/bonuses.

. . .

Keep flipping to find a sneak peek for book two of The Vikings MC, The Viking's Princess. It's available in KU and on Amazon now! Read toady!

SNEAK PEEK

Prologue

Bridget

"Bridget!"

I glanced over and stopped walking when my dad pulled up next to me in his Lexus. I shifted my school bag higher up onto my shoulder and smiled. "Hi, Dad." Stepping off the curb, I leaned in through the window and kissed his cheek. "Did I forget a lunch date?"

"No, sweetheart, but I thought I'd take you out if you had the time?" He smiled at me but looked a little stressed. I had a few more classes today, but nothing that I couldn't skip.

"Sure!" I walked around and dropped my bag and purse into the back seat before sliding in next to him. I watched my father's face as he navigated the roads leading us off the University of Texas campus and into the heart of Austin. His mouth was pinched at the corners and those heavy brows were furrowed with worry. I knew him too well for him to be able to hide it.

"Are we going to Masalinas?" It was one of my father's favorite restaurants and his go-to for comfort food. Although I wasn't sure you could count five-star dining as comfort food, but he did.

"Not today, Pumpkin." He tightened his grip on the steering wheel and glanced into the rear-view mirror before making a lane change.

"Okay, Dad what's going on?" I shifted in my seat so that I was facing him and folded my arms over my chest. His eyes met mine for a brief second before flashing to the road in front of us then again to the rear-view mirror. I looked through the back window. He was acting like someone was following us.

"Sit facing forward, Bridget," he snapped at me.

I immediately did as he asked, my mouth dropping open. My father rarely yelled at me and usually, it was only when I'd done something to test his patience, like bring home a guy I knew he'd flip out about. He wasn't in the habit of yelling at me for no reason.

"Tell me what's going on," I demanded. I realized we were leaving the Austin city limits and heading out of town.

He sighed and his gaze met and held my own. I searched those blue eyes that were so like mine and found doubt, fear, and an apology. "We need to leave town for a bit, Pumpkin. I've already sent your mother to her sister's." My mouth fell open, but he spoke right through my sputtered protests. "I'm in a little bit of a bind. It's not forever, just for a while."

"A WHILE?!" I stared at him in shock. "Dad, I have school. And my friends. What kind of trouble are you in?" I shook my head in disbelief. Dad was the former mayor of Austin. He ran in high society circles. *What could possibly have happened that had him spiriting his family away with literally the clothes on our backs?*

"I didn't say I was in trouble," he said indignantly, his face turning a mottled shade of red. It was the same shade it always turned when he was lying. I eyed the back seat where my bag and purse were. If he was going to force me to leave the city, the least I was going to do was text Gunnar. I'd dropped my cell phone into my purse before getting in the car though, so I was going to have to turn around to get it. He'd already yelled at me for turning around once. I'd bide my time; I'd get my phone in a few minutes when he was more distracted.

"Oh Daddy," I said softly. "What did you do?"

He glared at me and opened his mouth to speak, but before he could I saw a vehicle pull up alongside us and the world exploded. Or that's what it felt like anyway when the car sideswiped us. It took my breath away and I couldn't even scream as a car hit us so hard from Dad's side of the Lexus that it sent us careening off the highway and down a grassy embankment.

I gripped the door and my seat hard, trying to breathe. Dad's window had exploded upon impact and I could see blood running down his face from where fragments of glass had cut him. He was fighting with the wheel, trying to stop the car from spinning out of control in the grass.

I thought for sure he'd stop the car so that we could call the cops to report the accident. Instead, as soon as he righted the wheel and had the machine under control he stomped on the gas and shot along the embankment toward the exit ramp that was there. I let out a little squeal as we cut off a car and zipped down the lane. The long blare of a horn told me we'd come close to another collision.

Glancing behind us, I saw two black vehicles race after us down the exit ramp. "They're following us," my voice sounded hollow, even to me. Dad let out a string of curses that would have made my mother gasp and put on more speed. I whipped around just in time to see us shoot across the intersection at the end of the road, against the red light.

"Fuck!" I screamed and closed my eyes. I didn't want to see my death coming. When nothing hit us, I peeked one eye open. We were on the other side of the road and speeding away from the freeway. "Okay, enough of the bullshit, Dad," I spat out angrily. "Did someone just try to kill us back there?"

He sighed but started talking. "A cartel is looking for me."

My day had started out so normal and now here I was in the fucking twilight zone. "I'm sorry. Did you just say a cartel? Like... a drug cartel? From Mexico?" I asked in complete shock.

"Look, I don't have time to get into it, Bridget," he said irritably.

I started laughing. Okay, it was a slightly hysterical laugh, but a girl

SNEAK PEEK

was allowed in the current circumstances. "It seems to me we have nothing but time, Dad," I shot back. "Why is there a cartel looking for you? For us?" I amended. His mouth twisted into a hard frown at that.

"You aren't involved in this. You were never supposed to be involved," he muttered the last sentence.

I threw my hands up in exasperation. Clearly, he wasn't planning on telling me anything. He was driving like a mad man through some smaller town outside of Austin. All that lay beyond it, as far as the eye could see, was cattle farming land. I'd never been in this area before, so I had no clue where we were.

I also never knew my dad could drive like a race car driver, but he was doing just that. *I wonder if that's why he always insisted on driving a manual?* I eyed him as he downshifted around a tight corner then worked the clutch and shifter in tandem to gain speed out of the turn.

Suddenly, he slammed on the brakes and I thanked God I was wearing my seat belt as I slammed a hand on the dashboard to help stop my forward momentum. Dad was muttering from the driver's seat and I looked out in front of us. There were three SUVs blocking the road. He quickly threw the car into reverse and his arm over the back of my seat to look behind us. The sudden stillness that overcame him made dread pool low in my belly. I peeked behind us and found the cars that had chased us off the freeway idling there.

"Dad... What do we do?" I tried to keep the quaver out of my voice. I wanted to be strong. I quickly took my seatbelt off, just in case we needed to make a run for it.

"It's okay, Pumpkin. We'll be okay." He didn't sound very sure of himself. I wished I had some kind of weapon. Not that I knew how to use one. Now I wished I'd gone, all those years ago, when my best friend's dad had taken her to the gun range to show her how to shoot. He'd been a Marine and had insisted Remi learn how to safely handle firearms. I knew nothing about guns though. That brought me to my next wish. *I wish Gunnar was here.*

Gunnar was the sexy as sin MC guy I'd been dating, that my dad had made me break up with because 'he was too dangerous'. I sneered over at my father. *Who was the dangerous one now?* Of course, my dad didn't know I'd been in a warehouse a few days ago during a shootout between two rival MCs, trying to save Remi's life. He also didn't know that Gunnar and I had gotten back together the same day as the shootout.

What he didn't know wouldn't hurt him, I thought guiltily. My life sure had gotten exciting lately. I missed the good old 'boring' days sometimes.

Movement from the SUVs jerked me out of my thoughts. Three men stepped out and started approaching our car. Two were carrying really big rifles. My mouth went dry as fear raced through my body. I shot Dad a look and noticed he was pale and sweating slightly but he didn't say anything.

I went back to quietly watching the men approach. I thought about grabbing my phone out of my purse now, but I didn't want one of these men thinking I was going for a gun and shooting me. Instead, I stayed still. One of the men with a rifle opened my door and I shrank back. I felt Dad put a hand on my shoulder. I wasn't sure if it was supposed to be comforting, but it didn't have that effect.

"Brent. So good of you to save us the trouble of picking your daughter up ourselves." The man behind the one who opened my door spoke with a heavy Spanish accent. My eyes widened as we stared at each other. He was probably five-eleven, dark hair, dark eyes, and had a mean-looking face. Not one of these men looked friendly in the slightest, and not just because of the guns.

"Miguel, I told you before, she has nothing to do with this. I'll handle this little mishap, but you need to leave my family out of it." Dad's voice came out sure and strong. He was putting on a better show than I was. I could feel my body starting to shake. It was June, and very warm but I couldn't stop the tremors.

"You had your chance to fix it already. Now, we're fixing it. Take them," Miguel said with a little flip of his hand, as though we were nothing but a pair of pants he wanted brought home from the store.

The second man went around the car and opened the door. Dad stepped out, adjusting his suit coat, and stood next to him. Everyone stared at me. *Fuck all of them if they think I'm going to willingly just go*

SNEAK PEEK

with them. I glared at the man as he held his hand out to me and clutched the rifle in the other. Anyone who knew me would have seen my chin jut out stubbornly and would know they were in for trouble by that action alone. Luckily, this guy didn't know me. I was also thankful I was wearing shorts and sneakers today, instead of my usual skirt and heels. Thank God I'd been late for class that morning and had thrown on casual clothes.

Shimmying backward as quickly as I could, I squeezed through the front seats and into the back. This was one of those times when my five-four, smaller frame came in handy. The man frowned and started to move to the back passenger door, so I turned and bolted out the back driver's side door. The other gunman hadn't been watching or expecting this, so he wasn't blocking it. I quickly started running as fast as I could away from all of the cars. *If I could just find someone to help me.*

I heard shouts behind me, but I was making good time. I may be a girly girl, but I was still athletic. I knew I shouldn't look behind me. Every horror movie told you to keep running and just look forward. I glanced back and couldn't help the small shriek that escaped when I saw the gunman gaining on me. There were three more men not too far behind him. They must have come from the SUVs.

Shit! I looked forward but couldn't pour on more speed because I was already going as fast as I could. I was starting to tire out, too, and I'd run into a field that was across from the road we'd been stopped on so there was nothing around us. No buildings, no roads, no other cars, I started to lose hope. I doubted I could outrun these thugs and the heat had me sweating. I was sucking in deep pulls of the heavy, hot air. I wasn't willing to stop and give up though. *Think Bridget!*

I heard the pounding of footsteps behind me. *Oh God, oh God, oh God.* As soon as I felt the man's body get close to mine, I pivoted and switched directions, running off to my right. I was banking on the fact that the other three guys were still far enough behind that this wouldn't put me directly in their path. The plan paid off. With a curse the man who'd been about to grab me stumbled forward, off-balance, and crashed to the ground. The other men were still a little ways away, but far too close for comfort. I ran, kicking as hard as I could, lungs screaming at me for relief. I prayed I'd find something this way. I needed help because I couldn't keep going much longer.

All of a sudden, the ground started sloping downward. I slowed slightly and took in the valley below; we were on a hill that looked out over grazing land. There were cows and a cattle tank but no houses or barns to be seen. I started making my way down the sharp, rocky, drop as quickly and carefully as I could. It wasn't straight down but it was steep enough that I needed to be careful and find my footing. I froze when I heard something that caused me to glance up. A few feet up was one of the men chasing me. We locked eyes. I watched as he swept his gaze down the hill then looked back at me.

My eyes widened when I realized what he was about to do, but I couldn't make my body move quickly enough. Sure enough, wouldn't you know it? This asshole yeeted himself off the side of the hill and slammed into me, taking us both down in a rolling pile of limbs. I don't know how long we tumbled or how many times I caught an elbow or knee to sensitive areas but once we finally started to slow, I was about to be grateful, then my head slammed into a rock and everything went dark.

ACKNOWLEDGMENTS

A huge thank you to my partner in crime and Co-Author, Frank Jensen. I couldn't do this without you.

To my amazing beta readers Heather Ashley and Aurora Welkin, thank you so much for all of your time and effort you spent helping me make these books the best they can be!

Also a heartfelt thank you to my editor, Ce-Ce Cox of Outside-Eyes Editing and Proofreading! Thank you for catching everything I always seem to miss, especially those pesky commas.

Thank you to the awesome Kari March of Kari March Designs for giving me gorgeous covers each and every time.

To my wonderful and perfect fans! Thank you all for giving an unknown author a shot and for reading my books! I hope you love them and I can't show my gratitude for you enough.

Lastly, to my family, you're the best. Thank you for the love and support.

ABOUT THE AUTHOR

Cathleen Cole currently lives in Utah with her husband Frank, their six dogs, four goats, and flock of chickens. Cathleen and Frank have nomadic souls, so they don't expect to be tied down to one place indefinitely.

Animals, dog sports, traveling, scuba diving, and everything books are just a few of Cathleen's passions in life. She measures her quality of life based off the different experiences and adventures she gets to have.

You'll see every book written by either Cathleen Cole or Frank Jensen will always credit the other as co-author and that is because they use each other as sounding boards during their writing processes as well as they are each other's main beta readers. As husband and wife, they insist on sharing all successes and failures equally.

ALSO BY CATHLEEN COLE

The Vikings MC Series

Heart of Steel

The Viking's Princess

All's Fair In Love & Juárez

'Til Encryption Do Us Part

Bass & Trouble

War & Pieces

Heavy Is The Crowne

The Vikings MC-Tucson Chapter

Hush

The Discord Series

Havoc

Inferno

Deviant

Malice

Soldiers of Misfortune

Captured By The Mercenaries

Printed in Great Britain
by Amazon